THE FIVE *Minute* MISTAKE

HANNAH SHIELD

Cover photography by Wander Aguiar

Cover model: Andrew Biernat

Published by Diana Road Books

THE FIVE *Minute* MISTAKE

1

Nash

*F*our years ago, when I entered the police academy, I was no naive cadet. I'd just left the Navy after a decade-plus in the Teams. I'd served in war, buried comrades, killed my share of baddies. I thought I knew the worst the world could throw at me.

Yet I could've had stars in my eyes for all the big hopes and dreams I was harboring. Hopes of saving my marriage. Of reconnecting with my kid.

Past-me would've been appalled at how things turned out. But he had no clue what it would be like raising a teenager.

My thumbs fly over my phone screen, responding to my daughter's latest barrage of messages.

Emma: Dad, relax. This is not a big deal. Everybody does it.
Me: And that's a convincing argument since...when? Oh yeah, fucking never.
Emma: Don't think you're cool because you drop an f-bomb. And don't try to be funny. It doesn't work for you.
Me: You know what's not funny? Teenage boys. With penises.

Being invited to a sleepover where my fifteen-year-old daughter is present.

Emma: Dad, ew! OMG! [Vomiting emoji.]

Emma is at a slumber party tonight, but she "forgot" to mention there would be boys there. Apparently, co-ed sleep-overs with full parental approval are now a thing. If I'd tried that crap when I was in high school, my mother would have laughed through a solid week of grounding me.

Of course, Emma only admitted there'd be boys at this slumber party after the hosting mom sent a group text to the other parents, mentioning that "Chad" and "Toby" would be bringing the pizza, and could we all please Vemno money to chip in?

When I was Emma's age, Chad and Toby were number one and two on the list of *Dudes Up To No Good*.

Emma: We're just watching a movie. I'm not into anyone here, they're my FRIENDS. I know you don't have any, but I assume you've heard of them?

Me: Doesn't ring a bell. I'll be home in a couple of hours, and I'd better see you there.

I growl my frustration at the nearest object, a palm tree bordering the parking lot where I'm standing. It doesn't react.

When I joined the Navy at nineteen—not much older than my daughter is now—I intended to stay until I retired at the end of a long, full career. But being a SEAL is demanding. When my family started to fall apart, I made the decision to leave. It was one of the hardest of my life.

In many ways, it was already too late. Too late to fix my marriage. No question there. But at first, I thought I still had a chance with Emma. She was eleven when I returned to civilian life. A total sweetheart, excited to finally get to know this "dad" she'd heard so much about.

By now, though, the gimmick has worn off. My ex got remarried, quit her job at the hospital, and left the country on a grand adventure. Emma moved in with me. I have a rebellious fifteen-year-old who's picked *this moment* to make her stand.

Meanwhile, I'm supposed to be working. In fact, I'm supposed to be calmly preparing for the next scenario in the training that I'm running.

"Sergeant Jennings?"

I look up from my phone, which I'm squeezing so hard the plastic creaks. A West Oaks PD patrol officer in full body armor hovers a few feet away. The initials S.W.A.T. are emblazoned across his vest.

"I'm...reporting, sir," the kid says.

"We're meeting on the west side of the parking lot. In five minutes."

"Right," he squeaks, "sorry."

He scampers away, and shit, I wish I hadn't spoken so harshly. I don't mean to sound gruff. But more often than not, my voice comes out that way.

My phone buzzes again. Against my better judgment, I sneak a peek.

Emma: I'm not leaving. If you want, you can take me to brunch tomorrow at that place on Ocean Lane. The pancakes you like? With the whipped cream?

My daughter thinks she can manipulate me with frou-frou pancakes? They're delicious, but that's irrelevant. I take a deep breath, willing my heart rate to slow. Emma can push my buttons like nobody else.

Don't get me wrong. I adore my kid. I think she's incredible. Emma loves foreign arthouse films, the kind that're incomprehensible to me. She can play Led Zeppelin and Metallica on the violin like a total badass, but stops if she thinks I'm listening. She paints her nails with sparkly blue polish at the kitchen table, even though I've asked her not to.

She hates me. Except when she loves me. Sometimes, my status fluctuates by the hour.

The part of me that's outside the situation and can think objectively is saying, *Maybe you should let this go. Trust Emma. Let her make this decision for herself.*

But that's not the dad part of me.

Me: My decision is not up for discussion.

Why is it that I can keep myself under strict control in a damned war zone, to the point that my teammates accused me of being a lab experiment, but a teenage girl triggers my urge to explode?

THERE'S A SLIGHT NOVEMBER CHILL IN THE AIR. Not enough to warrant a jacket yet, because this is Southern California, but enough to notice the shift in season. Beside me, a flower bed brightens up the otherwise drab parking lot. The sky is so blue it looks painted on.

And over on the west end of the lot, sixteen trainees in full SWAT uniforms wait in the staging area. They keep sneaking nervous glances at me. I should head over there. Class doesn't resume until I appear, but still, I don't like being late.

I sigh. It's days like this I miss the military the most. While the views on-base might've been ugly, I knew exactly what I was supposed to do.

When I left the Teams, I moved to West Oaks, where my wife had relocated for her career as a nurse. For me, the police department seemed like a natural choice. I'd get to serve my community. Protect the innocent. Fight bad guys. All my favorite things, though on a far more local scale. And most importantly, I'd get to go home to my family each day.

Unlike most graduates from the police academy, I didn't go out on patrol. My situation was unusual. Because I'd been a SEAL, I was able to head straight into the SWAT team. What better way to put my sniper skills to good use? But my superiors seem to think my years as a SEAL mean I'm proficient at everything imaginable. Including training a bunch of candidates for a huge expansion of our Special Weapons and Tactics division.

Here's the problem.

In most military units, there's a guy who's in the background, cleaning his gun or contemplating the unknown or otherwise staying silent. His teammates joke and talk shit at him, and he sends back a sardonic glare. If he opens his mouth, it's only because he wants to. That guy is best behind-the-scenes. Not so much front of the classroom.

That guy is me.

Yet here I am, the teacher.

I jam my phone in my pocket and stalk across the concrete toward the staging area. My trainees go silent when they see me coming. I clear my throat and get started.

"Everyone, this is our final exercise of the day. A potential hostage situation."

After spending our first two days in class, we're finally out in the field. It's a little like a dress rehearsal. I've been setting up realistic scenarios for the trainees to tackle. This one will take place inside the sprawling brick structure behind me, the West Oaks First Methodist Church. The pastor graciously agreed to give us access.

"An armed suspect fled to the church after officers responded to a disturbance nearby," I explain. "There's a church employee trapped inside. You have all the intel our spotters have submitted, along with the building layout. Brainstorm your primary, alternate, contingent, and emergency plans. I'll select our final plans from those, and then we'll drill them and execute. You have fifteen minutes. Get to it."

I hold my breath, waiting and hoping for a reaction. A hint they heard a word I just said.

They drift into their groups and start muttering.

I make a mental note to buy extra-nice gifts for Emma's teachers this year. They must be saints to do this every day, and with teenagers.

As I make my rounds, my eyes catch on Madison Shelborne, one of the patrol officers in the class. Vivid green eyes, long lashes. Her cornsilk blond hair is pulled into a bun, though a few wisps have escaped onto her forehead. She's got her chin up, shoulders back, projecting an easy confidence while she strategizes with her teammates.

My eyes seem to catch on her a lot.

"Sergeant?" Madison says. "I have a question."

My pulse kicks. I head over to her, clasping my hands behind my back. "Yes, Officer?"

"What if we have to make a judgment in the moment, but we're not sure what to do? And the plan doesn't account for it?"

"Then you should've had a better plan. That's why we have back-ups."

"In hindsight, sure." The corner of her mouth pulls into a tiny smile. "But in the moment? What then? Do we follow our instincts?"

Instincts? Like the instinct that makes me keep noticing how beautiful she is?

Madison was my classmate at the academy. Now I'm the instructor, and she's the student. I suck at relationships, and even if I didn't? She's out of bounds. Full stop.

"Just focus on your plans," I say. "That's the assignment."

The small flicker of light in Madison's gaze goes cold. She's frowning when she replies. "Got it, sir. Thanks."

I linger there for a beat too long. If she didn't like my answer, I can't help that. Plans are safe. When you're out in the weeds, that's when the trouble starts.

My damned phone buzzes in my pocket. Emma, texting *again*. Somehow, I don't think she's going to cave to my demand. The war is not over.

I wish parenthood had plans and training sessions. Practice scenarios, when the consequences didn't mean so damn much.

2

Madison

"*Alpha team is in position.*"

My teammate Lia Perez lifts her handset to respond. "Bravo team is in position."

The call-outs continue, and she lowers her radio, turning to me. "Still up for drinks later?" Lia asks. "The guys were thinking Shore Lounge."

We're pressed against the stucco wall of the church. The temps have dipped below the sixties, but I'm sweating through my black T-shirt. My body armor is squishing my boobs, and my hair feels plastered to my head beneath my helmet.

It's a glamorous life I lead.

I thought trying out for the SWAT team would be exciting. Turns out, it's all *plans, plans, plans*, according to Sergeant Jennings. God forbid anyone has an independent thought. Or a question.

"I wonder if I can call ahead for the bartender to have a martini on standby," I say. "Preferably in an I.V. bag."

Lia wrinkles her pert nose. "A martini? Feeling high class, are we? Did you stash your heels in your gear bag?"

"Shelby wears heels?" Clint asks from his post a few feet away. Shaggy blond hair peeks out beneath his helmet.

"Hey, I can class it up when I want to. Might even put on some mascara."

Clint laughs, but the joke's on him. I'm wearing mascara right now. It's called *waterproof*.

Most everyone at West Oaks PD calls me Shelby, short for my last name, Shelborne. They say I'm one of the guys, and I take that like the compliment it is. I can kick their asses on the track or the sparring mat. But I enjoy being girly when the mood strikes. At holiday parties, I'm at least fifty percent sequins.

Not right now, though. At this present moment, I'm Kevlar and machine oil and layers of sweat. But at least it's Friday, and we have the weekend off.

We've got our dummy rifles ready, eyes on the east exit door. According to the primary plan, Alpha team will approach from the north with the negotiators. They'll make contact with the suspect—our pretend suspect, anyway—and that's where the action is.

My team is Bravo, and we're on containment, which means waiting and watching.

Then Lia's radio squawks, and we all freeze.

"Alpha team is under fire! Go to alternate! Bravo team, you're go for breach!"

Here's something I didn't expect. Jennings is giving my team a chance to show what we've got.

Lia nods at me. We fix our earpieces, joining the open channel.

"Bravo team is go," Lia says.

Tyler, the fourth member of Bravo, tries the door. It's locked, but a swift kick gains us entry.

The door opens into a long hallway. Tyler and Clint sweep

inside, their guns raised. Then they stand aside, guarding the hall, while Lia and I enter.

Sergeant Jennings' voice booms in our earpieces. *"Spotter reports suspect and civilian are in the north lobby. Civilian has been taken hostage. Sniper confirms no shot."*

"Bravo copies," Lia says. "We've breached the east entrance and we're on our way."

We have half a dozen rooms to clear. If this were a drive and drop, another team would be coming in right behind us to handle the clearing. But it's just us four. I know this is a training, but even so, my pulse surges. We might not get many chances to prove ourselves, so we'd better not screw this up.

Lia and I head for the nearest doorway to the left.

We enter a Sunday school classroom, where white boards and colorful artwork hang on the walls. SWAT has already cut utilities to the building, per standard procedure, so the lights are off. Sunlight barely penetrates through the curtains over the high windows.

I check along the right side of the room, while Lia covers the left. I peer into the shadows, my body tense and ready.

There's a faint squeak as my boot eases onto the wood floor. Another.

When I reach the far wall, I turn around.

"Clear," Lia says.

There's something nagging at me, but I can't put my finger on it. Do I stay here? Or do I continue on?

"Clear," I echo.

I give the room one last glance before following Lia into the hallway. We have to keep moving. Jennings is probably out there with his stopwatch, and if we let the "hostage" die, it won't look too good on our evals.

It's Clint and Tyler who check the next room, while Lia

and I keep watch in the hall. I'm standing with my back to the room I just cleared.

A bead of sweat rolls down my back. My grip is steady but loose on my rifle.

Then I feel a cold poke of metal against the bare skin of my neck.

"Boom. You're dead."

I turn around and find Detective Sean Holt from West Oaks PD's major crimes department behind me, a crooked smirk on his face.

Lia groans. "Aww, dammit." She pulls her earpiece free.

Holt lowers his pistol. Like us, he's using a dummy weapon for these training exercises. No live rounds. "Nice to see you, too."

Clint and Tyler have joined us. Tyler's mouth is hanging open, and Clint tugs off his helmet. "What the hell, Holt? The sergeant said on the radio that the suspect was in the lobby."

"I'm not the suspect. I'm his girlfriend." Holt poses. "Don't I look pretty?"

"Where were you hiding?" Lia asks the detective.

"Classroom. I climbed a bookcase. There's an alcove above the door."

Crap. I knew, I *knew*, that something didn't feel right in that room.

Clint nudges my elbow. "I can't believe that bookcase held Holt's weight."

"*That's enough, Bravo team,*" Jennings says on the radio. "*Charlie and Delta teams, continue with the scenario. Bravo, you're back to base with me.*"

We cringe and head outside. This is *not* going to be good.

Sergeant Jennings is waiting for us in the parking lot, thick arms crossed over his broad chest as we approach.

Lia leans into me. "Jennings is pissed. If I had balls, they'd be shriveling."

"Good thing we don't have any." I press my lips flat. This would be a poor moment to laugh. But I do have a tendency to laugh at inappropriate times. Like at church when I was growing up, and my eldest brother Jake would make faces behind his hand.

"Bravo team," Jennings says, deep and smooth and dripping with disappointment. "You want to explain how you missed an armed individual in a room you'd supposedly cleared?"

No one speaks.

Four years ago, Jennings and I were in the same academy class. But we couldn't be more different. Where I'm pale blond, his hair is coal black. I'm a hundred-twenty pounds soaking wet, and he looks like double that, and all of it muscle.

I came to West Oaks PD straight from college. Nash? He's a former Navy SEAL sniper with over a decade's military special ops experience.

People say I'm approachable, always ready with a smile. But Nash's dark-eyed gaze alone is hard enough to break rocks and demolish dreams. His jaw is razor sharp, and his muscles bulge under his long-sleeved T-shirt and tactical pants like he's made of stone.

No question, Nash is smoking hot. But he's the kind of hot that you don't want to mess with. Some people in our training call him "Sergeant Scary."

Back in the academy, he didn't seem so intimidating. Not to me. I guess things change.

But my friends and I? We work hard. We might goof around during downtimes, but we take our job seriously. And while I agree we messed up, I don't intend to cower at his feet.

"It was me," I blurt.

Everyone's eyes land on me, including the sergeant's. And they're all surprised. Hell, so am I. I didn't know for sure I'd say that until it came out.

Guess I'm following my instincts, even if Jennings wouldn't approve.

"*Shelby*," Lia whispers behind me, but I ignore her.

"I take responsibility. I said the room was cleared. The intel reported one suspect, and that's what I assumed."

"Intel can be incomplete. Even flat-out wrong."

"Yes, sir. But we only had so much time. We needed to reach the hostage. Holt had climbed up a bookcase and into an alcove. He got creative, and I didn't spot him."

"Sounds like you're making excuses."

I stand up straighter. "No, sir. I'm saying I made a calculated risk, even if it turned out to be the wrong choice. Because no plan accounts for *everything*."

There's silence.

"Do you agree, Bravo team? It was Officer Shelborne's fault?" Sergeant Jennings is speaking to my teammates, but his gaze hasn't wavered from mine.

Lia steps forward. "I was squad leader. I'm responsible too."

Tyler's glaring at both of us. Clint looks like he wants to run.

The rest of the teams are trailing out of the church, having finished with their part of the exercise. Some of their steps falter as they see us in the sergeant's sights, but others speed up, probably hoping to hear us get reamed.

Jennings doesn't seem to notice the audience. He clasps his hands behind his back again, legs spread. "Bravo team, you failed your mission today. We'll talk about what went wrong and what you'll do better when we're in the classroom on Monday."

There's a collective exhale from my teammates. Yet I'm holding my breath. I can sense this isn't over.

Then the voice of Sergeant Jennings booms out again across the concrete.

"Officer Shelborne, see me in twenty minutes. The rest of you can go."

Shit.

Lia gasps. Once again, I feel the stares of my fellow officers, but these are wide with horror.

"What did she *do*?" someone from Alpha team mutters, obviously late to the show.

Guess I'm going to be late to the bar tonight.

CLINT SLUMPS INTO LIA AND ME. "I NEED TEQUILA. That's the only way to get my mind off this afternoon."

"I was thinking vodka martini earlier, but you're right. Tequila's better." I could use some mind-erasure right about now.

We're leaning against the trunk of Lia's squad car, half out of our gear. Everyone else has been dismissed, and cars are pulling out of the parking lot, heading back to the station.

I don't see the sergeant. He and Detective Holt ducked inside the church a few minutes ago, probably talking to the SWAT commander.

What does Jennings need to say to me? And why couldn't he do it in front of everyone else?

Is he kicking me out of SWAT training?

"You look like someone who needs a distraction." Lia nudges my shoulder. "Has the rehearsal dinner started?"

"Yep. There's photo evidence." I take out my phone and open Instagram, showing Lia my siblings' latest posts. "They're having the dinner on a rooftop in Malibu. With

Grammy-nominated jazz musicians. Catered by somebody from a past season of Top Chef."

"Bleh. So basic."

"I know. Gross."

"So gross."

Clint is eying us, head tilted like a bewildered puppy dog. Lia and I crack up, but my laughter dies fast. I know she's trying to cheer me up. But this is yet another subject I'd rather not think about.

My high school boyfriend is getting married tomorrow. My entire family is going to the wedding weekend. I was invited too, but I skipped out. Both the rehearsal dinner and the wedding sound epic. Amazing. Worthy of the record books. And I swear I'm not jealous. At least, not jealous of the girl who's marrying him. I'm happy for my ex. I'm in no rush to fall in love and settle down for a baby, dog, and mortgage.

I just wish I could answer my parents' questions about *what I really want* and *where my future is going*.

Not heading for the SWAT team, apparently.

"You still coming tonight?" Lia asks me.

"I'm *definitely* coming, so don't let Clint drink all the Jose Cuervo. I'll meet you there."

"You don't want us to wait for you?"

"I'll catch up." If this is a bloodbath, I'd rather my friends didn't witness it.

She hugs me. "Whatever Jennings says, you're amazing. Don't forget that."

"Not as amazing as you. It'll be Sergeant Perez leading this training someday."

"Then I'd better work on my scowl." She makes a face, sticking out her lower lip, then dissolves into laughter.

Lia and Clint take off, and I sit on the curb. While I'm waiting, I scroll through my phone. My siblings have posted more photos of the rehearsal dinner to our family's group text thread. I send a response so they know I'm alive and not in any way jealous.

Me: You all look gorgeous. Steal some floral arrangements on the way out. Maybe some silverware? Bet it's expensive.
Aiden: Good idea, sis. We need supplies for the lunch we're catering at the West Oaks Country Club this week.
Mom: I would never allow such a thing. Madison, don't joke.
Me: It was Aiden!
Jake: I'm not bailing anybody out if this goes south. Will be LMAO when you're all explaining yourselves to the judge.
Mom: Madison, you should be here. Everyone's asking about you.

Aaaand I'm out.

I open my news feed instead. A headline blares from my screen. My smile vanishes.

Midnight Slasher Still At Large; West Oaks Residents Demand Answers.

It's from a local news blog, California Crimes Uncovered. I don't need to read the article to know what it's about. It's the case that's been dominating the attention of West Oaks PD and the rest of our Southern California town for months.

The Midnight Slasher is the reason we're having this SWAT training.

In the last several months, a ski-masked man has invaded homes at night, attacking the homeowners with a military combat knife and stealing thousands of dollars in jewelry and cash. The media gave him his nickname because he strikes in the early hours of the morning.

The slasher part? It's gruesome, but accurate. Thankfully, only one victim has died. But it's like the Slasher *wants* to keep his victims alive, left with skin-deep cuts but soul-deep terror after what they've endured.

With the Midnight Slasher's one-man crime spree, West Oaks residents want to see more being done. Faster response times, more manpower. They want the Midnight Slasher caught so they can sleep securely at night.

Meanwhile, my parents ask when I'll be done with this law enforcement phase and do something more practical. Something less dangerous. Something easier.

It's one thing for your brother, Mads. But you?

I thought if I could upgrade my job title, they'd finally understand why I'm working so hard. They'd be proud of me. But that's clearly not happening any time soon. Instead, my mom is at my ex's fabulous rehearsal dinner, wishing I was the one getting married.

And I'm stuck alone in this parking lot, waiting for Sergeant Jennings to hand me my ass.

Glamorous indeed.

3

Nash

$\mathcal{I}$ see the three dots bounce, then disappear, then appear again while Emma drafts yet another response. My kid is as stubborn as me. Some might call that irony, but I'm too frustrated to see the potential for humor.

A throat clears, and I look up to see Detective Sean Holt eying me with concern from the church steps. "Everything all right?"

I pocket my phone. "My teenager's giving me heartburn."

Holt smirks. "Along with half the students in this training?"

I groan. "Try more than half."

My commander was not impressed.

Bravo team did a piss-poor job with the last exercise. But Alpha, Charlie, and Delta weren't stellar today either. I'm used to working with operators who've surpassed every expectation set out for them. These kids are police officers, but still, I'm starting from almost the ground up. It's *my job* to get them ready.

When most of the students are failing, is it really their fault? Or does the problem lie with the teacher?

Holt and I walk down the steps and into the parking lot. Holt crosses his arms and rests his weight against my SUV. "If you don't mind me saying, I hope you aren't going to be too hard on Shelby."

"Shelby?"

"Officer Shelborne. Bravo team."

"Right. Of course."

I forgot that was her nickname. To me, she's Madison. Blond, green-eyed Madison, who stood in front of me and took responsibility and didn't wilt under my criticism. Meanwhile, guys built like linebackers struggled to maintain eye contact with me.

Even when I try not to notice her, it's impossible not to.

"She's one of our best patrol officers in major crimes," Holt says. "I don't want to lose her to SWAT, but that's me being selfish. She'd be an asset anywhere."

My phone buzzes in my pocket, and I cringe. Holt must think I'm reacting to what he's just said.

"You don't agree?" he asks.

"It's not that. It's Emma. We've been arguing over text, and my ex is out of town, so Simone's not going to swoop in to the rescue."

"Ouch. Henry's not even two yet, so I have a long way to go. Toddlerhood is bad enough."

"You have no idea what you're in for."

Holt claps me on the arm. "Good luck, then. Janie and I have a date night tonight, so I'm gonna take off. I'll check in with you on Monday."

"Thanks for helping out today, man."

"It was fun. I missed my calling. Should've been an actor."

"I'll have to take your word on that."

As he walks away, Holt crosses paths with Madison, who's right on time for our chat. They say hello to one another, and Holt murmurs something. Probably encouragement. She nods.

Then Madison marches over to me. She's got her hands clenched on the straps of her gear bag. Like she's bracing herself. "You wanted to see me, sir?"

For a brief moment, my attention lingers on her heart-shaped face. Her long nose, bowed pink lips, the slight flush to her cheeks... I scrub those thoughts from my mind. I'm a professional, and this is a professional conversation.

"I'd like to discuss what happened earlier."

"I hope I didn't offend you, sir. I was just trying to explain why..."

She trails off when she sees me shaking my head. "I heard your story. I don't need to hear it again. That's not why I wanted to talk."

"It wasn't a story. *Sir.*"

That's her third "sir" in as many minutes.

"Fair enough. But I know you weren't the only one who overlooked Detective Holt in that room."

"If you want me to rat someone out, I'm not—"

"That isn't what I mean. You took responsibility for your entire team, and I respect that. So now, I want you to step up for your teammates again. Tell me what I can do better as your instructor."

Madison's eyes narrow. There's a long pause. Way too long.

"Is this a trick?" she finally says. "Sir?"

She looks so skeptical and so damn *cute* that I almost crack a smile. Which is something that doesn't happen too often, at least not at work. Lately, not even at home. I spend too much of my time with Emma playing bad cop.

"Not a trick." I sigh. "I'm going to level with you. I've never actually taught anything before."

Madison shrugs. "I had a hunch," she mutters.

Thank you, I say silently. The last thing I want is for her to humor me.

At West Oaks PD, we have a full-time SWAT team, and most members serve a year or more. My commander wants to choose ten new operators to build up our tactical arm. At this rate, he'll be lucky to find half that.

And whose fault will that be?

I hate needing help and I *really* hate asking for it, but the commander doesn't want to hear my excuses. I didn't want this instructor gig, but now that I have it, it's my duty to excel.

And if the woman with the knowledge I need also happens to be stunning? That is irrelevant. Madison is the best person for this. It's not just that we went to the academy together, though that's a factor. It's Madison herself. The very things—apart from her physicality—that make me notice her.

"Here's how I see it," I say. "In the classroom, I've been looking at blank faces. I get almost no questions. Then today, there's screw-ups all over the place. As if they didn't hear a word I said."

"I was one of the screw-ups. I'm no teaching expert."

"But I'll bet you're an expert on your fellow students. I want full honesty. I won't get offended. Just think of it as helping out a former classmate from the academy."

She bites her lip. "I wasn't sure you remembered that."

"You think I'd forget you?"

My phone buzzes with a new text. I know I'm being rude, but I just can't resist looking.

Emma: You're always annoyed at me when I'm home, and then you get pissed at me when I'm gone. It's not my fault you have no one else in your life! If you're miserable, do something about it instead of taking it out on me!! [Angry emoji.]

I sputter as I read Emma's words.

"Is something wrong?" Madison asks.

"It's nothing." I switch my screen off. I'm sick of this back and forth with my kid. I'm sick of feeling like I don't have a *clue* what I'm doing. There's nothing I hate more. "Actually, a family thing came up. Can we finish this talk on Monday?"

She looks confused again. Then she shakes her head. "Sorry, yeah. Just trying to keep up. This has been a weird conversation, Sergeant."

"Didn't mean it to be."

"Okay, then." She smiles with her mouth closed. "I'm going to call a ride."

"You don't have a ride back to the station?"

"I rode with Officer Perez earlier, and I told her not to wait. But that's what Uber's for, right?"

Jeez. I'm being an asshole. I can't just leave her here by herself. If someone did that to Emma, I'd be mad as hell.

I point at my SUV. "I'll drive you."

"You sure?"

"Yeah, we can keep talking on the way. If you don't mind making a quick stop first?" I slide into the driver's seat. She dumps her gear bag in the trunk and gets in beside me. Madison buckles her seatbelt, and I steer the SUV out of the parking lot.

"What's the quick stop?"

"To pick up my daughter."

If Madison is present for this, it might keep me and Emma from going full nuclear on each other.

～

MADISON TUGS HER HAIR FREE OF ITS TIE. PALE golden waves topple over her shoulders. "So, what's she like? Your daughter?"

We've been making our way across town, stuck in Friday evening traffic. The cabin of the SUV is getting dimmer by the minute as the sun goes down. The streetlights along the route flicker on, and we're surrounded by the honking of horns and the revving of engines with nowhere to go.

Neither Madison nor I have brought up my request for honesty, and I get the sense she's stalling. But I don't call her on it.

"Emma's a sophomore at West Oaks High," I say. "A good kid. Most of the time."

"Why do I get the sense tonight is *not* one of those good times?"

"I just wish Emma would take things more seriously."

Madison stiffens beside me. "In what way?"

I know how gruff and freaking *old* I sound. I'm thirty-seven, which I still count as pretty young, no matter what my daughter thinks. But I can't help it. "Making smart choices. Being responsible for herself so I don't have to be the grumpy guy all the damned time."

Sometimes, I want to be the fun guy. Believe it or not.

The tension in Madison's shoulders evaporates, and she laughs. "Jennings, come on. Aren't you always the grumpy guy?"

At first, I'm speechless. Which isn't remarkable because I'm no prolific speaker as it is. But she just called me out, and I gotta say, I like it.

Her eyes widen. "Sorry. I shouldn't have said that. Sergeant."

You called me Nash in the academy, I want to say. Instead I go with, "Nah, I asked for honesty, didn't I? To respond to your question, I'm not the grumpy guy on purpose."

"Sounds like someone's making excuses."

"Oof. I walked right into that one."

Her teeth show as she smiles, and her emerald eyes shine

as they study me. I feel a warm glow of satisfaction. *See, Emma? Your dad can be funny.*

We reach the slumber party house and stop at the curb. I pick up my phone and open the messaging app. "It'll just be a moment. Emma's at a sleepover. I told her to come home, but I think I'm being ignored."

I'm going to give Emma one last chance to come outside before I make a scene in front of her friends.

"Wait. Why do you want Emma to leave this sleepover?"

I explain the whole boys-at-the-party situation, my pulse thundering again with indignation. Madison asks to see Emma's messages, and I scroll through them.

I've heard the horror stories about teens and social media. Videos that go viral and ruin girls' lives. That's not going to be my daughter. It's my job to protect her. And teenage boys? That's threat number one.

"Besides," I say, "if I don't do something now, my credibility is lost. She'll never listen to me again. And she'll end up in some terrible situation and won't come to me for help."

These are the thoughts that keep me up at night since Emma moved in with me full-time.

Madison doesn't say anything, but I can hear the gears moving in her head. "What about Emma's mom? What does she say about it?"

I don't want to explain that history. Tops on my list of failures. "I should be able to take care of this myself."

Madison nods. "Do you know the parents who're hosting this sleepover?"

"Yeah. Pretty well."

"Do you know Chad and Toby? Are they seniors? Trouble-makers with tattoos? Footballers with a bad rep?"

"No, I looked them up on social media. They're sopho-mores. No visible ink. In the debate club, like Emma. But..."

"According to Emma's messages, they're eating pizza and

watching a movie. Under the supervision of parents you know. And your daughter is otherwise level-headed?"

I sigh, slumping back in my seat. I can see where this is going. "You think I'm being an asshole."

"I wouldn't presume to go that far. But are you being *grumpy*?" Her eyebrows are trying to reach her hairline.

I throw my hands toward the windshield, as if that communicates something. "Sometimes, grumpy is warranted!"

"But you said you didn't want to be the grumpy guy with your daughter. This is your chance."

I glare at the house, with its lit-up windows. My breath catches when I spot someone pass by. It's Laura Chen, the mom, carrying a stack of pizza boxes. I see no signs of a raging orgy or meth lab. Or any other indication of trouble.

I'm calmer now. I realize if I storm in there and drag Emma out, she won't forgive me in the next decade. If that.

There's a reason my personal life is a mess. And that reason is me.

"Fine. You may have a point." I don't know why I sound so gruff. I could try for grateful, but the best I can manage is a slight movement at the corner of my mouth. I put the car in gear and drive away from the curb before I can change my mind. "I'd appreciate if you don't mention this to anyone."

"Mention what?"

"Thanks."

Traffic isn't so bad now. I exhale as I turn onto the main boulevard, leaving the sleepover behind. I hope I made the right choice.

No, I did.

"You're not as terrifying as some people think," Madison says a couple minutes later.

"*Terrifying*? You find me terrifying?"

"I didn't say that. But other people do."

"Who?"

"I'm not naming names!"

"Why do these nameless individuals find me terrifying?" I know I can be intense. I prefer being quiet over running my mouth. But it's never been a problem with my teammates, either in the Navy or on SWAT.

"It's because of your whole vibe. All scowly." She gestures at me. "The Navy SEAL sniper thing." She points. "See? That. Right there."

"What?"

"You're frowning."

That's just my face. "Do I come across as arrogant?"

"Not *exactly*. But you don't go out of your way to be approachable. If you want students to ask questions, they can't be scared of the teacher."

I grunt, thus proving her point.

She snickers. "Sorry you asked my opinion?"

"No," I grind out.

"Am I kicked out of SWAT training yet?"

"We're former classmates, remember? You're doing me a favor. This has no bearing on your standing in training."

"Careful. Former classmates almost sounds like friends."

"Can't we be friends?"

That sentence is out of my mouth before I consider it.

Danger, I tell myself. *She's your student.*

I remember the day she introduced herself to me at the academy. Somehow, everyone knew I was a former SEAL, though I hadn't said anything about it. I could feel my classmates' and instructors' curiosity, but nobody worked up the courage to ask how I'd ended up there. While tons of police are ex-military, ex-SEALs are rarer, especially among the rank and file. Everybody expected me to be a cocky asshole.

But when I arrived in West Oaks, fresh from my

discharge, I was a mess. Everything on my home front was falling apart.

And there came this vibrant girl with an easy smile, approaching me like I was the misfit loner on the playground.

Hey, I'm Madison. You're Nash, right?

I wasn't in the right place to accept her implied offer of friendship. But now, I wonder where we'd be if I had.

Since I left the military, I've been trying to hold together the remains of my family. I haven't had the mental space or energy for much else. Four years have passed, and I can count my friendships in West Oaks on one hand.

At the next red light, Madison bends one leg and twists her body so she's facing me. "Okay, I have a proposal for you. Between friends. You want to be a better instructor. And I could use some career advice."

"Career advice? About SWAT?"

She hesitates. "Yeah."

"My door's always open. That's what I said the first day of training. Nobody's taken me up on it yet."

"Well, here I am." She opens her hands. "Not asking for special treatment. Just some tips on how to improve."

That seems reasonable to me. "What's your proposal?"

"Drinks with your students. That's allowed, isn't it?"

There's a jolt down my spine. "Drinks with you?"

"With a bunch of people from the training. We're all meeting up."

A flash of disappointment cuts through me, and I ignore it. *Off limits*, I remind myself. But I can make this work. I don't have other plans tonight. When's the last time I had plans on *any* Friday night?

New plan: a drink with my trainees so I can get to know them.

"Why not? I'm in."

Madison's smile is dazzling. "I'll pull up the directions."

"Should I stop by the station first?"

"Nah, we're late enough as it is. You drive and practice not scowling."

"Two things at once? This is hard."

She laughs and shakes her head. That warm glow inside me is back, the flames catching and igniting.

Fuck. I am in trouble.

4

Madison

This is turning into a really strange night. But it's the good kind of strange. It's the kind of strange that excites me. Like I have no clue where it'll lead, but I'm pretty sure it's somewhere fun.

Major contrast to where this evening started.

"Where are we headed?" Nash asks.

I give him the address, which I've just pulled up on my phone. I'm still wearing my sweaty T-shirt, black tactical pants, and boots. But if I swing by the bathroom at the bar, I can freshen up. I tug my fingers through my hair to fluff it.

At the next red light, Nash drums his fingers on his thigh. "Should you warn them I'm coming? If they find me so terrifying, they might not be thrilled about me showing up."

"Don't worry. It'll be good. If they see you drink beer and eat nachos like a regular human, you'll be less intimidating."

"But you're not intimidated by me."

Earlier, I was. But I'd rather not admit that now. "That's because I have two grumpy older brothers." Aiden is a chef, and he's mellowed with age. Jake is a dad and works in drug enforcement for the feds. But unlike Nash, Jake usually won't shut up. I also have two younger siblings, who are even louder.

I side-eye Nash across the cabin. "You do drink beer and eat nachos, right?"

His mouth curves. "It's been known to happen."

My eyes are stuck on his mouth for a moment. Nash's whole aura changes when he smiles.

"I promise it will be fun," I say.

"Fun? I'm not familiar with this concept."

I snicker, watching as headlights wash over him.

I thought he was going to chew me out for my mistake. Instead he wants my advice. Weird, right? Though I'm not sure how useful I'll be. Compared to Nash and his impressive resume, I'm basically nobody. I'm squeaking by on patrol, despite trying for more. I'm still single, still the middle child, still never more than second best. Or maybe third. That about sums it up in my parents' eyes.

Back when we were in the academy, everybody knew Nash's military credentials. Even the instructors were deferential to him. Yet he always sat quietly at the back. He had this bewildered air about him. Like he wasn't quite sure how he'd gone from an elite operator deployed overseas to a police academy cadet with twenty-somethings like yours truly.

I tried a few times to get him talking because he looked lonely. Okay, maybe also because he's a smokeshow. He wore a wedding band, and when I chatted him up, I was careful to keep any trace of flirtation out of my tone. I wanted nothing more than to be friendly. I thought he gave me the brush off.

But talking comes naturally to me. Nash isn't the same. Waiting beneath his brawny, stoic exterior is an intriguing guy. He's like a painting that changes depending on your perspective. You have to catch him at the right angle to see his whole picture.

And this picture? Not too hard on the eyes.

His dark hair is short on the sides but long enough on top to fall over his forehead. His nose and jaw cut strong lines on his profile, but from the side, his lips look surprisingly soft. Especially with the hint of a smile that's lingering there.

When I subtly peer at his left hand, I don't see a ring anymore. Either way, it shouldn't matter to me. Whether he's married or not, he's my superior now. My instructor.

He's so far out of my league, he's in the next galaxy.

The sign for the Shore Lounge appears on the next block. "There's the bar. I texted Lia I was on my way."

"Is there a parking lot?"

"Try the next right. There should be street parking."

He turns at the corner. We're in a neighborhood, packed with rows of homes built in the last century. Nash parks in front of a brick house, careful not to block the driveway.

When I go to open the passenger door, Nash rests a hand on my arm. "I know today could've gone better. I'll tell you one thing. Detective Holt thinks highly of you. He said you'd be an asset no matter where you end up."

"That means a lot. Holt's a nice guy."

"True. But from what I can tell, he also knows what he's talking about."

"Thanks." Blood rushes to my cheeks. I'm not sure if it's the encouragement or his hand on my arm, but my body's reacting to him.

Back it up, I tell myself. He might be nicer than I thought, but he's still Sergeant Jennings.

This is not a date.

I push out of the SUV.

"I need to put the weapons and gear in my locker," Nash says. "It's in the trunk."

We lock away our belongings. There's my SWAT training gear, including the dummy rifle. But Nash and I stow our handguns as well. I usually carry when I'm off duty. But we'll be drinking, and West Oaks PD policy requires that we leave our weapons here.

The streetlight directly above us is out, casting this part of the block in darkness. Windows are lit up, TVs on, the residents oblivious to the fact that anyone out here can see inside. When I'm home, I keep my curtains closed even though I'm on the third floor. Maybe I've seen too many crime scenes. But Nash's presence keeps my mind from going anywhere too dark.

I can hold my own against bad guys. But a man like Nash on my six? I wouldn't say no.

We reach the bar. Nash opens the door. "After you." The light from the bright blue sign makes his hair look like spilled ink.

When I walk past him, I feel his warmth inches away from me.

The Shore Lounge is a dive, with sticky floors, bad lighting, and too few tables. But the energy's great here. It's always packed. Classic rock plays from the overhead speakers.

Nash stays close as we push through the crowd, angling his shoulder like a bodyguard might.

Lia and Clint both raise their glasses when they see me. They're at a long table with a dozen people from our training.

"Shelby!" Clint shouts. "Finally! We were worried you didn't survive having your ass handed to you by Sergeant Scary. Scale of one to infinity, how bad was it?"

Lia freezes. Her mouth forms an O, and she nudges Clint. Then, in less than a second, all activity at the table ceases.

They all stare. Clint's skin slowly turns pink.

"Do you think they've noticed me yet?" Nash murmurs. I feel his breath against my ear.

"Hey guys," I say. "I brought a plus one."

Immediately, I regret my word choice. *Not. A. Date.*

Lia's the first to move again. She gets up from her chair and heads over. "Sergeant. Good to see you, sir."

Nash steps out from behind me. "Hope I'm not crashing the party?"

"Of course not! More the merrier!" She's a little too enthusiastic. "Grab a chair!"

"How about I order a pitcher for the table?" He turns to me. "Madison, what do you like?"

"Fat Tire?"

Nash nods and turns to the others. "Anyone want to give me a hand?"

Wide eyes stare back until Tyler jumps up. "I will, sir." He practically salutes.

They head for the bar.

A bumpier start than I was hoping for.

Lia grabs my arm. "Um, what is happening?" she hisses.

Conversation among our friends has picked up slightly, but they're all whispering and casting nervous glances at Nash's back.

"What do you mean?" I ask. "He didn't have plans, so I invited him to get to know everyone. He's actually a decent guy."

She leans back and studies me like I might've been replaced by a body double. "Let me get this straight. You were supposed to be in trouble. Now you show up with Jennings like he's an adorable stray you decided to bring home?"

I scoff. "He's hardly a stray." We both turn our heads. Nash is leaning his elbows against the bar, all wide shoulders and curvy triceps. He's ready to burst out of that shirt. "He's more of a thoroughbred."

Her expression grows even more incredulous. "You have a crush on Sergeant Scary!"

"I do not," I hiss.

Clint pops up behind Lia. "Hey Shelby, why'd he call you Madison?"

I force my brain to switch gears. At least Clint didn't hear what Lia said. "When we met in the academy, I went by my first name."

He squints at me. "Wait, I thought your first name was Shelby."

"You thought my name was *Shelby Shelborne*? You're an idiot."

"Whatever. You're the one who brought Sergeant Jennings here. Tonight was supposed to be relaxing. He's freaking everyone out."

"He's standing right behind you," I whisper.

Clint spins around. Nash is still across the room, paying for the pitcher. I burst out laughing.

"Jeez, you spend an hour with Jennings, and you're already turning mean like him."

Clint jumps again when Nash actually appears, holding a pitcher of golden-brown beer, while Tyler carries a stack of glasses. We join the table, and the other officers make room. They're quiet and wary. But Lia and Clint say thanks and smile when Nash pours glasses of beer and passes them around.

Lia lifts her drink. "To bringing home strays."

Nash and half the officers at the table scrunch up their faces, confused.

I raise my glass. "How about, to new friends?"

"New friends," Nash repeats.

We all clink our glasses together and take a sip. It's cold and malty, a hint of hops spreading across my tongue. I'm close enough to Nash that his arm and thigh brush against me.

Nash said in the car that he wanted to be friends. I'm still not sure if it's possible. But do I mind having him here next to me?

Nope. I don't mind at all.

As we settle in, fresh drinks in hand, the conversation starts to flow more easily. But Nash is quiet, taking long pulls of his beer. A wrinkle settles in between his eyes. He's going back to brooding and intense. Nash's very presence is commanding. And yes, intimidating. But the others have it wrong. It's not scary so much as compelling. Nash is *someone*. A man who knows who he is. At least, that's how he seems to me.

But I genuinely want him to get to know the others. Not because I'm trying to score points with our instructor or prove that I'm useful. I like seeing the different angles of him. Everyone else should see them too.

I'm about to ask him a question and get him talking, but another of my teammates beats me to it.

"Hey, Sergeant," someone says from the other end of the table. "What's the real story behind the Midnight Slasher?"

5

Nash

*I*nstantly, our table goes quiet. A dozen pairs of eyes turn toward me.

"What do you want to know?" I ask.

I thought these patrol officers were going to turn tail and run when they saw me. Not the best start when they're supposed to be candidates for the tactical team. They might think I'm scary, but they'll have to be able to face a lot worse.

Lia brushes a thumb through the condensation on her glass. "The Slasher is the reason West Oaks is scrambling to add people to SWAT. So you must know a lot about it."

Everyone in West Oaks has heard a lot about the break-ins. The way the guy cuts his victims, attacks in the early hours of the morning when the homeowners are alone. But I suppose I have more intimate knowledge than most.

"I helped respond to the call to the Cowling residence," I say.

The Slasher's most recent victim.

It happened a few weeks back. An insomniac neighbor reported a possible burglary at the house next door. When patrol officers responded, they realized it might be the

Slasher. The guy was wearing a dark balaclava and had the homeowner tied up, bleeding from shallow wounds to his limbs.

Patrol called SWAT. We rolled in, treating it as a hostage situation. But by then, the Slasher had escaped.

I'll never forget the victim's face or name. Eugene Cowling, age sixty-five. Widower, parent of two. The attacker sliced cuts down Cowling's arms and legs. The other victims described the Slasher's knife as combat-style, similar to a k-bar. While the Slasher hasn't killed his other victims, Cowling succumbed to a heart attack—literally scared to death.

If we don't catch the Slasher, we're all worried Cowling won't be the last. Especially if the Slasher decides to escalate.

"We had a chance to catch him, and we were too late," I say. "Could we have helped save the homeowner if we'd made it there quicker? If we'd had a bigger team?" I shrug. "Mayor Ackerman and Chief Liu seem to think so." Cowling's son has been on every local news show and podcast, giving tearful testimonials about police incompetence.

"The chief has stepped up patrols at night," someone says.

"But we don't know *where* to do extra patrols," Madison chimes in. "The Slasher's been striking homes all over town in different neighborhoods. There are a few commonalities, like the fact that he always goes after people who are alone. But it's not enough to narrow the field."

Clint spins his beer glass on the table. "We've all seen nasty stuff before. But this guy? He's twisted." Clint glances around, lowering his voice, and the others lean in. "He must enjoy torturing them. Making them bleed. Why else would he do it?"

Madison chews her lip.

If they're looking for reassurance, I'm not sure I can give that to them.

"Trying to understand is a waste of time," I say. "Ninety percent of what we do in SWAT is executing high-risk search and arrest warrants. When we do it right, it's boring. We train for the hardest stuff, the situations we may never see. We plan for the 'what ifs' so we know that, if shit happens, we'll be ready. That's the *real* question. Not worrying about what motivates the sickos out there. When you get the call, are you going to be ready?"

Uneasy faces stare back at me.

TEN MINUTES LATER, THE SOMBER MOOD PERSISTS. They're staring into their beers.

I think I broke them.

Then Madison drains her glass and grabs the pitcher for a refill. "You must have some great stories, Jennings. What about the fun parts of SWAT?"

"Fun parts?"

Madison's eyes are so damn bright, full of good humor. "Yeah. You know. Tell us the sexy stuff."

Chuckles turn into laughs and jeers. But at least they're lightening up.

Fun stories. I can handle this. Right?

"Okay, this was a couple years back. We were called in on a bank robbery. The robbers were positioned in the front of the bank, firing AR-15s at patrol and getting more unstable by the minute. They'd herded the hostages into a back room. We got the order from the commander—get the hostages out of there. Whatever it takes. We decided on an extreme solution. A no-entry assault."

I pause for another sip of beer. No one else says a word.

"There were three walls between our operators and the civilians. So, what did we do? We set charges and blew our own exit path. *Boom. Boom. Boom.* It was like one of those old cartoons where Wile E. Coyote plows a hole through a bunch of brick walls. Then one of the robbers comes barreling through the smoke, waving his rifle. I was on the roof of the building across the street, saw him in my scope. *Bam.* Took him out. The negotiators got the other suspects to give themselves up. No other casualties."

"Whoa." Clint's eyes are wide. "What about when you were a SEAL? You must have even crazier stories from that."

"I do. But all the best ones are classified."

"Aw, Sarge. Not fair."

The others ask more questions, coaxing me into telling war stories from the SWAT team. Then some from BUD/S on Coronado Island, when I was going through my qualifications to become a SEAL. Even a few from my deployments overseas, with the details I'm allowed to share. Other patrol guys with military experience pitch in with their own stories.

The conversation moves onto their wildest nights on patrol here in West Oaks. Like that time a certain movie star stripped naked and ran down Ocean Lane, high on psychedelic mushrooms. Or a billionaire up in the hills who was inconsolable after his vintage porn collection was stolen. I enjoy hearing their stories, but it's Madison my eyes keep searching out. Her smiles as she fills in details. Her easy laughter, her head tipped back.

My students have finally relaxed. They're still green. But for the first time since this training started, I'm optimistic. Given the chance, I think I can make them into decent operators.

The only downside? I'm beginning to wish Madison wasn't in my SWAT training at all. For purely selfish reasons.

And that makes me a *real* asshole.

After a while, Clint gets up, then returns with a tray of shot glasses. There are cheers, and my students pass them around.

Madison ends up with two in her hand. "Want one?" she asks me.

I hesitate. This is probably a bad idea. But with Madison watching me expectantly, I can't bring myself to say no.

"Just one."

One shot can't do any harm.

6

Madison

*N*ash and I clink shot glasses. The tequila burns my throat on the way down, but it's a good burn.

He tips his back and swallows. I follow the bob of his Adam's apple.

"If Emma could see you now," I say, nudging his knee with mine.

He smiles. "She'd probably pour me another one."

"That could be arranged."

"Don't tempt me." The corner of his mouth ticks up again.

Temptation. I'm feeling that right now.

"What have you been doing since the academy?" I ask. "I knew you'd joined SWAT, but I haven't seen you around otherwise."

He shifts in his seat. "Emma's been living with me the past year. Before that, she spent the weekends with me. We worked on my house together, went to the beach." He shrugs. "I tried to stay out of trouble."

"You have a habit of getting into trouble, Jennings?"

"Usually, no."

Our eyes lock, and I'm the first to look away. "Speaking of trouble, do you remember in the academy when Chase Collins streaked all the way from headquarters to the beach?"

"Along with half our class? Yeah. Wish I could forget *that* image."

I snort. Lia and Clint were in the class below us. I have no idea if their group was as crazy as ours.

"You didn't streak though," I point out.

"I was still married then. I kept my behavior in check."

Still married. Which means he's not married anymore.

I've been reining in my thoughts—or at least, trying—because I wasn't sure if he was attached. But if he'd stripped down that night in the academy, there's no way in the universe I'd have forgotten the view. And that just makes me wonder. Does Nash have hair on his chest? Is he smooth? Does a happy trail lead down to his...

A wave of heat passes through me.

At the other end of the table, Clint and Tyler are singing along to the music. Lia's telling a story with big hand gestures. But she's also watching us.

"You didn't streak either," Nash says.

"Actually, I did. But I ran so fast, hardly anybody saw me." I had to cover my boobs along the way, just to fight the bouncing. *Ouch.* I close my mouth on a giggle.

"I can't tell if you're kidding or not."

"Guess you'll never know."

"Guess not."

A nearby group erupts into braying laughter. I lean closer so he'll hear me over the noise. "Be honest. Are you having fun?"

His only response is a half-smile as he watches me from the corner of his eye. We're not touching now, but his solid presence is like a magnetic field. I feel him even when I'm not looking.

Still my instructor. Still not happening. *But*, a naughty voice in my brain says. *But...*

Tingles rush through my body, and it's not just the tequila.

"Admit it, I have great ideas," I say. "I didn't even plan this out. Pure instinct."

"You're knocking my answer to your question earlier at training?"

"Just a little."

"Maybe your instincts are better than mine."

"What do you mean?"

He shakes his head. "Never mind. Ignore me."

Lia waves at me. Uh oh. I'm getting the signal. "Want another drink?" I ask Nash.

"A beer maybe. I can get it."

"No, I've got this round. I'll be right back." I go toward the bar, and Lia heads me off. We drop our elbows onto the bartop, waiting for the bartender.

"So, you and the sergeant are looking pretty cozy."

"He's a friend from the academy."

"You're friends with the guy suddenly? I get that you make friends just by breathing, but come on, Shelby." She turns to her side, facing me. Lia must've showered at the station before coming here. She's French-braided her dark hair, and shiny pink gloss coats her lips. "If you spend all tonight whispering with him and then make the tactical team, you know what people will say. Right?"

Acid rises in my throat. "That's bullshit for a million different reasons. Jennings doesn't pick the team. The commander does." I glance around, making sure none of the others are close enough to listen in. "And *nothing* is going to happen between me and him."

"You sure he knows that? 'Cause the way he's been staring at you could melt the North Pole in January."

Don't look, I tell myself. *Don't even think about it.*

I look over my shoulder. Nash is sitting back in his chair, arms crossed. His eyes are locked on me. They don't move away. But there's nothing lascivious in his gaze. If anything, it's protective.

I only glance away from Nash when the bartender asks for our order. "Two Bud Lights," I say. Then to Lia, "You're wrong."

"I just hope you'll be careful."

"I'm always careful."

But do I sometimes take risks? Risks that could end in disaster? I've already proven that today.

7

Nash

*A*n hour or two later, Madison and I are still sitting at the table, laughing about our academy days. It's not that I can't talk to people. I just choose not to. But Madison? She asks me a question, and suddenly I'm telling her my innermost thoughts.

I don't tell her *everything* I'm thinking, of course. That would be stupid. And could lead me to places I have no business going.

Tyler plunks down another tray of tiny glasses and a pile of lime wedges. There are shouts and cheers.

This is their third round. Or fifth? I've lost count.

Clint pushes a tiny glass into my hand. "C'mon Sarge. Have fun with us!"

"Nope." I set my shot glass back on the tray. "I'm done."

"No more shots?" Madison asks.

"We've had plenty." I grab an untouched pitcher of water instead. I pour a glass for myself and one for Madison. I hold it out to her, but instead, she downs her tequila. The shot glass thumps as she sets it on the table, and she flashes a sexy little smirk. As if she's saying, *You're not the boss here, Jennings.*

Shit.

My mind has been straying to dirtier places. Such as—I can't stop wondering if Madison streaked to the ocean with our academy classmates. I wouldn't have looked then, but I'd have no problem doing it now.

My dick's plumping up, and suddenly my dirty thoughts are translating into physical reality.

Nope. Not happening. Down boy.

"I'll stick with water." I lift my glass. "Here's to good behavior."

Madison laughs like I was making a joke.

Slowly, members of our group peel away. Lia and Clint remain, plus Tyler and a couple more guys. I can read their restless expressions, the way their eyes have been roving over the room.

Hookup time. And none of them seems to be finding suitable prospects. I'm glad they're not looking Madison's way.

I should be showing that level of judgment.

Clint slaps the flat of his hand on the table. "I'm ready to bail. The place across the street has a dancefloor. Who's in?"

Chairs scrape as Lia and the others stand.

Madison gives me a questioning look. "What do you think?"

The plan was one drink with my students. That's turned into several beers and a tequila shot.

I should say no. I'd better get myself to bed. *Alone.*

But when I open my mouth, that's not what comes out.

"I'll stick around. I should make sure you get home safely."

She rolls her eyes. "Don't make it sound like a hardship. I can find another ride."

That's what I'm worried about. I don't know if that makes

me less of an asshole, or more of one. "Not a hardship at all. I'm not ready for the night to end."

She smiles slowly. "Good. I'm not ready for that either."

Cold air blows into my face as we head across the street. The bouncer checks the others' I.D.s, but he barely glances at mine.

I pay Madison's cover. She seems surprised, but doesn't comment.

Once we're inside, a haze of heat and alcohol greets us. Pink and green and blue neon shimmer in the glass bottles behind the bar. An upbeat song plays by a singer I can't place.

It's a lot louder in here. Instinctively, I reach for the small of Madison's back as our group heads toward the bar. When we get there, I edge forward. "Two club sodas with lime," I shout at the bartender. I pass one to Madison without comment.

I'm probably being overbearing. I just feel like I should look out for her. But do I try ordering for Lia or Clint or my other students? No.

It's because I drove Madison here. I feel responsible for her.

Sure. That's it.

When we've got our drinks, we crowd around a bar-height table with no chairs. Madison's friends down their drinks and head for the dancefloor. I think she might follow them, but she stays at my side, leaving a couple inches between us. She sips her club soda and bobs her head in time with the music. She's like the kid at the prom hanging out with the chaperone.

"You don't want to dance with them?" I ask.

"I'll dance if you do."

"I don't dance."

"You don't have drinks with your students, either. Until tonight."

I'm still pondering that bit of wisdom when my phone dings. I see a new text message notification, and anxiety grips my stomach. It's from my daughter.

Emma: Dad, we're having a very PG night. Thought you'd want to know.

I huff a small laugh of both gratitude and relief. There's a photo attached showing all six of the teenagers at the sleepover. Two are vaguely boy-like. They're all grinning at the camera and flashing signs with their hands. I will assume those are not gang related.

"Looks like it's going well?" Madison's head is tilted in my direction, sneaking a peek at my screen.

I hold it up so she can see better. "Emma's that one," I shout over the music. I puff up my chest a little, pointing to my kid. She's got my dark hair, plus her mom's button nose. Emma's smile is pure mischievous magic. No clue where that came from. My ex is subdued like me.

"Beautiful. PG night indeed. I don't even spot any hickeys."

I make a horrified sound, somewhere between shouting and retching. She snorts.

Madison lifts up her phone. "My family's having fun without me too." She shows me a picture of a crowd in cocktail attire. Their arms are raised, holding champagne glasses. "There's my brother Aiden. And that's Jake. Those are the twins. I'm a double-middle child. Two older, two younger."

No wonder she's skilled at talking to people. She was constantly surrounded growing up. My skin itches as I imagine it. I had my older sister, but she left me alone, and I valued my space.

Of course, I'm not craving space as much at the moment. I shift an inch closer to Madison. So I can hear her better.

"I get along best with my brother Jake," she says. "He's one of my best friends."

"*One* of your best friends?"

"What? Everyone has more than one best friend."

"No, Madison. No, they don't. *I* don't."

"But are you the exception? Or the rule?"

"I don't know people's lives well enough to say."

"Exactly," she whispers, leaning into me. My hand ends up on her hip to brace her. But then, it stays.

I clear my throat.

"So, you have a lot of friends," I say. "What about a boyfriend?"

Her eyes slide to mine and hold. "Nope. I'm single."

I nod like this is mildly interesting. But I'm overheating. My heart's thumping to the beat of the music.

Dangerous fucking territory.

She's still got the photo on her phone screen. "What about those two?" I ask, pointing to the couple in the center of the group, their arms wrapped around one another. A guy in a suit and a girl in a white sequin dress. They have that kind of happiness that stock models do. So over-the-top it doesn't seem real.

Madison grumbles. "That's the bride and groom. The rehearsal dinner is tonight." She chews her lower lip. "My high school boyfriend is getting married this weekend. To my former best friend."

"Oh. Yikes."

"Yikes is the correct response. But it's not as bad as it sounds. They got together after he and I broke up. My whole family's still close friends with their families. There's no SWAT training tomorrow, so I could go to the ceremony. But really? I can't face it."

I study the picture on Madison's screen. There's a twinge in my chest. A discomfort as I look at this guy who once had his arms around Madison the way he's holding onto his fiancée.

"You can do better," I announce. I don't mean myself. My relationship track record is shit. She deserves somebody amazing.

She bows her head, laughing self-deprecatingly. "Not everyone thinks so."

Then they're idiots, I want to say. "This high school boyfriend. Is he the one that got away?" My lips almost brush her ear.

She looks confused for a moment. Then a grin breaks over her face. "No. That's not... That's not what I meant. At all."

"Then I'm lost."

"I'm glad they're both happy. I'm over him. I just don't like what he represents."

"Which is?"

She locks her screen and puts the phone away. "I'm warning you, this is going to sound dramatic."

"You witnessed my drama earlier. I almost did a breach and extraction on my kid's slumber party."

I shouldn't remind her of my grumpy asshole tendencies, but she laughs again. "I'll tell you. But we have to find a quieter place to stand. If I have to keep shouting, I'll go hoarse."

We retreat further into the club, away from the dance-floor. I don't see Lia or Clint anymore. Or anyone else we know.

We lean against a wall, turned slightly toward one another. The room is painted black. It's so dark I see her in shadows, in glimpses of washed-out color.

There's a charge to the space between us. Electromagnetism, making the hairs on my arms stand on end.

"My ex represents all the ways I've disappointed my parents. I dated him through high school, and we were off and on in college. Everyone had assumed I'd get married and join my parents' catering company. But then I decided to switch my major from business to criminal justice. My mother still isn't over it."

"She's not happy you're a cop?"

"She thinks it's dangerous. But both my older brothers were in the military. Jake did two tours in Afghanistan in the army, and he's with the DEA now. Nobody says boo about how his job is risky."

"That must be hard." If Emma wanted a career in the military or law enforcement, I'd worry too. But I have the utmost respect for women who serve.

"Jake is proud of me. But I'd love for the rest of my family to respect what I've accomplished, too. So far, being on patrol isn't enough."

"It matters that much what they think?"

She exhales. I feel the tickle on my cheek.

"Yes and no. I didn't care about their disapproval when I applied for the academy. But I still want to prove to them that I made the right choice. That I'm *good* at this and I belong here. You know?"

"Is this why you joined SWAT training? Because of what it would prove to your family?"

She cringes, looking away. "And why I took the detective exam a few months back. Sounds bad, I know. Like I didn't do it for the right reasons."

"Not necessarily." I can understand making career choices for other people rather than yourself. I'm in no place to criticize her for that. It's why I left the Navy. "But are you sure joining SWAT is what *you* want?"

"I don't know," Madison murmurs. "Honestly? I'm not sure what I want." Her full lips part. They look plush. Soft. "What about you?"

My throat goes tight. "*What* about me?"

"Do you know what you want out of your career? Out of life?"

"I want my daughter to be happy."

"I mean *you*. Not just your family." Those grass-green eyes look up at me, sparkling with light. Music thrums around us like the rapid beating of my heart.

What I want...

Her glossy hair falls over her shoulder, and I wonder what it would feel like between my fingers. I wonder what she'd feel like pushed against this wall, my body covering hers, her mouth on mine. In this dark corner past midnight, where we'd just be two people who crave each other.

I go lightheaded at the rush of need that pounds through my blood. It comes from nowhere, but it also comes from *everywhere*. It surges like the music pumping from the speakers. What I want... I know exactly what I want. It's pure, instinctual desire.

And fuck, this isn't good.

"I haven't got a clue." That's the first lie I've told her tonight.

I don't do this kind of thing. I haven't dated at all since my divorce, much less one of my subordinates.

But I'm right up to the line with her. So close, a single breath will take me over it.

She nudges my arm. "You're supposed to be encouraging me. You have a successful career and a daughter who loves you, no matter how much trouble she gives you at times. If *you* don't know what you want, then what hope do I have?"

I'm surprised by the low, rumbly voice that comes out of me. "If you're looking for a mentor, I'm not the right person."

"Why?"

"Because the thoughts I'm having about you aren't the kinds a teacher should have for his student."

8

Madison

I'm speechless. For maybe the first time in my life.
He just...

Did he mean...

Somehow, words surface on my tongue. "What kinds of thoughts are you having about me?"

Slowly, Nash's dark brown eyes trail down my body. Like his stoic mask has slipped, and underneath is pure longing, naked and raw. It sends a jolt of lightning into my veins, ricocheting up and down my arms and legs. The heat in his gaze burns me all the way through. Stealing my voice again.

Shadows pool around us like they're holding us close, and the melody playing from the speakers repeats, again and again, in an endless loop.

"As your instructor, I should probably say goodnight and see that you get home. I could leave you at your doorstep, watch you go inside, and see you again on Monday at our next training session."

"Or?" I say the word on an exhale. A breathy whisper.

"Or we could stay here." His voice has dropped another

octave. "But if we do that, we'll just be Nash and Madison. Friends from the academy. The choice is yours."

I don't want to break eye contact, but I quickly glance around for Lia and Clint. I don't see anyone I know. I'm not even sure the others are still in the building. Yet if she were here beside me, I know what Lia would say. *I just want you to be careful.*

But I'm not scared of Nash. I can't imagine ever being scared of him.

And if no one else knows? It doesn't matter what they'd think.

When I find his eyes again, they're back to inscrutable. They're the color of whiskey. Rich, deep brown, hints of smoke and earth and smoldering fire. It's like I'm drinking him in, and he hits me much harder than the tequila did. I can't look away.

I'm not inexperienced with men. But I've never been with a man like Nash. A guy who's got so much more knowledge of the world, who has a teenage kid. My superior. My instructor.

I asked Nash what he wants.

Is it possible that he actually wants *me*?

We stare at one another for a long, drawn-out moment. But it's the kind of moment that's unforgettable. That feels bigger than just a few ticks of a clock. The song ends and a new one starts. Someone shouts and laughs. A gust of cooler air winds through the club as the front door opens and closes.

My heart is still thumping in time with the last song.

He's still waiting for me to respond.

"I'll stay," I breathe. "If you dance with me."

His gaze drifts away from me, moving to the next room, where we can see the main dancefloor. Colored lights rove over the couples as they lean into one another.

He grabs my hand and tugs me along, moving with steady determination, his jaw set. When we reach a far corner of the dancefloor, he faces me. We're in each other's space. Noses, lips almost touching. I inhale his spicy, musky scent. But his arms hang at his sides.

"I'm gonna need you to take the lead."

He speaks with authority. This isn't a request, and I think I understand what he means. There's a skewed power dynamic between us, and each step closer that we take now —*now*, when we're just Nash and Madison instead of instructor and student—is a risk. If anyone sees us dancing like this, it would mean trouble for both of us at work.

But it's a risk that sets my blood on fire.

I want him. I want those rare, sexy smiles. The toe-curling way he just looked at me.

I take his big hands and put them around my waist. I hold on to his deltoids, squeezing the firm muscle. I'm tall, so I don't have to crane my head much to look up at him. We sway to the music. Nash's hard edges fit perfectly against my softer curves, like puzzle pieces.

One song flows into the next. Neither of us lets go.

Instead, I move closer, my arms circling his neck. Our stomachs press together. His palms slide down to my hips as we follow the rhythm of the music.

I imagine us in his bed. His firm touch running over my naked skin.

The blood rushes from my head. My vision goes blurry. Goosebumps spread across my skin. The night's turned dreamy and fluid, like it's no longer real. I have no idea what time it is. If time is still moving at all.

We dance and hold one another until I can't see anything but him. And the longer we dance, the less this seems real.

It was strange enough that Sergeant Jennings, our gruff instructor, ended up at the bar with me and Lia and the rest of us tonight. Taking shots with us, laughing, sharing stories and listening avidly to ours.

Except now, the only *us* is me and Nash.

Our arms are wrapped around each other, stomachs and chests brushing. My cheek rests on his collarbone, and my lungs fill with his masculine scent. His warmth floods into me through the barriers of our clothes. This man who, this morning, I thought didn't even remember my name.

It doesn't make sense. Which might explain why it feels so *right*.

I lift my head, and Nash's eyelids have fallen closed.

It's pure dream-logic when I touch his cheek. Stubble scratches my palm. The pad of my thumb. People and lights rotate around us, but we're in the center, unmoving. I'm not even breathing.

Nash opens his eyes. His lips part. I tilt my face upward.

And suddenly, my mouth is on his.

His heat, almost too intense, right up against my skin. The smooth softness of his lips. I taste his richness. His fire. My hand snakes around the back of his neck, pulling him closer. My fingers sift into the short, silky strands of his hair.

But just as quickly as it started, Nash breaks the kiss, pulling away from me. His chest heaves. His eyes are dilated. Shocked—at me, at himself, I don't know. He doesn't look happy.

And I'm crashing back to the ground.

Did I read this completely wrong?

"I'm sorry," I stammer. "I thought…" That Sergeant Jennings wanted me? *Really*?

Friends from the academy. That was what he said. *Friends*. And I threw myself at the man. Like a fool. Like a schoolgirl with a crush.

I have to get out of here.

"I'm just going to—" I start backing away, pointing my thumb at the bathrooms. I need to get away from this moment that's so mortifying, it's scraping my skin raw.

But the words cut off when Nash cinches his arms around me, and his mouth crashes down onto mine.

9

Nash

I'd almost forgotten how good this could feel. A sweet, beautiful woman up against me. Her mouth eager, opening to the demanding pressure of my tongue.

But Madison isn't just anyone. It's *this* woman I want.

This woman, who should be off limits.

When her lips first touched mine, I tried to stop. I really fucking did. I've built my life on doing the right thing, and this is wrong, wrong, wrong. But we've been edging toward this all night—maybe even since the academy—and I just want her too fucking badly.

My hands move downward, tracing the contours of her body. The curves and valleys along her sides. A lush landscape to explore. I taste her, drink her in, fill up my senses with Madison. Summer and sunlight, strawberries and fresh-cut grass.

I push my tongue deeper into her pliant mouth. She lets out this tiny moan, almost a purr, a vibration that makes my body hum at the same frequency. My fingers tangle in her cornsilk hair, thumbs stroking each side of her face.

Madison's hands flatten on my chest. They run along the

fabric of my shirt to my stomach, pause at my waistband, move back up again.

My dick hardens against the seam of my pants.

Still taking her mouth, I walk her further into the shadows until her back hits the wall. Music and lights pulse in the background. Sweat beads at my temples. I taste salt on Madison's lips.

I picture everything I want. Her long hair brushing my bare hip. Her tongue moving over my skin. Her body tangled with mine, the heat between us building until we can't contain it.

Come home with me. Those words are on the very edge of my tongue. An order, not a request. I'm taking her to my bed.

Fuck. I should stop.

I have to stop.

We both could be disciplined if anyone sees us. What the hell will happen on Monday when I go back to being Madison's instructor?

What will my daughter say if she finds out?

Stop. Stop. *Stop.*

I pull myself away. Our kiss breaks. I'm gasping for breath. Madison's eyes are wide, shining. Her lips are pink, swollen from kisses.

I want to dive back into her again, take her to my empty house—my *so very empty* bed—strip her and explore every square inch of her sweat-damp body with my mouth and my hands and with my aching cock and—

"Fuck, I have to go. I'm sorry. I have to go."

"But…" Her hand touches my arm, and I ease away.

"That was a mistake."

Her face falls. My guts lurch with guilt and everything else that's mixed up inside of me.

I might be sick.

I practically run out of there. I push through the exit onto the sidewalk, and cool air hits my skin, shocking me awake and all the way back to reality.

My pulse is still wild. I tell my vitals to slow down, but they won't. My body is in full rebellion, my testosterone spiking, tremors spreading to the tips of my fingers.

And I was worried about my teenage kid misbehaving?

Madison is my student. Even if I'm a shitty excuse for a teacher, that doesn't change my role. She asked for my advice about her career. She made it clear that she sees me as a mentor.

Then a few minutes later, I'm coming onto her? Shoving my tongue down her throat?

What the hell is wrong with me?

It doesn't matter that she chose to stay. That she kissed me first. I practically held her hand and pulled her along. *I knew* what I was fucking doing. I can't blame the alcohol because I haven't had a drink in hours and I'm stone-cold sober by now.

I expect more of myself than that. Better judgment. Better self control.

It must be nearly two in the morning. The street's nearly deserted. I know when the door to the club opens, because the music gets louder, then fades. "Nash?"

I can't even look at her.

"I'm sorry." I take out my phone, fumbling it as I try to unlock the screen. "I'm going to call you a cab."

"You don't need to be sorry. That was...um, well...I guess we got carried away."

"It was my fault," I say. "I take full responsibility." I hear the echo of her words from earlier, the training exercise at the church. My shame increases.

From the corner of my eye, I see her hugging her waist, shifting from foot to foot. "I just don't understand what happened."

"I wasn't thinking. You kissed me, and I reacted." God, I sound like an insensitive prick. Like I'm blaming her. I close my eyes and shake my head. "I wasn't thinking about anything except that I wanted to kiss you back. *Really* wanted it. In that moment."

"But I don't understand why you stopped."

I chew the inside of my lip so hard I taste salt and metal.

"Oh, shit. Are you still married?"

"*No.*" I spin around. "I'm divorced. And single. It's not that. But you're my student, and way too young for me, and—"

"That didn't seem to matter a little while ago. But if you're not feeling it anymore, that's fine. No need to say more." There's sarcasm behind these words. She's mad, as she should be, though not for the same reasons that I'm kicking myself.

"Madison…"

"I'm gonna go." She points her thumb down the block and then starts walking away.

"I was calling you a cab."

"So you don't have to drive me home? Yeah, I gathered that. I live a mile away. I'll get there myself."

"Are you going to *walk?*"

"Maybe. You wanted to be done with me, and now you are. I'm letting you off the hook. I'll get my gear from you on Monday."

Dammit. I can't let her walk home by herself. Madison is hardly defenseless, but it wouldn't be right.

Before, I needed space between us. I was worried about what I'd do if we were alone together. But I've very clearly killed the mood. Kissing me again won't be an issue.

I'll be lucky if Madison speaks to me after this.

"I'll drive you. Just wait. I'll get the car."

"No thanks."

"*Madison.*"

She's already halfway down the block. I curse and head in the opposite direction, running down the side street to get my SUV. The engine roars to life. I pull out and drive around the block until I'm back on the main boulevard.

But I don't see her. Where is she? I slam the heel of my hand against the steering wheel.

I wish I could go back in time. Stop myself from kissing her back. But that still would've meant rejecting her. Hurting her.

I should've stopped myself from dancing with her. I should never have agreed to come here at all. I knew I was blurring the lines between us long before I crossed them entirely.

But then, how would I have spent tonight? Lonely in my house? Pretending I'm satisfied with the piecemeal life I've allowed myself? Even before Madison kissed me, tonight was one of my best nights in ages. If I truly had the choice to take it back?

Enough. This is *exactly* why I keep this shit locked down. I know my job. I know my duty.

Rejecting Madison is the only right choice I could've made.

Finally, my body obeys me. My spine straightens, my racing heart slows. The world tunnels back into focus—the essentials. Like I'm staring through my scope.

I need to find Madison and get her home. I need to write up my notes from SWAT training today, something I should've done hours ago. I should get the house cleaned up and ready for Emma to come home.

And next weekend, I'll go out and find an attractive woman. Tall, slender, blond… I shake my head, forcing Madison's image out of my brain. I'll find someone and get myself laid. Someone warm and willing and uncomplicated.

Someone who doesn't expect anything from me but a wild night, because that's all I can possibly offer.

It's just been too long.

While I school my thoughts, my eyes scan street after street for a sign of Madison. She couldn't have gotten far.

I punch the brakes when I spot her, hair lit up like spun gold beneath a spotlight. I want to run my fingers through it, tug her close, cradle her against me.

Stop.

The engine revs as I accelerate into the turn, barreling over the asphalt. I buzz down the window, stopping beside her.

She's standing frozen in the middle of the street.

Words dry on my tongue when I see her expression. She's deadly serious, and her hand ghosts over her hip like she's searching for her gun.

"Burglary in progress," she says breathlessly, pointing at a house two doors down from where she's standing. "I heard glass breaking. Saw the perp enter. Dark ski mask."

"Are there occupants inside?"

"Don't know. I just called for backup, but we need to move, Nash. *Now.* It could be him."

She doesn't have to say the name. We both know who she means.

The Midnight Slasher.

Fuck.

10

Madison

*O*nce again, my night's taken another twist. I really don't like where this one is going.

I was heading away from the bar and away from Nash as fast as my feet could take me. I knew it was stupid to take off instead of waiting for a cab. But I just had to get out of there.

Nash kissed me back. Kissed me back thoroughly. And it was the hottest, most world-shaking kiss I've ever experienced. Nash's tongue and hands moved over me with wild abandon, like he wanted to strip me and devour me right on that dancefloor with strangers watching.

I wanted it too. Wanted Nash with an intensity I haven't felt in ages, if ever. I wanted to find out what his bronze skin is like under those clothes. Soft and smooth? Marked by scars?

Is he careful and deliberate in bed, controlled like he is at work? Or does he let go and turn into a man who's savage, primal, eager to take me over and give me the ride of my life? I'm guessing it's the second.

But then, suddenly, that incredible moment—that *yes, this is what I need* moment—vanished before my eyes when Nash pulled away. Because I'm still technically a part of SWAT training? Because I'm younger than he is? It's all bullshit. Excuses to explain whatever's really going on in his head.

I don't think Nash was trying to hurt me. But he wasn't trying *not* to hurt me either.

Why did he even kiss me if it was going to end like that?

So I was running away, my shoes tapping faintly on the concrete. And that's when I heard the tinkle of glass shattering. Everything inside me went cold.

A silhouette ducking into a window. A ski mask.

My mind skips back to the present. "We need to move, Nash. *Now*. It could be him."

Backup is a few minutes out, but we can't afford to wait. Thank goodness my last drink was hours ago.

Nash pulls his SUV to the side of the road. Throws it into park. Within seconds, he's unlocking the storage box in the back of his vehicle, pulling out our guns.

I feel naked without my belt and radio and all my usual gear, but I attach my holster to my waistband. I rack a round into the chamber of my gun.

"Put this on." He's holding out the body armor I wore for SWAT training, and I strap it into place. Nash has another vest in his locker, which he puts on. He's got a rifle in there too, but he leaves it behind, drawing his Glock.

We rush toward the house. Lights flicker in the windows. Looks like it's coming from a TV.

There's a broken window. Jagged glass sticks out of the frame.

A scream rends the air.

My heart lurches up into my throat, and my hand finds my weapon. "Cover me," I say to Nash, not hesitating a single second.

"*Madison*," he whispers. "Wait."

He might be a sergeant on SWAT, but he's not my

commanding officer here. I climb through the broken window into the house. I don't turn around, but I feel Nash there behind me.

We're in a laundry room. A washer and dryer sit to my left, a drying rack full of limp clothing to my right.

The doorway ahead of me is open. I go through it into a hallway. The scent of vanilla candles hits me, and beneath it something like roasted meat. Maybe the residents' dinner. Most of the lights in the place are off.

It's a comfortable home. Middle class. Typical, like so many others I've been inside before. A house that someone's cared for.

And now, it's been invaded. Not just by that man in the ski mask, but by us.

Nash steps past me, peering at the entryway of the house. From there, a staircase leads upstairs.

In the other direction down the hallway, I see the strobing flicker of a television. It makes me think of the lights on the dancefloor. The club was just a couple of blocks away, but it was like a different planet compared to this eerie, watchful stillness. A chill crawls through me.

Another scream. I feel it tearing at the underside of my skin. I want to run forward to help, but I force myself to remain steady.

Nash grabs my arm. I nod my head. *That way*. It came from the back of the house. He tries to hold on to me, but I shake him off. I know I'm being ridiculous, insisting on going first, but I can't stay still. I'm the one who saw that man go inside. I feel responsible.

I pad down the carpet toward the TV flicker. My gun is raised, level with my chest, my finger on the trigger guard. I reach the end of the hall. It opens into a room with a vaulted ceiling. A stuffed deer head stares down from the wall. From the TV, voices drone quietly, and garish colors paint the room.

A teenage girl sits on a straight-backed chair, sobbing. Her hands are behind her like she's tied up. The man in a ski mask stands over her, his back to me.

My whole body tenses. I'm starting to shake.

Tears stream down the girl's face. "Please let me go."

Is she a babysitter? Does she live here? I haven't seen any sign of other people in the home. If her parents were here, her screams would've woken them. Unless they're incapacitated. But the Slasher prefers to strike people alone.

The burglar pulls a knife. It's a military-style k-bar blade. Just like the Slasher uses. Without a word, he holds the tip to the girl's arm.

No.

I have to help her. Have to stop him.

My jaw clenches. I aim my gun at him, longing to pull the trigger, but the girl is directly behind him. I can't risk firing. The barrel trembles slightly in my hands.

Nash rests his palm against my back, and finally, I glance at him. His eyes are hard. Pissed. He tilts his head sharply, motioning for me to move. This time, I listen.

Nash steps forward to take my place at the mouth of the hall. His hands raise, the Glock held between them.

His body is as still and smooth as a glacial lake. Beautiful and starkly cold.

Suddenly, the girl shouts. Her eyes go wide as she spots us. "Help me!" she screams.

The Slasher spins around. His free hand goes to the girl's hair, his knife flying toward her throat.

Nash's finger twitches on the trigger. The movement is so subtle I almost miss it, and the rest of his body remains still as stone. The burglar's head snaps back, and at the same moment, there's a loud *pop*. The sound of a bullet lagging just behind its blinding speed.

The knife drops onto the carpet. The burglar's body falls onto the girl's lap.

She opens her mouth, drags in a ragged breath, and screams.

11

Nash

*M*adison races across the living room. I quickly lower my weapon. The scorched scent of gunpowder is bitter in the air.

Madison shoves the man's limp body off the girl, whose screams have turned to choked sobs.

"Oh my God. Help me. Please."

"It's okay," Madison says. "You're safe. We've got you. What's your name?"

"Bridget. Bridget Hanson."

When Madison and I emerged from that hallway and I saw Bridget, my first thought was of my daughter. Bridget reminds me of Emma. Dark hair, no older than sixteen. Shaking so hard her edges blur.

Holstering my gun, I go over to the burglar and rip off his ski mask. There's an oozing circle of red between his eyes. He's got a goatee, average features. Brown irises, staring at nothing. I check his pulse at his throat, but he's clearly dead.

"I want my mom."

I try to put myself between the man's body and the traumatized girl. I don't want her to look at him. "We'll find your mom, okay? Is she in the house?"

Bridget rubs her wrists, which Madison has untied. "Mom had a night shift at the hospital. Dad's out of town. I was watching TV, and that man came in and…"

Madison gathers Bridget into her arms. "Come on. We don't need to be here."

"I was so scared. I thought… If you hadn't come…"

"I know. It's going to be okay," Madison says soothingly.

She walks Bridget toward the back door, which is through the kitchen. We need to get the girl out of here, and I'll call dispatch with an update on the situation. The detectives will arrive to process the scene with the coroner and crime scene techs. Plus our backup to properly clear the house. There could be others here. We can't assume anything.

I don't hear sirens or see flashing lights yet. Where the hell is our backup?

"Bridget, are you the only one in the house?" I ask. "Are you alone?"

Then there's another scream, but it's coming from upstairs.

It's a baby's cry.

"My brother!" Bridget tries to turn around. "I have to get him!"

"Take Bridget outside," I tell Madison.

She nods. "I'll call dispatch and let them know what's happened."

Bridget's straining in Madison's grasp. "You have to get Stevie! Please. My brother. He's only a year old."

"I'll get him," I tell her. "I promise."

I take the hallway toward the front of the house. The wood floor groans under my feet.

Get the baby, get out of the house, I tell myself.

The baby continues to wail.

I reach the entryway. Opposite the front door, there's a staircase with a white-painted banister. I unholster my gun and raise it. My eyes scan back and forth, checking doorways for any sign of movement.

Smiling faces look back at me from the photos on the walls. Mom and Dad, Bridget. A swaddled baby brother, posed for a picture in his big sister's arms.

The baby pauses for a breath. The house goes quiet. From the second floor, there's a faint glow bleeding onto the landing. Pale blue. Maybe a nightlight.

My boot comes down on the first stair, and the baby's screams resume. My inhales and exhales are even as I climb, my heart rate steady. Every part of me is coiled and poised to react.

The shadows seem dense. Alive. Like there's something throbbing and shifting, just out of sight.

Then I pause. My muscles wind tighter.

There's somebody else here. A heavier presence. A threat. I can *feel* it. But where?

I came up here without a real strategy and no contingency plan. Exactly what I told Madison not to do.

Three rooms open off the landing. Three open doorways. The nightlight glows in one of them, and that's the source of the screams. The baby's room. I can see the child standing up in the crib, and I feel a twitch in my chest. A brief flash of memory. Emma, standing and crying during one of my visits home. Tight curls on her head. A tiny hand reaching out for me.

For a split second, I'm back in time. All the nights I was gone. The nights Emma needed me and I wasn't there.

Suddenly, there's another, deeper cry. A figure lurches toward me from the shadows of the doorway to my right. Another ski mask looms out of the dark. Eyes glittering with malice and fear.

Fuck.

A hail of gunshots, some of them mine. There's a heavy punch to my chest. My forearm. *God.* My weapon flies from my injured hand. I lose my balance, falling against the bannister railing.

He's standing over me. I see the yawning black circle of a barrel.

"Nash!"

Madison. It's hard to hear her over the ringing in my ears, but it's her. What is Madison doing here?

She fires.

The guy's arms pinwheel as he steps back. Then he takes aim with his weapon. Madison's down below in the entryway. An open target.

He pulls the trigger. Again. Again.

Bellowing, I kick the man's legs in a sweeping motion. He topples. There's a visceral *thump* as his head collides with the staircase bannister, and then he's tumbling end over end.

Terrible stillness falls over the house. A high-pitched whine fills my ears, but it's not the baby's cries. Those have turned to frightened whimpers.

"Madison?" I stand, pushing through the pain. My arm is limp at my side. I can't feel my hand. I have to look at it to make sure it's still there, and what I see is too much for my brain to process right now.

Wreckage. Like a bomb went off in my arm. I swallow down bile. Force myself to stay conscious.

I drag myself to the edge of the landing and stare down. The guy in the ski mask is sprawled at the base of the staircase. Blood spreads in a pool underneath him.

Doesn't look like the bastard's getting up again.

But I'm not feeling so great myself. My brain's commands to my body are misfiring. Adrenaline surges. I push upright and nearly pass out when my right arm brushes the railing.

The pain hasn't fully registered yet, not yet, but I can sense the blood pouring out of me like a molten river.

I need to get the kid and Madison. I need to get them out of here.

I have to get home to Emma.

Down on the first floor, Madison is standing over the assailant, her gun loose in her hand. Her pale skin stands out amid the shadows. Her eyes are glassy, her mouth hanging open.

"You okay?" I ask. "Madison?"

"I…"

She stumbles and falls backward against the front door. A streak of something dark and wet paints the white as she slides to the floor.

And finally, I notice the emergency lights strobing across the walls from the windows.

Our fucking backup.

12

Madison

*E*verything's dark. Murky. I can't tell which way is up. But I hear voices. They float away and disappear.

I try to open my eyes. Only a tiny sliver of light seeps in before the darkness presses in again. It's like trying to swim to the surface, but something underneath keeps catching hold of me and dragging me down. Over and over.

Nash. What happened to him? Where is he?

"Madison? Sweetheart, can you hear me?"

I hear a strangled-sounding moan, and I think it might've been me.

"Nurse! She's waking up!"

"Mom?"

My mouth is dry. Every part of me aches. I can't move.

"Sweetheart. I'm here."

A face comes into focus. My mom's blond hair, styled into a twist. Her green eyes, darker than mine. Perfect makeup in shades of pink and rose. A beige sweater. She grabs my hand, and I manage to wiggle my fingers.

"What...what happened?"

"You're in the hospital."

That much I've guessed, based on the machines beeping and the smell of cleaning fluid. My bed has plastic railings on it.

My brother's face appears. "Hey there," Jake says softly. "How you doin', kiddo? A little worse for wear?"

"I got shot." My voice sounds like tires over gravel.

"Don't see the point of that body armor," my mother says. "Doesn't cover your whole body, does it?"

Jake sighs. "You were wounded in your right arm and your leg. You had surgery early this morning after the ambulance brought you in."

Nash, I think. *Where's Nash?*

A woman in scrubs and a floral-print cardigan hustles into the room. "Look who's joined us." She peers at me, pokes and prods. I've got an IV drip. Bandages cover my right arm to the shoulder, a sling keeping it immobile. The nurse inspects the bandage on my left outer thigh.

"How's your pain? Scale of 1 to 10?"

Pain wraps around me, tight and unyielding, but there's already a narcotic haze blanketing my thoughts. "How bad was I hit?"

"Subjective question, honey," the nurse says. "I'll let the doctor try to answer."

"Where's Nash?"

I know I was with him. I remember...dancing.

A kiss.

After that, I know something went wrong. Terribly wrong. But it's fuzzy. Those memories are still underwater.

The nurse glances at my mom and brother. "I'll let the doctor know she's awake. Let me know if her pain bothers her."

Jake watches the nurse go, then turns to me. "Sergeant Jennings was admitted to the hospital as well."

My mother shushes him, and they exchange heated glances.

"What's going on?" I ask.

Mom gives my brother a warning glare. "Your dad and the rest of the family send their love. They'd be here, but I thought you would need quiet." She strokes my hand. "There was a burglary. Do you remember?"

I remember the sobbing girl. The man with a knife. Nash shot him. His hands were so steady.

I remember a baby crying.

And then...

I try to sit up. It doesn't go well. I end up sliding down the pillows. It feels like my mom isn't telling me everything. "Have any detectives come by? Do they need to talk to me?"

I discharged my weapon. I need to sit for my critical incident interview. There's a million things I need to do, need to know.

Jake leans his back against the wall, crossing his arms. "I spoke to Chief Liu. He asked to tell you hello and said not to worry about your interview yet. When you're up to it, the interviewers will come here to the hospital, and your union lawyer will be here as well. I'll get it arranged."

I relax. Jake has worked with West Oaks PD before. Drug task forces, that kind of thing.

"We practically needed a guard at that door to keep your friends away," Mom says. "Do you see all these flowers?"

Arrangements and cards crowd the table by my bedside. It just makes me feel more confused. How much have I missed?

"Can I have my phone?"

"Maybe after some healthy food. Everything else can wait." Mom eases me back so I'm lying against the pillows. She fluffs them and adjusts my blankets. "Jake, could you go get us something to eat? Something good. Not from the cafeteria."

"You're trying to get rid of me."

She doesn't deny it. "But we *do* need food."

He grumbles, giving me a kiss on the forehead. "Everything's gonna be fine. Okay, Mads? I'll be right back."

When he's gone, I say, "Mom, tell me what else is going on."

She watches me carefully.

"*Mom.*"

"All I know is that Sergeant Jennings—Nash—carried a baby and you out of that house even though he could barely walk himself. Believe me, I intend to thank him the first chance I get. But you won't help him by making yourself upset."

"What day is it?"

"Saturday. It's been less than a day, sweetheart. It'll be okay."

"You're going to miss the wedding."

"Do you honestly think I care about that? None of us are going to your high school boyfriend's silly wedding. Be serious. Sweetheart, what do you remember from last night?"

My eyes squeeze closed. More of it comes to me. It's like my mind is moving backward.

It's going to be okay. I remember saying those words.

Bridget Hanson. I remember untying her.

The man in the ski mask.

Nash and me, climbing through a broken window.

Then the picture moves forward again. I took Bridget outside. Went back in the house to find Nash. He was standing on the second-floor landing.

Gunshots. A man in a ski mask—another one.

There were two of them.

In my exhausted brain, the house merges with the church building from SWAT training. Two suspects instead of one. I didn't see the second guy. I didn't warn Nash.

My fault. It was my fault.

"I was at a training for the SWAT team," I say.

"I heard." Mom's voice is stiff with implicit disapproval.

"We went out for drinks after, and Sergeant Jennings came with us. He...he was going to give me a ride home. And I heard glass breaking. Saw a man go inside a house." A shudder runs through me, and pain jolts through my shoulder. "Mom, how bad was I hit?"

"You were very lucky. The bullets passed through without breaking bones or hitting anything vital. Lost some blood. The doctors patched you up just fine."

"What about Nash?"

A pause. "Last I heard, he was still in surgery."

I want to demand more information. But Mom is being difficult enough as it is. "How's the girl, Bridget? And her little brother? They're all right?"

"Jake will try to find out. I'll see to everything. Don't you worry." Mom smooths the hair from my forehead. "I already picked up some things from your apartment. Your pajamas, slippers, toothbrush. I asked your dad to wash those dirty dishes you left behind. And vacuum, because your carpets desperately need it."

That's my mother. She's the queen of taking charge. This is what she always does anytime there's a crisis.

It's kind of comforting right now.

My mom is the founder of Coastal Catering, a four-time winner of the West Oaks Small Business Owner Award. She started her business in high school, baking cakes and cookies for birthday parties and then weddings. Now, she manages over a hundred employees, including my brother Aiden. He's her executive chef.

"When I take you home tomorrow," Mom says, "everyone's going to be there. You'll be in the spotlight. Just like you always wanted, you poor middle child. We're going to spoil you rotten."

"All I had to do was get myself shot."

She tsks and shakes her head.

I sag against the pillows. I really do feel like crap. Every part of me hurts, but my leg throbs like it's being squeezed in a vise by a sadistic handyman. Might be time for some more of those pain meds.

Then I run her last few sentences through my head.

"Wait, what do you mean by 'home'? Are you taking me to my apartment? Or your house?"

"Your apartment is on the third floor with no elevator! How are you supposed to get up there on crutches? I mean *home*. You'll stay with us while you're recovering. That's non-negotiable. I told Aiden to plan menus. The twins are doing laundry and setting up a room for you."

"Which twins?" There are two sets. My younger siblings, and Jake's five-year-olds.

She waves her hand. "All of them. I don't know."

You'd think my mother would be too busy to take command of my life. You'd be wrong. When I was younger, I longed for her undivided attention. Ha. Be careful what you wish for.

I am *not* moving back home. That's not happening. But I'm grateful to have so many people looking out for me.

Who's taking care of Nash?

We need to talk. I need to see him and make sure that he's okay.

13

Nash

"*D*ad?"

Emma rushes into the hospital room. She runs toward me and barrels into the bed. I cringe at the vibrations that spread through my wounded body. But I don't care. I wrap my left arm around her shoulders and hold her tight.

"They wouldn't let me in to see you for *forever*."

"I'm okay now. I've been anxious to see you, too."

I haven't been awake for long, but Emma's been on my mind since the moment I came to. The nurse assured me that my daughter was in the waiting room and that she had an adult with her.

I was in surgery for a while, it seems. My body's a mess. But my mind's even worse. I'm glad I had time to compose myself before Emma came in.

I've been trying to make sense of last night. Process the fact that I'm hurt. Figure out what to do about Emma and all the basics of taking care of her.

And Madison. She's been in my thoughts too. An equal compulsion to make sure she's all right.

Last night...I wish I could say I don't remember. That it

was a blur. But every detail stands out in my brain like it was drawn in indelible ink.

Every. Single. Thing.

"Hello, Nash. How're you feeling?" Laura Chen hovers in the doorway to my room. She's the mom who was hosting last night's slumber party. She looks exhausted.

How do I feel? Awful. Like I was hit by a truck, and then the truck exploded.

"I'm okay," I say. "Thanks for waiting with Emma. I'm sorry about this."

"*No*. Are you kidding? I'm happy to be here."

"Dad, what happened? They've only told me parts of it. And there's stuff on social media, but nobody really knows." Emma's eyes are bleary, with smudged liner beneath. She's wearing ripped black jeans and her favorite vintage Pixies T-shirt. "They said you had surgery. You were shot. *Twice*."

Three times, actually. My armor stopped the shot to my chest, but the impact left a bruise over half my torso. It hurts every time I breathe. My calf got off easy, the bullet digging a hole through the muscle. Didn't even feel that one last night.

But then there's my right forearm.

I came in with open fractures. Extensive soft tissue damage. The surgeon screwed an external fixator into my bones to hold things in place until I'm healed enough to get more permanent plates. Lucky me. It'll be a long road ahead to get back full functionality, if I can get there at all. A nice fucking mess.

"I went after a bad guy, and he didn't go down easy. But I'm fine, Em. I promise. I'm fine." I wipe the tears from her cheeks, swallowing down the tight lump in my own throat.

She hugs me again, burying her face in my chest. "Don't do that to me again. Ever, ever, ever."

"You sound like me. Did we switch places?"

Emma lifts her head, scowling. "Don't try to be funny."

Laura steps further into the room. "I spoke to some of the other parents. We were going to organize a Meal Train and someone to come stay with you and Emma once you're home."

"That isn't necessary."

"But it is. We all love Emma, and we're going to pitch in. Never dealt with this kind of thing, but we're in this together."

This kind of thing? Does she mean a cop dad who was shot? Or a single dad who's injured and, by all appearances, helpless? Because that's how I feel. And it sucks.

It's pretty damn close to intolerable.

But the thought of these PTA parents swarming my house, taking over—it makes me want to crawl out of my skin.

"I appreciate it," I say. "I really do. But we're okay. You probably want to head home. Thank you. Again."

"If you're sure… Emma can stay at our place until you're out of the hospital, at least."

Emma gives Laura a hug goodbye. "Thanks, Mrs. Chen."

"Just let me know if I can pick you up later. Or if you need anything else." She gives me another anxious glance, then finally vanishes through the door.

Emma turns to me. "Dad, *what happened*? Tell me. For real. People are saying it was Bridget Hanson's house."

"You know her?"

"She goes to my school."

My eyes sink closed. While Emma's old enough to get the truth, I still want to protect her from the worst of it.

I think of Bridget screaming. The knife moving toward her throat.

"Another officer and I stumbled upon a burglary. We tried to help, but there were two suspects. Second guy got in some lucky shots." Because I screwed up. I let myself get distracted, as if my years as a SEAL meant nothing at all. I have *never* been so ashamed of myself.

"But they didn't get away, right?"

"No. They didn't."

She sits heavily in a chair, slouching in a way her mom would scold her for. "Did you kill them?"

"Em—"

"I'm not stupid. I know you've killed people. Probably a lot."

My mind goes back to last night, but it's Madison who appears this time. The blood when she slid down the wall. I remember a screaming baby in my arms. And setting Madison down outside in the grass, our stunned backup looking on as I yelled for a medic.

Is Madison somewhere in this hospital?

When I woke up earlier, I had narcotics in my system, and I asked the nurse not to give me any more. Pain is not something I've ever had a problem with. But I can't handle my mind being loopy. Being so far out of control.

Lying in this hospital bed is bad enough.

I've been spacing out for a while when Emma says, "Dad?"

"Yeah, Em?"

"I was thinking. It's only a few more weeks until winter break. I could arrange something with my teachers so I can do most of my schoolwork at home, and then I can cancel my trip to France. I texted Mom and asked her to fly here for the holidays instead. And maybe by January you'll be—"

"Whoa, whoa. Hold on. What do you mean, cancel your trip? And stay home from school?"

"Who else is going to take care of you? Look at you, Dad. You could've died." Her face crumples. "You can't do everything by yourself."

"Come here."

Emma sits beside me on the bed, and I pull her in close to me, ignoring the scream of the wound in my arm and the terrible ache in my chest. "That's not your job to worry about. I'm going to figure this out. I promise."

SEAN HOLT KNOCKS ON THE DOOR, PEERING through the crack. "Good, you're awake." He comes into the room, holding his girlfriend Janie's hand. "Hey Emma, how's it going?"

"Shitty."

"Hey," I say. "Language, please."

Holt and Janie Simon are trying to hide their smiles.

Emma gives me the kind of eye-roll that only a fifteen-year-old can achieve. "You got shot, Dad. It's shitty. And you say 'fuck' all the time."

Sean and Janie exchange a glance. She's a well-known West Oaks defense attorney. The two of them must go up against each other in investigations and in the courtroom, but they seem to make their relationship work. How, I really don't know. That kind of thing is beyond me.

Janie sets a flower arrangement on the table. "Emma, I was thinking you and I could swing by your house and pick up some things for you and your dad? Unless someone's done that already? I assume the doctors will have you staying here a few days."

Emma looks to me. "Dad? What do you think?"

I try to sit up higher in the bed. "That would be great. Maybe you could grab milkshakes or something, too. Get some fresh air and a shower. You've been stuck here all day."

Emma scowls at me, and I have no idea what I did wrong. But I usually don't.

She gets up and stomps toward the door. At least she

smiles politely at Janie and says thanks.

After they're gone, Holt pulls up a chair near my bed. He nods at the bandages and hardware on the lower half of my right arm. A few minutes ago, the nurse lifted my arm by the fixator bar like it's my own personal handle.

"How're you doing?" he asks.

"Shitty."

"So Emma got it right the first time."

I nod. "My leg will heal pretty quick. But I may have permanent damage to my right arm. Which would be a problem for a right-eye-dominant sniper." I try to paste on a wry smile, but I don't think it's working for me. "Full extent of the damage won't be clear for a while."

For a small county like ours, a full-time SWAT team is unusual. But it was perfect for me. Allowed me to devote myself to what I'm best at. With the wealth here, West Oaks has the tax base for the necessary funding, and the county loans us out as needed to other municipalities in the region.

But now? I might be finished with SWAT. Finished with being an operator. Of *any* kind.

"You could become a negotiator instead."

"*Me?*"

He's trying not to laugh. "Then move over to investigations. Run around and look tough and you'll be fine. Same thing you did as a SEAL, just without the sniper rifle. Easy." Holt was a Marine.

"Maybe a *little* more to it than that."

"Maybe." He stretches out his legs, crossing them at the ankles. "Besides, I'd be more concerned about other important uses for my right hand in the next several weeks. You are single and all…" He grimaces comically.

"Thanks for that. Very supportive." But I'm snickering. This is what I need. For someone to give me shit, not try to make me feel better.

"What have you gotten from the crime scene?" I ask.

"You know I can't tell you."

Holt can't discuss the shooting until after my use-of-force interview. Normally, I'd respect that. But I have too many questions. I can't hold them back.

"I'm asking for a friend."

"Oh. In that case." He grins. "We're working to identify our deceased suspects. One was shot in the head. Expert aim, by the way. Second also shot, multiple times, then kicked down the stairs. You and Shelby were quite the team. Which I shouldn't be saying, so ignore me."

"No names for the suspects yet?"

"They had wallets on them, but no IDs. Their car keys gave us a plate to run and a registration. I have officers following up to confirm their identities. The guy who shot you and Shelby was just a kid."

"That was a *kid?*"

"Compared to the other one, yes. The first guy you took out in the living room was older. They look alike. Could've been brothers."

"Was one of them the Midnight Slasher?"

"Million dollar question, isn't it?" Holt slowly puts his phone away, seeming to think. "The mayor's been calling us. The media's sniffing around. Everybody wants to know if the Midnight Slasher is dead, and who killed him."

Great. Just what I love. All the focus on me.

"Do *you* think it was him?" I ask.

"At the past crime scenes, we got no fingerprints or usable DNA. So we can't use those to compare."

"The guys last night weren't wearing gloves."

He nods, eyes sharp. "That's a difference from the Slasher's usual pattern."

"And there were two of them."

"A *very* clear difference. At the previous scenes, it was one person, working alone. But the perp could've changed his method after almost getting caught at the Cowling residence. If he's following the media at all, he'd know about the heightened patrols. But if that's the case, the absence of gloves is strange. I'd expect more care, not less."

Last night, neither Madison nor I said the name "Midnight Slasher" at that house. But I was thinking it, and I'm sure she was too.

A middle-of-the-night entry into an obviously occupied home. A burglar with a ski mask and a knife, tying up the girl inside.

"We found a k-bar at the scene," Holt says. "But the Midnight Slasher's preference for a k-bar wasn't common knowledge. West Oaks PD held the more gruesome details of the crimes back from the media. So it couldn't simply have been a copycat."

That makes me think it was the Slasher after all. But what the hell do I know? Can I even trust my own reflexes anymore?

My eyes sink closed as I force back the sucking hole of self-castigation and disappointment in my chest. Right where that bullet could've lodged.

"Whether it was the Slasher or not," Holt says, "You and Shelby took out two assholes who would've killed you and seriously traumatized or murdered an innocent girl. You're a fucking hero, Jennings. Don't forget that."

I'm not going to whine or complain that he's got it wrong. But I'm not feeling all that heroic at the moment.

"I'm supposed to be in the classroom on Monday," I say.

"Don't worry about SWAT training. Another sergeant will cover for you, I'm sure. It'll get sorted out."

"Any news about…Shelby?" Her nickname feels strange in my mouth. "I asked the nurse, but she wouldn't tell me anything."

"I've heard she's awake and expects to be discharged tomorrow. You could text her."

"I don't have her number."

He studies me. "I've heard from Lia Perez why you and Shelby were together. A bonding exercise with the patrol kids after training?"

"Yeah. So?"

He shrugs, all smug and sarcastic, as Holt can be sometimes. "Just surprised, that's all. You don't strike me as a let's-all-grab-drinks kind of guy."

"What're you talking about? I'm the life of the party." I say this with a stoney expression.

He smirks at me and laughs. "All right, Jennings. Invite me next time. I'd love to see you on the dancefloor."

I'm careful not to move a muscle, but inside I'm cringing.

After Holt leaves and I'm alone in the room again, my mind turns back to Madison. I made so many mistakes last night, I can't even pinpoint where it all went wrong. Or which mistake was worse.

If I hadn't pushed Madison away after kissing her, we never would've stumbled upon that burglary. Madison wouldn't be in the hospital now.

But that girl, Bridget Hanson, might have ended up in a far darker place.

Except for her baby brother, Bridget was all alone in that house. I want to believe her parents were doing the best they could. But that doesn't change the fact that they left their daughter vulnerable.

And now, my own kid thinks she has to take care of me.

Holt called me a hero. I'm not so sure. But Madison and I *did* help Bridget.

Does that make up for everything else I'm responsible for?

14

Madison

I wake up from yet another nap and find my mother gone. There's a new bouquet of flowers by my bed. According to the note, it came from Detective Holt and Janie Simon. *Sorry we missed you*, it says. *Didn't want to wake you.*

Then I hear snoring. Jake is sound asleep in a chair.

This is my chance.

Finally.

I have no idea what time it is, but there's no daylight in the window. I swing my legs to the side, then gingerly rest weight on my good leg, followed by my injured one. Gah, that sucks. I bite down on a curse. The wound in my thigh is throbbing.

Jake snorts, wiggling around in his chair. I don't know how dads can sleep sitting up like that, but it seems to be a talent they all possess. My father, my brother.

Though I can't imagine Nash asleep in a recliner with his mouth wide open. Nash is a dad, but he's not, like, *a dad*.

Ugh. I roll my eyes at myself. I can't go five seconds without thinking about Nash.

But I'm not someone who does well holding things inside. Nash is the only person in the world who knows what we went through last night, so he's the only person I want to talk to.

While I'm trying to psych myself up for the journey ahead, the nurse walks in. She takes one look at me. "Planning a field trip?"

"If I have to stay in this room any longer, I will scream."

"Please don't do that."

"You've been warned. Do you have any crutches?"

She scoffs. "I can dig some up somewhere. Can you wheel your IV behind you?"

The nurse sets me up with a single crutch so I can keep my IV with me. It's a bit awkward, but my bandaged arm is still functional. I can make this work.

The nurse also digs a robe and slippers out of the bag my mom brought me. Because my mom thinks of everything. I have to give her credit. She's pretty amazing.

When I'm ready, I ask, "Could you point me toward Nash Jennings' room?"

She smiles. "You mean Romeo?"

I feel my cheeks flushing. "What makes you say that?"

"He asked about you when I saw him earlier. And you asked about him. It's cute how anxious you both are, when you could just call the other up on the phone."

Nash's voice echoes in my head. *You're too young. You're my student.* Right after he kissed the hell out of me. And right before we got shot by the same guy.

That's one way to make a connection.

"It's complicated," I say.

The nurse relents. "What true romance isn't?"

In minutes, I'm hobbling down the corridor in my fleece robe, hoping that my hair isn't too crazy. And trying to remember if I've brushed my teeth in the last twenty-four hours. I slick my tongue over my teeth.

The nurse tags along behind me, probably making sure I don't lose steam halfway down the hall. "Psst. It's that one," she whispers.

I make my way to the partially open doorway.

Nash is asleep. His head lolls to one side of the pillow, hair across his forehead. I've never seen him like this before. So unguarded.

I scan for injuries. One of his arms is wrapped in bandages with a medical device sticking out. Blankets cover the rest of his large body. His tanned skin is pale, almost as pale as mine. His eyelashes are dark and full. And his mouth...

My insides tuck and roll as I stare at him, remembering those lips on mine. Needy and aggressive. Maybe the best kiss I've had in *ever*, and I'm not likely to get a repeat. Nash pushed me away, and his message was loud and clear.

What am I doing here? What's he going to think if he opens his eyes and finds me creepily watching him sleep?

I don't chase men who aren't into me.

"Madison?"

Shit, that came from behind me. And it was an all-too-familiar voice.

I look back. "Hey, Mom."

"Pulling a jailbreak, are we? I take it your brother fell asleep on the job?"

She's standing with a raven-haired teenager, both of them holding to-go coffee cups. I recognize Nash's daughter from the photo he showed me last night. Her hair is in two buns on top of her head, and electric blue lines her eyes. She's got a punk rock vibe with a little anime thrown in.

"You're Madison?" Emma asks.

"I am."

"You were with my dad last night." She scrutinizes me.

"I...was. I'm a student in his SWAT training. Everybody was grabbing a drink yesterday evening, and your dad was giving me a ride home. That's when we saw the burglar."

"That's what your mom said. But I wasn't sure if..." Emma trails off and nods, seeming to relax. "I'm glad you're okay."

"Thanks, me too." I turn to my mother. "Why are you two together?"

"When you sleep all day, you miss things," Mom points out.

I glare. But Emma grabs my IV cart, leading me into the room. "Dad, Madison's here. And her mom, Mrs. Shelborne."

Nash is now awake and watching this exchange with his brow furrowed. In annoyance or confusion, I can't tell.

"Oh, hi," I say.

Brilliant entrance.

Emma drags a chair across the floor for me to sit down.

His eyes are wide as my mother says hello. Emma babbles an explanation. Apparently, after she returned from getting milkshakes with Janie Simon, my mother caught up with them in the hallway and took Emma for coffee. Probably to keep Emma entertained and occupied while her dad rested. But knowing my mother, also to pump the girl for information.

Mom grabs Nash's uninjured hand. "It's a pleasure to meet you, Sergeant Jennings. I'm very grateful you were there with Madison last night. You can call me Heather."

"Thanks," he mumbles.

Nash's eyes meet mine. There's a dullness to his gaze, but I don't think it's pain meds. It's the same look he gave me last night when he was trying to call me a cab.

The look of a man who wants to get far away from me.

I've wanted to talk to him for hours, but now that we're

face to face, I have no idea what to say. And it doesn't look like Nash is too eager to listen, anyway.

I start to get up. "Maybe I should…if you and Emma are…"

My mother touches Emma's shoulder. "You know, I was just about to suggest we get some dinner. Nash and Madison could use more food in their stomachs."

Emma seems more reluctant to leave. "Dad, are you hungry?"

Nash doesn't get to answer because my mother talks over him. "Let's go corral my son Jake and figure out what to order."

They bustle out of the room, already chatting about Emma's school and her friends.

The sudden silence is jarring.

"Looks like we're being managed," Nash says.

I sink back down into my seat. "It's what my mother does. She must've seen Emma, realized who she was, and decided to take her under her wing. Sorry. She does mean well." As I keep repeating to myself. My mother means well, even when she's driving me or my siblings up the wall.

But I think Mom has guessed I need to talk things through with Nash. That's part of what makes my mother so frustrating. She's often right. But don't tell her I said that.

"No, I appreciate it. I'm…" He rubs his head. "Not totally sure what to do."

"With Emma?"

He nods, and I think he might elaborate on that. I wonder if he has family to help out while he's injured. And what about Emma's mom?

But he changes the subject.

Nash clears his throat, frowning deeply. "Lot went down last night."

"That it did."

I remember how well we got along at the bar. Telling stories with Lia and Clint and the other patrol officers. Laughing and joking.

Feels like another lifetime.

"What did the doc tell you?" he asks. "What's your recovery timeline?"

"One bullet grazed my left arm. Dug a nasty stripe, but didn't take too much other than skin. Road rash, basically. The other caught me in the thigh, but missed the important stuff." Like the artery that would've had me bleeding out in minutes. "I'll be on crutches for a couple weeks, but I'm sure I'll be on desk duty for longer, waiting for the use-of-force ruling. What about you?"

"Took one in the vest. Bruised ribs from that. Plus a small chunk missing from my calf. That'll be pretty."

"Ouch."

"And then..." He nods at the bandages on his arm. "Right forearm's all fucked up. I've got a fixator holding it together until I can have more surgery. It'll take a while to heal, plus the rehab." Nash shrugs. "I don't know."

The hand he shoots with. I'm not sure what that means for a sniper, but it can't be good.

"I'm sorry," I breathe, almost a whisper.

I want to comfort him. Tell him we both did the best we could, even if I'm not sure that's true on my part. I want to run my fingers along his arm and fit my hand into his.

But given his level of discomfort just sitting near me, that would be the last thing Nash would welcome.

He looks toward the window. A muscle in Nash's jaw pulses. He's doing that thing where he goes all stiff and scowly. "I'm sorry you got hurt, Madison. I should've kept that from happening." His lips barely move as he says this. "I'm sorry about everything."

"You can't blame yourself for that asshole catching us by surprise. I was there too."

"But I have more experience. I'm your sergeant. It's on me."

My sergeant.

He says this with finality. Like there's no possible room for argument or a different view.

"You're not my sergeant right now," I say. "We're just Nash and Madison. Remember?"

This is the closest either of us has come to mentioning the kiss. The scowl on Nash's face tells me he'd rather not talk about it.

But if he insists on feeling guilty, he can at least spread some of that around.

"All right. I didn't want to have to do this." I sigh and grab my crutch as I stand. "If you want the blame, you'll have to arm wrestle me for it."

At first, he just stares. *"What?"*

"We each have one functioning arm at the moment. Only way to settle this." I limp closer. "Come on, Jennings. Put your muscle where your mouth is."

"That does not sound right. At all."

There it is. The tiniest of smiles.

"Too scared to test your strength against mine?"

"Sit down before you hurt yourself. Hurt yourself *more*, I mean."

"Let the record show Jennings forfeited because he's chicken." I pump my fist in the air. "That means I win, and I can take whatever blame I want. I'll tell the critical incident team I took down both suspects. Do you think they'll believe it?"

There's no way I could've made that between-the-eyes shot in Bridget Hanson's living room. We both know it.

Nash snorts. But the tiny smile stays.

15

Madison

I'm still sitting in the chair by Nash's bed when my mom and Emma reappear. Jake comes in next, carrying a huge bag of takeout.

"I decided on sushi," Emma announces, "since my dad has to eat one-handed. But don't put wasabi on his. It makes him cry."

"Thank you, Em," Nash deadpans. "I'm glad everyone knows that now."

Mom introduces Jake to Nash. My brother distributes containers of nigiri, rainbow rolls, and spicy tuna. Emma sits on the bed beside Nash and opens the clamshell package for him, while his cheeks color slightly.

"Isn't this cozy?" Mom asks. "It'll be even better when we're able to sit at a real table at home." She turns to me. "Nash and Emma will be joining us once he's discharged. Won't that be lovely?"

I almost choke on yellowtail. "They're what?"

Nash is coughing too.

"I said we should ask them first," Jake mutters.

"We figured it all out," Emma says. "It's fine. Right, Dad? Can't we stay with the Shelbornes?"

I set down my food and grab my crutch. "Mom, could I talk to you outside, please? In the hallway?"

With a heavy sigh, Mom wheels my IV cart outside.

"What the hell are you doing?" I whisper when we're down the hall from Nash's room. "Managing me is one thing, but Nash is a grown man who you don't even know."

"His daughter told me they need help. Emma said they have no family in town, and Nash refused the help of other parents from her school. Nash is seriously injured, Madison. How is he supposed to take care of his daughter and himself?"

"You should've asked him!"

"So he could say no and end up struggling? Or possibly hurt himself when he tries to do too much? Emma told me he doesn't like accepting help. So I'm doing it for him. It's all settled."

Why does she sound so reasonable when she's being insane?

I have to fix this.

"Well, it's clearly not settled. Because Nash and I already have a plan. We worked it all out while you and Emma were gone. It's a SWAT team thing. Always have a plan."

"And what plan is this?"

"I…" Shit. What's the plan? "I'm going to stay with Nash while we're both recovering. At his house."

There. Brilliant.

One eyebrow slowly raises. "*You're* moving in with *him*?"

It sounds so much worse when she repeats it. I swallow. "Yep."

"Is there something going on between you and Nash that I should know about?"

"*No*," I sputter. "We're friends. From the academy."

"I don't think I'm unreasonable to be concerned over this, Madison. You have a tendency to make rash decisions."

Rash decisions? Okay, perhaps I've made a few. But is she referring to something specific? Or just my entire career in law enforcement? "And you have a tendency to butt in where you don't belong."

She smiles thinly. "I see you're not willing to have a mature discussion. I'd like to know what Sergeant Jennings has to say about this arrangement of yours." She turns on her heel and marches back into his room.

Crap. Why did all of that come out of my mouth?

I hurry to follow.

Nash and Emma are deep in conversation, and from their faces, I guess it's tense. They look up when my mom stops at the foot of his bed.

"Nash, my daughter tells me that she's going to be staying at *your* house while you both recover. Is that correct?"

Nash's eyes widen. Emma furrows her brow.

I nod vigorously behind my mom's back.

"Um, yeah," Nash says. "Madison is…staying with us."

My brother is watching all of this with an amused smirk.

I push forward on my crutches. I need to take over because Nash is not convincing. "We've each got one working arm. We're going to team up and help each other out while we're healing. So there's no need for Nash or Emma or me to stay at your place, Mom. We've got it covered."

"Can any of you cook?"

"I can use a microwave one-handed." I smile sweetly.

Nash opens his mouth, but his eyes are darting between me and his daughter. "I meant to check with Emma. She needs to be okay with it."

Everyone turns to the teenager.

Emma looks like she just bit into something terrible, but she's in front of the person who baked it. "Just Madison? Is she staying in the guestroom? Or..."

"Guestroom," Nash says quickly.

My mother sends a pointed glance my way.

His daughter's frown lessens, but only slightly. "Well, it would be way easier for me to get to school if I'm home. So I guess. Yeah. It's fine."

"It's just for a few days," I say. In fact, it'll be less than that. If Nash wants, I'll leave as soon as my mother's not looking. This is just to get her off our backs.

If Nash does need help? I'll happily step in. But not if Emma is uncomfortable with me around.

Mom is chewing the inside of her lip. "All right. This could work. And if it doesn't, we have plenty of room at my place. You just pick up your phone and let me know, Miss Emma." She winks. I'm guessing she and Emma already exchanged numbers.

Jake claps his hands together. "Then it's settled. Nash, if you're cool with it, we could get your fridge stocked before you're discharged. Mom, how about you and I make a list for the grocery?"

I see Mom's wheels turning. She can't resist a new problem to strategize and solve. My brother knows this. Thank goodness for Jake. "Very well. We should get Aiden's input, too. And Madison, I'll need to go back to your apartment to pack more of your things." She taps a finger on her chin. "And possibly drop by Target for new pajamas, because yours are atrocious."

Soon Jake, Mom, and Emma are on speaker phone with Aiden, arguing over food options. I sneak over to Nash's bedside. "Sorry," I whisper. "That was all I could think of. I don't really have to stay with you."

He shrugs. "Maybe it'll be good. An extra set of hands. Or...hand."

I laugh so loud, the others stop and stare.

16

Nash

Madison is extremely persuasive. Or maybe I'm just groggy from the few pain meds I've allowed myself. Either way, those are the only explanations for where things end up a few days later.

Madison's moving in with me. I'm getting the far better end of this deal.

How the heck is this going to work?

Emma pulls our SUV into the driveway. She's only got a learner's permit, but she insisted on driving me. I'm in the back, surrounded by pillows that my kid spent ten minutes arranging carefully around me. Like I'm one of the stuffed animals she liked to make a nest for when she was little.

"We're home, Dad." She turns around in the driver's seat, smirking at me. "Your girlfriend's waiting."

Emma's been testy with me all morning. But every time I offer to scrub this move-in plan, Emma insists it's fine.

"I already told you, she's not my girlfriend," I grunt in response. "She's my coworker. And friend. It's completely platonic."

Of course, my kid knows I'm full of shit.

"Sure, Dad. Whatever you say. But the next time you claim I can't go to a sleepover with guys present, I'm calling you a hypocrite."

"That is *not* the same."

"Isn't it?" Emma gets out and opens my door. I grab the cane I received at the hospital, warring with the pillows as I try to push them out of the way with my left hand.

"Just wait a sec. Jeez." Emma helps me extricate myself. Finally, I'm out of the car, and we're heading toward the front door.

Madison and her brother are just stepping onto my porch. Jake's got a rolling suitcase in his hand. They must've arrived right before us.

"Hey, Emma," Jake says. "Nash."

Madison leans against her crutches, smiling uncertainly.

She checked out of the hospital a couple days ago. I had to stay for the doctors to monitor my injuries for complications. While I was there, I had my interview with the critical incident team, who will review my use of deadly force. So that's out of the way. Today, I got a tutorial from the nurse on how to clean the pins of my fixator and dealt with hospital paperwork while Madison's mother borrowed my keys to stock up our fridge. I'm also going to have physical therapy to look forward to for my calf. PT for my arm will have to wait until I'm healed, except for some flexing of my fingers.

I had some anxiety over the dirty dishes that must've been littering my kitchen. When I left the house last Friday morning, I wasn't counting on strangers coming in. Though I guess the Shelbornes aren't strangers anymore.

My life has collided with Madison's, and we're now stuck together for the time being.

Or rather, she's stuck with me.

Emma unlocks the door to let us in. "Where's Mrs. Shelborne?"

Jake shrugs. "She said something about you needing toilet paper? I think she's on a Costco run."

"Oh, jeez," Madison mutters.

She crutches inside first, and Jake and I play chicken over who will go next. He wins, his feet staying planted until I limp inside with my hospital-provided cane. Going to ditch *that* nuisance as soon as possible.

The small entryway opens into our great room. My house is a mid-century ranch. Exposed brick covers one wall, and a floor-to-ceiling window looks over my postage-stamp back-yard. There's a sectional couch in front of a stacked-stone fireplace, above which a big-screen TV hangs.

Madison goes right to the couch and plops down, sighing as she sets her crutches aside.

Jake points at the suitcase. "Where should I put this?"

Emma has already zoomed into the kitchen, where she's inspecting whatever's inside the fridge.

"I'll show you." I nod toward the hallway and limp toward my tiny office/guestroom. When I reach it, I try to push aside the clutter on the desk. Was it always this dusty in here? "The couch pulls out. I can grab some sheets from the hall closet. Just leave the suitcase here."

"I'll make up the bed."

"Don't worry about it, I can—"

But Jake's already in the hall. In moments he's back with a pile of mismatched sheets. I stand back as he moves the couch cushions and yanks the hideaway open.

"You don't have to do that."

"Trust me, I can handle making a bed. Did it just this morning after one of my five-year-olds had an accident. Not the kind you're thinking, though. Cereal and milk. I'm on the phone for half a second..."

"*One* of your five-year-olds?"

"I have twins." He pulls out his phone and shows me the

lockscreen picture. A boy and a girl smile and wave from a grassy lawn. They look like Madison, except with dirty blond hair like Jake's. A golden retriever sits in front of them with a huge smile and lolling tongue.

"They just started kindergarten," he says. "The kids, not the dog."

I recognize the light of pride in his eyes. "Cute."

Jake has a vibe and posture that makes me think military, and I don't miss those hospital corners as he efficiently yanks the sheets into place. I remember Madison saying something about a brother doing two tours in Afghanistan.

"Did you serve?" I ask.

"Army. Madison and I are the odd ones in the bunch. We didn't go into the family catering business. We use guns instead of spatulas for a living."

"I don't know a thing about cooking. But guns, I understand."

Jake nods, eyes crinkling in a friendly way. "Thanks again for looking out for my little sister. Making sure she got home. She's tough, but we worry about her. Hearing she was injured…" He shakes his head. "It's hard."

"She looked out for me too."

"That doesn't surprise me."

I half expect some pointed questions or a lecture about my intentions toward Madison, but they don't come. Jake puts a case on a pillow and spreads out a blanket.

"Talking about me?" Madison's in the doorway, balanced on her crutches.

"Naturally." Her brother walks over to kiss her on the forehead. "You're all set up here, so I'll get out of your hair."

"Can you keep mom from coming over with her bulk toilet paper? Tell her we can handle it."

Jake grimaces. "You know there's no stopping her sometimes, but I'll do what I can." He nods at me. "Let me know if you need anything. Otherwise, I'm out."

Madison shifts aside to let her brother through. I start toward the door to follow him, but Jake says, "I can find the exit. You two sit down. I'm scared you're going to fall over." He winks and strides down the hall.

I hear Emma in her room, listening to music and Face-Timing with her friends by the sounds of it.

"So..." Madison says.

We're alone, with our injuries and bemused expressions.

Sunlight streams through a large window. Worn paper-backs line a bookshelf. The desk is covered with dusty framed photos of Emma and me, most from the last year. I bought some abstract paintings at a local artist's fair to decorate the walls, but otherwise I've gone with simple black furniture and light blue accents.

She makes her way to the bed and sits down, leaving her crutches propped against the wall. "Thanks for making room for me. I spent the last couple days since I got discharged at my mother's house, and I *really* needed an out."

"Glad I could serve as your excuse."

Madison stretches out her legs on the blankets. "I meant what I said before. If you don't want to do this, I can take off once my mother's not paying attention. I don't want to impose."

Is she looking for a way out of this? I wouldn't blame her.

Does she really want to spend the next several days with the guy who made an utter ass of himself in front of her? Who kissed her and then rejected her, and then fucked up so catastrophically we both wound up in the hospital?

She's got far more sense than that.

Which makes what I'm feeling all the more pathetic. Underneath my annoyance at needing help—I'm willing to admit now that I do—there's a flicker of excitement in my stomach at the prospect of seeing more of Madison.

I like being around her. I like her warmth and her jokes, the way she forces me out of my shell, no matter how much I try to retreat into it.

I sit on the edge of the thin mattress, ignoring the painful twinge in my bruised ribs. "At least stick around to eat the food your family dropped off. Looked like there was enough to feed all of West Oaks PD for a week."

"My mother likes to go big."

"I'm grateful. It was kind of her. Your family seems like good people."

"I like to think so. Yours too."

"It's just Emma and me."

"Exactly. I've met you both, and I give you my stamp of approval."

Pleasure glows in my veins.

"You might as well sit next to me," Madison says. "You look really uncomfortable hanging off the edge of the bed."

She's right. My ribs are killing me, and my shoulder muscles ache from keeping my right arm steady. "Or I could let you rest, if you'd—"

Madison cuts me off. "I'm calling an end to all weirdness between us. I'm staying here at least a few days, and we're friends, and we've been through some shit together. So you can sit wherever you want. We can both be cool." She sinks into the pillows and sighs. "See? Making myself at home. It's your house, so you should do the same."

I slip off my shoes, move around to the other side of the bed, and settle in beside her. We're both lying on top of the blankets.

"I'm relaxed," I say.

"You sure about that?"

"I am, actually." We both turn our heads, facing one another.

It's like the air between us is vibrating.

My phone rings in my pocket. My stomach sours when I see the name. "It's Emma's mom. Mind if I answer it here? Not sure how fast I can get up." It took me a while just to sit down.

"Go ahead. No weirdness, remember?"

Not sure about that, but I answer the call anyway. "Hey, Simone."

"Nash! I've left like a million voicemails."

I grit my teeth. I saw the missed calls, but I've been avoiding calling her back. The difference in time zones is part of it. But not all. "Emma said she'd texted with you."

"Yeah, but I wanted to hear from you."

"I've been sleeping a lot. And France is eight hours ahead? Or nine? I keep forgetting."

"I just…" She breathes heavily into the phone. Sounds like she's fighting back tears. "I've been really freaked out."

"I know. But you don't need to be."

Even after four years of being divorced, we still care about each other. We're raising Emma together, and we get along well. But sometimes, I'd prefer indifference. I don't want Simone to mother me.

"I've been looking at flights," she says. "Makes the most sense to fly out of Marseilles, but—"

"No, don't do that. We're okay. A friend is helping us out." I glance at Madison.

"A friend? What friend?"

"From work. Why do you sound surprised?"

"It's you, Nash. I know how you are. You sure you don't need me there?"

"Completely. I promise."

"You'd better let me know if that changes. Are you still

good with Emma coming to me for the holidays?"

"Of course. It'll be a great trip for her."

"If you're sure." There's a pause. "Take care, Nash. I know you'll look out for our girl, but don't forget about yourself."

"I'm fine."

"Yes, I was married to you for thirteen years. I know that's what you always say. Whether it's true or not."

When I finish the call, I set my phone on the nightstand.

"Where's Emma's mom?"

"In France with her new husband. He's a travel blogger, and they're living abroad in different tiny towns in Europe."

"Sounds incredible."

"Yeah. They asked Emma if she wanted to go, but she chose to move in with me instead. She'd never lived with me full-time before that."

Throughout her childhood, I was deployed six months out of the year, busy training the other half. I wonder if my marriage would've lasted so long if I'd been home. Hard to say. All I know is, I ended up with a wife who felt more like a sister and a preteen daughter who hardly remembered me.

I'd only been back a few months when Simone asked me for a divorce.

Took me a long time before I stopped wearing my ring, which is dumb. I wasn't in love with Simone anymore. But it was like a security blanket, one I'd relied upon through so many lonely nights. That promise that somebody was waiting for me.

It's good that Simone moved on and found happiness with someone else. A guy who could give her what she needed.

"I'm still surprised Emma chose California instead of Europe," I say. "But she didn't want to leave her school or her friends." I shrug. "I'm trying not to screw her up too badly."

"Give yourself some credit, Jennings. Emma's handling all this really well. She's resilient. A lot of kids would be a wreck in her situation."

"I'm proud of her. I just don't want her to think it's her responsibility to take care of me. That's too much for a fifteen-year-old."

Madison sighs dramatically. "Then you and I will have to take care of each other. That's the only solution." Her green irises are pale in the sunlight, glinting like seaglass. Or shallow water that I could fall into and never come up for air.

I might've pushed her away last Friday on that dancefloor. But I did want her. And I still do. That hasn't changed. Not one fucking bit. I still feel that pull, that urge to reach out even though I know it's a bad idea.

Madison is hurt because of *me*. I can't do it again.

She blinks and averts her gaze. "I've been thinking about what happened."

"I have too." Shit, I wonder if she's having the same doubts. That living together is too much temptation. Even if I could start something with Madison—if she really was just a friend from the academy—she deserves a lot better than me.

She takes a shaky breath. Suddenly, her lips are trembling.

"Hey," I whisper. "What is it?"

She starts to turn away. "Sorry."

"No. It's okay. Tell me."

"I keep imagining the bullets hitting me a few inches differently. I can't get it out of my mind. But I couldn't say that to my family. It would scare them too much, knowing I'll be back on duty once I'm healed. Jake understands better than any of them, but he sees me as his little sister, too. He worries."

Not what I thought she'd say. But it makes my chest ache to know she's upset, and it's nothing to do with my bruise. "I get it. I can't tell Emma this stuff either. But I think about it.

What could happen to me, and what she'd do with her mom out of the country." Emma has emergency numbers to call, including her grandparents. But they all live out of state. We're not that close. And while Laura Chen offered to keep Emma, my daughter insisted on staying beside me in the hospital.

"I'm glad we can tell each other," Madison says.

I don't have much faith in my instincts right now. But I decide to follow this one.

I lean into her. Touch my forehead to hers. Madison grips my shirt in her fist. I put my left arm around her and pull her close, and she presses her face into my neck.

We breathe against the other's skin.

The relief is tremendous, a weight lifting off of me. Consciously, I didn't know how much I needed this. Being close to her, touching her after what we shared. But it feels right. So, so right.

I hope this is what she needs, too. That I'm giving her something instead of taking. Please tell me this isn't an asshole move.

After a while, Madison pulls back, lifting her eyes. "That helped. Thanks."

"Any time." I brush a stray teardrop from her cheek with my thumb.

I imagine touching her lower lip next. Bending down. I can still feel the shape of her mouth in my memory.

Then my daughter's voice rings out from the hallway. "Dad! Are we having dinner or what?"

Madison and I jerk away from each other.

"Just a sec, Em." I clear my throat. "Be right there." I scoot to the edge of the mattress. "We should…"

"Yeah. I'll be out in a minute."

I get out of the guestroom as quickly as I can. I'd rather Emma didn't see that I was in here.

17

Madison

I wake to sunlight streaming through a gauzy white curtain. Springs squeak and my body aches as I sit up. For a moment, I can't remember where I am. Then it all comes rushing back. But it's not as overwhelming as before.

And I smell bacon. So that probably helps.

I get out of bed and fish around in my open suitcase for clothes. Last night, I went to bed early after we ate lasagna and chocolate cake for dinner. Hard to be annoyed at my mother when she provides like that. Nash wasn't kidding about the supplies filling his kitchen.

My warm fuzzies last until I look at my phone.

Mom: Are you sure you don't need me to drop by with the toilet paper? The bathrooms looked low when I was there.
Me: Mom, enough about the toilet paper!

Then I feel guilty.

Me: Thank you for all the food and taking care of me. You're amazing. I love you.

Mom: All in a few days' work. I love you too, and I want you to let me know if you need anything at all. And if you have anything to share about your romantic entanglements, I would appreciate not being the last to know.

I clench my teeth and switch my screen off.

There are not going to be any romantic entanglements. My attraction to him is as strong as ever. Judging from the look in his eye yesterday, when he was comforting me, he might feel it too. But at the hospital, I told the nurse that Nash and I are complicated. That was an understatement.

I throw on a pair of jeans under my West Oaks PD T-shirt. Then I make a trip to the bathroom, where I change the bandages on my arm and leg. After that, I brush my teeth and tame my hair. Nash and I are just friends, but that doesn't mean I want to look like a beast around him.

Finally presentable, I head into the great room. Emma's in the kitchen, bent over the oven.

"Morning." I slide onto a bar stool and rest against the upholstered back, my bandaged arm tucked against my side.

She gives me a wary smile. "Hi."

"Sleep well?"

"Not bad. I was just heating up the bacon and cinnamon rolls."

"Perfect."

Her hair is piled into a bun on top of her head, and she's washed off the eyeliner from yesterday. After dinner last night, I went straight to bed. I was too exhausted to do anything else. Plus, I wanted to let Nash and Emma have time together without me as a third wheel.

"Do you have school today?" I ask.

"Nope. I already told the attendance office I was staying home for my dad. I wasn't sure if you were still coming."

"Ah."

There's a long pause. Neither of us says anything.

Emma pulls the cinnamon rolls from the oven, and I inhale the sweet, spiced scent.

"Aiden puts orange zest in the icing. There's always a batch in the freezer at my mom's house on standby."

"Did he make the food from last night? It was good."

"He did. Aiden teaches cooking classes, if you'd ever be interested. A lot of teens sign up."

She shrugs and goes quiet, taking out her phone instead.

Dang. I probably sounded like I was trying too hard. But I'm nothing if not persistent. I'm staying in this girl's house, and I want her to like me.

"I love this kitchen," I say. "It's so retro."

Emma looks up from her screen. "Isn't it? We took off all the cabinet doors, sanded them, and re-painted them the original color. The appliances are new though. My dad got them from some kitchen supplier that makes things that look old-fashioned."

The cabinets and appliances are pale green, straight out of the 1970s. All that's missing is the old-school laminate countertops. Instead, they've gone with butcher block.

"The backsplash is a nice touch." The tile has a subtle paisley pattern. I've never seen anything like it.

Emma beams. "I picked that out."

I gesture at the great room. "The whole house is gorgeous. Did you guys decorate it?"

"We did more than that. Dad bought this place after a bank foreclosure. You should've seen it." She shakes her head. "Water damage, holes in the walls. Nasty shag carpet and dingy bathrooms. It was a disaster. We've been working on it for the past two years. It was our project on the weekends when I was staying with my dad."

"Nash must be pretty handy."

"You'd think so, but no. My dad looked up everything on

YouTube. But he just had to do it all himself. To absolutely no one's surprise."

I grin. I don't know Nash well, but that sounds like him.

Only, he asked *me* for advice on being a better instructor during SWAT training. I'm just now realizing what a big deal it was. That he would trust me that way.

Emma takes the food out of the oven and sets it on the counter. "Coffee? It's done brewing."

"Please. You're my hero."

She pours me a cup from the coffeemaker, then hands me the cream from the fridge. I add a splash.

I've just taken a sip when Emma asks, "So, are you and my dad hooking up?"

Coffee shoots straight down my wind pipe.

I spend the next solid minute coughing. I did not expect those words to come out of her mouth. But Emma doesn't seem fazed. She watches me hack up my lungs and hands me a napkin. "I just want to know what I might walk in on."

"It's…not like that." I wipe my mouth. "Did your dad say something?"

"He said you're friends. But of all the people who offered help, you're the only one he accepted it from. Not even me. I appreciate it, I do. He can't do everything on his own. I'm just trying to figure out what it is about you."

That sounds a little like an accusation, but I try not to take it personally. Because I don't know either.

Plus, it's natural Nash's daughter might feel some jealousy. I've been worried about this since I came up with this plan.

"Maybe it's easier to accept help from someone who needs it too," I say. "If I wasn't here, my mother would expect me to recover at her house, so you're saving me."

"I don't know. Your mom seems nice. And super generous."

"Yeah, she seems that way. Until she's sorting through your underwear drawer to replace the old ones like you're in preschool and not a grown adult." Luckily, my younger siblings are enough of a handful that she lacks the time to focus on me. Until now, anyway. Getting shot put me front and center.

Emma doesn't laugh at my joke, but she's not frowning either. "Bossy parents are something I can understand. But I wish I had a big family like yours. It gets too quiet around here. My dad can go days without saying a single word."

"I heard that." Nash limps into the kitchen. "And it's not true. I'm saying words right now."

"That's because Madison is here." Emma tilts her head in my direction. "But maybe you can liven up this place while you're around?"

"Just wait," I say. "By tomorrow, you'll be begging me to shut up."

"Bonus points if you can get my dad to watch something on TV besides ESPN or football."

"That can be arranged."

"I'm not sure I like this," Nash says. "You two are uniting against me."

Emma ruffles his hair. "What did you expect? Madison's cool, so obviously she sides with me."

Yes. I'm doing an internal victory dance.

Emma grabs some plates and dishes up breakfast. We eat there at the counter. She takes the stool next to me, leaving Nash the one on the other end.

He smiles tentatively at me over her head. His chin is dark with stubble, and he's got a messy bedhead. "Sleep well?" he asks.

I open my mouth, but Emma answers first. "Fine," she says.

I busy myself with my cinnamon roll.

"Dad! You need to see this." Emma holds up her phone. "There's an article about you guys!"

Nash and I both lean in.

It's from California Crimes Uncovered. The same website that coined the name "Midnight Slasher."

The headline reads, *Is the Midnight Slasher Dead? West Oaks Residents Demand Answers.*

Sources report that, over the weekend, West Oaks PD officers confronted two suspects in a brazen home invasion. Police gunned down both suspects. But Police Chief Alex Liu is still refusing to comment.

Some speculate that one of the suspects could be the vicious Midnight Slasher, who is wanted in a number of recent West Oaks home invasions. The Slasher is known to torture his victims, and his reign of terror has had much of West Oaks on edge for months. Those victims include Eugene Cowling, who tragically died of a heart attack following the Slasher's attack. The West Oaks SWAT team responded, but failed to save Cowling's life.

'I've heard almost nothing from police,' Landon Cowling, the victim's son, says. 'Is the Slasher dead? Is he still alive? The victims deserve to know what's going on. The whole town deserves to know.'

The officers involved in the shooting are Sergeant Nash Jennings and Patrol Officer Madison Shelborne. They were off duty at the time of the incident, and witnesses spotted them drinking at a bar shortly before the shooting.

Asked for a statement, West Oaks Mayor Norman Ackerman said, 'Rest assured, our community is safer as a result of the heroic efforts of our police force.'

But that remains to be seen.

Mayor Ackerman faces a runoff election next Tuesday after failing to garner the required fifty percent of votes during the general election last month. His opponent has accused Mayor Ackerman of being soft on crime and unable to handle the startling increase in violent incidents in West Oaks. Residents are wondering the same thing.

When will we get answers?

Heat spreads over my skin. I look over at Nash. He's rubbing a hand over his jaw.

"I think we've seen enough," Nash says. "This blog isn't a news site. It's a tabloid. Just trying to get as much attention as possible."

"It's working." Emma turns off her screen. "Tons of people are talking about this on social. People in West Oaks. Not like, the whole world. But still. People are saying you stopped the Midnight Slasher."

Nash pushes away his plate. "Detective Holt told me they're still investigating."

"Wait, do you mean the Slasher *is* still out there? Or..."

Nash reaches out for her, and Emma hugs him. Suddenly, in her dad's arms, she looks far younger than fifteen. "I know we're safe here. Okay? We don't have anything to worry about."

His eyes meet mine over Emma's shoulder, and I wish I could believe that, too.

A MAN IN A SKI MASK STANDS OVER ME. THERE ARE two black voids where his eyes should be. He raises a knife.

"Please," I beg. *"Don't."*

The knife slashes downward.

I jolt upright in bed, gasping, my fists gripping the blankets. My teeth clench, fighting off the pain in my body.

My eyes blink in the darkness.

A nightmare. It was just a nightmare. It wasn't real. But I'm wired like a taser just unloaded its charge into me.

I scramble off the mattress, stumbling as my weight lands on my injured leg. My shoulder hits the wall, and *fuck*, that's my hurt arm. Finally, I find the light switch and flick it on.

My heart's beating so hard, I feel like it'll burst out of my chest. I find my phone, and it says it's three in the morning. There's no way I'm getting back to sleep.

Yesterday, Emma and I started binge-watching a murder mystery series on Netflix. Why did I think that was a good idea? Nash knew better. He hung out in his room most of the day. It was good, in a way. Gave me and Emma a chance to hang out more. She showed me her violin, too, though she would only consent to playing a short rendition of "Blister in the Sun" that was pretty amazing.

After that, I tried texting with my family and friends, but they only asked questions I wasn't able—or ready—to answer. I went to bed early again, hoping for another solid night's rest. No such luck.

As quietly as I can, I twist the knob on my door. I step out into the dark hallway.

The silhouette of a man stands there, looming out of the shadows. "I heard a noise. Are you okay?"

Nash.

My heart won't slow down. "Sorry. I tripped."

He steps toward me. "You're hurt?"

"More than usual? Nah." I realize I'm wearing just a T-shirt with nothing but panties underneath. And Nash doesn't have a shirt on. Just sweatpants and his bandages. The fixator is a thin bar that's pinned through the skin into his hand and in his forearm. There's also a huge splotch of purple over his chest and trailing along his stomach. The bruise from the gunshot to his vest. I have an urge to kiss it. Make it better.

The rest of him is golden skin, thick muscle, a dusting of dark hair…

This is not helping my elevated heart rate.

I force my eyes to stay on his face and cross my arms over my chest. "What are you doing up?"

"Couldn't sleep. You?" His hair sticks up wildly, like he was rolling around in his bed.

"Same."

"Want a drink? I was heading to the kitchen."

"Okay. I just..." I look back at my room. "I left my crutches by the bed."

I think Nash might go get them. But instead, he wraps his arm around my waist. "Come on. I've got you."

"You don't have to." But am I going to refuse putting my hand on his back? A very broad back that tapers down to his narrow waist. The man's skin is so hot against mine it's searing.

I close my mouth on a moan.

"You sure you're okay?" he asks. We're limping toward the kitchen. Mostly he's supporting me, while I brace against him. Even though he's far more injured than I am.

I make a sound that's vaguely agreeable.

In the kitchen, Nash doesn't turn on the overhead light. Instead, he flips a switch, and a dim glow comes from beneath the cabinets. It's just enough to see by.

My rebellious eyes try to stray down his body before I stop them. "What drink are you making?"

"Hot water with lemon," he says.

I wrinkle my nose. "You don't have anything better?"

"I could add rum and brown sugar." He smirks.

"Now you're talking." I need something stronger than lemon. *Nash is plenty strong*, a naughty voice says in my head. But I'll have to settle for the rum.

This is only my second night staying at his house. I should be able to behave myself. There will be no repeats of what happened on that dancefloor.

Nash grabs the kettle while I work the tap. We end up

laughing after the water nearly overflows. He gets the kettle onto the stove, then digs into the fridge for lemon wedges and a cabinet for rum and sugar. I watch his back muscles flex.

"Why were you really stumbling around in your room?" he asks.

"Nightmare."

He looks over his shoulder. "What about?"

"I'm sure you can guess." I sit at the counter, and Nash follows, sliding onto the stool beside me. He puts the liquor bottle and bag of sugar down in front of us. I hear the rush of the water in the kettle as it heats.

"Do you think the Slasher is really dead?" I ask. "Like that article said?"

"I hope so. If not, we got rid of a couple of bad people. I'm not crying. Neither should you."

"I wish I knew their names. I'm not sure why that matters, but it does."

"I get it."

I figured he would. Nash is right beside me, an inch away, and I can't resist. I rest my head on his bare shoulder and close my eyes. I feel him turn his face into me, stubble scratching my forehead. My body finally relaxes, letting go of the fear from my nightmare.

"I worked on the Slasher case before this," I say. "Not as a detective, obviously, but I'm assigned to major crimes. I got all the briefings. Saw photos from the crime scenes." My stomach twists as I remember them.

Nash holds out his hand. I squeeze it, then force myself to let go. Comforting each other is one thing. I can't get carried away.

The kettle whistles. "I'll get it," I say, ignoring the pain when I jump up.

"Do *you* think we killed the Slasher?" he asks.

"Maybe. A lot of it fits. The ski masks. The k-bar knife." I pour hot water into two mugs, then stir in the sugar and add a squeeze of lemon. Nash holds out the rum bottle, and I unscrew it for him. He adds a little to each mug.

I take my seat again, and we sip our drinks. Another bit of comfort that makes me toasty inside.

"I've been thinking about the article Emma showed us," Nash says. "What do you know about the Crimes Uncovered blog? I don't love that she was reading it."

"Just that they write everything for maximum effect—to scare people. They have a true crime podcast too. Pull it up on your phone, and I'll show you."

Nash takes his phone from his sweatpants pocket. I navigate to the website. The front page has the article we read. And below, there's a list of other articles and podcast episodes on the Slasher. I'm sure some of it's nonsense, but I'm curious what else they say.

We spend the next half hour reading as we sip our drinks. There are no major revelations. Yet I'm impressed by how much info this blog has. Makes me wonder about their sources.

Eventually, I start yawning and sagging into him.

"Let's get you back to bed," Nash says.

We limp down the hallway together. At my door, he stops. His arm's around me, and it doesn't let go.

"I'm sorry you had a nightmare."

"Same here."

"If you need anything, anything at all, I can…"

"You'll what?" I whisper.

It's like we're drawn together by some invisible force. Without saying a word, we take a step toward one another. Our bodies meet, and my nipples press into his bruised chest through my thin T-shirt.

I feel the ache pouring off of him in waves. My body's

alive with longing. Nash cups his hand at the side of my neck. My pulse thrums against his palm. The pain of my injuries, I can handle. This pleasure is unbearable.

Our noses touch. Our breaths mingle. His lips barely brush mine. We just stay there. Not quite a kiss, but almost. Almost. The moment hums with potential.

And I do want it. I want *him*. God, I do.

But kissing him last Friday was a mistake. We both know that. Now would be even worse. The fact that we're right outside his daughter's room is only part of the reason. We're both a mess after all that's happened.

If I let him kiss me now, what's to stop him from changing his mind again? Just one more thing for us to regret.

"Nash." I have to force the words out. "We shouldn't."

"Fuck. I'm sorry. I'm...yeah." He pulls away, arm dropping to his side. "Goodnight, Madison," he says firmly. "I'll see you in the morning."

"Night."

I watch his back as he walks down the hall. One last glance, and he vanishes into his room.

18

Nash

*M*adison's stay of "a few days" has now become a week. Neither of us is in a rush for her to leave. At least, not from my perspective. It's been good having her here. And not just for the help getting shit done around the house.

Whenever Emma's home, the three of us hang out, cooking or talking or bingeing Netflix shows. But I'm happy to just sit back and watch them. Emma and Madison, laughing over videos on Emma's feed. Racing around the kitchen on Madison's crutches. Or more often, laughing at something I said or did. They *love* ganging up on me. I've rarely seen my daughter smile so much at home. She's been downright pleasant instead of angsty. Madison seems happy too.

But right now, Emma's at school. It's just Madison and me. And the dynamic is…different.

Madison tucks her legs beneath her. Her foot almost nudges my knee, but not quite. "I may have found something. I'm not sure yet. It could be a lead on the Slasher."

She's got her hair in a messy ponytail, and she's wearing

leggings and a soft-looking oversized sweater. I've noticed she likes shimmery eyeshadow, something she never wears at work. A long silver chain hangs from her neck, with the pendant tucked inside her sweater.

"Yeah? What is it?" I shift an inch closer, my left arm draping over the back of the couch.

She lifts her phone to show me, but I'm struggling to focus on anything but *her*.

Outwardly, I'm fine. A couple times a week, we go for our respective physical therapy appointments. When Madison and I are alone at home, we talk about guns and tactics. We scour the Internet for any mention of the Midnight Slasher or similar knife-wielding burglars. It's not much of an investigation, but it's what we've got. And it keeps us both busy.

She's still having nightmares, and our nightly insomnia sessions haven't veered beyond the platonic again. Not since I almost kissed her. Almost, as in one fucking millimeter away. I don't want to be selfish with her, yet I keep doing it.

Not only that, she's become my *daughter's friend*. A fact I have to constantly remind myself of.

My left hand is getting more skilled, though. There's that.

"What do you think?" Madison's eye catches mine, and I feel that electric charge move through me. Singeing my nerve endings. Making me long for things I can't allow to happen.

"Um, sorry. Still reading."

She's showing me a news article on her phone, but this one's not from the Crimes Uncovered site. It's from a Northern California newspaper. I take the phone from her hand and try to focus.

Burglary Victim Reportedly Slashed, Like Others.

"There was a series of home invasions in Mammoth Lakes," she says. "This was published ten years ago."

"Ten *years*?"

Mammoth Lakes is five hours north of here, near

Yosemite National Park. It's a ski resort town. A small community, like West Oaks, though we're much closer to a big metropolitan area.

"The burglar in Mammoth was never caught," Madison says. "But he tied the victims up and cut them with a knife. Always superficial wounds. But enough to terrify them before he robbed them."

"Like the Slasher's crimes in West Oaks. Eugene Cowling only died because of his heart condition."

"Exactly. It's similar enough to look into."

"Are you going to forward this to Detective Holt?"

"Already have."

I hand back Madison's phone. Our fingers touch. Just that brief contact, and heat rushes into my stomach.

Her phone chimes in her hand. We both startle. Madison checks the notification.

"Lia texted." She glances up at me. "The mayor and Chief Liu are holding a press conference on the Midnight Slasher in an hour."

"Want to get out of the house? See what it's about? Emma won't be back from school for another hour or two."

"Yeah," she breathes. "Out of the house sounds good."

I wonder if she's feeling the same unrelenting tension that I am.

IT'S COOL ENOUGH THAT I WISH I'D WORN A heavier coat. I hear waves crashing into the nearby shore, and pedestrians mill along the sidewalks. The light poles have green and red garlands wrapped around them. Barely into December, but the town's getting ready for the holidays.

Madison looks back over her shoulder. "Pick up the pace, gramps. At this rate, we'll miss the whole press conference."

She's gotten quick on her crutches. I didn't bring my cane because I hate that thing. We had to park a few blocks away from city hall because parking around here sucks.

"Working on it," I say. "You can go on without me."

"But then you'll probably forget where you are. Emma will be pissed if I lose track of her elderly father."

"Ha. Ha."

When we reach city hall, there's already a crowd gathered in front of the steps. A podium is set up with microphones, and reporters mill around, cameramen at the ready. It looks like this story has gone beyond West Oaks. The LA Times is here, as well as other regional papers.

I look for someone from California Crimes Uncovered, but I don't see a microphone or camera with their name.

We keep to the edges of the crowd, trying not to be noticed.

Finally, Mayor Ackerman appears, followed by Police Chief Liu, who's dragging his feet. I see lights on video cameras flicker on.

"Thanks for being here, everyone. I'll get right to it. For the past several months, a criminal known as the Midnight Slasher has terrorized West Oaks residents." The mayor pauses, eying the cameras. "Today, I'm pleased to tell you that his acts of terror will never occur again. The Midnight Slasher is dead, killed by devoted officers of West Oaks PD."

Madison shares a look with me. My hand goes to the small of her back.

The mayor flips a page of his notes. "The Midnight Slasher was a man named Jeffrey Nichols. We're still gathering information about his life, but I can confirm that Nichols was killed by Sergeant Nash Jennings when the off-duty sergeant was responding to a home invasion. Nichols had an accomplice, his younger brother Thomas Lipinski, who was seventeen years old. Mr. Lipinski was also killed after he opened fire on Sergeant Jennings and his fellow West Oaks PD Officer Madison Shelborne, wounding both of them."

In my peripheral vision, I notice someone glancing at me and Madison. Whispering. But then the crowd shifts, and the gap closes up again.

"While the official investigation into the deadly use of force by Sergeant Jennings and Officer Shelborne remains ongoing, I'm pleased to share that I received a preliminary report from the District Attorney just this morning. The DA's office expects to rule that Sergeant Jennings and Officer Shelborne acted within legal bounds."

My heart kickstarts in my chest. I drag in a breath. Madison's eyes find mine again.

Mayor Ackerman nods to someone in the crowd, and another man steps up to the podium. This guy is in his thirties, with shoulder-length hair and thick-framed glasses.

"My name is Landon Cowling. My father Eugene Cowling died at the hands of the Midnight Slasher earlier this fall. I'm grateful to Mayor Ackerman for stepping up West Oaks PD's response."

I remember Cowling's quote from the Crimes Uncovered blog post a few days ago. He was pissed off at the mayor and West Oaks PD then. He's changed his tune.

"Sergeant Jennings and Officer Shelborne," Cowling says, "if you're watching, I want to thank you for bringing my father's killer to justice."

Again, I feel eyes on me. There—a girl is watching us through the crowd. Then her hand claps over her mouth, and she starts pushing toward us. "Sergeant Jennings! Officer Shelborne!"

It's Bridget Hanson.

A man and woman follow after Bridget, reaching for the teenager with fear and exhaustion in their eyes. Like they haven't slept a whole night in a while. The woman's carrying a toddler. I remember his curly hair, and carrying him and Madison out of the house when I was only half-conscious from the pain and blood loss.

Other people in the crowd are turning toward us.

"*Bridget?*" Madison gasps.

"Mom, Dad, this is them! The police officers who helped me!"

"Oh my God, thank you," Mrs. Hanson says, tears rolling down her face. "You saved my kids."

The mayor and Cowling have stopped speaking, but nobody's paying attention to the press conference anymore. Someone jostles my fixator, and I bite down on a curse. I cinch my arm around Madison, keeping her close so we're not separated.

Microphones appear in front of our faces. "Sergeant Jennings! Do you have any comment?" a reporter shouts.

"What was it like to kill the Slasher?" another asks.

Somebody else bats the microphone away. "Move, coming through. Out of the way, please." It's Detective Holt. He hustles me and Madison through the crowd.

It's chaos. Cameras point at us. People shout. Up on the stage, the mayor's noticed us and he's calling our names.

Landon Cowling stares, eyes wide.

Holt pushes us both along with a hand on our backs. Madison is struggling with her crutches. "Maybe this wasn't the best idea," she says.

"You think?" Holt mutters.

A couple of West Oaks PD officers step in behind us, holding back the media.

Then Chief Liu blocks our path. "This way. *Now*." We follow him across the street. Not like we have much choice, with that stern look on the chief's face and Holt right behind us.

The chief reaches a black sedan. There's a driver waiting in the front, and he nods at the chief.

"Get in. Not you, Holt."

Madison and I slip into the back seat. The chief gets into the front passenger side, and the doors shut and lock. I see Holt through the window, standing on the curb. His chest moves like he's sighing, and his eyes say, *Nice one, Jennings*.

The chief turns around, unbuttoning his suit jacket. "What the hell are you two doing here?"

There's a tense pause. We're catching our breaths.

Madison speaks first. "It was my idea. I wanted to see what the mayor would say."

"Couldn't watch it streaming on Facebook?"

"In retrospect, that would've been less conspicuous."

"I hope you're not making light of this situation, Officer Shelborne."

I force my mouth to open. I can't let Madison take the blame, though she often seems determined to do it. "We didn't see the harm. We didn't plan on being recognized."

Madison frowns at me.

"I didn't want to be here today at all." Chief Liu stretches his long legs, shifting in his seat. The leather creaks. "This whole Midnight Slasher situation…it's a shitshow. You heard about the mayor's runoff election next week, right?"

His driver is silent, facing the windshield.

From here, we can see the mayor on the steps of city hall. He's got Bridget and her family up there with him now. Bridget and her mom are crying, and the cameras are no doubt catching every tear. Her dad stands stoically behind his family. I'm not sure if the mayor invited them to the press conference or what.

And there's Landon Cowling, his hand on Bridget's shoulder as they speak into the microphones. Victims of the Midnight Slasher.

"Are you saying the mayor's office is manipulating the investigation?" I ask.

"I'm not saying *anything*. And neither should you, Sergeant." The chief glances back at me, eyes cold. "It's true that Jeffrey Nichols is our top suspect in the Midnight Slasher attacks. Our *only* suspect, since Lipinski's girlfriend provided an alibi for at least one of the prior incidents, so he wasn't the Slasher. We got absolutely nothing from the previous crime scenes."

Madison leans forward. "We might have found another lead. Ten years ago, there was a similar string of burglaries up in Mammoth Lakes. A guy with a knife broke into homes, slashed the homeowners, robbed them. Sound familiar?"

Chief Liu glances from me to Madison and back again. "I can see you both have been busy while you're convalescing." I open my mouth, but the chief raises a finger. "I'm going to say this exactly once. *Don't.*"

"Don't what?" Madison asks, chin lifting in defiance.

Careful, I think.

"Don't ask questions. Don't get involved. The district attorney is going to rule you followed all procedures, as he should. Because it was a clean shoot. But you never know with the media. They're fans of you both now, singing your praises as heroes, but that could change any moment."

"Is the Slasher investigation still open or not?" Madison says. "Are you going to look into the Mammoth Lakes connection?"

Liu twists fully around, gripping the seatback. "*Don't. Ask. Questions.* The two of you need to stay out of it. That's an order. Is that, or is that not, understood?"

There's a pause, and silence settles over the cabin. The chief's eyebrows raise toward his hairline.

He's our commander. There's no choice but compliance.

"Yes, sir," I say.

I feel Madison's disapproval radiating from her. But she nods. "Yes, sir," she echoes quietly.

"Good answer." He tugs the lapels of his jacket. "Now, where can I drop you off? Can't have my heroic officers limping down Ocean Lane."

"We're parked a few blocks away," I say.

ON THE WAY HOME, MADISON IS QUIET.

I pull into my driveway and reach across to put the SUV in park with my left hand. It's annoying to drive with my injuries, but what can I say? I like to be in the driver's seat.

Madison doesn't get out. I sit and wait to hear what she has to say.

"What're we going to do?" she asks.

"About what?"

"The investigation!"

"What the chief said. Nothing."

"You really want to let this go? After everything that's happened? We killed those men, Nash. I want to know who they really were. I want to know if the Slasher is really dead or not."

I want all those things too. But the chief has given us no leeway.

"If people think the Slasher is dead," Madison says, "and that allows him to move to some other town and hurt more people? I'm not okay with that. Jeffrey Nichols was bad. But the Slasher is worse."

"I'm not okay with it either. But I don't see what choice we have."

"Well, I think that's bullshit." She pushes out of the SUV.

The sun is starting to set, and the lights are on inside my

house. Emma must be home. I don't like that she beat us here. These days, I don't like her being here alone.

But when Madison and I get inside, I find Bridget Hanson sitting with Emma at the kitchen table.

Both girls stand up. Bridget's eyes are red like she's been crying.

"Dad, Bridget asked if she could come over and talk to you and Madison."

"I would've done it before," the other girl says. "But I wasn't sure if you'd want to see me."

I try to cover my shock at seeing Bridget here in my home so soon after the press conference. I look around as if I'll see reporters here too, though of course there are none.

"It's all right," I say. "You two are in the same class, I remember. Do your parents know you're here?"

Bridget nods. "Yes. I can give you their numbers, if you want. Catherine and Steve. They wanted to say thanks again as well. They feel bad about causing a scene at the press conference."

Madison steps forward and gives her a hug. "I'm so sorry we ran off. It got a little out of hand."

Bridget rubs tears from her cheeks. "I didn't mean to make everybody descend on you like that. I was just surprised."

"So were we," Madison says.

The four of us sit at the kitchen table. The conversation starts slowly, with Bridget telling us how the last week and a half has gone. Interviews with the police. Then the news today, proclaiming the names of the men who attacked her.

Emma nods along sympathetically, and I get the sense she's heard some of this already.

I knew Emma and Bridget were classmates, but I hadn't realized they were friends. I wonder how much they've been talking, and then I feel shitty about my discomfort.

Bridget is just a kid. She shouldn't have to go through this. Especially not alone.

She asks us more questions about what happened that night. Our jobs with the police. Then, finally, Bridget comes to the question I'm expecting. "Was Jeffrey Nichols really the Midnight Slasher?"

I feel Madison stiffen beside me.

What am I supposed to say to this terrified girl? And to my daughter? Am I supposed to tell them we're not sure?

Jeffrey Nichols is our only suspect. That's what the chief said. The guy had a k-bar knife. A ski mask.

There are always doubts. But should the girls let their fears rule their lives? Shouldn't they be able to move on?

"Well, we're—" Madison begins.

I cut her off. "Nichols was the Slasher. And he's dead. He's not going to hurt you or anyone else ever again. The important thing is to lock your doors, be aware of your surroundings. But you don't have to be afraid."

Bridget exhales. "I've been scared thinking about it. Like, I know the men in my house are gone, but if there was somebody else out there? I just wanted to know it was over. I'm glad that it is."

"Me too," I say. "Me too."

But Madison doesn't look up from the table. And Emma is watching her.

19

Madison

*L*ia spots me from down the hall, and she does a double-take. Then she rushes over and drops a stack of manila envelopes onto the counter in front of me.

"Look who it is! Why didn't you tell me you were coming back? And what're you doing working the evidence desk?"

"Just got clearance from my doc for light duty." I point at the stack of envelopes she delivered. "Long night?"

"Like you wouldn't believe."

I scrunch up my face. "Pretty sure I would. If I dig *way* back in my memories."

It's been a week since the mayor's big press conference announcing that the Midnight Slasher is dead. Since then, my phone has been blowing up with requests for interviews. Same with Nash. We've said no to each one.

Some of the Slasher's past victims and their families have contacted us, too. Like Landon Cowling. But aside from talking to Bridget Hanson, I've tried to keep a low profile. Just like Nash wanted.

"I'll trade with you," she says. "I could use a few shifts on the evidence desk."

"Get shot and then tell me how great it is."

Lia snorts. "Jeez, you're grumpy. Has Jennings been rubbing off on you?"

"Way to make it sound dirty."

"I meant it to be dirty."

A passing officer raises his eyebrows at us.

"Kidding!" Lia shouts after him. She props her elbows on the counter. "How much longer till you're back on active?"

"No idea."

The DA's office still hasn't finalized its report on Nash and me using deadly force, because that shit takes *forever*, but with the preliminary decision, I should be okay to return to regular duty as soon as I'm fully healed.

I shuffle through Lia's envelopes. Each is labeled and sealed with evidence tape. I have to log them in. But then she takes the envelopes from my hands.

"Take a break with me."

"I can't right now."

"Three minutes. We need to talk. Come *on*." She practically drags me to a little-used stairwell.

The heavy door swings shut, and quiet falls around us. Lia crosses her arms. "How are you doing? *Really*?"

"I'm good. Healing."

"Then why haven't you been responding to my texts?"

I shrug, grasping for a way to explain it. It's like there's a barrier between me *before* the shooting, and me *after*. Lia still expects me to be the same Shelby I was.

But I'm not so sure I am.

"The SWAT guys have been asking about Jennings," Lia says. "They haven't heard much from him. And I haven't heard much from *you*. Not until right now. Are you and Jennings still living together?"

Here we go. "It's only been a few weeks."

"*A few weeks?* That's longer than most of my relationships."

"This isn't a relationship! We're friends."

"I get that you shared an intense experience. But before the shooting, you barely even knew Jennings. He was our instructor, and then suddenly you're living with him full time? People are talking."

"I don't care what anyone says."

"Yeah, I get that." She shuffles her foot against the concrete floor. "When are you moving back to your own place?"

Ugh. "I don't know."

"When *will* you know?"

"I *don't know.*"

This past week, Mayor Ackerman defeated his opponent. The media accepted his word that Jeffrey Nichols was the Midnight Slasher, even though West Oaks PD is technically still investigating. The whole town is breathing easier and feeling safer.

I guess I should be, too.

I've been doing my PT exercises, and I'm off the crutches. The scars on my arm and thigh look less angry by the day. And while I've still been researching those burglaries in Mammoth Lakes and reading every article I can find about the Slasher, they've led nowhere. I've reached a dead end.

Yet my thoughts go back, again and again, to the night of the shooting. I still have nightmares. I tense each time I hear sirens, as if I'm waiting for the Midnight Slasher to reappear.

Nash and I have reached an uneasy equilibrium. Chaste touches. Occasional brushing of fingers. He got his sutures out, and sometimes I help him clean the pins of his fixator. If Emma's not around, I might rest my head on his shoulder. But that's it. Nash hasn't tried to kiss me again. Though sometimes, I'd swear he wants to.

It's mixed signals all over the place.

The only thing more frustrating than being around him? The idea of not having Nash nearby. Because even when we disagree on things, we still understand each other. He might prefer acting like the Slasher is dead. But I don't think Nash is ready to move on any more than I am.

How do I explain this feeling to Lia? This sense that things are unfinished, and I can't just pretend it's over when it's not?

"I'll probably go back to my own apartment in a few more weeks. Once I'm sure Nash and Emma don't need me anymore."

Lia whistles. "Holy crap. You're really hung up on this guy, aren't you?"

"*What*? No."

"Whatever you say." She pushes back from the wall. "Just be careful. Don't make a bunch of sacrifices for a man who won't return the favor."

"I don't know what you're talking about."

She leaves the stairwell, shaking her head.

When I get back to the evidence desk, I know right away something's out of place. I left my purse in a cubbie beneath the counter, but now it's up top.

What the hell?

I grab the bag and rifle through. My wallet's still here, thank goodness. Nothing seems to be missing.

But I find something new here instead. It's an evidence envelope, unsealed and unlabeled. The flap has *Shelby* printed across it. I flip it open, and there's a USB stick inside. Nothing to indicate what this is supposed to be.

"What's that?"

My head pops up. Lia stands on the other side of the counter.

"Um, nothing." I tuck the envelope back into my bag.

Her brow wrinkles. "Is that evidence?"

"Obviously not. I wouldn't be taking it home with me. What do you need?"

She slides another sealed envelope across the counter. "Forgot this one earlier."

"No problem."

"Hey." She drums her fingers on the desk. "I'm sorry. I don't want to argue with you. I've really missed you, that's all. I hate to think that you're not okay."

The regret in her eyes makes me sorry I've been distant. "I know. I've missed you too."

"Can I have a hug? Will you talk to me if you need anything?"

"Yeah. I will." We embrace across the counter. Then I get busy logging in her evidence, and I leave the mystery USB stick in my bag.

It's just one more thing in the tangle of my thoughts.

NASH HAS LEFT HIS BEDROOM DOOR PARTLY OPEN. I hear him breathing heavily inside. When I look, I see him in a plank position on the floor, doing one-armed pushups. He holds his injured arm against his chest, while the other bends and straightens. The muscles all over his back and arm bulge and flex. His olive skin glistens with sweat, and his black hair hangs over his forehead. He's skipped shaving in the last week, and his stubble has darkened into the beginnings of a beard.

Now *that's* a sight I won't forget anytime soon. My mouth goes dry as I stare.

His knees drop to the carpet. Nash glances up and sees me. "Hey." He sits back against his heels, panting. His pecs rise and fall. The bruise is fading at the edges.

I lean into the door frame. "Hey."

He gets up and grabs a water bottle from the dresser. I watch his throat work as he swallows. For a brief moment, it makes me forget that mysterious USB stick in my bag.

Nash grabs a clean T-shirt from a drawer and puts it on, careful around the fixator on his injured arm. The movement is smooth and practiced. "How was the evidence desk?"

"Boring." I shake off my brain-haze. "But I got an anonymous gift." I dig out the envelope and hand it to Nash. "Showed up in my bag while I was taking a break. Somebody at the station must've left it."

He pops the envelope open and pours the contents into his palm. "Have you seen what's on this?"

"Not yet. It's fun to imagine it's the clue to some mystery. But also seems like a good way to give my computer a bunch of viruses."

"Easy enough to check." Nash goes to his laptop, which is set up at a small desk by the window. "I'll switch off Wi-Fi, just in case, and scan the drive."

He takes a seat at the desk, and I sit on the bed nearby. "Wait, are you a computer nerd, Jennings? How did I not know this?"

"I'd love to claim the credit, but Emma set this stuff up for me. Can't even change my own oil in my SUV. They should revoke my man-card."

My eyes trace the long line of his shoulders. "You're right. Nothing manly about you at all."

He grunts. Why do I find those grunts so sexy?

Not where my mind should be going. I haven't stopped noticing how attractive he is, but we truly are friends. Nothing more.

The anti-virus program scans the USB drive and gives it a green check-mark. Nash opens the contents, and a list of folders appears, each labeled with a date.

One date jumps out at me. It's from last month, November, and it's a day that neither of us will ever forget.

"That one," I say, pointing.

He clicks on it. Inside, there's a police report. It's from the night Nash and I were shot at Bridget Hanson's house.

It doesn't take us long to realize what the other folders contain—reports on each of the Midnight Slasher's crime scenes. Some of these I've already seen.

But there's more.

Crime scene reports from the sheriff's department in Mammoth Lakes. Dating back ten years ago.

The lead that I found. Someone else has been investigating it.

"Where did this come from?" Nash asks.

"Somebody at West Oaks PD. Or somebody from the outside who wandered over to the evidence desk. But that's hard to believe."

We're glancing through the police reports and pondering the mystery when an email dings on my phone. I check the notification. It's a press release from West Oaks PD's public communications department.

West Oaks Police Department Closes Case on Serial Slasher Jeffrey Nichols.

"Did you see this?" I show Nash my screen. It went out to our entire department. He picks up his own device.

"I got it too."

Nichols has been called the Midnight Slasher, the press release says. *His younger brother, Lipinski, was his accomplice, and was likewise killed in November by West Oaks PD officers responding to a crime scene.*

I lower my phone and stare at the USB stick. It's still plugged into Nash's computer. "This can't be a coincidence. The department announces the Midnight Slasher case is officially closed, and I receive the police reports the same day?

Plus the reports from Mammoth Lakes? Somebody must have doubts about the official story. I can think of a possibility."

"Detective Holt?" Nash asks. "If he disagreed with the chief about closing a file, he wouldn't sign off on it."

"Unless he didn't have a choice."

Holt has gone rogue on an investigation before. Well, he had the help of Janie Simon, his girlfriend. That case involved Janie and Holt personally. Someone was trying to kill them, and they teamed up to catch the guy.

And this time? The Midnight Slasher case affects Nash and me in a way few other people could understand. Even *I* don't completely understand its pull on me.

"Whoever left this," I say, "they want me to keep investigating. And they're giving me the keys to do it."

"Madison…"

I look at the laptop screen, which still shows the list of folders labeled by date. One for each of the Midnight Slasher's crimes. A homeowner he terrorized.

"Do you want me to move out?" I suddenly ask.

His expression turns bewildered. "*What*? Why are you asking me that now?"

"Because I need to know if we're in this together. What happened to us that night? It *isn't over*. No matter what you say to Emma. Or what you want to believe. Look at us. We're still messed up about it, and I don't just mean our injuries."

He looks down at the bar screwed into the bones of his arm. The scarred, puckered skin.

"Nash, I can't ignore this. If West Oaks PD isn't going to look into it, I'm going to try. Even if I have to do it alone."

He rubs his chin. "You want to defy the chief's explicit orders."

"I've never been a stickler about rules. Not like some people."

He walks over to me. Lifts his eyes. And they're liquid,

whiskey-brown fire. "I don't want you to move out," he says softly. "Not yet."

When he looks at me like that? I'd probably say anything. "Okay. I won't. If you'll agree to help me."

He runs his hand through his sweaty hair. "You're persuasive, you know that? Maybe you should be a hostage negotiator."

"Or maybe you just have an inner rebel who's dying to get out. Are you going to help me with the investigation or not?"

He blows out a breath. "I'm with you. Where do we start?"

20

Nash

I'm not sure if I have a rebel hiding inside me. But if I do, Madison is responsible for bringing him out. If anyone makes me want to break the rules, it's her.

We sit down in the living room and skim the crime scene reports. Both those from ten years ago, and more recently. The crimes in Mammoth Lakes bear a striking similarity to those in West Oaks. A suspect in a ski mask broke into occupied homes, tied up the solitary residents, and cut them with a knife. The man seemed to enjoy inflicting pain for no reason at all. Afterward, he stole as many valuables as he could carry. He wore gloves. Left no physical evidence.

All things we already know. The guy had his M.O. down pat.

Only two victims stand out as different, and they're the most recent ones. Eugene Cowling, who was the only victim to die. And Bridget Hanson, whose home was invaded by *two* perps instead of just one.

"I've tried, but I still don't get it," Madison says. "If Nichols was the Midnight Slasher, why would he bring his younger brother along when he'd always acted alone before?"

"No clue." I asked Holt the same thing when I was in the hospital, though I didn't know the names Nichols and Lipinski then. The answer's no clearer to me now. "But there were enough similarities between the attack on Bridget Hanson and the others to conclude Nichols was the same guy."

"So, let's learn more about Nichols. Was there a link between him and the Mammoth Lakes crimes?"

Emma comes home from school, and we have to take a break for dinner. Afterward, Madison and I retreat to my room to read through Jeffrey Nichols' file.

We're sitting on my bed, shoulders leaning together, the laptop balanced on our thighs. I'm making a valiant effort not to notice the soft tickle of Madison's hair on my neck.

Nichols' mugshot stares at me from the screen. In the photo, his brown irises peer out from hard, narrowed eyes. The last time I saw this man's face, he had a bullet hole between his eyebrows that I put there.

According to the file, Jeffrey Nichols had quite the checkered past. He grew up in Reno, Nevada, and had his first conviction as a juvenile for grand theft auto. He was in and out of jail, entered some diversion programs.

Then he moved across the border to Tahoe, California. A couple of hours from Mammoth Lakes.

"So Nichols was in the Sierras ten years ago," Madison says. "He could've spent time in Mammoth. But there's nothing that *specifically* ties him there. No mailing address, no work history."

In other words, no proof that Nichols committed the crimes in Mammoth.

But eight years ago—two years after the last Mammoth burglary—Nichols was convicted of robbing a convenience store in Truckee at gunpoint. He spent the next seven years in prison at California City Correctional.

"Which could fit with the Slasher's timeline," I say.

"True." Madison points to the screen. "If Nichols was the Slasher, this prison stint would explain the gap in time between the Mammoth Lakes burglaries and now. No new victims because he was off the streets."

"Until he got out a year ago."

She clicks through the pages of the file. "After he was released from prison, Nichols came down to the LA area. He lived with Thomas Lipinski, his younger brother. Nichols worked on road construction crews, which is common for an ex-con."

"But if he was living in LA, why come to West Oaks? If he was looking for rich houses to target, there were plenty closer to home."

"Maybe that was the point. Didn't want to make a mess in his own backyard. He didn't *want* any ties between him and the community he targeted." Madison clicks on the next file. "All right. Thomas Lipinski. Seventeen years old. Born in San Bernardino. Mother deceased. He and Nichols shared the same father."

"Why did they have different last names?"

"That was in the Nichols file." Madison clicks back over. "Nichols used his mother's last name, rather than his dad's."

"Family drama?"

"Sounds like it."

It doesn't take long to go through Lipinski's file. Unlike his older brother, Lipinski had almost no criminal record. Only a citation for truancy. Like Nichols, he had no ties to West Oaks that we can see.

The gun Lipinski used to shoot both of us? He'd bought it just a week before.

Madison exhales, wiggling against the pillows, which in turn makes her wiggle against me. "The only thing we can say for sure is that Lipinski wasn't the Slasher. He would've been seven years old ten years ago."

There's nothing here to prove Nichols was the Slasher. And nothing to prove that he *wasn't*. Just circumstantial evidence. But plenty of cases are built on less.

"But somebody left these files for you. What did they want you to find?"

"Guess we'll have to keep looking." She smiles wryly. "Welcome to the wild world of investigations."

"Is it always this exciting?"

She laughs. In truth, my pulse is racing while we sit here, reading page after page of dull police reports, and it has nothing to do with our investigation.

It's just her.

For the past week, I've been trying to keep busy instead of spending endless hours with Madison. First, it was easy, because she was annoyed at me after the mayor's press conference and what I said to Bridget and Emma. Telling them the Slasher was definitely dead. But then Madison got over it, and she's been her usual self again.

Her usual enticing self.

So I've been getting out of the house more. Heading to the range to practice shooting my Glock with my left hand, meeting with Emma's math teacher for a conference. I even got beers once with Madison's brother Jake. We avoided the subject of his sister. I appreciated that.

"If I don't go back to SWAT," I say, "maybe I'll join major crimes with you. Will you show me the ropes?"

"I could try. Lesson one, not pissing off the chief. Lesson two, gun safety and avoiding injury." She grits her teeth. "Wait, maybe I'm not the best teacher after all."

I hold up my right arm. "I'm no better. I'm the cautionary tale."

Madison's expression softens as she looks at my injured

arm. "If you want to go back to SWAT, you'll get there. You'll get better."

"Maybe." Maybe not.

A few days ago, I had a doctor appointment to get my sutures removed, and I got the news I've known was coming. More surgery on my arm. That was always a given. But now the doctor's worried that the bones aren't lining up right. It could mean a longer recovery and a more doubtful prognosis for regaining full dexterity. I haven't told Emma or Madison yet. The longer I can avoid *that* subject, the better.

That's me these days. The guy who avoids things.

She runs her fingers gently over the mangled skin. I want to sigh. Lean into her. But in my bed? Not the best idea. We probably shouldn't be sitting in here at all. But I guess we're both rule-breakers, aren't we?

"Does it still hurt?" she whispers.

"Not much."

Not when you're next to me. Not when you touch me like that.

My left arm has gone numb. Something warm and soft is lying on it, tucked against my chest, smelling of sunshine. As if the rays of light shining through the blinds have taken physical form.

I startle, snapping to full alertness. It's morning. Madison's still in my bed. The laptop has slipped down between us.

And there's a raging erection tenting my sweatpants.

My left arm is trapped beneath Madison. If she wakes up, there's no hiding what's happening downstairs. I try adjusting with my other hand, but the fingers don't move well. I'm not doing much of anything except adding friction, which is *not* what I need right now.

I breathe out slowly, counting down from twenty. As a sniper, I use biofeedback exercises to regulate my vitals before I take a carefully timed shot. I've got more than a little practice. But Madison's summer-scent and lithe body aren't making it easy.

This is getting ridiculous. I don't do this kind of thing, get so caught up in someone that all my usual defenses are... well...defenseless.

Get control of yourself.

When I open my eyes again, Madison is staring at me. "You okay over there? You're breathing all weird."

I sneak a peek down south and see nothing obvious. Thank God. "I'm great. You?"

Furious knocking interrupts us. "Dad!

"*Shit*," I hiss, knocking into Madison as I try to sit up. I get my arm from beneath her.

"Dad, are you up? I need my charger. Did you take it? I'm coming in."

"I don't have it!" I scoot off the bed in full panic mode. Madison's still lying down, her expression frozen with shock.

The thought of Emma seeing Madison in my bed makes my insides twist the wrong direction.

I grab the end of my comforter and throw it over Madison's head just as the door opens. I bar my arm across the doorway. Emma almost runs into me.

"Jeez. Dad. Is my charger in here?" She waves her glittery blue phone case at me. "I'm going to be late for school, and my phone's almost dead."

"Why would I have it?"

"Can I come look for it?"

"Em, I'm telling you. It isn't here."

She scowls. "What about Madison? Where is she?"

There's a faint snicker behind me. My heart gallops at a pace that can't possibly be healthy.

"What do you mean?" I choke out.

"Her door's open, and she's not in there. Or in the bathroom. Where'd she go?"

"I guess she had an early shift. But I doubt she'd know where your charger is either."

Emma makes an infuriated sound and stomps into the great room. Five seconds later, she says, "Oh, never mind. Here it is. See you later!"

I don't breathe until I hear the front door opening and closing.

That probably took a year off my life.

"Can I come out now?" Madison whispers behind me.

I sigh and turn around. Madison's sitting up, the comforter still on her head. I flick it off of her. Golden hair sticks up crazily around her head, catching the sun. "Shouldn't the Navy have taught you to be a better liar?"

"I'm a Teamguy, not CIA."

"You could've told her the truth."

"You wanted my daughter to know you spent the night in my room?"

"It was just a platonic, co-ed sleepover. No big deal." Her mouth makes an exaggerated *O*. "Wait...You don't approve of those. Gah, the irony. I can't take it." She grabs her chest over her heart. "Irony is my greatest weakness. Now I'll never have the strength to leave this bed."

Sounds good by me, that rebellious voice says in my brain.

"I need to get dressed. So should you." I tug on her arm, trying to make her get up, but a mischievous gleam appears in her eye. She tugs back. *Hard.* I land on the mattress on my knees, just stopping before I crash into her.

We're inches away from each other. Her exhale ghosts over my cheek. I can see the strands of her eyelashes and the flecks of amber in her green eyes. My gaze strays down to her mouth. Her lips part, pupils dilating.

My thumb strokes across her knuckles, and an electric shock pulses through me from my neck to my toes. My cock takes notice. It's waking up again.

Shit.

I scramble backwards off the bed, nearly falling over. "I should get moving. I…have an appointment."

Madison smooths down her hair and gets up. "I should move too. I actually do have an early shift."

"Great. Coffee. I'll make some." I race out of the room before I climb back in that bed and do what I *really* want.

The more time I spend alone with Madison, the more rebellious I want to get.

21

Madison

*E*very night for the next week, Nash and I pour over the files on the USB stick. On top of the eleven different crime scene reports, there are hundreds of pages of photos, interview transcripts, and forensic summaries.

Emma realizes pretty quick that something's up. She's a smart cookie, that one. But after that impromptu sleepover in Nash's room, we've been avoiding each other's bedrooms.

I thought Nash was going to kiss me, again. And he freaked out. *Again.* I'm officially over it. No more flirty nonsense.

See, Lia? I think. I'm not hung up on him. I can quit Nash anytime I want.

Instead of cuddling up in Nash's bed, which is a definite no-no, we sit on the couch or at the dining table to work. Emma's annoyed when we won't give her the details on our project, but thankfully she's distracted by her upcoming trip.

In just a few days, Emma will jet off to France to spend the holidays with her mom.

And Nash and I will...I don't know. I've been trying not to think about what'll happen after Emma goes. At the very least, I'll be spending Christmas at my parents' place with my entire family. After I skipped Thanksgiving dinner to spend that day with Nash and Emma—we got Thai takeout—I can't skip Christmas too. But it'll be good to spend time with my family again. I've missed them, especially my niece and nephew.

The rest will figure itself out.

Tonight, we're at the kitchen island, going over some of the files from Mammoth Lakes. Emma's already said goodnight, withdrawing into her room with her headphones on and the door closed.

I'm frustrated. Whoever left the USB stick in my bag must've believed I'd find something important. But we haven't yet. There's plenty here to shed doubt on Nichols being the Midnight Slasher. Enough to give a defense attorney wet dreams. But Nichols doesn't get a legal defense. He's dead.

So, what am I missing? What clue am I supposed to find that will lead us somewhere new?

I sit back in my chair. "Is it break time yet?"

"Jeez, I hope so. I've been dying over here."

"Why didn't you say something?"

"Didn't want you to give me shit about my lack of investigative endurance."

"Luckily, that's not a thing," I say.

Nash slides out of his seat and opens the pantry cabinet. His limp is almost imperceptible now. "Want some hot chocolate? There's marshmallows."

"*Marshmallows*? Careful, Sergeant. Someone might think there's a warm and gushy center beneath your tough exterior."

"You won't tell anyone, will you?"

He's sporting one of those rare, full-out smiles where his incisors are showing. The kind that makes my chest clench and my insides spin. Grumpy Nash is sexy, but when he smiles like that, he's gorgeous.

I wish he wouldn't look at me like that.

I wish he'd *always* look at me like that.

He grabs the tin of hot cocoa mix, balancing a bag of mini marshmallows on top. Nash sets down his supplies by the stove and grabs the water kettle. "Give me a hand?"

I press down the filtered water tap, while Nash holds the kettle open. Water pings against the metal. We're standing close enough that his stomach brushes my side.

"You must like hot beverages," I say. "First the rum with sugar and lemon, now hot chocolate."

He shrugs. "Only when you're here. I don't make stuff like this most of the time."

I don't even think before I ask, "What're your plans for Christmas?"

There's a flicker in his eyes, and that brief smile evaporates. "Not sure." He puts the kettle on the stove and switches on the heat. "The past few years, Emma has done Christmas Eve at her mom's and Christmas Day with me. We make the whole traditional dinner. Ham, green beans, mashed potatoes. She's the cook, but I make a decent assistant. I'm glad she has her trip this year, but I'll miss her."

"You're not going to see the rest of your family?"

"I'm not that close to them. My parents are still in the small town in Nebraska where I grew up."

"A farm?"

"Nah, my dad's a mechanic. Mom runs an antiques store. I love them, but my family was never close like yours. My sister left as soon as she graduated." His eyes move to the corner of the room, going distant. "I was on the track team in high school, and I'd run for hours on end, imagining what it would be like if I could just keep on going. Never return.

Eventually, that's exactly what I did. Simone grew up in the same town. When I enlisted, she came to California with me."

Nash hasn't said much about his marriage or his family before. But I'm glad he's telling me now. That's what friends do.

Because that's what we are. Friends. And it's a good thing. A *great* thing.

"Crazy idea," I say. Like I just thought of it. "Why not spend Christmas with me at my parents' house? They'd love to have you. Aiden will make way too much food. Jake will buy an insane amount of booze for everyone to share. We'll play board games and watch cheesy classic movies, and my niece and nephew will be excited about Santa."

He presses his lips together. He's going to say no. I can feel it.

But then, he doesn't.

"That sounds fun. I'll think about it. Thanks."

I exhale, feeling ridiculous about how happy his *maybe* makes me.

"But there's something I should tell you," he says.

"You're part grinch?"

"That's true. But this is something else." He frowns at his right arm. "My next surgery is going to be while Emma's in France. I'm worried she'll try to cancel her trip if she finds out, so please don't mention it to her."

I don't like hiding things from Emma. But Nash feels differently, and he's her father. This isn't my call to make. "I guess I can keep it quiet. Will you need someone to drive you or help out afterward? I know we haven't talked about how long I'm staying, but…"

"Yeah. I'd appreciate that."

His eyes meet mine again and hold. Two deep pools, fire and whiskey.

The kettle shrieks, making us both jump.

I'VE STUDIED THESE CASEFILES LIKE THERE'S going to be an exam. I practically have the things memorized. And there's no secret info. Nothing that proves Nichols isn't the Slasher.

Except...maybe one tiny hint of doubt. A nothing that could, possibly, be a *something*.

After reviewing the Mammoth police files for a second time, a detail pops out at me.

"Ten years ago, the police in Mammoth Lakes had a suspect," I say to Nash. "A guy named Kent Kaylor. He purchased a knife used in the Mammoth home invasions."

"Right." He nods, hand on his stubble-covered jaw. "I saw that in the file. But Kaylor had an alibi, and he was completely cleared of all wrong-doing."

"But here's the interesting part. In the transcript of his interrogation, Kaylor claimed that a neighbor stole the knife. But the neighbor is never mentioned again in the file. As far as I can tell, the police in Mammoth never followed up."

I show Nash the interview transcript, and he reads over the page I'm referencing. "I missed that before. Did anyone from West Oaks PD talk to Kaylor?"

"Not as far as I can tell."

"Does Kaylor still live up there?"

"I did a quick Internet search and found a property tax payment in his name from this year. Has a Mammoth Lakes address. We could drive up. See what he has to tell us." It's always better to interview a witness in person rather than by phone.

Nash exhales, almost a laugh. "If the chief finds out, it's not going to be pretty."

"He won't find out. We'll ask Kaylor our questions as private citizens. He doesn't have to know we're cops. If Kaylor has something important, I'll tell Holt. And at that point, the chief won't be able to do a thing to us. If Nichols wasn't really the Slasher? The media will be all over it."

"But if Holt gave you the USB stick, we have to assume he knew about this loose end. Why didn't he go question Kaylor himself?"

"The chief's watching him too closely. Maybe the mayor is, too."

Nash takes a moment to consider. But his decision comes faster than I expected it. "Then we're going to Mammoth. This might be a long shot, but it's our only one. We'd better take it."

We decide to visit Kaylor the following weekend, right after Nash drops Emma at the airport for her Christmas vacay. I make a surreptitious call to the Kaylor residence and claim to be UPS. He says he'll be in town.

Nash is impressed when I tell him about my spy tactics.

On Saturday morning, he loads Emma's suitcases into his SUV. I've packed my puffy coat, as well as a bag in case we have to stay overnight in Mammoth. According to the forecast, it'll be cold up there, on the edge of a stormfront that's moving in later this weekend and bringing snow. Hard to believe it down here in West Oaks, where December means thin sweaters and lights strung around palm trees up and down Ocean Lane.

I'm in the kitchen, finishing up the last of the dishes, when Emma comes in.

"Hey, Madison?"

"Yep?"

She leans against the counter and checks over her shoulder like this is a clandestine meeting. "I have a gift for my dad, and I want him to open it Christmas morning. Could you make sure he gets it? We don't have a tree, otherwise I'd put it underneath. My dad's not so big on decorations. As you can tell."

"I'm not sure I'll see your dad on Christmas. I invited him to my parents' celebration, but he hasn't committed."

Emma makes an exasperated sound. "I'll guilt trip him into it. That's the only thing that works. He never does anything for himself."

"If he doesn't want to go, you shouldn't force him."

"No, that's not what I mean. Trust me, he wants to hang out with you. It's obvious." She rolls her eyes. "But he thinks he has to be a martyr or something. I dunno."

I'm not so sure. Nash is a grown man. If he wanted... certain things, he could just say so. "Well, the invitation's open. Whatever he decides. I can give him your gift either way." If I have to, I'll drop by here on Christmas morning with Emma's present and an egg nog latte. A friendly gesture. Purely platonic.

Emma cocks her hip. She's wearing her ripped black jeans and an ugly Christmas sweater. It has kittens in Santa hats all over it. "Are you planning to keep staying here over the holidays? While I'm gone?"

She's trying to act casual, but I can tell there are bigger questions beneath what she's said.

And I don't know the answers, either.

I wipe my hands on a dish towel. "I haven't figured that out. I usually spend a lot of time with my family this time of year. But your dad has his surgery coming up, and—"

Shit. The moment it comes out of my mouth, I realize the mistake I've made.

"What surgery?"

I grit my teeth. "I shouldn't have said that."

"Madison, is my dad having another surgery on his arm while I'm gone?"

"I'm sorry. You'll have to ask him."

Emma's tan face goes pale, then bright red. "He said the doctor hadn't scheduled anything. He fucking *lied* to me. And so did you." She spins, storming away from me. I go to follow her.

But Nash opens the front door that minute and says, "Everybody ready to go?"

Emma blows past him, heading outside. She's got a murderous scowl on her face.

"What's that about?" Nash asks.

"I screwed up. I mentioned your surgery. I didn't mean to."

His head falls back against the door, and he mutters a curse.

"I'm sorry. Really."

"No, it's okay. This is my fault. I'll explain it on the drive. It'll be fine."

~

It's definitely not fine.

It's a two-hour drive to Hollywood Burbank Airport, and every minute is excruciating.

Nash looks in the rearview mirror. "Em, what are you and your mom going to do when you arrive? Are you still spending a couple days in Paris?"

His daughter's got her headphones on and doesn't answer.

"Can't we have a nice few minutes before you leave for three weeks?"

No response.

I want to say something, but I don't know what. I shouldn't be in the middle of this. But as the miles pass, I feel Nash's frustration growing. His left hand grips the leather steering wheel so hard it squeaks.

"*Emma*," he finally barks. "I've had enough of your attitude."

She pulls off her headphones. "Oh, really? You don't like asking questions and being ignored? At least I didn't lie to you."

"Is this about my surgery?"

She sneers. "So Madison told you she let that slip? Big fucking surprise."

"*Excuse* me? That's not the way you speak to me. Or to Madison."

Emma stares out her window, shaking her head.

Nash is quiet for several minutes before he speaks again. "I didn't tell you about my surgery because I didn't want you to worry. It's my job to deal with stuff like this and not put it on you."

"But you told *Madison*."

I slump down in my seat. As if that's going to hide me.

"I get it," she says. "Madison's going to take care of you after your surgery, so you don't need me."

"Emma—"

"You and Madison have your secret investigation thing that you think I don't know about. And you have this weekend trip you're taking together the minute I'm gone. No wonder you wanted me to go to France so bad. Can't wait until I'm out of the way."

"That is not true."

"Whatever. I hope you and your secret girlfriend have a *great* Christmas all by yourselves, having all the sex you want without your kid interrupting."

"Jesus, Emma, that is *enough*. There is nothing going on between us. I'm not spending Christmas with Madison!"

Silence falls in the car. The sounds of traffic and the

whisper of the tires fill the space. Emma scowls at her window. Nash glares at the cars ahead.

Neither of them looks at me.

At the departures area, Nash grabs Emma's bag from the trunk. I stay in the car, watching them on the curb. He's talking to her, trying to smooth things over. She's not having it. Finally, Emma heads inside the airport, dragging her bags behind her.

Nash gets in and slams the door closed.

"I'm sorry. I didn't mean to cause problems between you and Emma," I say.

"I know. I shouldn't have put you in that position. But when it comes to my daughter, I always manage to fuck things up. Guess it's my thing." He pulls away from the airport, merging onto North Hollywood Way, and then the I-5.

"I was fifteen once," I say. "It was intense, and I didn't have to deal with my dad getting shot. I'm sure she'll calm down while she's on the plane."

"Maybe."

There's a long pause. Miles fly by, highway concrete disappearing beneath us.

"I missed most of Emma's childhood," he says. "I've been trying to make up for it. And she still thinks I'd rather not have her around."

Because Emma thinks Nash is choosing me instead. But his daughter has nothing to worry about. She's got it so wrong.

It's just like Nash said. There's really nothing between us. Nothing beyond this connection we share because of one terrible night.

"When we get back to West Oaks," I say, "maybe I should head back to my apartment."

He glances over. "Oh?"

"We've been giving Emma the wrong idea. Besides, you must be ready to have your own space again."

"Space." Nash clears his throat. "Space is good. That's probably for the best."

"Just what I was thinking."

"It was nice having you around."

"It was." *While it lasted*, I finish in my head. "If you need anything when it's time for your surgery—"

"I could ask Holt. I'm sure he and Janie wouldn't mind driving me. I can handle the rest myself."

"Yeah. I'm sure." My chest tightens up even more, and I'm afraid he'll hear it in my voice. This ridiculous crush that I can't seem to shake. A kiss that I wish I could forget.

He smiles, but it's not a real Nash smile. The real ones appear spontaneously, transforming his whole aura. They're rare and beautiful. Those smiles, I've come to live for. This one doesn't reach his eyes.

Well, my smile right now is bullshit, too.

After we return to West Oaks, we'll go our separate ways. Colleagues and sort-of-friends.

I settle back in my seat. We have a purpose for this trip, and I'll do better if I focus on that. This all started with the Midnight Slasher. Now, if we're lucky, we can end it there too.

We can figure out if Jeffrey Nichols was really the Slasher, and then move on. Put the last few weeks behind us and never look back.

22

Nash

We arrive in Mammoth Lakes in the early afternoon. The snow-streaked Sierra Nevadas expand around us, bright sodium white on dark sapphire. Somehow, the drab, overcast sky makes the landscape glow in richer colors.

"We're not in So Cal anymore," I say. Lame comment, but it's all I can think of.

Madison hums in agreement. She hasn't said a word since we passed through Lancaster. Hours ago. I'm supposed to be the grumpy, silent one. I'm not enjoying this reversal.

I feel terrible about what happened earlier with Emma. Especially the fact that Madison ended up in the middle of it. I should've told my kid about the surgery in the first place, but I thought I was avoiding unnecessary conflict. Didn't turn out that way.

The hurt look in her eyes when she said, *You told Madison* —that hit me straight in the chest.

And the accusations about Madison being my secret girl-friend? That made the guilt even worse. Because I *do* want Madison, even though I shouldn't. The temptation has been getting stronger and stronger. Harder to ignore. Which is the reason I agreed when Madison said she'd move out, even though I'd rather she did the opposite. I don't want her to leave.

But I am not boyfriend material. And what about my kid, and what she needs?

What about what's right?

I sneak glances at Madison as I drive. I study the different threads of bronze and wheat in her pale hair. The occasional freckle that dots the tops of her cheeks. I want to kiss every single one. I want to pull her close and bury my nose against her skin and breathe her in. Her endless-summer scent. Grass and jasmine. I want that so badly I feel an ache in my ribs, and it has nothing to do with taking a bullet to my body armor weeks ago.

"Hungry?" I ask.

"Mmm-hmm."

I pull the SUV into a shopping center parking lot. There's a grocery store and a strip of shops and restaurants. People bustle across the concrete in their puffers and beanies. Christmas lights decorate the eaves of the buildings.

We grab our coats and walk into a deli to grab sandwiches.

Madison's expression has barely changed in the last four-plus hours, but when the guy behind the counter asks what she'd like, she turns her mega-watt grin on him. "What do you recommend? Turkey club or the grilled cheese?"

"Gotta go grilled cheese on a day like this. Something warm and cozy." Then the dude actually winks.

"Grilled cheese it is."

He flirts with her while he makes her sandwich. Madison tells him that we just drove up from West Oaks.

"Staying for the weekend?" the guy asks hopefully, and

nobody in the vicinity could miss the suggestiveness of his question. "Got plans?"

I'm standing right here, I want to say. Contrary to my daughter's assumptions, I'm not Madison's boyfriend, and I shouldn't be. But this dude doesn't know that.

I take a step closer to her, hovering at her shoulder.

"We're just here for the day," she tells him. "We'll be in and out."

We are? We brought overnight bags to find a hotel if the meeting with Kaylor runs long. Two rooms, obviously. But it seems Madison is eager to get back to West Oaks.

"You'd better be out before nightfall, then," Sandwich Guy says. "Big storm's coming."

"That's not until tomorrow," I cut in. "That's what the forecast said."

He shrugs, pressing down the lid of the sandwich griddle. "Forecast changes, man. Weather in the mountains is unpredictable. Gotta keep up."

I order the turkey club and make a point of paying for both sandwiches. Madison and I sit down to eat. A moment ago, she was plenty talkative with Sandwich Guy. But now, she's gone silent again.

I check my phone and find a text waiting. We had no service for a lot of the drive, so it must've been delayed. "Emma wrote while we were on the road. She was boarding. Should be in the air by now." She's still pissed at me, as shown by her lack of emoji or GIFs. But at least she wrote.

There's a message from my ex, too.

Simone: Hey, sorry to hear about your surgery. Glad you won't be alone. We'll Skype on Christmas Day, K? Hard to be away from our girl.
Me: Yeah, it is. Skype would be great. Thanks.

So Emma told her that Madison would be with me. She's wrong, but I don't want to correct it. Did Emma complain to Simone that Madison's really my girlfriend, despite my denials? That I'm a liar and a horrible father?

Thankfully, my ex doesn't mention any of that. I'm glad Simone doesn't use this kind of stuff against me. I can dig myself into a hole just fine on my own.

I look up, and Madison's studying her grilled cheese like it's the most interesting thing in the room. She takes a bite, and gooey cheese rushes out. She licks it from her fingers.

I've told myself, again and again, that I can't have her.

I've been trying so fucking hard to do the right thing, even if it makes me absolutely miserable. I didn't want to hurt Madison again.

But am I hurting her now?

Do I even know what the right thing is anymore?

MADISON FINDS KENT KAYLOR'S ADDRESS ON HER maps app and gives me the directions. The road winds into the mountains. It's a secluded area, with cabins visible between the trees here and there.

Just before we reach the turn, Madison says, "What do you think? Go in armed?"

Our handguns are in the locker in my trunk. I like having my weapon close, even if I'm nowhere near as accurate with my left hand. "Your call. I don't want to offend the guy, but the last time we went into a stranger's house together, we both got shot."

"Excellent point."

I pull over, and we put on our holsters, making sure our weapons are out of sight.

The driveway to the Kaylor property takes us about half a

mile into the woods. Madison parks in front of a stone cabin. Smoke puffs from the chimney.

Outside, the cold air makes my skin feel tight. We approach the door. Madison knocks. A man answers. He's wearing a thick sweater and khakis, and silver threads his beard. His eyes are bloodshot, and a whiff of alcohol hits me.

"Can I help you?"

"Mr. Kaylor?" Madison asks.

"What's this about?"

"This request might sound strange, but we wanted to ask you a few questions about some burglaries that happened in this area. About ten years ago?"

"Why?" He glances past our shoulders like he expects to find someone else. "Are you more reporters?"

More reporters? "No, sir," I say. "Just interested citizens."

"Why are you interested?"

We didn't discuss a cover story, but Madison has one ready. Either that, or she's a better bullshitter than I realized. "We're from West Oaks. We've had a string of home invasions that seem similar to the ones that happened here. We're friends with one of the victims."

I figure Madison is thinking of Bridget Hanson.

Kaylor nods at my fixator, which is sticking out of my coat where it attaches to my hand. "Is that how you got hurt?"

I'm not sure if I should lie. But Madison goes with a version of the truth. "He was trying to help our friend escape."

The door opens a bit wider. "Is your friend okay?"

"She is," Madison says. "But she's shaken. It was a rough experience."

"I still don't understand why you're here. Or what I have to do with any of this."

He starts to shut the door, but Madison puts her hand on the frame. "The police and the West Oaks mayor say the suspect is dead. But some people in West Oaks are questioning that. We can't get straight answers, so we're trying to find out for ourselves. A knife you owned was used in the crimes here, right? It was stolen?"

"I had an alibi. I was completely cleared of—"

"Of course. We know that. But did you have any theories about *who* could've stolen your knife?"

"I told the police."

"But did they follow up?" Madison asks. "Those crimes were never solved. Not until now, or so the police say. But what if they're wrong?"

Kaylor shifts his weight from foot to foot, and I think he's going to say no. He's going to shut that door in our faces.

But instead, he steps back, and the door opens wide.

"I guess you can come in. Just until my wife gets home."

23

Madison

*K*aylor doesn't let us far into the house. We sit down in an enclosed porch area, just past the front door. Even from here, the smell's not pleasant. Like unwashed socks and cheap whiskey.

"You mentioned 'more' reporters," I say. "Have reporters come to see you recently?"

"Not that recently. But in the past, they have. Last year, it was somebody from that podcast about unsolved crimes."

"California Crimes Uncovered?"

"That's the one, yeah." He sniffs. "I didn't want to talk to them. Afraid they'd blame me for things I didn't do. I'm so tired of that kinda bull."

"Can't blame you." I'm sitting on a small loveseat with Nash crammed in beside me, taking way more than his half. Kaylor took the seat to our diagonal, so Nash and I have to turn our heads to look at him.

Exotic indoor plants fill the rest of the porch, some of the trees as tall as me. But their leaves are wilted like they haven't been watered in a while.

"When all that stuff happened, ten years ago..." Kaylor

scrubs a hand over his face. "It was hell. First these awful attacks in our town. The police kept calling them burglaries, but they were *attacks*. Some psycho breaking into people's houses, cutting them? Sick."

"In West Oaks, the media started calling him the 'Midnight Slasher,'" I say.

Kaylor shudders. "Yeah, that fits."

Nash's leg presses harder against mine. I try to inch away to give him a little space. That's what he said he wanted. But his body heat bleeds into me wherever we touch, despite the layers of clothing separating us.

I can't take it anymore. I jump up from my seat and stand instead, crossing my arms.

Super nonchalant. That's me.

But Kaylor doesn't seem to notice. "When the crimes happened ten years ago, the police showed up at my door and harassed *me*. Saying my knife was found at a crime scene."

"A k-bar?" Nash says.

Kaylor shrugs. "I guess. I thought it looked cool. The guy who sold it to me said it made a great hunting knife."

"How did they know it was your knife?" I ask.

"They said something about tracing it to the store. I'd used a credit card. The police took me down to the station, read me my rights, interrogated me like they believed I was the attacker. But I was on vacation in Mexico during two of the break-ins."

"You told the police the knife was stolen?"

"Yeah, out of my hunting shed. And I told them who'd taken it. The jerk who'd been renting the house next door a few months beforehand."

"You know his name?"

"He called himself Steven, and that's what I told the cops. But it was a fake identity or something. The landlord was taking the money under the table so he didn't do a credit check or copy the guy's ID."

"Can you describe him?" Nash asks.

"In his twenties, back then. Average height, slim but muscular. Light brownish hair."

"Eyes?"

"I think brown?"

That fits the description of the Midnight Slasher, and also Nichols. But it could fit a lot of people.

There has to be more. Some clue, however small, that we can go on.

"Did he have family?" I ask.

"None that I saw."

"Anything particular about him? Distinguishing? Was he ugly, attractive?"

Kaylor thinks for a few seconds. "I wouldn't say he was ugly. He was quiet, lived alone. I think he was a handyman. I didn't mind him until I saw him poking around my shed. Trying the lock. I yelled at him for it, and he claimed it was some misunderstanding. But months later, the day after he moved out, I noticed the lock on my shed was broken. Some of the stuff inside was missing. I even filed a police report about it. Had to have been him."

I pace across the porch. "No tattoos? Scars?"

"Not that I know of."

I take out my phone and load an old mugshot of Jeffrey Nichols. "Did Steven look like this?" I turn the screen to Kaylor, and he squints at it.

"Could be. Yeah. That could be him."

"You're not sure?"

"No, I'm sure. Maybe?"

Nice and specific, I think. *Thanks.*

Even if he'd talked to California Crimes Uncovered, I doubt they'd have gotten anything interesting. I'll have to check their blog archive and see if they posted anything about the Mammoth burglaries. Kaylor said they came to talk to him last year, long before the Midnight Slasher struck in West Oaks.

It annoys me that a tabloid blog knew about Kaylor, yet West Oaks PD didn't bother to talk to him.

I keep quizzing him, but Kaylor doesn't seem to know much else. If anything, he gets more agitated as we sit there. He's scratching his arms and glancing around, eyes flicking again and again to the door.

Kaylor mentioned a wife earlier, but there's been no sign of her.

Finally Nash stands up and puts his hand on my arm. "We should go before the storm hits."

I don't want to give up. But he's right. We aren't going to get anything more here. We thank Kaylor and head back outside to Nash's SUV.

The sky's turned white, and flurries blow through the air. We didn't spend long in the house, but already the temperature in the SUV has dropped. Snow is starting to stick to the windshield.

"I'll drive," I say. I have too much energy. I need a place to focus it. But Nash is frowning, and I can tell he doesn't want to agree. My frustration bleeds through. "Do you have a problem with that?"

"I drove us the whole way here."

"So?"

"So, it's my car. I'm more comfortable driving."

Really? He can't give me this one thing? "Fine." I slam the passenger door as I get in. Nash drives us back toward the road. "Please tell me you got more out of Kaylor than I did," I say.

"You were sitting there with me. You heard his answers."

"I know, but I was hoping you learned something more

between the lines. Do you think Steven the Renter was really Jeffrey Nichols?"

"The description sounded a little like him. Or like anyone."

"Not you," I point out. Nobody would use "average" to describe Nash. For example, he's above-average infuriating.

"He sounded like a lot of people," Nash says. "Kaylor thought the photo looked like him. But the whiff of bourbon on the guy's breath didn't inspire confidence. If Steven was really Nichols, he could've used a fake identity because of his criminal record."

I hit the heel of my hand against the steering wheel. "Kaylor gave us nothing. Which means we have *nothing* to go on. This was our only lead."

The snow is falling harder now. The air is thick with swirling white. We can barely see the trees anymore.

"Do you have cell reception?" I ask. "I can't pull up the current forecast."

"I need to watch the road." He holds out his phone to me.

No service.

I curse under my breath. The guy at the sandwich shop said the storm would move in after nightfall. We should still have another hour or two. I guess somebody should've told mother nature the schedule.

There are two headlights behind us, but I can't even see the vehicle. If there are cars more than a few yards ahead of us, I can't tell. There's no view outside but a chaos of white.

Nash heaves a sigh. "This storm is bad. It's getting dangerous."

"What do you suggest? Sitting around and waiting?"

"No, we need to stop for the night."

"Where?"

"In town. We'll find a hotel."

That was what we'd planned on before. But after the

awkwardness with Emma, I just want to get back to my own apartment. My own *space*. "I don't want a hotel. I want to get home tonight."

"Getting back to West Oaks is no longer an option." He's using his gruff Sergeant Jennings voice. As if there's no possible argument. "The roads will become icier by the hour. If the storm gets any worse, it'll be blizzard conditions."

And I know he's right. But my frustration has been building all day, and now it boils over.

"Okay, *Dad*," I snap.

He purses his mouth. "That's uncalled for."

"You're using the same tone with me that you do with Emma."

"I am not."

"I'm surprised you're willing to stay in a hotel with me at all. Won't that be too much temptation? You've been struggling not to throw yourself at me since I moved in."

His head whips toward me, eyes wide.

Gah, why can't I stop the words from leaving my mouth?

"You know what?" I say. "This was a mistake. This has *all* been a mistake. I wish none of it happened."

"Which part?"

How does he sound so calm?

I'm in the middle of a snowstorm, trapped with a man who doesn't really want me, both of us still reeling from a terrible night we can't escape.

Time is supposed to heal you. But I'm more of a wreck now than when I first got shot.

Because of Nash.

I finally allow myself to admit what I've been denying. This isn't just a crush. It's gone so far beyond that. So far that it scares me, because I have never felt this way. Not for anyone.

And it *hurts*. Like nothing else.

I force my tone to match his. I will not lose my composure. Not with this man. But I need to get this out. I need to say what I've been holding back.

"I wish I'd never kissed you that night at the bar. I wish those two assholes hadn't broken into Bridget Hanson's house. I *definitely* wish we hadn't gotten shot and spent so much time together, because now…"

Now, I know him. I know how impossible it will be to forget him when this is over.

"Now, what?" he asks softly. Soft as the snowflakes falling on the windshield as the car creeps toward town.

I've said more than I should already. "Let's just get back to West Oaks, and I'll never bother you again."

"Madison, I—"

There's a loud *crunch*. We're both thrown forward against our seatbelts. Something's just hit the back of the SUV. Nash grips the steering wheel, trying to keep control.

"Look out!" I scream. But our tires are skidding. The SUV jerks, bumping up and down as we leave the road. The headlights swing across snow and trees. Then we slam forward again. The airbag deploys in front of my face.

We've stopped, but everything's tipped forward. There's rushing in my ears.

Nash reaches for me. His warm hand touches my neck. "You okay?"

"Just surprised. What about you? Your arm?"

"I'm fine. We're in a ditch. We need to get out of the car."

I try my door, but it won't open all the way. I crawl through Nash's side instead. He helps me out. Wind blows icy droplets into my face. I pull the hood up on my coat.

I look for whoever hit us, but I can't see much of anything. Snowflakes sting in my eyes. "The other driver. I don't see them."

"Come on," Nash says, "let's get back up to the road. Hopefully the other guy can give us a—"

There's a high-pitched whine, a snap, and a window on the SUV fractures into a spiderweb of cracks.

Nash and I both dive for the ground. *"Rifle,"* he screams into my ear.

Another crack hits the SUV.

My head lifts a little, searching the surroundings for cover. "Can we get to the trees?"

He draws his gun. "On my mark. I'll cover you."

I draw my gun as well. I'm shaking. Adrenaline scorches my veins.

"Go." Nash pops up, firing toward the road. I sprint for the trees, keeping to a crouch. My boots slip in the snow. I careen into a tree trunk and duck behind it.

"Nash!" I yell, raising my weapon. "Come on!"

He's running and firing behind him. Rocks and snow explode from the ground a few feet away from him.

Beyond the car, a dark silhouette stands on the roadway.

I step into the open, firing at the shape. Nash reaches me just as a shot rips into the tree trunk nearest me. Splinters of bark scratch my face. Nash tackles me to the ground.

We're both gasping. Our breaths cloud in front of our mouths. I can still hear the echo of the last gunshot and the chattering of my teeth.

In half a second, Nash is back up, grabbing onto my coat. "We gotta keep moving." He pulls me upright, and we're running.

We weave between the trees. Nash keeps his head on a swivel, watching for whoever was shooting at us. But the woods have become jarringly peaceful. There's no sound but our breaths, our footfalls, and even that is muffled by the snow.

In my four years on patrol, I've been in some dangerous

situations. I've seen the world shift into sudden, stark violence. I've been shot at twice now—both times with Nash. After the first, I thought I'd be ready if it happened again.

The second time is worse. Much worse.

My wounds have healed, but it's like they've opened up again. Gaping and raw. The pain and the fear claw at me. I can almost see the dark spatter of blood against the white, like that night at Bridget's house.

Not real, I tell myself. *Keep it together.*

I'm falling behind. The cold is seeping into me. That initial rush of adrenaline is freezing in my veins.

Nash stops and turns, looking back at me. "You okay?"

I open my mouth, but I can't find the answer. I can't stop shaking. I don't know what's happening to me. I'm *stronger* than this.

"Madison." He runs back to me. I stumble into his side. He braces me, and I feel the hard press of the gun in his hand.

"Look at me. Okay?" He pushes his forehead to mine, dark eyes bright. "I've got you. You can do this." His breath on my skin warms me. Steadies me. "Are you with me?"

"I'm with you," I whisper.

"Hold on to my jacket. All right? Don't let go."

I twist the fabric in my stiff fingers. *Don't let go.*

24

Nash

We run through deep snow, leaving a clear line of tracks. Our steps might be invisible after a couple more hours of snowfall, but that's time I can't count on having. We have to get to cover.

Protect Madison. That's my priority above anything else. I have to get her somewhere safe. There were houses along the road when we came up here. That's where we need to go. Find one of those houses and get help. But I have no idea if I'm going the right way.

I stop briefly to check which direction we're going, but there's no telling. Even our tracks behind us are hard to see for all the trees and the swirl of white.

"N-Nash?"

I realize I've slowed down. "We need to find a place to wait out the storm. There's bound to be a house or a cabin around somewhere."

Madison's shivering. Thank goodness we've still got our coats on, but they won't keep us warm for long in this weather. I pocket my gun, hold her closer, and pick up my pace, choosing a direction on instinct alone.

After a while, I spot a dip in the landscape. Maybe a creek. Sure enough, when we get close enough, a sloping bank appears. This is a good place for us to cross. Might help obscure our tracks.

"This way," I say, nudging Madison forward. Her teeth chatter, and her eyes are glassy.

It feels like we've been going for an hour when a clearing opens, and a large, dark shape looms ahead. A cabin. It's rustic, but it's the kind of rustic that has money behind it. The lines of the home are elegant, blending into the surroundings. Probably someone's vacation ski chalet.

I race toward it, half dragging Madison along with me. We're both covered in wet snow, our jeans soaked through.

It doesn't look like anyone's home. All the lights are out, and when I rap on the front door, there's no answer.

I avert my face and knock a pane from the sidelight by the front door. My arm reaches through the broken window. A moment later, I've got the door open and we're stepping inside.

"Hello?" I call out. "Anyone here? We need help!"

No security alarms are going off. But even if there were, would local police respond in this storm?

When I try a light switch, it flicks up and down with no effect. The power's out.

Madison slumps against the closed door, eyes glazed.

"You with me?" I ask again.

"I'm okay. Yeah."

We've got a host of problems, but the gunman who ran us off the road is still threat number one. "We need to get everything locked up and that broken window covered," I say.

She's still shivering, but she pushes off from the door. "I'll help."

We use the flashlights on our phones to search the kitchen. Madison grabs a container of plastic wrap, and I dig a roll of duct tape from a drawer. We use our supplies to tape over the gap in the broken sidelight. We lock the door, and then barricade it with a table that we carry from a dining room.

Then I take a look around.

The house is one story, with a huge living room in the center. It's clean and uncluttered, as if nobody's been here in a while. Banks of windows create a panorama of the woods.

The view is peaceful, almost idyllic. Like a Robert Frost poem. Dark lines of trees, snowflakes whirling between them. All that white reflects the sky, amplifying what little light there is. It's enough to illuminate the interior of the house.

We take up defensive positions and keep watch from the windows. Outside, snow falls in ever-deeper drifts.

Nothing stirs in the woods.

As the minutes stretch, I steal more glances at Madison. Her breaths condense with every exhale, and her shaking's only gotten worse.

"I'll make a fire," I say. "We should get warm. Not much point in keeping watch if we freeze to death while we're doing it."

"But that guy c-could be out there." Her teeth chatter as she speaks.

"We haven't seen any sign of him for a long time. The guy can't search for us in the woods all night. He needs shelter just as much as we do."

But I understand what Madison's feeling. It's based on primal terror. The knowledge that we could've died. *Again.* It would get under anybody's skin, including mine.

I grab both our guns and set the weapons nearby, within easy reach.

I take a blanket from the couch and drape it over her

shoulders. She looks down at her hands like she doesn't recognize them. Her fingertips are pale. Loss of circulation.

"Keep the surrounding blanket," I say. "I'll work on the fire."

There's firewood stacked on the hearth, along with kindling and a box of long matches. Madison waits beside me as I get the fire going, tending it with a metal poker until the logs start to catch. Finally, tendrils of warmth roll toward us from the fire.

I stand up. "How you doing?" I rub her hands and her arms until her eyes start to brighten.

"These are some shit accommodations, Jennings."

At least she's able to joke with me. "I'll try to do better next time."

"I don't think I've ever been this c-cold."

"We won't warm up unless we get rid of our wet clothes."

"You t-trying to get me undressed?" Her attempt at a smile makes my heart twang with worry.

She's putting on a brave face. But I know her well enough now that I can see through it.

In the car earlier, I talked about space. I knew we needed distance. But my entire world has collapsed into this room, the few square feet around us. The terror in Madison's face. The shivering that won't cease.

I tug off my coat and shuck my jeans next. I throw everything into a pile by the fireplace next to my wet socks and shoes. I'm left in my T-shirt and boxer briefs.

"I can't get my f-fingers to work." Madison's still struggling with her coat zipper, so I place my hands over hers, steadying them.

"Let me do it." I get her jacket off, then peel her jeans down her legs, keeping my eyes averted. I kneel, working the denim over her ankles. Her skin is so cold.

Standing in front of the fire, I take the blanket from her

shoulders and pull it around the both of us. Madison's ice-cold. I try to wrap her up as best I can, my feet on either side of hers, her head tucked beneath my chin.

We stand there, flames climbing in the fireplace behind us, until the last of her shivering fades away.

"Who the hell was that guy?" she asks. "How did he find us? Why?"

All questions I'm asking, too. "I don't know."

"Was it random? Has he been following us since West Oaks?"

"I don't know." If he did, I failed to notice.

"When I heard the gunshots… Realized what was h-happening…"

We're warm now, but a tremor still moves through Madison. I pull her even closer to me, cinching the surrounding blanket.

"It's okay now," I murmur. "You're okay."

Madison lifts her head and looks up at me. "What about you? Are you okay?"

I'm not. Nothing about what just happened is okay. But I don't want to let it show.

I could've lost her. We could've lost each other.

Every cell in my body is on alert. Every sense is heightened. But now that we're still, now that we're safe, all of my attention has zeroed in on Madison. Her body, leaning into mine. The scent of her hair right beneath my nose.

"Madison," I whisper. "I'm sorry about all this."

"You blaming yourself again? You know I hate that."

I manage a weak smile. "I know. But you said in the car that you regret everything that's happened. Us…getting close. It was a mistake."

"You don't think so?"

Her green eyes glow in the firelight, like sun on a stream, and I'm caught somewhere inside of them.

There are reasons I've held back from her. Rules I've tried to follow, like the objectives set out before a mission. *These are my responsibilities, my guidelines, and it's my duty to follow them. Because the team is counting on me.*

Number one, be a good father. Be a good man. As if those are jobs with established expectations and rulebooks. As if that was enough to keep Emma and Madison from getting hurt.

But now, my justifications are like scraps of paper trying to hold back the tide.

I'm not an impulsive person, but some impulses run too deep. They won't be denied. And maybe I've made things worse by fighting it.

"I'd never want you to be in danger, but I wouldn't take back the rest of what happened," I say, and it feels like a sinful confession.

Not even my injuries. Fucked up as that might sound. Because if it all hadn't happened, if fate hadn't led us here, then she wouldn't be in my arms right now.

I kiss her forehead. Her temple. Her cheek. Her skin warms beneath my lips.

Madison's breath catches, and I feel the thump of her heart through the thin fabric of our shirts.

In this moment, after we've just run for our lives—nearly lost each other for the second time—all my rules and reasons might as well not exist. They're swept away by the currents in Madison's eyes. By the snow filling the windows, the crackle of the fire. The beat of Madison's heart with mine.

"Nash," she whispers.

"Tell me if you don't want this." I hesitate only a moment.

Then I press my mouth to hers, feeling the shape of my name on her lips.

I kiss her slow and deep. Madison opens to me immediately, her head tipping back. My tongue licks into her mouth.

Tasting what I've craved these past weeks. And *fuck*, it's even better than I remembered.

What I feel now, it's beyond words. It's relief, and it's longing. It's the sense that so many things are wrong in this world, but this isn't one of them. This, the two of us wrapped up in each other—how did I ever think this could be wrong?

I only want more, but I force myself to ease back. I rest my forehead against hers, and our noses brush. My lips find hers again. Gentle touches. Nibbles.

In between, I ask, "Do you want me to stop?"

"Never. Please don't stop."

My tongue surges into her mouth. My eyes flutter closed, and it's just Madison's taste, her warmth, filling up my world.

God, I've ached for this. For her.

Madison's fists clench on my T-shirt over my chest. Her mouth closes over my tongue, sucking me deeper.

My cock was already hard, but now it's throbbing. If she keeps kissing me like that, I'm not going to last long. And I want to make this good for her.

I intend to take my time, even if it's going to torture me to do it.

I break our kiss and reach for the bottom edge of her shirt, teasing my fingers underneath it. She lifts her arms, and I pull it over her head one-handed. The blanket's fallen away from our shoulders, but I've barely noticed. Every inch of me is on fire, and as my eyes take in Madison's smooth skin, the lacy bra cupping her breasts, the moment only burns hotter.

We kiss again. Now that we've started, it's like we can't go too long without it. We nip each other's lips, suck them. At the same time, my hand wanders over her newly exposed skin. Lace tickles my fingers. Her heartbeat pulses just beneath. I fit my hand around her breast, imagining how it'll feel weighed against my palm. I want it. I want all of her, right now. Again and again.

My right arm cinches around her waist, holding her to me. I wish I could touch her with no limitations, in every way that she needs. But even if I could, that probably wouldn't be enough. If I had two working hands on her, I'd just want three.

She pulls at my shirt. "Get this off."

I strip it over my head and throw it aside. With frantic movements, Madison reaches behind her back and unhooks her bra. The lace falls to the rug. She pushes her breasts against me, and the sensation is overwhelming. So much soft skin. The stiff points of her nipples. Her smoothness against my dusting of hair, my years' worth of scars.

And then my eyes find the raised marks on her right arm. The gunshot that dug a furrow from her elbow to her shoulder. The low light from the fire sets off the contrast, the wound still dark as it heals.

I bend to kiss the scar.

"It's ugly, isn't it? The one on my thigh is worse."

"No, you're beautiful. Every part of you. You're perfect."

"So are you." Her fingertips trace my pecs and my stomach, then play along the edge of my briefs. There's no way she doesn't feel my erection against her hip.

And somehow, we're still standing.

I need to remedy that.

I give Madison another slow, open-mouthed kiss, and then sink to my knees. As I go, I reach for her panties and tug them down. She steps out of them, bracing one hand on my shoulder. My fingers drag over the raised starburst-scar at her thigh.

I hate that she was hurt. I'd take her wounds away if I

could, put them on myself. Yet it's part of what brought us here. Part of *us*.

I tilt my chin up and devour her with my eyes. She's made of firelight and shadow. The subtle curve of her hips and the long lines of her legs. The swell of her breasts. The shiny pink buds of her nipples.

My cock jerks. I have to squeeze the base of my shaft through my briefs to keep myself calm. Precome dampens the fabric.

I'm going to worship every inch of her. But there's one spot I want to touch most, to taste, and fuck it, I'm not strong enough to resist for a second longer.

I dip my nose into the juncture between her thighs. Madison gasps, her free hand flying to my other shoulder. She spreads her legs wider for me.

My finger pushes into her tight channel. My tongue darts out, parting her folds and seeking the center of her heat. Her arousal is sweet and heady. As intoxicating as any liquor I've ever tasted.

"*Oh.*" She chants my name, and fuck, do I like the sound of that. "Nash, I can't...I can't..."

I tear myself away from her. Does she not want this?

But Madison drops to her knees, mirroring my position. She grabs my face and crashes her mouth against mine.

This kiss is wilder, barely contained. Madison bites at my lips, my jaw.

Then her hands leave my face. She paws at the waistband of my boxer briefs, yanking them down. My erection pops out. She breaks away from my mouth and she's instantly on my cock, sucking me down.

"Oh, *fuck.*" I sit back against my heels. My left hand falls behind me to keep me upright.

Her hair falls across my lap, a wave of softness caressing my skin. Her mouth works me over. Fast and hungry before switching gears. Her tongue swirls around my glans, probes my slit, moaning at what she tastes.

Madison's turning my bones to liquid fire.

"Wait, wait. That feels too good. I need a minute." It's been a really long time for me. Not that I could compare Madison to anyone else. It's never been like this. Like I'll lose my mind if I can't have her.

She sits up, wiping her mouth and licking her bee-stung lips. I reach between my legs and tug my balls to bring myself down.

I need to be inside her. I need her on my cock.

"C'mere," I say. That's all the eloquence I'm capable of at the moment.

My hands go to her hips, guiding her to straddle my lap. I position her over me and sink her down onto my swollen, aching shaft. A guttural moan rumbles from my chest as her pussy envelopes me.

Madison tips her head back, a breathy groan issuing from her lips. Her legs wrap around me and her thighs tighten on my hips. Her hands flutter, reaching out, and land on my shoulders.

"Nash," she pants. "Don't stop. Please don't stop."

We're not even moving, but I could come from this alone. She keeps taking me right to the edge. Her pale pink nipples and creamy skin, contrasting my darker olive tone. Her tight body clenched around my shaft.

Then I notice the view in the dark window across the room. I can see us both in profile in the reflection. I have never seen anything so intensely erotic as the two of us. Me, still sitting with my knees bent. Madison impaled on my cock. My fingers spread wide and digging into the flesh of her ass. Her hair cascades down her back, shimmering in the fire-light in different shades of gold.

My next groan is even deeper. Savage.

Her back arches, everything exposed to me. I lean forward and press my lips to her throat. My tongue traces the throbbing vein there.

Finally, I start to move.

With my hand on her waist, I lift her and pull her back down, again and again, onto my dick. I'm slicked with her arousal. My hips thrust. Sweat beads on my upper lip, between my pecs.

The scent of sex makes my eyes roll back, my chest go tight. She's sopping wet, dripping onto my lap and dampening my pubic hair.

Adrenaline and lust swim in my brain.

I need more. More speed, more heat, more friction, more of her. Just *more*.

I cradle my arm around her and tip her until Madison's lying back on the rug. Her hair spreads in a halo around her head. I hover over her, resting my weight on my elbow. Madison's legs wrap around my waist, my cock still filling her.

She's so beautiful. I don't even know how to describe it. No words could do her justice. This incredible woman who took care of me, who's brave and persistent and so giving.

How did I ever think I could move on from what we've shared these past weeks? From what we've become to each other?

I want to hold on to her and make her mine. Take care of her. Never hurt her, and never let her go.

And in the searing heat of this moment, that doesn't seem so impossible.

25

Madison

My world has turned to ice and fire. And Nash is at the center of it.

He pulls his hips slowly back, then snaps them forward again, pushing deep until I feel his balls up against me. I cry out with each surge of his thick cock inside me. I'm delirious with need for this man.

I didn't know anything could feel like this. So perfect it's almost painful, like a live wire is touching my heart.

The flames in the fireplace dance in his dark amber eyes. Nash's hair is unruly, tumbling over his forehead. I run my fingers through it, then cup his face. My hands trail down his shoulders, his torso. Over scars and soft hair, his muscles, bunched and flexing underneath. Our bodies undulate together, his cock spreading me open again and again.

I want all of him. He's giving me so much, but it isn't enough.

Don't stop, I think. *Don't ever stop.*

"Nash, I need…"

"Tell me."

"You," I murmur. *Just you.* I suspect I'm not making sense, but all the blood's rushed out of my brain.

And that's good. I don't want to think about what this means. What kinds of risks we're taking.

He's balancing all his weight on his uninjured arm. The other hooks beneath my knee and bends my leg up. Opening me even more. His dick sinks deeper into me, stretching me wider than I've felt any man before. He's breathing hard, groaning, and each sound ratchets my pleasure higher. He fills me with his cock, and my hips lift to the rhythm he sets.

I'm exposed and vulnerable. But it's not just my body. It's what's inside my heart. What I feel must be plain in my eyes, my expression. Obvious for him to see.

Keep me safe. Don't let me fall.

We're surrounded by cold, by dark and cruel things, but the heat between us is like the center of the sun. That heat and that pleasure keep intensifying, taking me higher with each pump of his swollen shaft. Nash is everywhere, solid and strong. It's his inner fire. His confidence. A steadiness that makes me feel steady too, even now when I'm nowhere near in control.

I've got you, he said in the woods.

I want to believe that. I have to.

I want Nash to keep pushing away everything I'm afraid to think about. To make love to me as if nothing exists but the two of us.

I don't want this to end.

But my body has other ideas. My breath skips. I can't get enough air. I crave release, I'm desperate for it, as if this is too much sensation for me to bear.

Nash's beautiful body, his strength, and the unrelenting thrusts of his cock—it's all too much.

I sneak my hand between our bodies, reaching for the spot just above where we're joined. My fingers massage my clit, and it's the final, unbearable pleasure to send me right over the edge.

My pussy clenches around him. For a brief moment, my vision goes as white as the storm outside. My body quakes and shudders with each wave of delicious sensation.

Nash throws his head back and shouts. He thrusts wildly into me as his cock jerks. His heat scalds me from the inside out. But he doesn't stop. He keeps fucking me through the aftershocks until neither of us can take any more.

Finally, his weight lands heavily to one side of me. Our chests heave, struggling to catch our breaths.

One of his legs is tangled between mine. His arm rests against my stomach.

I seek out his gaze for reassurance, even though I can't stand this needy feeling. I'm afraid of what's beyond this house, what could be waiting for us, but I'm afraid of what I feel for Nash too. It's somethings so big I can't even see it all at once. It's enough to fill up every empty space inside me, everything that's missing.

But it's enough to break me too.

When I look for him, he's there. Eyes locked on my face.

"Hi," he murmurs, and drops a kiss to my shoulder.

"Hey."

"How're you doing?"

"I…" There are too many thoughts warring in my mind, trying to come to the surface. Nash's brow creases with concern. He sits up, and I reach for him by instinct. "Don't go."

"I'm just getting the blanket." He grabs a couple of pillows from the couch and drags the blanket over us, cuddling me close to him. We're tangled up together again. I touch his cheek with my fingertips.

"Get some rest," he says. "I'll keep watch."

I want to stay awake with him, but exhaustion is pulling me under.

He's the last thing I see as I fall asleep, and his eyes don't close before mine.

A MASKED MAN BENDS OVER ME. I SMELL HIS SWEAT. His smile chills me. I'll never be warm again. His knife glints, flames shivering in reflection on the metal.

No, please.

You can't stop me.

He presses the tip of the knife against my heart.

No!

I jolt upright with a scream caught in my throat.

I'm in a strange house. Embers glow in the fireplace. There's a huge window with snowy woods outside, glowing in a strange sort of twilight.

Nash isn't here. I'm alone.

I search for my gun, but it's gone.

"Madison?" Nash races toward me from another room. "Something wrong?"

"Just...forgot where I was for a minute." I clutch the blanket to my naked body. Nash has his jeans on, no shirt. His gun sits in its holster, and my weapon is tucked into his waistband.

My eyes graze over his chest, then away.

I grab for my T-shirt and pull it over my head. My panties are halfway under the couch. I reach for them and tug them on beneath the blanket.

My jeans are on the hearth. Nash must have laid them there to dry.

When I look up, he's watching me warily. "You all right?"

I nod, even though I'm not sure. I feel unbalanced, that

nightmare still lingering in my head. And what happened before, having sex with Nash...

I wanted it. But that doesn't mean it was a good idea.

I get up and put on my jeans. The denim is still damp, and it's cold on my overheated skin. "What time is it?"

"Three in the morning."

Of course. My usual nightmare wake-up time. "Did you get any sleep?"

"I've been keeping watch."

Right. I remember him saying he'd do that.

I remember every moment of what we did. How incredible it felt. How reckless. We didn't even use a condom. The slickness between my legs is Nash's come.

I've got a birth control implant, and I trust him. But it just shows how little I was thinking.

"Madison? Are you sure you're okay?"

I hum a response. "Power still out?" I wander into the kitchen.

"Yep. No cell service either. And no sign of anybody coming near the house. We have a solid vantage point from here. There's a ton of snow out there, and it's still coming down."

I go to the window over the kitchen sink and look out. It's almost the same view as from the living room. Trees bowing under the weight of snowfall. I can make out the slight depression where our tracks lead out of the woods and toward the front door. But everything else is pristine white, tinged an unearthly pale blue beneath the dark gray sky.

"I think this cabin is a vacation rental." Nash points at the fridge, where there are paper printouts taped to the side. "There's instructions here for working the Wi-Fi, working the dishwasher. Phone number for the owner. Makes me feel a little less guilty about breaking in. I can pay them for the cost of staying. Plus that broken window, obviously. And if there's any other damage."

Nash sounds like he's rambling. Like he can tell I don't know what to say and doesn't want to let the silence fall between us. But he's never minded that before.

"I'm not sure if they have a backup generator," he says, "but it hasn't kicked on. It'll probably be a while before the roads are cleared."

"Okay." That probably means nobody has found Nash's SUV yet. Nobody knows we're in trouble, and we have no way of getting help.

Emma's the only person who knows we went to Mammoth.

Her plane has probably landed in France by now. I hope she's having fun with her mom. Not worrying about Nash or me. If she writes her dad and doesn't hear back, she'll assume he's asleep.

And what about my family? When will my mom realize I'm not answering my texts? Tomorrow?

Hugging my elbows, I walk from room to room. Nash follows me.

When we got here, I guess I was in shock. He told me we were safe, and I believed him because I needed to.

I *should* believe him. He's handled far more dangerous situations than I have. But getting naked with him... Then waking up after that nightmare, seeing that he was gone...

My knees go weak, and I sit heavily on the couch.

Nash lays the guns on the coffee table and sits beside me, facing me. He reaches for my hand. "Will you talk to me?"

If I were feeling more like myself, I might laugh. Nash asking me to talk, when I'm usually the one who's coaxing him. "I can't think straight. My thoughts are all over the place. And I don't know why I'm reacting this way." I search for the words to explain it. "When we got shot before, I kept it together. But this time we're not even hurt, not any worse, and I'm a mess."

"Can I hold you? Can I make it better?"

Nash pulls me into his lap, and I go willingly. I burrow against him, my face in the crook of his neck. My body shakes. Nash rubs my back.

It's exquisite torture. Having him so close, knowing how it feels when our bodies are joined, when Nash is deep inside me. But not knowing what any of it means.

Flames crackle and the logs shift in the fireplace.

"Were you ever shot before a month ago?" I ask.

"Some shrapnel wounds, but I was lucky. I never took a bullet."

"But you were shot at. You've been in war."

"Yes."

"Do you get used to it?"

"In some ways. But knowing you were in danger last night was a lot worse. That's the part that terrified me."

That terrified me too. And not just because *I* was afraid of losing him. Emma loves her dad so much. She needs him. How could I tell her if something happened to him while he was trying to protect *me*?

But once I knew we were safe, that relief overwhelmed every other thought in my head.

He brings his lips to my ear. "Madison." His thumb strokes my cheek. "Do you regret what we did?"

Would I have gotten naked with him if we hadn't just been in danger? Did the stress scramble my brain? Maybe. But not enough to make me say yes to something I didn't want—the opposite.

I wanted Nash so badly, I chose to ignore everything else.

"I don't regret it," I say.

"We didn't use a condom. I should've asked."

"I should've thought of it too. But I'm fine with it. I just keep waiting for you to change your mind. To say it can't ever happen again."

To leave me on that dancefloor.

He palms my cheek, and his eyes are as intense as I've ever seen them. "I have wanted you *every single day* since you first kissed me. I fought what I wanted because I thought I had to. But I can't anymore. My only mistake was pretending I could deny this. But if you don't want it to happen again, it won't."

My heart opens up, just a little. "I've always wanted you. Even when I knew I shouldn't."

He kisses a path down my face. He's holding me so tightly there's almost no space between us. We're as close as we can get while still wearing clothing, and I'm tempted to get rid of that barrier too.

I sift my fingers into his dark hair and breathe in his scent. Woodsmoke and musk and sex. His whiskers are soft against my cheek.

"What about all the reasons we shouldn't do this?" I ask. His daughter. Our careers. Our ages, though that hardly matters to me.

His kisses pause, but he doesn't pull away. "I don't know. I didn't say I have it all figured out."

"Neither do I."

My colleagues are talking shit about me at work. And Emma's furious with her dad for getting so close to me.

But all of them already think we're sleeping together.

"Do you want to be with me?" he asks. "The decision is yours. I'm done fighting it. If you say you're mine, I'm going to hold on to you as long as I can."

I can't stop the elation that bubbles inside me, even though he hasn't made any promises. *As long as I can* is pretty vague. But I'm not ready to make promises either.

I already told him I want him. It's everything else that's

been the problem. Nash and I are complicated. There's no getting around it. But when I'm in his arms, when he kisses me, the rest of the world falls away.

Right now, it's just the two of us. This refuge is only temporary, and we could lose it any second. But isn't that the point? When you find something this perfect, you should hold tight to it. Even if it won't last.

"I'm yours," I say.

His mouth slants onto mine, our connection even deeper than before. It's just Nash and me, and it's right.

We can deal with the complications when we get back to West Oaks.

26

Nash

The world outside the living room window could be a painting, it's so peaceful. All looks clear. The sun is out, and the ice crystals on the top layer of snow glitter like a million diamonds.

But the woman sleeping in my arms is far more dazzling.

We slept like spoons, Madison's body curved into mine like she was made to fit me.

We've scavenged more blankets and pillows from a hall closet to make a bed here on the couch, close to the fire. The flames have died down to embers, and the air outside our blankets has a distinct chill to it. But underneath, where we're curled together, it's toasty. My arm drapes over her stomach, holding her to me.

In the back of my mind, I'm thinking of all I need to do. How to get us out of here, how to notify the local police of the attack on us last night. For whatever good that will do. But after all we've been through, Madison and I deserve this brief respite of calm. If for no other reason than the power's still out, and we're cut off from the outside world. For better or worse.

I can't resist kissing her shoulder and nuzzling her neck.

"Hmm?" She inhales, eyes blinking. "What is it?"

"Nothing." Contentment sings through my body. I feel a little bad about waking her. But only a little.

Madison yawns and wiggles even closer to me, her ass against my crotch. I rock my hard-on against her.

"Somebody's having a nice morning." She sounds sleepy, but I hear the smile in her voice.

"Could be better."

She turns her head to kiss me. We're a mess from making love during the night—twice—but I don't care. Madison doesn't seem to either. There's no self-consciousness about her. Our kisses are lazy, all tongue. She reaches back to squeeze my thigh.

Then she lifts her knee and guides my cock between her legs.

I slide all the way into her wet, tight heat. Sweat beads over my body, slicking my skin everywhere we're touching, her back to my chest and stomach.

"That feels…" I grunt the rest. I can't think of any new words to capture this.

Perfect. Amazing. Exactly what I need.

"The sounds you make drive me crazy."

"What sounds?"

"You know. Those caveman noises."

"Like this?" I growl against her ear and suck the lobe into my mouth.

"Mmm, *exactly* like that."

I'm not usually talkative during sex—go figure, right?—but I like being vocal. So does Madison. Her sighs and whimpers make my head spin.

I grunt and groan to my heart's content while I fuck her. We're on our sides, still spooning, kissing, equal parts passion and ease. It's been many years since I've had this much sex in a twelve-hour period. If ever. But somehow, my balls are already full and eager to empty into her again.

"Touch yourself. Want you to come." I'd do it for her, but with only one functioning hand, my options are limited in this position.

"Yes, Sergeant."

Her answer thrills the inner rebellious side of me. The part that secretly craves what's forbidden. Until Madison, I hadn't even acknowledged that side of me existed. Now, I'm setting that desire free, and *fuck* does it feel good.

Madison's fingers dip downward. Her spine arches, and I plunge even deeper inside her. I push the blanket out of the way so I can see what she's doing. Madison's hand works fast in the cleft between her legs. I feel the added pressure on my cock. That extra stimulation, the visual—it sends my arousal spinning higher and higher.

Then it's just our rhythm and our breaths and heat fogging up all the windows in the living room.

She comes a half second before I do. My balls draw up and spill my release into her, my cock jerking, white-hot pleasure ripping through me.

We snuggle and don't bother to move as I soften inside of her.

"Can't wait until I'm healed," I murmur. "Then I can touch you however I want."

Her eyes are round when they find mine, but the surprise in her look disappears so fast I'm not sure what it meant. I guess I was talking about the future. Does Madison not believe I want that with her?

I told her I didn't have it figured out, but I do want that. I want days and nights spent together, making love as if we don't have another care in the world. Exploring every part of each other. I want to know how to drive her crazy, how to make her completely lose control.

But then, imagining my arm healed makes me think of my surgery, and that leads back to the argument I had yesterday with my daughter.

My mind instantly pulls away from it, like touching a hot stove.

I have no clue how to handle Emma. How to make my role as "father" merge with what I want with Madison. I don't even know what word to use to describe this. She's not just a friend with benefits, because that's not my style. I feel much more for her than that. Is Madison my lover? My girlfriend?

I imagine saying either of those words to Emma, and my throat seizes up.

For years, Emma has been the number one person in my life. But I need Madison, too. I've tried to keep her distant, and I've already proved that's impossible.

Somehow, I'll work it out. I have to.

I tap the flat of my hand against her butt. "We'd better get up."

"Before we go at it again?"

I answer her smirk with one of my own.

I clean up with ice-cold water in the bathroom. While Madison takes her turn, I pull on my clothes to go outside and check our perimeter. The frigid air focuses my attention on our surroundings instead of the beautiful woman waiting for me inside.

As I saw from the windows, there's no sign of anyone coming near the house. I can't even hear any cars. Birds chirp, and a clump of snow falls from a tree branch.

We're going to need more firewood, so I poke around until I find the wood pile. There's plenty here beneath the layer of snow. The owners of this house take good care of the place. As soon as the Wi-Fi or cell service are up and running again, I'm going to call the phone number I saw on the fridge to let the owner know we're taking shelter here. I don't like taking things that don't belong to me, but it's the best I can do.

Back inside, I take off my coat and boots and leave them by the door. I set down several pieces of snow-damp firewood to dry out. We'll have to deal with a chilly house until I can get the fire stoked again.

I haven't examined the bathroom cabinets fully yet, and I'm hoping there's an extra toothbrush or two in there. I could use it.

I find Madison in the kitchen inspecting the cabinets. She's dressed in her jeans and coat. "I found some crackers, canned soup. Jars of tuna packed in olive oil, the fancy kind. And peanut butter."

"Peanut butter and crackers happens to be a speciality of mine."

Madison grabs a plate and a butter knife. We spread peanut butter onto the wafers, taking turns feeding them to each other as we lean against the kitchen counter. My right arm isn't good for much, but I can link my fingers with Madison's. Every once in a while, I brush my nose against hers, or kiss her temple.

We're being disgustingly cute. Emma would definitely send a vomit emoji if she could see us right now.

I hide my inner flinch. *Don't think about Emma.*

"This is nice," Madison says, tracing her fingertip down my chest over my shirt. "Getting to touch you."

"You like me?" I ask with a smile.

"Eh, you're not bad."

"That day you introduced yourself to me in the academy, I had to work very hard not to notice how beautiful you are."

"You did a good job, then. I never would've guessed. When I started SWAT training, I thought you didn't even remember me."

"Trust me, you were the first person I noticed in the class-room every day. I couldn't keep my eyes off you." I kiss the corner of her mouth, where there's a dab of peanut butter.

"Is *that* why you really wanted my advice on your teaching? To get me alone?"

A denial leaps to my tongue. But did I subconsciously want to be near her? Maybe. It's never been just her physical beauty that attracted me, though. I've been around stunning women before and they never tempted me.

"Did you really streak with our classmates in the academy?" I ask, answering her question with one of my own.

She presses her lips together, laughing silently. "Yep. Totally did."

I reach for her, grumbling under my breath. "Tell me who saw you. If it's any of the guys in SWAT training, I'm going to make his life hell."

She wraps her arms around my neck. "Don't be jealous."

"Can't help it. I want you to myself."

"You've got me," she whispers.

Usually, I'm not the jealous kind. Besides, I doubt I'll go back to being an instructor anytime soon. But Madison has an effect on me that no other woman does.

Thirteen years I was married, almost all of that while I was in the Navy. I was a shitty husband in many ways, gone far more than I was ever around. But I was loyal. In all those years, I got used to letting my eyes skate past attractive women in bars. Every time a woman approached me, touched my arm, batted her eyelashes, I made a quick exit. Steered her in the direction of a teammate who'd be all-too-happy to take her to his bed for the night.

Even after my divorce, I kept acting like I was taken. When I needed relief, I rubbed one out in the shower. Rinse. Repeat.

Madison has been the only person to break open the parts

of me I'd closed off. Being around her, I realize how lonely I've been. How unsatisfied. I can't go back to that.

But this is more than just filling an emptiness inside me. I'm greedy for *her*. I'm jealous of all the time we could've had together if I hadn't fought this attraction.

We snuggle into each other and are quiet for a while, just enjoying this moment together.

"Why'd you go to the academy at all?" Madison asks. "I'm sure a former SEAL could do all kinds of exciting things. Like join the CIA or be a bodyguard for celebrities or who knows what."

"I served my country, and now I'm serving my city. Though I might need to reconsider my options with my arm busted up."

She gently strokes the bar of my fixator. "You're going to get better. I know you will."

I swallow around the lump that rises to my throat. "But if not, I could use a few more backup plans."

"How about motivational speaker? Teach your acolytes about the sniper way of life."

"Me? I'd inspire exactly no one."

"That is not true."

"I hate talking to people. I prefer to grunt and point."

She laughs. "You're doing just fine talking to me."

"But you're different." Different from everyone.

"Why am I different?" Her tone is light, but her eyes are searching mine.

I wish I could explain everything I see in her. How my world is brighter when she's in it. How, despite our differences, she makes me feel understood.

"I like how you dive in, even when you can't see where you're going."

She rolls her eyes. "That's just another way of saying I

make rash decisions. Exactly what my mother accuses me of."

"Not rash. You're more careful than that. But you don't let uncertainty stop you, and I admire that." I kiss her softly on the lips.

"Well, I like how deliberate you are," she says.

"Stubborn?"

"Some might call it stubborn. But even when you're breaking the rules, you're thinking of what's right. You're someone people can count on. I've never trusted anyone the way I trust you."

I don't always feel so grounded, but Madison makes me want to live up to the man she sees. "You're the one who's good at talking. Maybe that's *your* career future."

"Hmm, maybe talking is overrated."

"I've always thought so." I take her hand and press it to the erection crowding my pants. She squeezes my hard length through the fabric.

Then her gaze flicks past my shoulder. Shifts into shock. Panic.

Madison gasps and points at the window. "*Nash*. Someone's out there."

I spin, already reaching for my gun. "Hide."

27

Nash

I press myself to one side of the window and look out. There's a person standing in the gap between the trees, about where I'd expect the driveway to be. The figure is dressed in a heavy black parka and black snowpants. A hood is up, obscuring his face.

He carries a rifle loosely at his side.

I sidestep toward the back door, grabbing my coat and putting it on. Either our visitor knows we're here, or he suspects it. Either way, I don't want to wait here for an ambush.

"I'm going out there," I say. "Stay out of sight."

"No way. You can't go out there by yourself. I'm going with you."

"The impulse is admirable, but I need you to cover me. No sense giving him two targets instead of just one."

"Except it would mean two guns on him. How am I supposed to cover you if I can't line up the shot?"

"I'll draw him closer."

"You just want to protect me."

She's got me there. But I'm not arguing about this. "Wait for my signal. If you see it, then come out guns blazing."

"And if the asshole takes a shot at you before I see the signal?"

"Then get out of the house as fast as you can. Head north towards town."

She frowns like she's going to refuse. But when I step outside, Madison hangs back as I've asked.

The snow buries my legs up to the knee. Keeping my arms at my sides, I wade forward. The figure between the trees hasn't moved. The rifle still points at the ground.

My fingers flex, itching to grab the gun in my waistband. "Morning," I call out. "What can I do for you?" I put my hand on my hip, inches from the gun.

"I was going to ask the same thing." The figure pushes back the hood of the parka, revealing a weathered face. Deep-set wrinkles surround narrowed eyes. A woman.

Whoever this is, she isn't the Midnight Slasher. But I don't have a clue who shot at us yesterday after forcing us off the road.

"We're renting the house for the weekend," I say, painting on a smile.

"Who's 'we'?"

"My wife and me," I improvise. "It's our honeymoon. Bad luck on the weather. You live nearby?"

She nods. Her grip hasn't loosened on the rifle, but it's still pointing down. "Next property over. Saw the smoke from the chimney, wanted to check on things over here."

If she just wanted to check on the rental property next door, why bring the weapon?

Neither of us makes a move. But the tension runs between us like a current.

"Funny thing is," she goes on, "I spoke to the owner of this house just yesterday. Guy lives in San Fran. He said he wasn't in Mammoth and didn't expect any renters either. So, who the hell are you?"

Behind me, the door slides open. Madison appears in my peripheral vision, taking up position next to me. I can read the defensiveness in her posture.

She didn't follow my directions. But really, should I be surprised?

The hand at my hip slides closer to my gun. My fingertips brush the grip.

"We're not looking for trouble," I say to our guest. "We crashed our car, got stuck in the storm, had to find shelter. I have every intention of paying the owner for our unexpected stay here."

"Then why didn't you say that in the first place?"

I shift slightly, trying to put Madison behind me.

The woman barks a laugh. "Trying to protect your lady. I like that. But a big, strapping man like you can't be scared of little old me."

"Guess I'm a paranoid kind of guy."

She nods slowly, assessing me. "Then you and I have something in common. I'm Tonya."

"Good to meet you, Tonya. I'm Nash. This is Madison."

Tonya still looks skeptical. But she lowers her rifle completely. "Well, I suppose you could use some supplies. Got about ten pounds of beef thawing in my freezer with no power. Happy to share some with you so it doesn't go to waste. But in exchange, I'd like the truth."

"Truth?" I ask.

"Not many newlyweds would go on vacation packing heat. I know the look of somebody carrying when I see it. But, as we've established, a little healthy paranoia isn't a problem. I'd just like to hear your story. How does that sound?"

Madison stays quiet, looking over at me. It seems she's

letting me decide. Maybe it's an apology for not waiting for the signal.

"Sounds good by me. But you're not bringing that rifle inside."

Tonya smiles, and deep furrows appear by her mouth. "I'll leave my weapon at the door, long as you leave yours."

I GO INSIDE FIRST. TONYA COMES IN AFTER ME, AND we both lay our guns on the tile floor. Madison takes out her Glock and lays it beside mine. All three of us give the weapons a wide berth.

Tonya wanders into the living room, her sharp eyes taking it all in. Our nest of blankets and pillows, the broken window we've covered with plastic wrap.

"You're law enforcement," Tonya announces. "I can tell from your weapons. But even without that, I know military." She nods at me. "Army? Navy?"

"Navy," I say. "Retired."

"And now?"

Madison walks forward, resting her hand on my back. "You're right, we're police officers. We did crash in the storm, but we came up here to look into an old case."

"I guessed as much. But why lie?"

"Because somebody ran us off the road yesterday," Madison says. "Shot at us. That's why we're a little nervous."

Tonya whistles. "Can't blame you there. Have you notified the sheriff? No, I suppose you wouldn't have been able to. Unless you've miraculously had cell phone service?"

I shake my head. "You're the first person we've seen or spoken to. I've been keeping an eye out in case the guy who shot at us managed to follow. As far as I can tell, he gave up."

"I don't like the thought that he's prowling around my neighborhood."

"What makes you think he's not from around here?"

"Listen, son, I know the people up here. I know my neighbors. I've lived here forty years, and spent half that as a sheriff's deputy myself. So I can sympathize with you. *But.* Seems to me you must've brought this shooter along with you from wherever you came from. What's this case you two are investigating? What's it have to do with Mammoth?"

Madison opens her mouth, but I reach for her elbow. She turns around and drops her voice to a whisper. "You trusted her enough to let her in. Maybe she's heard something that could help us."

Tonya watches us, waiting for us to explain.

I debate for another moment. "We're from West Oaks. Investigating a series of home invasions that match some that took place here about ten years ago."

Tonya's face changes completely. Her stoic skepticism morphs into understanding, and then something resembling regret. "All that happened after my time. I was already retired from the force by then. But I know the people who worked on it. That case haunted them." She sneaks a look out the window behind her. "I heard through the grapevine that the West Oaks police requested our casefiles on those incidents."

"That's right," Madison says. "We've seen them."

"But I also heard the suspect in West Oaks is dead."

"That's what we're hoping to confirm," I say. "But if the guy's dead, why would someone be trying to stop us from asking questions about him?"

"You think the attack on you yesterday had something to do with that case?"

"Quite a coincidence otherwise."

Tonya thumps toward the back door with a sigh and picks up her rifle. "Now that I know why you're here, I guess I'd better help you however I can. I'll go grab that beef and some salad greens, and how about you cook me lunch while I tell you what I know." She pauses, a hand on the door knob. "And I'll bring you some spare 9-millimeter rounds as well. I imagine you'll want to keep your weapons fully loaded."

"I WASN'T IN THE SHERIFF'S OFFICE ANYMORE when those burglaries happened ten years ago. But I had friends there still, and I heard plenty."

We're sitting at the dining table, which I've returned to its rightful place after using it as a barricade over the front door. Noonday sun shines through the windows. The glare outside is so bright it leaves spots in my vision.

I slice my knife through the steak on my plate. Tonya brought three New York strips from her freezer, along with a bouncy Jack Russell terrier named Captain Jack. Madison and I asked her if she needed help carrying things back here from her house, but she declined.

We cooked the meat in a cast-iron skillet right over the logs in the fireplace. Tonya told us how long to heat the pan, when to flip the steaks. I helped throw together a salad with oil and vinegar. The food is simple, but it's some of the best I've ever tasted.

"Of course, all of Mammoth was sharing details and rumors about it. The victims always had their curtains open. The perp could see them inside their homes."

"The reports on the West Oaks crimes were similar," I say.

Tonya feeds a scrap of meat to Captain Jack. "People speculated on what motivated the guy. Greed or hatred or whatever. They thought he was jealous of these happy people in their comfortable homes. Wanted to punish them, take their belongings away. But I don't think that was really it. The guy struck people who were *lonely*."

Madison frowns and her gaze moves to the distance. I wonder what she's thinking. Beneath the table, I rest my foot against hers.

When we left Kent Kaylor's house yesterday, I believed Jeffrey Nichols really could be the Slasher. Just like West Oaks PD had already decided. If he was as twisted as Tonya thinks, then I have no problem being the one who ended the guy.

But after Madison and I nearly got assassinated? By someone who was very much alive?

I don't give a shit what makes the Midnight Slasher tick. Thinking about his inner motives gives me the creeps. But I care who he is. I care if he's still coming after Madison or me or anybody else.

"We drove up to Mammoth Lakes to speak to one of your neighbors," I say. "Kent Kaylor. We met with him yesterday."

Tonya harrumphs. "I can guess why you'd talk to him. The knife he claims his neighbor stole? What a mess that was."

"You don't believe him?" Madison asks.

"Oh, I do. But Kaylor…" Tonya shakes her head ruefully. "The man's memory isn't exactly crystal."

I wonder if that's a reference to the cloud of alcohol surrounding him. "Kent Kaylor's house smelled like bourbon."

"His poison of choice. Man's wife finally left him a couple years back."

Madison turns to look at me, probably remembering what Kaylor said. He was waiting for his wife to come home.

"If you wanted a reliable witness, you should've come to me in the first place." Tonya taps the side of her nose. "My memory's sharp as it ever was, and trust me, I pay attention."

Madison grins. "Of that, I have no doubt."

"You implying I'm a busybody? Hush, child." Her laugh is husky and well-worn.

"Why do you believe Kaylor's story?" I ask.

"Because his knife *did* end up at that crime scene, and Kaylor had an alibi. How'd the knife get there otherwise? His ex-wife said they kept that knife with their hunting equipment, and then it vanished. Her word, I did trust."

"But what about Kaylor's claim that it was a neighbor named 'Steven' who stole it?"

"I believe that part too, but only because I met Steven myself. There was something off about him. Have you ever known someone who has the lights on, but nobody's home? I don't mean stupid. I mean *empty*. Soulless. I know how dramatic that sounds, but it's the only way I can describe it. I have no proof whatsoever that Steven committed those attacks. But would I believe it? Without a doubt. He disappeared right after the knife was found at the last crime scene."

Suddenly, Madison jumps out of her seat.

Tonya and I both look up. "Everything okay?" Tonya asks.

"Your guess is as good as mine."

"I very much doubt that." She gives me a knowing grin.

In a moment, Madison returns with her phone. "I haven't got much battery power left, but I want you to look at this picture." She's pulled up that mugshot of Jeffrey Nichols, the same one she showed Kent Kaylor yesterday. "Do you recognize him?"

Tonya studies the image. "Can't say I do."

"Are you *sure*? He's not Steven?"

"I don't forget faces. And I've never seen this man before.

Whoever he is, he's not the gentleman who lived next to Kent Kaylor and called himself Steven."

Madison's gaze meets mine, and I see all my questions echoed there.

If the guy who stole Kaylor's knife wasn't Jeffrey Nichols, then who was he?

28

Madison

We're still sitting around the dining table when the lights flicker, and the house comes to life around us. The power's back on.

Tonya hits the table with the flat of her hand. "About time. Our tax dollars at work."

We go around switching on lights while the heating system kicks in. "I'm going to check the furnace and the water heater," Nash says. He gives me a kiss, then heads off, searching for a utility room.

Tonya grins, watching him go. "You two may not be newlyweds, as your man claimed, but you've got something special. That's clear to see."

"I think it's special. I hope so."

"I had a romance or two when I was on the force. Good way to stay warm on a cold night."

I laugh. "It's a little complicated between us, but we're trying to figure it out."

"I'm not a fan of complications myself. Probably why I'm happy with Captain Jack here, and my own little corner of the

Sierras. But if I'd ever consider complicating my life, it's a man like yours who would tempt me."

"Tempting doesn't begin to describe him."

"To be young again." She winks. "Is the Wi-Fi connecting? I'd appreciate the password."

"It's on a paper taped to the fridge." I take her into the kitchen and show her.

Within minutes, notifications fill my phone screen, many of them texts from my family. That'll take a while to sort through. We'll need to update Detective Holt about all that's happened. Getting shot at, all this stuff about Kent Kaylor. And now, Tonya's witness statement as well.

Could Steven have been the real Midnight Slasher? This info could break West Oaks PD's case wide open. But I can't imagine the chief will be happy to hear it.

I can already imagine the skeptical response. If "Steven" wasn't Nichols, then who was he? Where did he go?

What frightens me is the idea that he's been wandering around West Oaks. That he actually followed Nash and me to Mammoth and shot at us yesterday.

But at the same time, the Midnight Slasher hasn't struck once since Jeffrey Nichols died. There's still so much we don't know. So many pieces of this that don't make sense.

Tonya holds up her phone. "If you've got some time now, we'd better call the sheriff's department about your misadventure yesterday."

We head into the living room to make the call. It takes a while to get dispatch on the line, and then even longer to explain everything that's happened.

I sit on the couch beside her, filling in the gaps as Tonya speaks to a deputy. At the same time, I catch up on my buildup of text messages.

Jake: Mom says you're missing. Can you please reply so she knows you're alive?

Me: It's been one day!

Me: I'm with Nash.

Jake: I figured, since I couldn't reach him either. Mom thinks you two eloped to Vegas or something.

Me: Does everyone think Nash and I are seeing each other?

Jake: Aren't you?

Was it that obvious? To everyone except Nash and me, anyway. If we're going to get so much judgment for it, at least we get to enjoy the benefits.

Me: Yeah. But it's new.

Me: And we are NOT eloping. To Vegas or otherwise.

Jake: Just don't break the guy's heart.

Me: The opposite is far more likely. I'm your little sister. Aren't you supposed to be overprotective?

Jake: I know you can handle yourself. But if he does break your heart, I'll have to work on my stealth tactics. Don't want him to see me coming.

Finally, Tonya ends her call and sets her device on the coffee table. Captain Jack is curled up in my lap and snoozing, a warm snuggly ball of fur.

"They said they found your SUV crashed in a ditch this morning. All kinds of questions about that, and from the sounds of it, they're happy to know you're safe and accounted for. They're on the lookout for the shooter, but with how long it's been, and how chaotic the storm was, it's not likely the guy stuck around."

"What about Nash's SUV?"

"It's been towed to the impound lot."

It won't be drivable with the airbags deployed. Hopefully there's not more damage.

"I was thinking you might want a ride into town?" Tonya says. "You could stay at a hotel tonight and see about your car in the morning. Plus meet with a deputy to give your statement."

Relief washes over me. We won't be stranded here. If the shooter is still looking for us in this area, we'll be a step ahead. "That would be amazing. Thank you. Nash and I are beyond grateful for everything you've done."

Tonya and I both get up from the couch. Nash wanders in, wiping his hands against his jeans. "Got the water heater going."

I rest my weight against him. "What a big, strong man you are."

Tonya brays a laugh. "Just in time for us to leave. Afraid you'll have to take your hot shower at the hotel. Get packed up, and I'll give you a ride into Mammoth."

Nash grumbles. "I shoveled snow, too. Isn't anyone going to enjoy the fruits of my labor?"

I check the view from the window. There's now a long path cut through the snow toward Tonya's property. A snow shovel leans against the side of the house by the back door. The man did all that shoveling one-handed.

But I can believe it. I've seen those muscles in action more than once.

"You get all the credit," I tell him. "And my admiration."

He wraps his arms around my waist and kisses my neck. "I can live with that."

THE ROADS ARE MOSTLY CLEAR BY THE TIME TONYA drives us into town. I take shotgun, while Nash sits in the back with Captain Jack, who seems to enjoy licking Nash's face. Something I can understand.

We cleaned up the house to the best of our abilities, ran a load of blankets and towels in the laundry, and left our contact info for the owner. Tonya's arranged a rental car for us, which we'll pick up in the morning.

With luck, we'll be back on the road to West Oaks tomorrow.

Tonya pulls into the parking lot of a hotel. "I called ahead for you, and they've got a room reserved under my name. I figured you'd want to be discreet, just in case someone nefarious is trying to find you?"

"We appreciate that," Nash says. "You sure you won't have dinner with us? Room service, my treat."

The Jack Russell terrier perks up, resting his paws on Nash's leg, but Tonya shakes her head. "I'd better head home and see to my fridge and freezer. Hoping some of it is still salvageable. You just let me know how this mystery turns out."

We say goodbye, then head into the hotel lobby. The clerk checks us in. "Need any help with your luggage?"

"We've got it, thanks," I say. "We travel light."

Nash and I are both wearing our guns under our coats. Aside from our phones and wallets, which we were lucky not to lose in that first mad dash through the storm, we don't have anything with us. I saw a couple of clothing boutiques on the drive in, and I long to refresh my outfit. But we're trying to keep a low profile around here.

Then the hotel clerk surprises us. "What about the bags that were sent ahead for you?"

We're confused for a moment until we realize these are the overnight bags we packed in Nash's SUV. Tonya must've arranged for a sheriff's deputy to bring them from the impound lot.

"I'm going to order her a gift basket or something," Nash says on our way to the elevator. "What do you think she'd like?"

Then we look at each other and say the same exact thing. "Steaks."

I crack up. "Tonya deserves a whole cow's worth of prime cuts for all the ways she's helped us."

The hotel room is simple and comfy, decorated with skinny vintage skis and rope-covered snowshoes. I've never been so happy to see my own toothbrush. Or my phone charger—my battery was in low-power mode.

We strip and jump into the shower. The hot water feels like paradise. But enjoying it with Nash is even better. His dark hair is plastered against his forehead. Water droplets run over the planes of his muscles, accentuating his golden skin. I try to lick them as they fall.

We soap each other up, our hands wandering over our scars. I'm trying to be gentle with his injury, but Nash backs me up against the tile wall and kisses me until I'm breathless.

With one powerful arm, he lifts me up, and I wrap my legs around him. His hard cock nudges against me. "You want this?" he asks.

"Yes. Give it to me."

It takes a little maneuvering, which makes us both laugh. But that turns to moans as our bodies slide together. I feel every inch of his cock as he fucks me up against the shower wall. I kiss him and suck the water from his lips.

Nash's cockhead rubs a spot inside me again and again, and I just might lose my mind, it's so good. I try to memorize all of it—this fullness in my body and in my heart. The heavy-lidded way he's looking at me. The flush of lust in his cheeks, and the water trailing over him. The firm contours of his muscles. So much strength.

My screams of pleasure echo against the bathroom tile.

Half an hour later, we're both dressed and feeling refreshed. I curl up on my bed and open the browser on my phone. The mattress compresses as Nash sits next to me. He's wearing a dark green v-neck sweater, his damp hair is tousled, and the scruff on his chin is long enough to be soft. He's got a sexy mountain-man vibe going.

I'm tempted to climb into his lap and forget the rest of the world for a while longer. But the next thing he says drags me back to reality.

"Did you see the latest post on California Crimes Uncovered?" Nash asks.

"You're that much of a fan?"

"Hardly. It's my Google alert on the Midnight Slasher."

My pulse races. "There's news?"

"In a way." He shows me the post.

Landon Cowling, Son of Midnight Slasher Victim, To Tell Father's Story In Upcoming Book.

"Remember Eugene Cowling?" Nash asks. "He was the only Slasher victim to die. Heart attack. His son Landon has been all over the media."

"He was at the mayor's last press conference."

"Yep. Well, the guy's been busy."

The article says that Landon Cowling has sold both book and movie rights to his father's story. It's going to be an exposé of the Midnight Slasher—supposedly Jeffrey Nichols —told from the "perspective of the victims." Though I can't tell that Cowling got input from the other victims or their families.

"And look at this." Nash scrolls further down the article. "Cowling is working jointly with California Crimes Uncovered on the book."

Why does this Crimes Uncovered site come up whenever the Midnight Slasher is involved? Is it because they coined the "Midnight Slasher" nickname, and now they want to capitalize on it?

I'm surprised Cowling is willing to be a part of that. Sensationalizing his father's death that way.

I guess I shouldn't judge anyone for the way they manage their grief over the loss of a loved one. But this news leaves a bad taste in my mouth. The book deal seems exploitative.

"A couple weeks ago," I say, "Cowling tried to contact me through the victim resource officer. He wanted me to meet with him for coffee. I said no."

Nash scowls. "This guy asked you on a *date*? Now I *really* don't like him."

"Not a date. He probably wanted to get info he could use in his book deal." There's something else about this that bugs me in a deeper way. Like there's an itch under my skin, and I don't know where it's coming from.

But so many aspects of this case have bothered me that way. My investigation with Nash has raised far more questions than it's answered.

"We'd better call Detective Holt," I say. "That conversation is going to take a while."

∼

"WHERE HAVE YOU BEEN?" HOLT BARKS.

"I'm with Nash. You're on speaker, by the way."

"I assumed you were with Jennings. But what the hell are you doing?"

We're both sitting on the bed. Nash leans back against the pillows beside me. He's staying quiet, the corner of his mouth twitching sardonically.

"Your mom said you and Jennings are both missing."

Ugh. My mother. How did she even get Holt's number? "We were snowed in."

"*Snowed in?*"

"We're in Mammoth Lakes?" The second word comes out sounding like a question. This is not going to be good.

There's a pause. A long one.

"I doubt Jennings was skiing with a broken fucking arm. Do I want to know what you're doing there?"

"Probably not," Nash chimes in.

"Are you somewhere you can talk?" I ask. "*Really* talk?"

"I'm in my truck. Alone."

"Someone left a digital copy of the Midnight Slasher files in my bag near the evidence desk last week. Know anything about that?"

"I have no clue what you're talking about," Holt deadpans.

So he won't admit it. Fine. Holt has wanted deniability. But if the detective left me that USB of Midnight Slasher files, then he wanted me to investigate.

Well, we did. And the Mammoth Lakes police have gotten involved. It won't stay quiet.

Nash eyes me like he's asking, *You going to explain, or should I?* I can guess which he'd prefer.

"We found a possible lead in one of the transcripts of a witness interview. It led us here to Mammoth Lakes. Ten years ago, a man named Kent Kaylor was brought in for questioning because he'd purchased a knife used at one of the crime scenes."

"And?"

We tell him everything. The trip up here, speaking to Kaylor and learning about his neighbor, the mysterious "Steven."

Then getting run off the road and nearly shot.

Sean curses under his breath during that part. "But you're both okay? You're safe?"

"We're fine," I say. "But there's more."

"Of course there is. What now?"

I tell him about our new friend Tonya, and how she's convinced Steven the Renter wasn't Jeffrey Nichols. He was some other creep. But who was he?

Could he have been the real Midnight Slasher?

"I knew I wasn't going to like what you had to say." Holt heaves a sigh into the phone. "You want me to go in to Chief Liu and tell him to reopen the case? That the Midnight Slasher is still alive?"

"Some asshole tried to kill us," Nash snaps. "Getting yelled at by the chief is far lower on my list of concerns."

I can hear him drumming his fingers against the dashboard of his truck. "All right, here's what we're going to do. You're going to send me all you've got. Write up your statements of speaking to Kaylor. Then everything you can remember of what happened after. The description of the guy who shot at you, exactly how it went down. And this Tonya person. I want last names, phone numbers. Got it?"

"Yes, sir," I say.

"Quit it with the 'sir', Shelby. I know you're being sarcastic. Listen, I want you to use my personal email, not my department one. This needs to stay under the radar until we know exactly what we're dealing with. I don't want anyone else finding out and betraying us and causing havoc."

"Got it." I'm not trusting this info with a single soul apart from Holt and Nash.

"Any other bad news you want to lay on me? Because now's the time."

I think of my hunch from earlier and decide to follow it. "Did you see the story about Landon Cowling? The book deal?"

Nash crosses his arms, watching me curiously.

"I heard. What does that have to do with anything?"

"That's what I'm trying to figure out. What do you know about him?"

Holt grumbles. "Let's see. The guy's a pain in the ass, but I try to be nice because his father was killed, and that's some shit nobody should have to deal with."

"Agreed." I can tell this is just a preamble. "Go on."

"We looked into him as part of our investigation. Landon stands to inherit from his father's estate. Over a million, plus the house."

I whistle. "Wow. A classic motive if there ever was one."

"And that's on top of this book deal," Nash says.

"True. But there's no law against being a jerk or inheriting money from your murdered father. Cowling had an alibi for that night. And besides, our main suspect for his father's death has always been the Midnight Slasher, who chooses his victims at random. What's this really about, Shelby?"

"I'm not sure yet. But I wonder about Landon Cowling's ties to California Crimes Uncovered. They're writing this Midnight Slasher book with him."

"That blog and podcast? They've been even worse than Cowling about blowing up public sentiment on this case. If there hadn't been such an outcry in the media, I doubt Mayor Ackerman would've demanded we close the Slasher case so fast."

I raise my eyebrows at Nash.

"Could you poke around?" I ask Holt. "See if there's anything else to find out about Cowling? Anything we should know?"

"It'll have to be off the record. I could give our friends at Bennett Security a call. Private company, so they don't have to deal with government red tape. They could take a deeper look at Cowling. Unofficially."

"Unofficially? You mean illegally?" Nash asks.

"Of course not. I'd never tell anybody to do something

illegal. But Shelby and I are close with a few people at Bennett, and they know how to get shit done without involving paperwork. Maybe you know a couple of them, Jennings. Noah Vandermeer and Tanner Reed. Former SEALs like you."

Nash laughs silently, shaking his head. "Not all Teamguys know each other, Holt. That's a stereotype."

"Suppose I wouldn't know. But I'll talk to them, see what they can do. I'll be in touch."

He hangs up.

"What're you thinking?" Nash asks. "What's your theory?"

"I don't have one yet." But I'm still pondering Landon Cowling, his inheritance, this book deal. Kent Kaylor's knife. And the Crimes Uncovered site... Connections that my brain wants to make, but it can't quite get there.

"Do you remember what Kent Kaylor said yesterday?" I ask. "He mentioned that someone from California Crimes Uncovered got in touch with him last year, asking questions about the burglaries in Mammoth. *Last year*. Before any of the new incidents in West Oaks."

A crease appears between Nash's eyebrows. "But that's what the site is about, right? Investigating unsolved crimes."

"Awfully convenient that the same burglar resurfaced in West Oaks, committing more crimes after a ten-year hiatus. And then they worked with Landon Cowling to get a book deal out of it."

Detective Holt might be looking into Landon Cowling, but I want to learn more about this blog.

29

Madison

The California Crimes Uncovered logo sprawls across the top of the webpage in vivid red. A bloody outline of a knife runs through the "o" in "Uncovered." I've seen that graphic too many times now, more than I can count, yet it makes me nauseous every time.

"Subtle, isn't it?" Nash murmurs.

"No kidding."

"What are we looking for?" he asks.

I scroll through the most recent blog posts. "We know someone from Crimes Uncovered came to visit Kaylor last year, asking about the home invasions. But I wonder if they wrote any articles about the crimes in Mammoth Lakes on the site."

Using the sitewide search, I type in "Mammoth Lakes." Two articles come up, published last year. They describe the Mammoth home invasions and the police investigation, along with details about the suspect's use of a combat knife to terrify his victims.

A *k-bar* blade.

West Oaks PD kept that particular detail hidden from the public. But it seems the Mammoth police did not.

Nash and I are still snuggled against one another on the bed, using the browsers on our phones. We keep poking around the Crimes Uncovered site. It's only a couple of years old. They've reported on dozens of crimes, from murders to fraud to kidnappings. Most of the older articles have just a handful of comments.

But that changed with the most recent Midnight Slasher articles.

"Looks like the site wasn't getting many hits until recently," I say. "After Crimes Uncovered coined the name 'Midnight Slasher,' the comments for its new posts have numbered in the *thousands*." And a quick Google search shows that plenty of other news sites are now cross-referencing Crimes Uncovered. Its popularity has skyrocketed.

Nash runs a hand over his beard. "Do any of the posts about the Midnight Slasher mention Mammoth Lakes?"

"No. Not one. Which seems weird, don't you think? I'm surprised the site editors overlooked the similarities between the crimes in the two towns." As far as I can tell, nobody in the media has linked the Mammoth Lakes break-ins to those in West Oaks. Not publicly, at least. The police departments have been keeping it quiet.

And I'm the one who told Chief Liu about the connection in the first place. But I don't think I'm some investigative genius. Anyone who read about the crimes in Mammoth Lakes and in West Oaks would see the similarity. Right?

Nash leans into me. "I know gears are turning in that brain of yours. What're you thinking?"

In my head, I list what we know for sure. Somebody broke into homes in both Mammoth Lakes and West Oaks, ten years apart. Somebody hurt the homeowners. Somebody also

—if we believe Kaylor—stole a knife used in the Mammoth crimes.

Right now, the world thinks that man is Jeffrey Nichols. But we have some glaring reasons to suspect Nichols didn't commit *all* of those crimes. The biggest reason being that asshole who tried to kill Nash and me two nights ago. Plus, Tonya's witness testimony.

Who was Steven?

How do all these pieces fit together?

"I'm thinking plenty of things," I say, "but I can't make it add up."

"Don't forget, there's also the part about Landon Cowling writing a book with the Crimes Uncovered blog. So Cowling's wrapped up in this too. In multiple ways."

I sink back against the pillows. "Maybe I should accept Cowling's offer to have coffee. See what he has to say."

"*What?*" Nash jolts upright. "You're not going on a date with that guy."

"Not a date. But it's cute that you're jealous."

"Don't turn this around." He frowns disapprovingly. "If you think Cowling has something to do with...*any* of this, then you are not meeting with him."

"I'm a police officer, Nash. This is my job."

"But you're also..."

"I'm what?"

He presses his mouth into a thin line. "You're someone I care about."

I reach out and trail my fingers down his sweater. I don't mind Nash's protectiveness. But he's not going to stop me from taking part in this investigation. "I've been undercover before. You know those stings where we catch sickos who think they're meeting teenage girls? Who do you think plays the teenager?"

He makes a low growl in his chest. "I know you can look

out for yourself. But if I'm around, I'm going to look out for you too."

"Because I'm younger and less experienced?"

"Because of what you mean to me." He kisses me gently on the lips. "I don't want anyone touching you."

"Do you have a possessive streak? Not sure how I feel about that."

"When it comes to you, I do." His big hand moves along my side. "Do you have any idea how incredible you are? You could have anyone you want."

I whisper in his ear, "I just want you."

He kisses me again, tilting his head to deepen it. All the nerves in my body light up. He licks my lower lip, and if he's trying to make my head spin so I'll agree with him, it's working.

Our breaths mingle, and we're so wrapped up in each other that everything but Nash fades from my mind. Our investigation, Cowling and Kaylor and the rest. That keeps happening with Nash. Like there's a gravity between us, pulling us together and leaving the rest of the world behind.

We're on the second floor of an anonymous hotel, and nobody but Tonya knows exactly where we are. I'm sure she's not telling. There's no way we can solve this mystery tonight. But we can get lost in each other. We can make sure this is a night we won't forget.

Who knows how many we'll get to have?

As good as he looks in this sweater, I want it off. I tug the fabric over his abs, revealing the hard planes of his stomach. I drop forward to run my nose along his trail of hair. The sensation makes us both shiver.

I can't imagine anyone being sexier than Nash.

He tugs off his shirt. I lift my arms, and he pulls off mine. I sink into his arms, our bare stomachs pressed together. We kiss and touch. Fingers brush teasingly over skin.

I kiss my way down the center of his chest, into the hollow between his pecs. My teeth bite gently at his hardened nipples. I feel his cock straining at the fly of his jeans.

I reach for the button. Pop it open. A second later, I've got his zipper down. But he stops my hand.

"Uh, uh," he says. "I'm in charge here. We're doing this at my pace."

"Feeling bossy, are we? What do you want, Sergeant?"

"I'll show you." His left arm traps me around the waist, and he flips me onto my back. Somehow, he has my jeans open and down my legs without any help from me. Seems like he's getting efficient working with one arm.

Nash throws my jeans to the floor, then sits back, looking down at me. There's fire in his whiskey-brown eyes. So much heat as they move over me. My nipples bead against the translucent pink fabric of my bra.

"I love these," he breathes, fingertips touching the pink ruffled trim of my matching panties.

I had these packed in my overnight bag. Guess my subconscious was feeling optimistic about this trip. "I like being girly."

"You ever wear these under your uniform?"

"Sometimes. I wore them to SWAT training once."

He groans and cups his erection through the denim. "Now you're just teasing me."

"Guess you'll never know for sure."

Nash flicks my bra straps over my shoulders and yanks the fabric down. He dives onto my breasts, sucking one nipple between his lips, then the other. At the same time, he tugs at my panties, sliding them over my hips.

"Mine," he whispers. "Tell me this is mine."

My eyes flicker closed. "All yours."

Nash works his way down my body until he's between my

legs. He pushes my knees open and kisses a line along my inner thigh, inching closer and closer to my center.

I'm panting with anticipation. His beard tickles my inner thighs.

Finally, his tongue flicks over my clit, and I cry out, grabbing for his hair.

I can't believe I get to have Nash this way. His mouth and hands all over me. Driving me wild.

Nash licks and sucks at my folds. His tongue dips in and out of my pussy, his whiskers rubbing my thighs. It's so good it makes me delirious, pushing me right to the edge of my control. I'm moaning and yanking his hair at the roots.

I come so hard it steals my breath. Convulsions rocket through my body. But I want more. I don't want Nash to ever stop making love to me. I want him to feel this intensity. To know, bone-deep, that he needs this as much as I do.

He stands and strips off his jeans and boxer briefs. Nash crawls onto the mattress and kneels over me. His cock juts out, bright red and engorged. "Touch me," he rasps. "I'm so fucking close."

I lick the palm of my hand, adding that to the precome leaking from his tip. My fingers wrap around his thick shaft, and I jack him tight and fast.

In seconds, his cock swells in my grip. He growls, his mouth a sexy snarl, and ropes of his release spill onto my stomach and hand.

Nash falls forward over me. I pull him down the rest of the way.

"I'm crushing you."

"I like your weight on me."

"There's a *lot* of me on you."

I grin. "I'm not complaining." We both need another shower, but I'm in no rush. Keeping eye contact, I suck my thumb into my mouth, licking it clean.

"Gonna make me hard again."

"You say that like it's a bad thing."

"I'm older than you. I need to catch my breath." Nash dips his head to suck the skin at my neck. "I'll be right back."

He returns with a warm washcloth. Nash wipes us both off and tosses the cloth into the bathroom.

Then he snuggles up with me under the blanket. I draw lazy circles on his back with my fingertips. Part of me wishes we never had to leave this bed. We could exist in this moment, where almost nobody knows where we are and we have no responsibilities.

Of course, Nash loves his daughter, and I care about Emma too. And there's my family, my friends...an entire life that existed before Nash eclipsed the rest of my world.

I want *both*. Everything I was before him, and everything I feel with him here.

I don't want to spoil this moment. But there's something I have to ask him. "Are we going to tell people about this? Us?" I told Jake, but my brother doesn't really count. I mean everyone else.

A lot of people assume we're together, but that's different from confirming it. That's going to have consequences. For our families, our careers. But if Nash says no, he doesn't want to tell anyone? That'll have consequences too. For me.

I'm brave enough to admit, at least to myself, that I've fallen for him. He says he cares about me too. But I don't really know what that means.

He blanches, but only slightly, then recovers with a kiss to my temple. "I want to be with you. I don't want you to be my secret."

"But what about Emma?"

This time, Nash goes quiet. And my anxiety increases with each moment that passes in silence.

30

Nash

W hat do I tell Emma? The very subject I've been avoiding.

I've been worried about my daughter rebelling, but really? It's me who's broken every rule I set for myself. Putting Emma and my responsibilities first... All of it has paled compared to what I feel for Madison.

But when I think of confessing that to Emma, my insides shrink away from it. I remember the hurt in her eyes, the accusations dripping from her words.

I hope you and your secret girlfriend have a great Christmas all by yourselves, without me, just the way you want it.

I love my kid. I don't want to hurt her.

I don't want to hurt Madison either.

I wipe a hand over my face. I'm not good at these things. Navigating these nuanced emotions, even my own. When I'm operating, I live by orders. Intel. My trust in my teammates. My world narrows to what's in my scope.

But my relationships at home have always refused to fit into the narrow boxes I've assigned them. My marriage failed because *I* failed it.

Is the same thing going to happen with Madison?

"I hate it when you go silent on me, Jennings." Madison blinks rapidly and looks away, turning her body to face the ceiling. Her strength and intelligence have blown me away, time and again. But right now, her green eyes are hesitant. Vulnerable.

Suddenly, there's this gulf between us, though our legs are still tangled together beneath the blankets.

I reach out across that space. Her glossy hair slips through my fingers.

"Hey." I cup her cheek so she'll look at me. "I will tell Emma the truth. I'll tell her about us and try to make her understand that it's separate from me being her dad. But can it wait until she's back in West Oaks? I don't want to have that conversation over the phone."

Slowly, Madison nods. "Maybe I should move back to my apartment, though. So you can talk to her and she'll have time to get used to it without me...there."

Fuck, I don't want her to go. I want to keep Madison close. To share the small parts of my days with her, the way we've been doing. But now, I'll get to have all of her. Madison in my arms. In my bed.

"Stay with me until she's back?" That's three weeks from now. I know I'm buying time with shoddy currency. But I'm greedy for Madison. For every moment we can steal together before I figure out how to blend these two parts of me.

From the moment I met Madison in the academy, I've been drawn to her. The night we talked and danced after SWAT training—when we kissed—our attraction was stronger than everything that should've kept us apart.

With every day that's passed since then, our bond has only grown stronger.

I have to believe that, somehow, my daughter will forgive me. What else can I do?

"When Emma's home, I'll talk to her," I say.

I hate that there's still doubt in Madison's eyes.

No matter how I've tried to deny them, my feelings for her keep rising up again. Refusing to be ignored. Now that Madison's a part of my life, I want her with every part of my being. I want something *real* with her.

I press my lips to hers, chaste at first. I feel the tension in her. She's holding back. My tongue slides over the seam of her lips until she finally opens up and melts into me.

"Please?" I say.

"Okay. I'll stay with you until Emma's back. Then we'll see."

"I'll make this work. I promise."

"Then I believe you."

We're still naked, and my cock needs very little encouragement to stiffen up again. "Can't control myself around you."

"You know, you don't really have to."

I kiss a trail down her neck. "Those are dangerous words."

"I told you I trust you."

"I trust you too. I want you. Always."

"Good," she whispers. "I want *you*."

I roll onto my back, pulling her on top. Madison sits upright, straddling me. She leans forward to kiss me, and I cup a round breast in my hand.

She sits up and holds my cock at the base, lining herself up over me. But she doesn't sink down. She swirls her hips instead, teasing us both.

"*Ughn,*" I grunt. I grab her thigh and squeeze.

"Like that?"

She lowers onto my shaft an inch at a time. She has to stop and breathe a few times as her body makes room for me.

I caress her hips and thighs. Finally, she's all the way in my lap. Nothing between us.

The rightness of this moment settles over me.

"Can't believe I've been missing out on this," I say.

"Now we get to make up for it."

"As much as possible."

I grab the blanket and wrap it around Madison's shoulders. She bends over me so we're in a warm, cozy cocoon. Our mouths are greedy, hands all over each other. Madison slides herself up and down my cock. I pump my hips to meet her. Faster. Harder. I lose myself in the rhythm. It's heat and sweat and the smooth glide of our bodies. Everything I want and need.

A coil of pleasure starts in my balls, her tight pussy squeezing my cock until I think I'll pass out from the intensity. We orgasm together, shuddering and swallowing each other's moans.

As we come down, I dig my fingers into her hair, our foreheads touching.

I've never made a relationship work in my life, but I'm going to figure this out. Somehow. I won't accept anything else.

WE'RE TEN MILES OUTSIDE MAMMOTH, DRIVING south along I-395 in a rental car, when Holt calls.

Madison's fingers are twined loosely with mine. I let go so she can answer. "Hey, you're on speaker," she says.

"Are you still in Mammoth?" There's honking, distant voices. Sounds like Holt is outside near a street.

"We're on our way home, and we have cell service at the moment. Have you found anything?"

"Matter of fact, I have. Bennett Security had their research team dig into Landon Cowling's background overnight. They found some very intriguing details that our regular investigation missed. You were curious about Cowling's ties to the Crimes Uncovered blog, I believe?"

Madison gives me a sardonic glance. "You have our full attention."

"Just wanted to make sure. Turns out, Landon Cowling is the founder and sole proprietor of the Crimes Uncovered website. He owns it through a bunch of shell companies. He tried to keep the 'who is' data on the domain anonymous, but Bennett Security tracked it down."

Madison huffs, shaking her head. "Unbelievable. So it was *Cowling* who invented the Slasher nickname? And then, Cowling's own father ends up being one of the victims? What are the chances of that?"

"None that I'm comfortable with," Holt says.

Scenery flies by as I drive. "Have you read the blog posts on the Slasher? They don't sound like the perspective of a grieving son."

"I agree," Holt says. "When you add that to Cowling's inheritance? The money he's making from his book deal? This is starting to give me an ulcer."

Madison chews her lower lip. "Holt, Crimes Uncovered got in touch with Kent Kaylor last year about the Mammoth Lakes break-ins. *And* they've been reporting on the Midnight Slasher from the beginning. What if Cowling wanted his father dead, and this unsolved series of burglaries was the perfect cover?"

The three of us let this sink in.

"Wait, are you suggesting Cowling is the Slasher?" Holt says. "He had an alibi for his father's murder."

Madison taps her fingers on the dashboard. "I don't know *what* I'm suggesting. Not yet. I'm still working it out."

"Can we go to the chief with what we have?" I ask. "It's

enough to raise serious questions. At the very least, about Eugene Cowling's death."

Before Holt can answer, Madison says, "We need more before we go to the chief. Cowling wanted to have coffee with me, supposedly to thank me for helping take down Jeffrey Nichols. I'll meet with him, get him talking."

I grumble under my breath. Madison brought up this idea last night, and I don't like it any better now.

"You can't secretly record him," Holt points out. "That would violate California's anti-wiretapping law."

Madison smiles. "Sounds like Janie's been teaching you things. Good for you, Holt."

"Hey, I knew that one already. I don't want to taint my evidence."

"Neither do I," she says. "I won't record him. I'll just ask questions and listen. He won't be in custody, so I don't have to give him Miranda warnings."

"Can we go back to the part about you meeting with Cowling?" I cut in. *That's* the part I have a problem with. If anyone's meeting with him, it should be me."

"So you can put him at ease with your relaxed demeanor?" Madison says. "You'll get him to open up and tell you his secrets?"

She and Holt are both snickering.

"I can do just fine. What you're both really thinking is that I can't *flirt* with this asshole. But you shouldn't be flirting with him either. Cowling could be dangerous."

"And I'm a cop. I'll be armed, and I'm trained for this."

"I agree we need to talk to Cowling," Holt says. "You two can fight it out and let me know what you decide. I'll be waiting."

He ends the call. The jerk. No fucking help at all.

～

MADISON TAPES THE MICROPHONE JUST INSIDE HER collar. "I get that you'll be listening, but you'd better not storm in until I give the signal."

Like you did when Tonya appeared at the house in Mammoth? I want to ask. But I don't.

"I can behave," Holt says. "But I can't speak for lover boy over here."

I'm scowling at them both, arms crossed over my chest. We're sitting in Holt's truck, which is parked in a public beach lot. In five minutes, Madison will walk across Ocean Lane to meet up with Landon Cowling for their coffee date.

I don't like this. But I've been overruled.

At a gas station halfway between Mammoth and West Oaks, Madison texted Cowling, who promptly agreed to meet. Madison and I drove straight here to coordinate with Holt. We didn't even drop our bags at my house or turn in our rental car at the nearest agency.

We're not going to record her conversation with Cowling, but Holt and I will listen in to make sure nothing goes awry. If Cowling does anything I don't like, I'm charging in there.

Do they think I'm going to hang back if Madison could be in trouble? Not fucking likely.

"Your gun's fully loaded?" I ask.

"Yes, Sergeant. Same as it was this morning. And ten minutes ago when you last checked."

It's not that I don't trust Madison's skills as a cop. I just don't see why she should go in there instead of me. We don't know what role Cowling played in this twisted saga. I've gone up against bloodthirsty terrorists. I've killed more people than I'd like to count. Even with a busted right arm, I'm still a special operator who served with some of the most elite badasses on the planet.

Madison is strong and capable. But I'm sorry, her four years on patrol simply don't compare.

Every instinct in me is screaming to shield her. Protect her. The thought of Cowling laying a hand on her makes me physically ill.

But I'll be cooling my heels in Holt's truck while Madison walks into the line of fire.

This is why you can't date someone in your chain of command. I'm not objective when it comes to her.

Holt tests the listening device. When Madison's ready, she opens the door and hops down from the truck.

I jump out and catch her before she's gotten too far. "Wait."

Madison turns around. I quickly check our surroundings. We're shielded from view by a dumpster and several other high-profile vehicles.

I pull her up against me, laying my best kiss on her. We're talking dip-the-girl back, old-fashioned style. I put everything I feel for her into that kiss. I'm making a wordless promise. I'm going to make this work between us, and I'll be there for her any time she needs me.

Always.

When I set her upright, she's blinking in surprise.

"I'll be listening every second. If Cowling winks at you funny, give the signal. Okay? You have nothing to prove to anybody."

Her lips twitch, not quite a smile. But her eyes go soft. "I'll miss you too, Jennings. I'll see you soon."

Then she turns on her heel and jogs toward the street.

I get back in the truck, slamming the door. Holt's got his elbow resting on the driver's side door, grinning at me.

"So. You and Shelby."

"Can you give me shit for this another day? I'm not in the mood."

"Why would I give you shit? You're technically not her

instructor anymore. If you mean her age, that's nothing but a number. Except for the fact that you're *way* older than me."

"Are you incapable of shutting up?"

"Janie asks me that sometimes. Answer's always yes. But I like this feisty side of you, Jennings. I'll bet Shelby does, too."

31

Madison

The coffee shop is decked out in silver and gold for the holidays. Oversized ornaments hang from the ceiling, and tinsel garlands drape over the windows and the coffee counter.

I walk inside, running my fingers through my hair as I glance over the customers.

Landon Cowling is already at a table. He smiles at me, standing up. He's wearing a button-down white shirt and a pair of khakis. Thick-framed glasses dominate his face, giving him a nerdy vibe. But the guy must work out. His frame is all lean muscle. He's not bulky and tall like Nash, but Landon moves like someone who's comfortable in his body.

"Officer Shelborne. Can I get you something to drink?"

"A latte would be great. And you can call me Shelby. Or just Madison."

He grins, adjusting his glasses. "Madison. And you should call me Landon."

I imagine Nash's face as he listens to this. I have no doubt he's scowling. It sometimes annoys me when he's overprotective, but that's just who he is. And really? Nash isn't wrong about Landon Cowling. It's entirely possible the guy is dangerous. At the very least, he's been lying about his true affiliations.

Now that he's standing in front of me, I'm not sure what to think.

Landon orders two lattes, and we sit at a corner booth. "Thanks for meeting with me. It's been a while since I asked the victim resource officer to pass on my message. I thought you weren't going to get back to me."

"I wasn't sure if I should." I sip my latte, glad to have something to keep my hands occupied. "But I really am sorry about your father. That must've been terrible, losing him that way."

"It has been, yes. My dad was my best friend. I moved in with him when his health worsened. I'm a web developer, so my work is flexible." Cowling's eyes glisten. "We weren't that close when I was younger, and I was so grateful to have that extra time with him. Before the end."

"Are you still living in the same house?"

"I am. It's been difficult to be there after what happened. But Dad wanted me to keep the place. It's full of so many memories of him."

He's laying it on a bit thick. But it's hard to get a read on him. Is his grief authentic, or just an act? "I can imagine."

"It's a relief to know his killer is dead though. I couldn't sleep at night when the Midnight Slasher was still out there."

I swear, that was Cowling's official quote from the ten o'clock news. The anchors had it on replay. *I can't sleep at night while the Slasher is still out there.*

"That's why the mayor had to take action," I say.

"That's right. Thank goodness he did." Cowling smiles at me, taking a drink of his coffee. Christmas music plays in the background.

Cowling's foot brushes mine beneath the table, and I

draw back. I'm not scared of this guy, though. I don't know if it's the holiday bustle of the coffee shop or Cowling's demeanor. I'm getting sleazy vibes from him, not vicious killer.

Yet if I've learned anything on patrol, it's that outward appearances don't always match the cruelty that people are capable of.

Did this guy actually have something to do with his father's death?

"Why did you want to get in touch with me?" I ask.

"I wanted the chance to thank you. Jeffrey Nichols would still be out there hurting people if it wasn't for you."

The hidden microphone scratches at my neck. "I wasn't the one who fired on Nichols. That was Nash. Sergeant Jennings."

He glances into his coffee cup. "So I heard."

"But you didn't get in touch with the sergeant. Just me. I was curious why."

Cowling shrugs. "You seem easier to talk to."

I can't disagree with that.

"But I'm curious about something as well," he goes on. "Why you got back to me now, after weeks have passed."

I flutter my eyelashes. I'm not above it. But I'm glad Nash can't see. "I saw the news. Your book deal?"

"I thought that could be it." Cowling shifts forward, elbows on the table. "I'd love to interview you, quote you in the book. I'm imagining a whole chapter about what happened at the Hanson house, and your help with that would be amazing. But I'm not doing this for money, just so you know. I want the real story to be told. After losing my father, I couldn't get straight answers."

I mirror his posture, leaning forward, even though I'd rather not get closer. "That's why you went on the news and spoke to the media? Why you came to the mayor's press conferences?"

"Yes. Exactly. I just want people to know what happened."

"What *did* happen?"

He gestures at me, his hand almost brushing my elbow. "You must know more than I do. Since you're in West Oaks PD. And you were there that night. When Nichols died." Cowling shudders, but the movement is too much. He's putting on a show. I'm sure of it.

Just how much is he hiding? Is it the truth about the Crimes Uncovered blog, or far more?

"I do know a lot," I say, "but not everything. I've been mostly off duty after being wounded and because of the internal use of force investigation. There are some things I don't get. Like, why did Jeffrey Nichols choose to come to West Oaks? He had no ties here, as far as I'm aware."

"That's an interesting question."

"And how exactly did he choose his targets? Was it just random, or more planned out? Do you think your book will talk about that?"

"I assume so."

"You'll have a co-author, right? California Crimes Uncovered?"

Cowling's throat works as he swallows a gulp of coffee. "They've done a lot of reporting on the Midnight Slasher."

"You're interested in true crime?"

"Sure. A lot of people are interested in true crime."

My finger draws a circle around the rim of my mug. "You're not just interested, though. You own the website."

He makes a choked sound. Coffee dribbles from his mouth, and he wipes it away.

"Why didn't you mention that to the detectives?"

His coughing morphs into a nervous laugh. "Is it so important? I guess I wanted to be a cop when I was younger, but I got into the journalism side of it." He licks his lips, glancing around at the other patrons. "Why are you asking me about this?"

"I'm just trying to understand where you're coming from. Your side of the story."

"My side? My side of what?"

"The book deal. That's what we've been talking about, right?"

"Sure." Cowling's shoulders relax slightly.

I give him my warmest smile. "I'm in law enforcement for a living, but we have so many rules we have to follow. I admire what you're doing with the Crimes Uncovered website. Going deeper, asking the tough questions? I can't say this officially, but between you and me, it's people like you who keep this system honest."

"Thank you. I appreciate that."

Things were getting tense for a moment, but now Cowling's defrosting. Letting his guard back down.

Exactly what I want.

Now, I'll get to why we're really here.

"Since we're speaking candidly," I say, dropping my voice, "I'll tell you what I really think. There are plenty of unanswered questions about the Midnight Slasher case."

He leans toward me again. "Such as?"

"The Mammoth Lakes connection. I've wondered about that."

"Mammoth Lakes?"

"The Midnight Slasher was active there ten years ago. Did you know that?"

He looks thoughtful. "If there's a connection, I expect I'll look into it when I'm researching the book."

"I've already been looking into it." I glance left and right, as if I'm checking who's listening. "That's why I went to Mammoth Lakes this weekend."

Cowling's pupils dilate. "You and Sergeant Jennings went there?"

I keep myself from reacting. But inside, everything's gone cold. I feel the comforting weight of my Glock against my lower back, underneath my sweater.

"How'd you know Jennings was with me?"

He bats his coffee cup from one hand to the other. "Just that you were wounded together, and I saw you both at the press conference. I assumed you were close." He's smiling, but I don't miss the sweat beading at his temple. The jump of his pulse at his neck. "What were you doing in Mammoth?"

"We went to see Kent Kaylor. Do you know who that is?" I move slightly closer, and Cowling inches back an equal amount.

"Not familiar with the name."

"Kaylor believes the Midnight Slasher rented the house next door to him ten years ago," I say. "He thinks the Slasher stole a knife from his shed. And you know what else Kaylor told me?"

Cowling's gaze is locked on mine, though he keeps shrinking back.

"Someone from Crimes Uncovered came to see him last year," I murmur. "Was it you?"

"I...don't remember."

"If I show Kent Kaylor your photo, will *he* remember?"

His face goes pink. "Maybe it was me. I talk to a lot of crime victims, police, witnesses, you name it. About all kinds of incidents. It blurs together."

"I'm sure. But here's what I don't get. When the Midnight Slasher started his home invasions in West Oaks, the pattern matched the one from Mammoth Lakes perfectly. Yet you claimed you didn't realize the Slasher had been active before."

"I *didn't* know."

"But your website posted about the Mammoth burglaries last year. Did you write those articles?"

He sucks in a breath, and his eyes break from mine. He looks around like he's hoping for an escape. "I don't remember every post."

"You seem to have a faulty memory."

He says nothing.

"But it gets even stranger, doesn't it? Because then your father happens to become one of the victims. He was also the only one to die of his injuries."

Cowling jaw shakes. "I don't need a reminder of that."

"Did you know about your father's heart condition?"

"His health wasn't great, but…"

"Did you realize after your father's death that your blog had already written about his killer? That the man you called the Midnight Slasher had been active ten years before in Mammoth Lakes? I guess you must have. Because you wrote those two articles."

"It wasn't me."

"Wasn't you who wrote the posts?"

"I…"

"Or, it wasn't you who hired Jeffrey Nichols to kill your father?"

32

Nash

The cabin of Holt's truck is so quiet, I can hear my own heartbeat in my ears. The only other noise is the faint background of the coffee shop coming through Madison's microphone.

"How'd you know Jennings was with me?" she asks.

Cowling knew that Madison and I were together in Mammoth Lakes. How the hell would he know that unless he was the guy who shot at us?

Hell, no. I'm not just going to sit here.

I've tried to stay calm and let Madison handle this. And I'll readily admit, she's got some interrogation skills. Cowling doesn't have a clue that she's spun a web around him. He's already trapped. Madison's pushing him hard, and the guy is bound to give more away. But when he realizes she's outwitted him? When he tries to force his way free?

I push the truck door open.

"Jennings," Holt hisses at me. "Get back here. If Cowling sees you—"

I slam the door and jog across the street.

There's a couple heading into the coffee shop, and I duck

behind them. The door jingles as we enter. I join the line to order.

Madison and Cowling are in a corner booth, bent close together. Close enough the guy could reach out and grab her throat. Acid churns in my stomach.

Madison has her back to the wall, the more defensible position. She's got a view of the rest of the shop. I keep my head down, but she doesn't look up and spot me. I can't hear the transmission from her microphone anymore, and Holt's stayed outside.

Sticking my hands in my pockets, I leave the coffee line and stroll around the edge of the shop like I don't have a care in the world. A couple of women glance up as I pass. I keep a neutral expression on my face, slumping my shoulders to minimize my frame.

I slide into an easy chair and pick up a forgotten copy of the LA Times. I'm glad that I'm just a few steps from her. But if I could have my way, I'd have Cowling sighted in my scope. The chair has its back to Madison's table, and I can hear her and Cowling's conversation.

"But your website posted about the Mammoth burglaries last year," Madison says.

"I don't remember every post," Cowling responds. He sounds agitated.

Customers mill around the coffee shop, and my eye roves over them as I listen. One of the women I passed a moment ago lifts her head. She sees me looking and smiles.

She gets up.

Shit. Don't come over here to chat. If Madison hears my voice, she'll know what I'm doing.

Meanwhile, I can hear Cowling's agitation increasing. "I don't need a reminder of that," the man says.

"Did you know about your father's heart condition?"

"His health wasn't great, but..."

The smiling woman has almost reached me. I bow my head, pretending I don't see her. *Abort. I wasn't flirting with you.*

"It wasn't me," Cowling says tightly.

"Wasn't you who wrote the posts?" Madison asks.

And here she is—the woman from across the coffee shop. "Excuse me. You look so familiar. Didn't I see you on the news? Or…"

At the same moment, Madison says, "Or, it wasn't you who hired Jeffrey Nichols to kill your father?"

My eyes dart away from the flirty woman. I twist in my seat, checking Madison's table.

It's just in time to see Cowling explode.

He leaps up from the booth. Both coffee mugs topple, milky liquid sloshing across the table. "Kill my *father*?" His eyes are wild with panic and rage.

"I know you did it," Madison says.

Cowling's hand shoots out and cinches around her upper arm.

I launch out of my seat, brushing past the woman who's trying to talk me up. There are shocked gasps all over the coffee shop. In a split second, I've got Cowling's arm wrenched behind his back.

"Keep your fucking hands off of her," I growl.

He twists in my grip, whining and collapsing into himself. "Ow! That hurts, man!"

"Nash." Madison stands with her arms crossed. She doesn't look thrilled to see me. "What happened to waiting for the signal?"

"The guy grabbed you. Wasn't that enough?"

"Enough for me to arrest him for battery on a police officer. But I don't need your help with that."

I loosen my grip on Cowling's arm, but only slightly. "Let's go," I tell him. "You're under arrest. Like she said."

"BATTERY ON A POLICE OFFICER MIGHT BE A stretch," Holt says.

We're standing in Holt's office at the station. Cowling's being booked as we speak. He didn't put up much of a fight when Holt cuffed him and pushed him into the back seat of the truck. But Cowling didn't spill any further details about Jeffrey Nichols or the Midnight Slasher, either.

"It'll keep him in custody overnight," Madison says. "We can question him more. Put pressure on."

"Sure. But I have the feeling Cowling will lawyer up quick."

Madison sinks into a chair by Holt's desk. "I'm sure video evidence of his arrest is already circulating, thanks to Nash's theatrics." Her eyes glitter with amusement.

"Hey, Cowling was causing a scene on his own," I say.

"Yeah, but the entire coffee shop wasn't staring at us until *you* rolled in, busting out submission moves with only one working arm."

"The two of you are cute together," Holt says, "but let's focus on logistics. Because any minute, Chief Liu is going to hear what we've been up to. He's going to want explanations, and let's face it, you didn't get much out of Cowling at the coffee shop."

Madison scoffs. "I tried to push him, get a reaction, and I succeeded. He's hiding things about his father's death."

"And he knew Madison and I went to Mammoth together," I say.

She nods. "We should check his alibi for the weekend. Find out where he was."

I meet her gaze. "You think Cowling was the one who shot at us?"

"The guy seems like a coward face-to-face, but he'll lash

out if he feels cornered. Cowling could've tracked us there and gotten scared of what we'd find."

Holt rests his weight against his desk. "We can request a CDR from his cell carrier to see if Cowling was in the Sierras over the weekend. Same with Geo-fence data. But we'll need a subpoena or a warrant, and that's a big *if*."

This conversation is taking me back to my academy days. A CDR—Call Detail Record—shows a phone's location at a particular time. Geo-fence data will list all cell phone numbers that were in a defined location. Either one could prove that Cowling was in Mammoth Lakes when we were. Assuming he had his phone powered on.

Holt rubs his eyes. "Shelby, you accused Cowling of hiring Jeffrey Nichols to kill his father, and it's an intriguing theory. But what do we have to back it up? So far, we've got mysteries upon mysteries, leads that go nowhere, and fewer answers by the day. And I'd love to not get fired over this, if I can help it."

"Might be asking a lot," I mutter, and Holt fixes me with a smirk.

"Jennings, I'd think you'd be worried about the same thing."

He's right. I don't want to get fired either. But I've made my choice already. I'm sticking with Madison to the end of this, wherever it leads.

"If we're going to the chief," Holt adds, "we need a coherent theory."

She points at the whiteboard on Holt's wall. "Would you like to do the honors?" she asks him. "Or can I?"

"Go right ahead. If you've got a theory that can make sense of this mess, be my guest."

She grabs a blue marker, yanks off the cap, and starts writing names and places in seemingly random spots on the whiteboard.

Mammoth Lakes

West Oaks

Kent Kaylor

Steven

Eugene and Landon Cowling

Jeffrey Nichols and Thomas Lipinski

The Midnight Slasher

Then, in the center of all this, she writes *California Crimes Uncovered* and underlines it twice.

"The only thing we've found that ties all the major pieces is the Crimes Uncovered blog," she says. "Here's what I think happened. Landon Cowling wanted his inheritance. He had a brilliant idea—have somebody break in to his dad's house and terrify his father so badly his weak heart couldn't take it. Landon himself would make sure he had an alibi."

I see where she's going with this. "But he worried he might still be a suspect," I say. "Because of the inheritance. It's an obvious motive."

Madison points the marker at me. "Exactly. But Cowling, true crime fan that he is, also owned the Crimes Uncovered website. It wasn't popular, probably wasn't making any money. He wanted to get rid of his father *and* give Crimes Uncovered a bigger claim to fame. He already knew about the unsolved burglaries up in Mammoth Lakes. Sounded like a perfect M.O. to use on his father. Plus, Crimes Uncovered would get much-needed attention for reporting on it. He just needed someone to play the burglar."

Holt crosses his arms. "And to target other houses first to make it believable. Enter Jeffrey Nichols?"

"We don't know yet where Cowling met Nichols," Madison says. "But somehow, Cowling ended up hiring him."

"And Nichols agreed to this scheme?" Holt asks. "Slashing people with a knife? That's extreme."

"But Nichols had a history of violent crimes using guns,"

I say. "Maybe he wouldn't have chosen to use a knife on his own, but if Cowling requested it? Some people are just that cold-blooded if it means making money. Targeting houses in West Oaks netted Nichols a lot of jewelry and cash."

"We assume," Holt says. "We didn't find any jewelry or cash at Nichols' house in Los Angeles. But go on."

I shake my head. That's another tidbit we didn't know—and another weakness in West Oaks PD's case against Nichols. But maybe Nichols stashed the money somewhere else.

Maybe Cowling has it.

Madison paces across the small office. "Nichols begins his burglary spree, as inspired by the old crimes in Mammoth Lakes. Meanwhile, Cowling plays it up on his Crimes Uncovered blog to make sure it gets plenty of attention. He invents the 'Midnight Slasher,' driving West Oaks into a frenzy. Then his father dies, according to plan, and Cowling demands justice. But...Nichols doesn't stop. He brings in his brother to target the next house. Or maybe Cowling encouraged it. He liked reporting on the Slasher."

Holt chews his lip as he considers. "Cowling couldn't have expected you two to stumble on Nichols and his brother in the act at the Hanson home."

"True," Madison says. "But for Cowling, it was a perfect stroke of luck. Nichols and Lipinski both dead, unable to point a finger back at Cowling. The book deal was probably just icing on the cake. I'll bet Cowling intended for the Midnight Slasher case to remain unsolved. That might be the only part that didn't work out for him. A book about an unsolved case could sell better than one with all the answers. But now? Cowling can't afford for anyone to question whether Nichols was the same burglar as the guy in Mammoth Lakes. He's strategized himself into a nice, tight corner."

And that would provide a motive for Cowling to follow us. To run us off the road and try to kill us.

It could fit.

But it's a complex, tangled story. And there are still loose ends.

"Who was Steven?" I ask. "Who really committed the Mammoth Lakes crimes?"

Madison shrugs. "We might never know. That man could be dead or in a different state by now. It's the West Oaks crimes we're responsible for solving. Maybe Jeffrey Nichols really *was* the West Oaks Midnight Slasher. But Cowling was the brains behind the entire plan."

Her theory makes more sense than anything else we've got. Gotta say, seeing her at the whiteboard is hot. She has a bit of a teacher thing going. I don't mind sitting back and being the student for once.

I must be smiling, because she asks, "Something to say, Jennings? Do you have any better ideas?"

"No, ma'am. Just enjoying watching you work."

"You weren't saying that in the coffee shop."

"I don't like seeing you in danger, and I'm not going to stand by while someone hurts you. You want me to apologize for that?"

The look she gives me could melt all the snow in the Sierras. "You could make it up to me some other way."

Holt groans. "Enough with the mating dance. Shelby, your theory is solid. The problem is, we have barely a shred of proof to support it. I'll question Cowling and see what I can get out of him. And maybe the Geo-fence data will fill in some gaps. I'll keep you posted. But until you hear from me, please tell me you'll stay out of trouble."

Madison grins at me. "We can keep ourselves busy."

I'm liking the sounds of that.

33

Madison

*A*fter leaving Holt's office, we walk out to the station parking lot. We get in the rental car, but Nash doesn't start the engine yet. My head falls back against the seat, eyes slipping closed.

I've been wired since the coffee shop. But now, all that tension is bleeding out of me.

"How are you feeling?" he asks.

"Like we might've solved the case." That isn't the same as proving it. But knowing what really happened? It's a relief.

There wasn't truly a Midnight Slasher in West Oaks at all. It was a fiction created by Landon Cowling and Jeffrey Nichols, working together. Even if there's still a lot more we don't know, this part feels true.

Now, Nichols is dead and Cowling is in custody. At least for tonight. I'll sleep soundly. Especially because I'll be in Nash's arms.

"You mean, *you* solved it." Nash reaches for my hand and squeezes it. "You did great today. You're going to make a hell of a detective someday, assuming you want it, and you'll be running this place."

"Maybe."

"You don't believe it?"

"Who knows." I roll my head so I'm facing him. "What if I want to try for SWAT again?"

"Then you will, and I'll be rooting for you. Even if I'm not your sergeant."

"Don't you want to be my sergeant? You like being the boss."

"Hell yeah, I do." Nash leans in to kiss me.

We really shouldn't be doing this here. Anyone could walk across the station parking lot and see what we're up to. Holt knows about us, but that's not the same as announcing it to the entire department. Lia has already voiced her disapproval, and she's a close friend. What's everyone else going to say?

But when have I ever been able to resist Nash?

I grip his shirt and open to his kiss, savoring him for a few more seconds.

Then I pull back, licking my lips. I joked about joining SWAT with Nash, but we both know that isn't possible. His arm might not heal the way he needs it too. And if it does and he goes back to being a tactical sergeant, I can't be in his chain of command. Not if we're together.

"You okay?" he asks.

"Thinking."

"About the coffee shop? How I didn't wait for your signal before charging in there and making a scene?"

"Not really." But it's a little about that. "I know I freaked out in Mammoth after we were attacked. If I'd been with Holt or some other coworker, I'm sure I would've hidden that better. But it was *you*. When it comes to you, I can't seem to keep a professional distance."

Even in the academy, it was that way. The man just does something to me.

"I have the same problem. I'm not objective when it comes to you." His fingers brush my cheek. Tingles spread through me.

"I just don't want you thinking I'm weak or that I need my hand held." Part of me is still trying to prove I'm good at this job. My parents don't quite believe it. When Nash charged in today and dealt with Cowling, it felt like he was saying he didn't believe in me either.

"I don't think that," he says. "If I was going into battle, I'd want you on my team. Maybe I'd take you under my wing for some special ops training first…"

I nudge his shoulder playfully. "Always lording that over me. *SEAL this, SEAL that.*"

"But I want you with me," he finishes. "If we have to face something, I'd rather we do it together."

Ugh, he's getting romantic on me. The ultimate trump card. "I guess I can work with that." I indulge in one more slow kiss.

Nash starts the car.

"Your place?" I ask.

"Yeah, let's head home."

Home.

I've been living at Nash's house for about a month, but now, everything's changed between us. When we left for Mammoth, I was just a houseguest. Now…am I his girlfriend? We haven't even used that word.

There's so much we need to work out. I'm staying with him until Emma's back, but what then? Nash said he'd take care of it, but what does that mean?

Thank goodness we have several more weeks until that happens.

We stop at the grocery for some dinner supplies. When we get to Nash's street, he drives by and around the block, casing the place to watch for anything suspicious. But everything seems normal. No unusual cars at the curb, nothing amiss about the house.

"Looks okay," I say.

"Good thing." Nash laces our fingers together. "Because I have plans for you the minute we get inside."

"You going to make your caveman noises?"

He grunts and scowls, and *ugh*, does this man turn me on. I need Nash's arms around me, his mouth on mine, and the knowledge that we're safe. We're home. For however long this version of "home" lasts. Maybe we haven't settled everything yet, but we're together. After all we've been through, we deserve to enjoy that.

We park and grab our bags and the groceries.

The moment we're in the house, we drop everything on the floor. Nash pushes me against the closed door, fusing our mouths together. I shove my hands under his shirt.

There's a noise, and I realize it's the warning sound on Nash's alarm system.

"Shit." He hurries to the panel and types in the passcode, disabling it. We almost set it off.

"Would've been awkward if someone from West Oaks PD showed up, and we were half naked in your bed," I say, smothering a laugh.

"Only half naked?"

I shrug. "You're right, not realistic. Also, I don't think we'll make it to your bed."

We collide and stumble across the great room, knocking into furniture. We're too busy making out to watch where we're going. He grabs my ass with his left hand, squeezing hard enough it almost hurts.

I recall the weeks I spent with Nash in this house, wanting him so badly but thinking I'd never have him. All the things I imagined us doing. I plan to act out every fantasy.

Starting with me on my knees for him, right here in his kitchen. I'm going to suck him down my throat until his eyes cross.

He's got his back to the granite-topped island. I unzip his fly and slide my hand down his pants. Nash moans into my mouth, bracing his hand behind him on the countertop. My fingers wrap around his cock. He's rock hard, burning hot against my palm.

I don't have a clue we're not alone until a voice shrieks, "*Dad?*"

34

Nash

$\mathcal{M}$y daughter is standing a few yards away in our kitchen. And Madison's got her hand down my pants.

Shock and mortification infuse my body. Instantly, I spin to face the kitchen island. "Emma, what—what're you—" My fingers shake as I adjust myself and zip up with rapid, halting movements.

Fuck. Fuck. *Fuck*.

"What're you doing here?" I choke out.

"What am *I* doing? What about *you*?"

I turn around. Emma's blushing from the neckline of her black T-shirt to the two buns in her hair. She's pressing her lips together so hard they're white. One fist clutches the band of her headphones.

Madison stands off to one side, arms wrapped across her middle.

"You're supposed to be in France!"

Emma scowls. "And you said you weren't dating Madison!"

I dig my fingers into my hair. "This isn't how I wanted you to find out."

"Didn't want me to see you and Madison going at it? Yeah, I'd bet not. I need to scrub my eyeballs with soap. Sorry I interrupted. I'll go, since you clearly don't want me here."

"Em, you told me you got on the plane!"

"Then I guess we're both liars."

"You'd better start fucking explaining," I say. The initial shock is wearing off, and now I'm pissed. Why isn't Simone freaking out? Unless she knew. I only got a single text from Simone, saying she was glad I wouldn't be alone for my surgery.

Was *this* what my ex meant? She thought our daughter would be with *me*?

If Emma didn't get on the plane, where has she been the last two days? Has she been here alone?

"I don't owe you an explanation. I don't owe you *anything*. This is such bullshit." Emma storms toward her room.

"Excuse me? Get back here, young lady."

"No one says 'young lady' anymore."

"I don't care! Sit the fuck down and explain yourself."

She glares at me as she throws herself onto the sofa. "I didn't get on the plane because I felt bad about what I said to you. I made all those accusations about you and Madison, and when I was in the airport, I calmed down. I thought, gee, maybe I'm being unfair to my dad. Shows what an idiot I am."

"How did you get back here?"

"I took an Uber. I put it on your credit card."

I groan, closing my eyes. She rode with some stranger all the way back to West Oaks? Some stranger who'd know exactly where she lives?

I glance around for Madison, but she's disappeared. I'm

nervous about how she's reacting to this, but I can only deal with one thing at a time.

"Why didn't you tell me?" I ask.

Emma shrugs. "I lied because I figured you'd be mad, so I decided to surprise you. Like some stupid little kid." She points at the corner, and I finally notice a Christmas tree where there wasn't one before. With ornaments I don't recognize.

"Where did this stuff come from?"

"I bought it online. You never put up a tree or anything."

"Emma…"

Tears well in her eyes. "I get it. You don't want me here, Dad. Just let me go to my room. Please."

Dismay overtakes me. I can keep yelling and insisting I'm right. But my kid is sitting here about to cry. Because of *me*.

I scrub my hands over my face. "Let's back up. Okay?" I sit on the couch beside her. "I didn't lie to you about Madison. This thing between us is new."

"You felt something for her before. I could tell."

"I did. I *do*. But until this weekend, I'd decided nothing was going to happen with her."

"Why?"

"A lot of reasons. Part of it was…you."

She's blinking back tears again. "So you decided to be with Madison in secret. Just like I thought."

"No, that's not it. I planned to tell you when you got back from your trip, but *not* like this."

She looks away from me, her jaw set.

"Em, you mean everything to me. I love you so much. I would *never* want to hurt you."

"Am I *really* that important to you, Dad? Because it doesn't feel like it."

When she was a kid, I wasn't around. She's right about

that. But for the past few years, Emma has been the *most* important part of my life.

Now, I have someone else I care about too. But my responsibility to Emma and Madison isn't equal. My daughter is supposed to take precedence, isn't she? Over my career, over anything else that might come between us. That's why I left the Navy. That's why I've put almost the entire rest of my life on hold while I tried to make up for the ways I've failed my family.

I've tried to do the right thing. And I've still managed to mess up at every turn. Is it because I didn't sacrifice enough? Didn't rid myself of every selfish desire?

There's a fist squeezing my heart in my chest. It's everything I know I'm supposed to do. My duties and obligations. My responsibility as Emma's dad. As Sergeant Jennings.

And Madison's on the other side. From the moment we met in the academy, she's been on the other side of every duty I owe. First, I was married. Then I was her instructor.

Madison. This incredible, beautiful, strong woman. Who makes me smile. Who draws me out of my shell. Who makes me want to break every rule if it means I can be with her.

This is where I'm supposed to give her up, isn't it?

But I can't.

"You *are* that important to me, Em. I love you. But Madison's important to me too."

"Do you want to be with her? Just tell me the truth."

"Yes," I murmur. "I do. But I need you in my life too. I need you both."

A tear rolls down Emma's cheek. "And you think I don't want that for you? That's the kind of daughter you think I am?"

I open my mouth, but nothing comes out. That's not what I expected her to say.

Emma gets up from the couch, facing away from me. "Do

you know why I chose to stay with you when Mom left for Europe earlier this year?"

"So you wouldn't have to leave your school and your friends."

"No. It's because, if I left, you wouldn't have anybody. *That's* why I didn't get on the plane to see Mom two days ago. I yelled at you about Madison, and then you said you weren't spending the holidays with her. And I felt so awful. I thought you were really going to be alone on Christmas. Alone when you had surgery. I told Mom I couldn't go to France, and I came home. I stayed here for you." She shrugs. "It seems stupid now, but it made sense to me at the time."

"Em. You shouldn't miss out on things because you're trying to take care of your dad. That's not your job."

She spins around, fury in her features. "You always say that. You don't tell me things because you think I can't handle it. And that's why it hurt my feelings that you told Madison about your surgery, and not me."

"I thought you might've been jealous."

"Maybe I was, a little bit. You wouldn't let me take time off school to help you recover, but you let Madison move in with us. You told her about your surgery and talked to her about what you were investigating. But the problem isn't Madison. It's that I want to know what's going on with you. And if I can help you, I want you to let me. Dad, if you're happy with Madison, I'm glad for you. You deserve that. But I want to be a part of your life, too. I want to be included."

All I can do is stare at her.

She hasn't said any of this to me before.

My kid is a heck of a lot more mature than I've been giving her credit for. But this has been my problem for a long time, hasn't it? Holding myself back and not opening up to the people I care about. I want things to be different with Emma. It still goes against my nature to lean on her. To let her take care of me. But she's telling me this is what she needs. Am I going to keep refusing?

"I can try to do that," I say.

"You're the most amazing person I know." Emma sticks out her tongue like this admission makes her gag. "You can do anything, even talk to me. I believe in you. Insert other inspirational phrase here."

I chuckle. "Thanks for the pep talk."

She shrugs, toeing at a piece of tinsel on the rug.

"I'll talk to you more," I say. "And I'm sorry it took me this long to understand how much you need that. But I'm still not okay with you lying to me and ditching your flight." A flight that cost me and her mom a lot of money, but I'm not going to mention that. "Please tell me you didn't have any parties here while I was gone."

She rolls her eyes like I'm the most absurdly impossible person she's ever met. "Does this place look like I had a party? I haven't left the house, and I kept the security alarm set except for when I was bringing online orders inside. I haven't even gone to see my friends. I've just been Face-Timing them. And mom."

"Does your mom know you were here without me?"

"Uh, no. Because she'd flip out like you did."

Glad to know I'm not the only overbearing parent. "Can I have a hug?"

She wraps her arms around my neck, resting her cheek against my shoulder.

"We're okay?" I ask.

"We're okay." Emma sniffles, but she's got a tentative smile. "I guess I should apologize to Madison for things that I've said. Like on the way to the airport."

"Yes. You definitely should."

"But if you can ask her to never mention what I saw a few

minutes ago, I'd appreciate it. I'm going to scrub that from my memory."

"That sounds about right to me."

"I'm glad it's Madison though. I could imagine someone a lot worse than her. Like my geometry teacher." She shivers.

"Your geometry teacher, who's seventy?"

"I said that would be worse! But not because of her age." She shrugs. "It's because she makes us listen to opera in class and smells like blue cheese."

I smile and shake my head. "You don't think Madison's too young for me?"

"Madison's not that young. She's great and all, but I still had to explain to her who Charlie D'Amelio is."

"Who?"

She pats my cheek. "Exactly, Dad. Exactly."

35

Madison

I'm sure I've had more embarrassing moments than this.

I just can't remember a single one right now.

While Nash and Emma are arguing, I slink toward the back door. Neither of them notices me leaving. But I can't just stand here while they talk about me, and I certainly can't speak up either. I need to stay way, way out of this conversation.

I close the door as quietly as possible. Nash's backyard has a patio and planting beds along the fence. Emma told me once that they've been planning a vegetable garden, but haven't gotten around to it yet. Everywhere in this house, there are joint father-daughter projects. Evidence of the life they've built, of what they mean to each other.

And now, they're inside fighting. I guess their relationship wasn't perfect before I showed up, but have I helped matters?

How did this happen? Emma wasn't supposed to be back in West Oaks for weeks. I wasn't ready to face this, but more importantly, Nash was nowhere near ready. That was probably the worst way it could've gone. And I'm nervous what Nash will do as a result.

Should I go somewhere else for a while? Head back to my own place? That's what we agreed. Hell, it was my idea. Maybe it would be easier for them if I'm not here.

But I'm not ready to give up yet.

Instead, I sit in a sunny patch of grass and take out my phone. I think about calling Lia, but there might be an "I told you so" in her tone, even if she'd never say it explicitly. I'm not sure my other friends will be sympathetic either. *A guy with a teenage daughter? What did you expect to happen? That she'd welcome you as her new best friend and start planning her dad's wedding?*

There's only one person I can think of who's always understood me. I pull up his number, and Jake answers the video call.

"Hey, sis."

"Hey. Is this a good time to talk?"

"For you, always. What's wrong?"

Of course he can tell. Jake knows me. He's the first person I called when I decided to apply to the police academy. I'm the first person he went to when he found out his wife—now ex—was pregnant with twins and he had an existential crisis.

"Emma didn't leave for France after all. And she just walked in on Nash and me."

"Oh, damn. In a compromising position?"

"You guessed it. She didn't know about us before. Not the best way for her to find out."

"How compromised are we talking?"

"We still had clothes on. But my hand was…busy."

"Ugh. Jeez, I'm sorry. That sucks."

"It certainly does."

"But it's not as bad as when mom walked in on me and

that girl from across the street in high school. Not a stitch of clothing in sight."

I grimace. "Wait, do you mean *Harper*?"

He nods ruefully.

Jake and Harper Kendrick were tight before she moved away to parts unknown. "I've never heard this story."

"Because it's horrifying and traumatizing. For mom and me both. Anyway, my point is, it sounds like your surprise interruption wasn't as bad as that."

I glanced at the back door. I can still hear raised voices. "Emma might disagree. Horror and trauma may be exactly how she describes it."

"I'm sorry, Mads. But it'll get better. You just have to ask yourself if Nash is worth going through the hard stuff."

I don't hesitate a second. "Yes."

"Then you have your answer."

I guess I do. I just hope Nash feels the same about me. "If you're so wise, why are you still single?"

"Oh, did you miss the part where I have twin five-year-olds? And a demanding job? My life is nothing but hard parts. No woman is willing to put up with this."

"Then you haven't found her yet."

"Or I did, and I missed my shot."

"Way to be positive. Who are these women who got away? Do you mean Harper Kendrick?"

"I don't know." He laughs. "You've got me all philosophical. And that leads nowhere good."

"Come on. I need to hear about your mistakes to make myself feel better."

"You'll have to settle for funny stories about the twins."

I grumble like I'm annoyed, but really, I'm happy to hear about my niece and nephew, and whatever craziness they're up to. I lie back in the grass, closing my eyes as I listen to Jake.

The snick of the back door opening makes me turn my head. It's Nash. He closes the door behind him and sticks his hands in his pockets, his eyes sliding away from me.

My stomach drops. I dread what he needs to say to me. But I'd rather hear it now than drag this out.

"I gotta go," I say to my brother. I lower the phone, my thumb hitting *end* on the screen.

Is that what I should say to Nash too? Should I put him out of his misery and offer to leave, so he doesn't have to ask me?

Nash walks over and holds out his hand. He helps me up.

I'm holding my breath.

Then he cups my face, drawing me closer. "I'm sorry about earlier," he murmurs. "I was afraid you'd left. Was about to jump into the car and chase you down."

"That would've been tough, if I'd taken the rental."

"Then I would've run down the street after you."

He kisses me. It's soft at first, as soft as a whispered apology. But the heat between us builds, as it always does. Our lips slot together and hold. I feel his reluctance when he pulls away. But his hand stays on my cheek, keeping me there.

"Emma's okay?" I ask.

"She'd like to talk to you. But she asked if you could avoid the subject of, you know, what we were doing when she walked into the kitchen earlier." Red inches up his neck into his cheeks.

"That will not be a problem. Collective amnesia it is."

He nods, exhaling. "She's going to make some food. Don't know about you, but I'm starving. We skipped lunch to deal with Landon Cowling. Up for an early dinner?"

"I could eat," I say. Even though my stomach is still tying itself into knots. "Do you want me to stay here tonight? Or will it be—"

"Please stay." Nash brushes a kiss over my nose. "Emma and I both want you to stay."

That's exactly what I was longing to hear.

NASH HOLDS MY HAND AS WE WALK INSIDE. BUT when we reach the kitchen, I gently let him go. I'm relieved that Emma has calmed down, but I don't want to push my luck.

She's spreading tortilla chips on a baking tray. "Nachos?" I ask.

"Yep. My dad's favorite. You liked the ones I made before, right?"

I slide onto a barstool. "With the green chilies? Yeah, those were amazing."

Nash kisses my head, then says, "I'm going to unpack my bag from this weekend." His footsteps recede.

Now it's just Emma and me. I'm not sure if I should make the first move. Or even how.

"He thinks he's so subtle," Emma says.

I remember sitting in this kitchen on the day I arrived here. Weeks ago. That day, Emma asked me point-blank if I was hooking up with her father. I told the truth when I said no. But I did want him.

Does she think I seduced him? That this was my plan all along?

"I never wanted to come between you and your dad."

"I know. That isn't the kind of thing you would do." She opens the bag of shredded cheese and sprinkles it over the chips. "I'm sorry about, um, the shrieking…"

"It's okay," I rush to say. "I understand." Emma doesn't want to relive those details, and neither do I.

"But it's not okay how I acted." Emma turns to face me,

leaning against the stove. "My dad... He always thinks he has to give things up for other people. But I don't want him wasting away like it's his duty to be miserable just because he was gone when I was a kid and couldn't work things out with my mom. I've never blamed him for that. I want the chance to know him *now*. And more than anything, I want him to be happy. Around you?" She shrugs. "He's happy."

"You think so?"

"Trust me, I know him. He's much easier to deal with when you're around. Way less grumpy."

I smile. "Don't tell him, but I like when he's grumpy."

"Then you're both weirder than I thought. But weird can be good." She studies me a moment. "Are you serious about him?"

"Is this the third degree? Does overprotectiveness run in the Jennings family?"

"My dad would say he can take care of himself. But I have my doubts."

I look down at my hands. "I'm serious about him. I've never felt this way about anyone else. But if he needs someone to take care of him, it should be a joint effort. You and me both." When I lift my eyes, she's beaming. And the tightness along my spine finally unwinds.

"You're right," she says. "It'll take us both to manage him. I need you to run interference for me when I'm going out with my friends. Think you could get me a later curfew?"

I hold up my hands. "You're on your own there."

"Madison, come on," she begs. "I'd like you sooo much better if you could talk my dad into one a.m."

"Not falling for it."

When Nash returns to the kitchen, the cheese is melted, and Emma and I are laughing over a TikTok video on her feed. "Dad, you have to see this!"

He grabs a nacho. "Nope."

"Madison is way more fun than you."

"I know that. Everyone knows that." Nash gives me a crooked half-smile, sliding his arm around my waist.

We eat standing at the counter. Emma keeps scrolling through her phone. Then she gasps. *"Dad.* Seriously?"

"What?" Nash asks.

"Bridget just sent this to me. What the heck?"

She shows us the screen. It's a video of us from that afternoon at the coffee shop.

Oops.

The Nash in the clip wrenches Landon Cowling's arm behind his back. *"Keep your fucking hands off of her."* Cowling struggles and protests.

"This looks worse than it was." Nash scratches his head sheepishly.

Emma narrows her eyes at her father. "Really?"

I knew people were filming at the coffee shop, but I still hoped this wouldn't be all over social media. If the chief and the mayor hadn't heard about Cowling's arrest before, they probably know about it now.

"Bridget Hanson sent you this?" I ask. "How's she doing?"

"She's okay, but don't change the subject, Madison. What happened?" We don't respond right away, and Emma scowls. "Isn't this the guy who was at that press conference? The Midnight Slasher killed his father? Why was he bothering Madison?"

"You sure you want to hear this, Em?" Nash says. "It's upsetting."

"I'm almost sixteen. You said you'd tell me things."

He still looks doubtful, but I nod. Emma's going to hear about it through the news anyway. She should get the truth from us.

"You wanted to know before if the Slasher is dead," he says. "It's a more complicated question than we realized."

Nash starts with Jeffrey Nichols. Then the mysterious casefiles showing up in my purse, which led us to Mammoth Springs and Kent Kaylor. Emma listens, rapt.

Nash downplays the shooting incident. But when he mentions us getting snowed in, Emma's face turns beet red. I've got my fingers pressed to my lips, trying not to laugh.

She's fifteen alright. She can guess where *that* part of the story led.

Nash skips ahead to our suspicions about Landon Cowling. "Madison figured out the rest of it." He gestures for me to take over.

"We found out that Cowling owns California Crimes Uncovered," I say. "*And* he had motive to kill his father. We're still trying to prove it, but it's possible Cowling hired Nichols. The whole 'Midnight Slasher' thing was a charade."

"Bridget is not going to believe this!" Emma starts texting.

I cover her hand with mine. "Whoa, hold on. You've still been talking to her about the Midnight Slasher?"

"The same people who broke into her house were the ones who hurt you guys. We talk about it all the time." Emma's face pinches. "Who else would get it?"

I share a glance with Nash. We can understand a bond forged by a traumatic event better than most.

"But news like this could be hard for Bridget to hear," Nash says. "That someone else was responsible for what she went through."

"Bridget's a lot stronger than you think, Dad. We *both* are."

"But you're still my little girl."

She makes noises of protest, but she lets Nash hug her. She holds him tightly in return.

Emma goes back to texting after that, while Nash and I sit in the kitchen holding hands and stealing kisses. It's such a simple moment, but I can't stop smiling. I can imagine lots more days like this. The three of us together, doing nothing in particular.

"Are you happy?" he whispers to me.

"Yes. Are you?"

"More than I've ever been."

Emma looks up from her phone. "Bridget and I are going to meet up with some other people. Toby's going to give us a ride."

"If you're back by ten," Nash says.

"But Dad." She tilts her head and flutters her eyelashes beseechingly. "Can't I have until midnight? You'll have more time with Madison."

I cover my laugh.

"Where are you going to be?" he asks.

"We're going to Chad's house."

"In that case, make it nine."

"Dad! Madison, can't you do something with him?"

"What if your friends come over here instead?" I suggest.

Nash and Emma both eye me. I don't think either of them is thrilled with this idea. But Nash nods his head. "Sure, why not? Invite your friends here."

"Really? You hate when I have people over."

"No, I don't."

This is obviously a lie. Emma's eye-roll says she knows that as well as I do.

Nash frowns at us both. "I promise I will be nice around your friends."

"Better yet, could you and Madison hang out in your room?" Emma asks. "And not bother us?"

He's grumbling. I grab Nash by the arm and steer him

toward his bedroom before he can protest any further. "Have fun with your friends," I shout behind us.

We go into Nash's room, and he shuts the door. "I think I handled that well."

"Masterfully." I smirk. "Emma will have a great time, and you won't have to worry about where she is."

"She's had to grow up too fast. So has Bridget Hanson."

"But they have family who love them. And friends. That's what they both need."

I'm glad Emma and Bridget found one another, even if a dark moment forged their connection. They'll be stronger for it.

Just like Nash and me.

Since that night at Bridget's house, our lives have been bound together, to the point that I don't think it's a choice anymore. I couldn't turn away from him if I tried. We need each other.

I need answers, too. I want Cowling to face punishment for what he's done, and I want the world to know who's truly behind the Midnight Slasher's crimes.

But if I have to settle for just one—having all the answers to the mystery, or having Nash—there's no question which I'd choose.

His arm wraps around me and he leans his forehead into mine. "I'm so glad you're here."

"Me too."

36

Nash

I hover by my bedroom door, listening as the doorbell rings and teenage voices start to banter.

"Are you really that concerned about Emma having her friends over?" Madison asks. She's settled onto my bed, looking extremely enticing.

I sit down next to her and wrap my arm around her. My fingers stroke her cheek. "No. I'm just...letting it all sink in."

Even this morning when we left Mammoth Lakes, I didn't think this was possible. Having Madison here with me and having Emma be happy about it. This is a *pinch-me* kind of moment. A chance to fix the ways I've fallen short in the past.

My arm is still a mess. I might never go back to SWAT. But if Emma and Madison are both happy, if they're in my life, does it matter?

What I'm feeling now is more powerful than anything I've experienced, except for being a dad to Emma. That's love, but it's a different species entirely. It seems like there should be a different word for it. What I feel for Madison and what I feel for Emma isn't the same. Yet both are all-encompassing.

I can't lose either one of them, and I have to do whatever it takes to make sure I don't screw it up this time.

Madison rests her head on my chest, nestling into my side. "I was thinking. Maybe I should head back to my apartment tomorrow."

My arm tightens around her. "So soon? Why?"

"That's what we agreed, isn't it? Last night. That I'd go back to my apartment after Emma got back."

"That was supposed to be weeks from now."

Her thumb strokes my shirt over my stomach. "Yeah, but now she's back. And me living here is different from before. With us together. Sleeping in your bed, I assume."

"This is a co-ed sleepover I approve of."

She laughs. "And I like it here. But I have to move out sometime. Right?"

That's what we've both known since the beginning. But now, I don't see the point. I want her with me.

I smooth the hair back from Madison's forehead. "Don't go yet. Stay through the holidays at least. Emma's good with it, as we've seen."

"Since you asked so nicely." She smiles, but that smile morphs into a grimace. "I have to spend Christmas Day with my family though. It's great, actually. I love it. But...would you and Emma want to come along? To my parents' house?"

"Your parents wouldn't mind?"

"Of course not. But make sure you know what you're getting into. It would be with my whole family. Kids and dogs and everything. Would Emma be up for that?"

"My extroverted daughter? Are you kidding? She'd love it. But will your mom be okay with it?"

"The woman runs a catering company. She's the ultimate hostess. She'll make you and Emma feel welcome."

That isn't what I meant. I'm thinking of the Mrs. Shelborne who gave me the stink eye when I was lying in a hospital bed. She was great with Emma, but I don't think Madison's mother is a fan of mine. "What about being okay with *us*? You and me, together?"

"If she's not, she can keep that opinion to herself."

"Will she?"

Another grimace. "Probably not. She always lets me know what she thinks. But Nash, I don't care anymore. I'm so tired of chasing their approval. After everything that's happened?" She shakes her head. "I can't spend my life dreaming that if I find the right job title, they'll be proud of my law enforcement career."

"If they're not proud, I don't get what they're missing. But I'm happy to tell them how impressive you are at Christmas dinner. I was your instructor. I should know."

"Might not help to bring up the teacher-student thing."

"Maybe not. But you have a lot to be proud of. You're a hell of an investigator, and a great cop." I catch her chin with my finger. "You listening?"

"Yes, Sergeant." She's smirking, but her eyes are soft. I'm starting to know Madison's looks, and this one's sincere. She's blinking fast. Like there are tears in her eyes, and she doesn't want to let them fall.

So I kiss her eyelids and her nose, and finally her mouth. Until any trace of tears is gone.

I could fall in love with her so easily. I think I'm already nearly there.

But I can't shake this dread in my gut. This feeling that I could still lose her or Emma. That I can't possibly have both people I care about most and hold on to them.

I'm not pessimistic by nature, but I'm a realist. You have to be, when you've been to war and seen the worst shit people can do. Having something this precious makes me want to shield it. Keep it safe and protected.

Because I know how easily it could all go away.

AFTER A FEW HOURS—AND A LENGTHY MAKE-OUT session between Madison and me—the front door opens and closes, and the voices out in the living room quiet down.

There's a knock at my bedroom door.

"Dad?" Emma calls out.

"Come in," I say, smiling at Madison. Emma's trying to give us fair warning. Madison's got her legs draped over my lap, but she swings them forward as Emma opens the door and peeks in.

Bridget Hanson is right behind her. She waves at us tentatively.

"Can Bridget spend the night?" Emma asks.

"That's okay with me. If your parents gave their permission, Bridget?"

Emma answers for her. "Yeah, Dad. Obviously." She grabs Bridget's wrist. "We're going to bake cookies."

They head into the kitchen, whispering and laughing. Madison and I both get up, and I hook my thumb into her back pocket.

"Sorry, I didn't ask what you thought. Is it all right with you if Bridget stays tonight?"

"Of course it is. But it's not my call, anyway."

"You belong here too. I want you to be comfortable."

"I promise I'm very comfortable." She steps into me, and my hands go to her waist. You would've thought we didn't spend the last few hours kissing, because I can't resist pulling her close and capturing her lips.

Things start crashing in the kitchen.

"If you're going to do that, can you close your door please?" Emma shouts. "We can totally hear your lips smacking. Gross."

There's snickering, which I assume came from Bridget.

"We should probably set a better example," Madison whispers.

"Do we have to?"

She takes my hand, and we wander out into the kitchen. There's flour and sugar and butter on the counter. Emma takes a baking sheet from a cabinet.

"Did you have a good time with your friends?" I ask.

"Yup." Emma exchanges a meaningful glance with Bridget, which looks like the universal sign for *Dads are the worst*.

"Was Chad here?" I say.

"You don't have to say his name all weird like that, Dad. Yes, we had fun. We played video games and stuff."

Madison and I sit down while Bridget and Emma make cookies. Bridget keeps glancing at us before she works up the courage to say what's on her mind. "So you guys are officially together now? You fell in love because of getting wounded, right? It's like fate or something."

"Or something," Madison says, cheeks coloring.

I rest my hand on her leg, trying to hold back my grin.

"Did Emma tell you about Landon Cowling?" Madison asks. "How he was arrested?"

I huff slightly. I don't think she needs to bring that up. But then again, there's no way Bridget missed the video of us in the coffee shop. Emma already said she was going to tell Bridget about it. So I guess Madison is trying to address the subject openly. Exactly what I need to start doing.

The girl nods. "Yeah. It's crazy. Mr. Cowling called my parents a couple times right after the break-in at my house. He wanted all the Slasher's victims to meet and talk about putting pressure on the mayor. That was before the police said, you know, that Jeffrey Nichols was the person who hurt us."

Her eyes dip down as she says this. It can't be easy for her to discuss what happened, and my first instinct is to change the topic. But Emma and Madison would both probably tell me not to do that.

If Bridget needs to talk, we should listen.

"Did your parents meet with Cowling?" I ask.

Bridget shakes her head vigorously. "My dad said Mr. Cowling was just trying to get attention for himself. And maybe get money out of it. I guess that was true, wasn't it? You really think he hired Jeffrey Nichols to kill his father? And do those other things?"

"That's what it looks like," Madison says. "We don't have proof yet."

"But do you really think there was more than one Midnight Slasher?" Bridget's eyes are wide.

"It's possible," I say carefully. "But we're pretty sure that Nichols was the West Oaks Midnight Slasher. It's just that Cowling came up with the idea."

Emma puts her arm around her friend. Bridget scowls at the kitchen counter, tears welling in her eyes. "I don't understand people like that. Who do awful things just to get money. Hurting innocent people."

My stomach burns. I wish I could take her fear away. Hers, and my daughter's too.

Madison reaches across the counter and puts her hand over Bridget's. "I don't understand it either. But there are also people who care, and who want to help."

She glances up. "Like you all."

"Exactly. If you ever want to talk, we're here," Madison tells her.

For a moment, I think Bridget is going to say more. The girl inhales, as if she's working up to something. But then she blinks, and she seems to deflate.

She turns to Emma instead. "Do you need me to mix the dough?"

Emma gives her a tentative smile. "Why don't you add the chocolate chips?"

Madison and I watch the girls scoop out cookie dough onto the tray. Then they set the timer and wander off to Emma's bedroom.

Madison leans into me, her head dropping to my shoulder.

"You're great with Bridget," I say.

"So are you."

"Me?"

"Absolutely." Madison looks up at me. "When things are scary and the world feels out of control, you just get steadier. You project confidence. Trust. Bridget needs that."

I kiss her. Because I can't *not* kiss her. Not now, when I have no reason to hold back.

"She needs someone like you, too," I say. "So does Emma. Someone who can actually talk to them."

She shrugs. "Maybe Bridget will take me up on my offer later. We've got all night."

I nod. "It seemed like she had more to say."

"Right. I thought so too. It's just a hunch, but—" Madison's phone buzzes. "It's Tonya." She answers with a grin on her face, putting it on speaker.

"You missed us already?"

"I'm sorry, Madison," Tonya says in her scratchy voice, "but this isn't a social call. I have bad news."

Madison glances at me with concern. "What's going on?"

"Kent Kaylor is dead."

37

Madison

I jump up from my seat. "Kaylor's *dead*? How? When?"

"We're still trying to determine that. Captain Jack and I were visiting the neighbors, making sure everyone's got their power back and their vehicles dug out. Kaylor's place looked untouched. He didn't answer the door. So I called the sheriff." I hear her swallowing. "They found him on his sunporch. Stabbed. Been dead a couple days."

"That's horrible."

I feel Nash's hand on my arm.

"I'm going to give the deputy your number," Tonya says. "I just wanted to give you a heads-up. They need to talk to you about when you last saw Kaylor. What you spoke about, how you left him."

"Of course." I run through it in my mind. It was two days ago, on the first day we drove up to Mammoth. Just before the storm hit.

Just before that attacker—maybe Landon Cowling—tried to kill Nash and me.

Did he go back for Kaylor afterward?

"I wonder if this could have some connection to that mystery of yours," Tonya says. "The gunman who forced you off the road. Set you running."

"Just what I was thinking." My stomach wrenches, and I stumble on my way to the couch. "We've had some updates in our case here," I say, though my voice doesn't sound as steady as I'd like it to. "We might have a suspect for you. I'll give your deputy the contact info for West Oaks PD."

"I think police here have already been in touch with West Oaks, but you might as well grease the wheels. I'm retired from the force myself, but I'm doing whatever I can to help. We don't see too many crimes like this."

"I'm sorry. If we led the guy up there—"

"It's a terrible shame. But Madison, we don't know yet what happened. If the same madman came after you and then Kaylor, it sounds like the perp was a powder keg waiting to go off. You'd better not be blaming yourself. You just be careful. And stay safe."

Tonya says the deputy will be in touch, if not tonight, then in the morning. Then she hangs up, and I set my phone on the coffee table.

Nash sits down beside me, reaching for my hand. "It's a good thing West Oaks PD already has Landon Cowling in custody."

"Right." The nausea in my stomach increases. "But *was* it him? It's one thing to shoot at a target with a rifle. Another to stab a man to death. Don't you think?"

Nash nods, his gaze going distant. "Yes. The second act is far more visceral. More personal."

I get the sense he's speaking from experience.

"And Cowling hired Nichols to do his dirty work before," Nash adds. "Cowling had never slashed anybody, at least not according to your theory. But there's always a first time. If he got desperate enough?"

"I have to call Detective Holt," I say.

We head into the living room and sit on the couch. It's getting late, but Holt picks up on the first ring. "Shelby. Have you heard?" I've got him on speaker. "A call just came in from the sheriff in Mammoth Lakes."

"Kent Kaylor is dead. Yeah."

Nash stands up, crossing his arms. "Holt, it's Jennings. Anything on Cowling's whereabouts over the weekend? Did you get the Geo-fence data?"

Exactly what I was about to ask. If police can link Cowling's cell phone to the Mammoth Lakes area, then it'll be a key piece of evidence against him, and not just for the attack on Nash and me.

"Look," Holt says. "I was going to update you both, but this is the first chance I've had. It *wasn't Cowling.*"

My eyes fly to Nash as shock takes over my system.

"Cowling's lawyer gave us access to his phone GPS voluntarily after I asked some probing questions. Cowling was in West Oaks. He hasn't gone anywhere."

"Do we have corroboration of that?" Nash asks. "We can't just accept—"

"He also provided a credit card receipt from a restaurant Saturday night. The night of the storm in Mammoth. There's no way Cowling was up there."

"But then who the hell shot us?" I say. "Who killed Kaylor?"

"It's still possible Cowling hired someone to go after you. We think he hired Nichols, so why not someone else? But that means this hitman is still out there."

My mind is spinning. The answers I thought I found are now up in the air again. Thank God Emma's here at the house. If she wasn't, I'm sure Nash would be out the door already, tracking her down.

"I've gotta go," Holt says. "The police from Mammoth are calling again."

"Wait," I say. "Did Cowling give you anything else when you questioned him? Any hint that we're right about him?"

Holt sighs. "If the guy was lying, he's a great actor. He would have to be in order to orchestrate this entire scheme. But we don't have enough to keep him in custody past tomorrow morning. The battery charge is a misdemeanor. He'll be released. Now, I've really gotta go."

I curse and set down my phone.

"Dad?" Emma asks. "Madison?"

I look up and find Emma and Bridget standing in the great room, watching us. I wonder how much they've heard. Dammit, I didn't think about that when I put Holt on speaker.

Emma looks like she's about to cry. But Bridget looks even worse. It's like she's turned to stone. Her face is a mask of utter shock.

"Dad, somebody shot at you in Mammoth Lakes? And murdered some witness?"

Nash stands up. "We didn't want to frighten you."

But Emma backs away from him, wiping roughly at her eyes. "You told us the Midnight Slasher was dead."

"And that's still what we think," Nash says gently. "I told you about Landon Cowling. We think he's behind it, but the police are investigating as we speak. They're going to figure out what really happened."

"Dad, I'm scared."

He pulls Emma into a hug, and she clings to him.

I walk over to Bridget and put a hand on her arm. "Are you all right?"

She's gazing into the distance. "You and Sergeant Jennings were in Mammoth Lakes this weekend?" she asks softly. "Someone...shot at you?"

"That's right. But like Nash said, the police are investigating. You don't need to worry."

I feel like an idiot saying that. Of course, Bridget is worried. This must be terrifying for her to hear. For the past month, she's been living with what happened to her, praying that it was really over.

She's just learned that it's not.

Honestly, I'm just as freaked out. But I'm a trained police officer. I'm better equipped to handle it. Bridget is just a kid, and it isn't fair that she has to deal with this.

Every bit of color has drained from Bridget's face. "I'm not feeling that well."

Nash lets go of his daughter. "Bridget, maybe I should take you home for tonight. We'd love to have you another time."

"Dad, no!" Emma protests.

Bridget doesn't say anything. She just goes to Emma's room and emerges with her backpack. She's still got that shellshocked expression.

Nash grabs his keys and squeezes Emma's shoulder. She flops down on the couch, dropping an arm over her eyes in dramatic teenager fashion. I feel for her. Tonight was supposed to be fun, and now it's deadly serious.

"I'll be right back," Nash says, fitting a ball cap onto his head.

I grab his elbow before he can leave. "Check on Bridget," I whisper. "I don't think she's handling this well."

"I will. And I'll let her parents know what happened. I'll see you and Emma soon." He kisses me on the cheek. But just before he leaves, a thoughtful look crosses his face. He goes into the bedroom, and when he comes out, I can tell he's wearing his gun holster under his jacket.

Nash opens the door, and Bridget walks out first. He smiles at me once more as he heads out. "Lock the door behind me, okay? I'll be back in a few minutes."

And then, he's gone.

38

Nash

I jump into the rental car, and Bridget slowly gets in beside me. She sets her backpack between her feet on the floor.

The engine roars to life, and she jumps slightly.

I might not be able to read my daughter perfectly, but I can tell when something's wrong. Bridget is giving off those same vibes. Shoulders tight, head bowed, arms wrapped around her stomach.

I pull away from the curb. "There were a lot of developments today. This news about Cowling and Kaylor."

"Yeah," she says quietly.

"I hope you'll talk to your parents about it. Or Madison. Or me."

"I know. I bet you don't want me talking to Emma about it."

Guilt twinges in my chest. "I didn't mean that. But an adult might be a better option. Whatever you're feeling, it's okay. We want to help."

Bridget looks out her window instead of at me.

We're rolling steadily down the street. The clock on my

dash says it's nearly midnight. A few houses on my block still have lights on, but most are dark.

"Do you need my address?" Bridget asks.

I smile ruefully. "I remember it." It would be hard to forget.

She grimaces and shakes her head. "Sorry. I forgot for a minute. I'm...kinda distracted."

"Do you want to talk about it?"

Her expression is pensive. She doesn't answer.

I wish she and Emma hadn't overheard that phone call. I thought they were in Em's room with music playing. But I'm coming around to Madison's point. The girls are old enough that it's better to give them the truth. It saves a hell of a lot of headaches. Plus, it's the right thing to do. I see that now.

As much as I want to protect my daughter, it's just not possible. Not entirely. All I can do is be there when she needs me.

I'm not Bridget's father, and I don't have any right to make decisions for her. But I want to be here for her if I can.

The tires roll over the asphalt. Streetlights glow as we pass them, and I see people moving around in lit-up windows.

Bridget's face is in shadow.

I think she isn't going to answer my question. But then her small voice fills the silence of the cabin. "Emma's friendship has really meant a lot the past few weeks."

"I'm sure it has. I'm glad she was there for you." I might've been nervous about their connection before, but I'm speaking sincerely. "And your friendship means a lot to her. Any time you want to come over, you're welcome. Tonight was just—"

"I get it," Bridget says. "You want to be with your family, and that's Madison and Emma."

Damn it, that guilt is rising higher in my throat. I wasn't

trying to push Bridget away. I was trying to do the right thing, taking Bridget to *her* family. "If our positions were switched, and Emma was at your house when she got this news, I'd want your dad to bring her home. I'm sure your parents will feel the same."

She's still staring listlessly through the window. "Emma's lucky to have a dad like you."

"I'm not so sure she would agree with you, but I appreciate you saying that."

Bridget shifts slightly, turning her shoulders toward me. "No, Emma says that all the time. She was really scared when you were injured."

"I hate that I frightened her. But I'm relieved that Madison and I were there for *you* that night. That's our job as police officers. And we'd do it again. No matter what."

"You're not afraid of getting hurt again?" she asks.

"No. Not if it means saving someone else."

I glance away from the road, and Bridget's eyes finally lift to meet mine.

We turn onto the boulevard, and the sidewalks glow yellow in the wash of artificial light. There's more traffic. Red brake lights, and pedestrians heading out to bars and clubs for the night.

A familiar strip appears up ahead. The sign for the Shore Lounge blinks in blue and green. It's where Madison and I had drinks with the other trainees on that night a month ago. When all this began. At least, when it began for me and Madison.

Like it's fate or something, Bridget said in the kitchen.

It does feel that way now. I've never believed in things like fate before. But how else can I explain this connection between Madison and me? Like we were meant to collide that night. Like two stars trapped in the same orbit, destined to meet by an invisible gravity. To be there for each other.

And for Bridget.

There's a honk behind me, and I realize I'm stopped at a green light. I accelerate, and the Shore Lounge passes us by.

Two more streets, and I turn onto Bridget's. More memories appear out of the ether.

Searching for Madison after our disastrous kiss. Seeing her frozen in the middle of the road.

Burglary in progress.

"Emma and I didn't know each other well before all this happened," Bridget says. "We had history together last year, and English Lit this semester. It was like we knew of each other, but our groups didn't really overlap. You know?"

"Sure."

"But then, after that night, when Nichols and Lipinski broke into my house and you and Officer Shelborne saved me, Emma DM'ed me. A lot of other people did too, but she's the only one I responded to. Because *you* were her dad. I know it sounds weird, but it made me feel like, in a way, you were my dad too. Like you were watching out for me. If I knew Emma, that meant you were still nearby. And that meant I was safe."

I'm surprised by her sudden rush of talkativeness, but I'm also touched. "It's not weird. We find different ways of coping. Don't we?"

I remember how Bridget reminded me of my daughter when I first saw her tied up. Nichols standing over her, the vicious gleam of the knife. I've never felt the slightest remorse about putting a bullet between his eyes. I would've done the same if I were protecting my own daughter that night.

I've never thought about it, but it does make sense that Bridget experienced something similar. Identifying me with her dad once she learned I had a kid in her class.

I see Bridget's house just ahead, and I pull up to the curb.

I don't see any lights on inside. Maybe her parents are already asleep. I wonder if I should've called ahead. Let them know we were on our way.

The last time I saw this house, I'd just carried Madison and Bridget's brother outside. I was nearly delirious. My body was in shock.

The engine's still running. I reach to put the car in park, and my right arm aches.

"But you have your own dad, too," I say. "I know he wasn't there that night, but I'm sure he wants you to come to him about stuff like this. He wants you to feel safe." That's the impression I got when I saw her father at that press conference, anyway. A guy who worried he had failed his family and wanted to make up for it.

Or maybe I'm just projecting my own past failings onto him.

My mind wanders for a moment until I realize Bridget hasn't responded.

"Don't you think your dad wants that?" I ask.

"Sort of. He used to. My dad always made me feel safe when he was around. My real dad, I mean. He died." She shrugs. "My stepdad is okay. But it's not really the same."

I twist to see her better. "I didn't know that. I'm sorry. So it was your stepdad at the press conference?"

"Yeah. My mom wants me to call him Dad, and I do. But…"

"But what?"

"It's just not the same."

My eye is pulled toward Bridget's house. All the windows remain dark, just reflections of streetlights and the night sky. But the shape of the house pulls more images and impressions from my memory.

My right fingers twitch, remembering how I squeezed the trigger. The loud pops and the jarring impact when the gunshots hit me. But even worse, seeing the trail of blood when Madison slid down the wall to the floor.

I blink, pushing the images away.

Madison is home with Emma. They're safe. But adrenaline courses through me all the same.

Suddenly, I want to get out of here. I want to see Bridget safely with her family, and I want to get home to mine.

I switch off the engine. Go to open the door. But Bridget speaks up again.

"Have you ever realized things aren't the way you believed? And you're not sure what to do?"

I'm unsettled by this new subject. I want to ask what this is really about. But if Bridget is anything like my daughter, she needs to tell me at her own pace. I just have to let it play out.

I settle back into my seat.

"I think so. Going through trauma changes you. Changes your brain. It takes time to adjust to that." I'm not thinking of trauma in my own life, exactly, but I've faced my own revelations. It's not easy to re-order everything. To know how to move in a different direction.

"That isn't what I mean. I don't mean...what happened to me. Not exactly."

Impatience seeps into my veins, but I hold it at bay. "Can you tell me more about it, then? So I understand?"

Her next sentence is a whisper. "I'm afraid to."

39

Madison

I let Emma pout a few more minutes after her dad and Bridget leave. Then I walk over to the couch, grab her wrists, and pull her up. "Make hot cocoa with me."

She groans, standing. "Whatever. I guess." But she gets more enthusiastic as we take out supplies and heat the water. Emma piles a few fresh-baked cookies onto a plate.

"Should we eat the rest before your dad gets home?" I ask.

A smile pulls at her mouth. "Nah, I'll save one for him."

"What a good daughter you are." I wink at her.

Emma grabs a cookie and nibbles the corner. "This has been one of the weirder days I've had," she says.

"Me too. But that seems to happen when I'm around your father."

She scrunches her face up, turning contemplative. "What's next on your investigation?"

"I think your dad and I are officially out of it. The detectives at West Oaks PD and in Mammoth Lakes are taking over."

"Are you just saying that because you still don't want me involved in your case?"

"I'm really not."

I don't know what to think about the latest news. I still think Cowling is guilty, but how many other people are involved in this? Is there another Jeffrey Nichols doing Cowling's bidding? It gives me the creeps.

I locked the doors after Nash left, you can count on that.

But at this point, what would be the purpose of Cowling sending someone after us again? We've shared everything we know with the police.

"I showed that video of you in the coffee shop to Bridget and my friends," Emma says. "I know my dad was stomping around being the hero, as he does, but you must've really pissed off Cowling on your own. You were meeting him to get evidence? That's so badass."

"Not sure I got anything useful though."

Emma spoons cocoa mix into both of our mugs. "You still did it. I freaked earlier when I heard about the guy shooting at you and my dad when you were in Mammoth. But you confronted Cowling *after* that. Weren't you worried?"

"Not much. He wasn't going to surprise me again. We were in public, and I had my weapon. And...your dad was nearby. That helps. Even when he's stomping around."

She smiles. "I've thought it could be cool to become a police officer. Investigating crimes and stuff. Maybe you could tell me more about it sometime."

"I'd love to." I know I'm beaming at her, but I don't even try to stop myself. I want to keep this camaraderie going. "How did Bridget seem when she heard what happened in Mammoth Lakes? I thought she was really upset by it, but I don't know her as well as you do."

"Bridget has strange moods sometimes. She gets really

down. So do I, and I didn't even go through what she did."
Emma takes another bite of cookie, brushing away the
crumbs before she goes on. "Bridget told me she saw Dad
carry you and her little brother Stevie out of the house. You
guys were both bleeding, and my dad's arm…" She doesn't
finish, her throat working as she swallows. "It's especially
strange when I'm at Bridget's house, and I think about what
happened there."

"I'm sure." I haven't even thought about Emma going
over to the Hanson residence.

It seems like every time I turn around, there's another
terrible moment rising up to the surface from that night. So
many angles that I haven't even considered. For Bridget, for
Emma. For everyone still being affected in ways I can't even
understand.

Emma's expression has shifted into a frown. "I *hate*
feeling scared. But sometimes…it gets to me."

"I know what you mean."

I've never hugged her before. But this feels like a moment
that she needs one. I circle my arms around her, and she
gives me a tight squeeze before stepping back.

When the water boils, Emma adds it to the cocoa mix,
then drops marshmallows into the steaming mugs.

"How are Bridget's parents handling it?" I ask.

Her frown deepens. "Bridget said they've been fighting a
lot. Her mom Catherine is a nurse, and she gets night shifts
at the hospital. That's where she was the night of the
break-in."

"Right. I remember that." Bridget has mentioned her
mom's demanding schedule before.

"But her mom's been trying to take only day shifts ever
since. I think it's been hard with her work."

"What about her dad?"

"Steve's gone a lot. He's her stepdad, really. Bridget said he's a handyman, and that's how her mom met him. Doing work on their house after Bridget's dad died. A few years back, I think? Bridget said he's okay, doesn't bother her much. Except he likes to go hunting, and she's not a fan of that. Bridget's vegan."

"Hunting?" I ask. "What does he hunt?"

"Deer, maybe? I don't know. But that's where he was when their house got broken into. On a hunting trip."

An image flashes into my mind—a deer trophy hanging on the wall of the Hanson house. I'd forgotten that.

There's a loud bang in the backyard. My spine goes rigid, and I set my mug on the counter.

"What was that?" Emma asks.

"No idea." It sounded like a metal door closing. Could it be Nash? Is he back, and he went into the yard for some reason? But why would he do that?

By instinct, my hand goes to my hip, but I'm not wearing my holster. My gun is in Nash's bedroom with my other things from our trip to Mammoth.

I walk toward the back door. The curtains on the rear windows are open, and I see my own reflection. I cup my hands, pressing them to the glass. It's cold on my skin.

Nothing stirs outside. But a thread of unease moves through me.

Something doesn't feel right. The yard is too dark. There's usually a light beside the garage door. It has a sensor and turns on every evening when the sun sets.

But right now, it's off.

I take the phone from my pocket. Should I call Nash? Or should I go straight to 911?

Am I completely overreacting?

I wonder if Lia or Clint are on duty. If they'll respond and laugh at me for turning paranoid.

But someone drove Nash and me off the road. Stabbed Kent Kaylor.

"What is it?" Emma asks. "Do you see anything?"

"No. But I'm going to call West Oaks PD. I don't—"

Before I can finish, every light inside the house goes dark.

40

Nash

"What are you afraid of?" I ask Bridget.

A tear rolls down her cheek. "I'm afraid to tell anyone. But I'm also afraid *not* to tell. And it's like I'm paralyzed. Like I'm in one of those nightmares where I can't move, but the bad thing could be coming for me. And I can't get away. I don't know what to do."

Dread washes over me.

I look from Bridget to the house. The last time I was here, blue and red lights were splashed across the pale brick facade. But tonight, no other cars drive on the street. No neighbors are walking their dogs or stepping out to smoke. It's as if we're the last people left after everyone else has been evacuated. It's a strange impression, but I can't shake it.

"Are you afraid of your stepdad?" I ask. "Is that what you're trying to tell me?"

She whispers, "Yes."

I don't move a muscle. If I make a single motion towards Bridget right now, I'm afraid she'll jump out of this car and bolt.

"Why are you afraid of him?" I ask gently.

She sniffles. "My mom met him when he answered her ad online for a handyman. He seemed really nice, and she was probably lonely after my dad died. She got pregnant with my baby brother Stevie just a few months later. Then they got married. But even at the wedding, none of his family came. It was like he had no past at all. Or like he didn't want to remember it? I don't know."

"That didn't bother your mother?"

"Back then, I don't think so."

"But now?"

Bridget twists the edge of her sweatshirt in her fist. "My stepdad has always traveled around for his job, doing work wherever it comes up. And when he's not working, he likes to go hunting. Elk and deer, mostly."

"I saw the trophy hanging in your living room."

"Yeah. That's one of his. But my mom, she's been getting madder and madder about how much he's gone." As she speaks, her voice gets quieter and quieter. "Last week, I found her going through his things. A box of old stuff he keeps in the basement."

Unease fills me like a spreading poison. "What did she find in there?"

"I don't know. She didn't tell me. But whatever it was, it upset her. Really bad."

"Did she ask him about it?"

Emma nods. She's quiet for a moment, and it seems to stretch endlessly. Like the silence is echoing. Getting bigger.

"He hit her," she whispers.

Every part of me clenches. I want to track down Bridget's stepfather right now. Make him answer for hurting her mother and frightening this already traumatized girl. He's a fucking coward, not a man.

I'll need to report this to West Oaks PD.

I fight to keep my voice steady. "I'm really sorry that happened. What about you? Has he laid a hand on you?"

"No. That's not..." She presses her fists against her eyes. "That's not what I'm trying to say. Steve has always been distant to me. He's left me alone. That's not why I'm afraid."

"Okay." I keep my tone easy and light, though it goes against every impulse inside me. "Take your time. I'm listening."

I check the house again. Windows still dark. No sign of anyone inside.

More tears roll down Bridget's cheeks faster than she can wipe them away. "This past weekend, Steve went on a hunting trip. But this time, my mom couldn't reach him at all. For like, two days. She was getting really upset. She had to miss a shift at work because she didn't want to leave me and Stevie alone."

I force myself to take a breath in. "Did Steve come back?" I ask.

"Last night. There were scratches and a dent on the front of his car. Like he ran into something. I was too scared to ask him what happened. But he had a heavy winter coat with him. Thick gloves."

The world seems to stop. I'm not breathing.

"Then today, when Emma and I heard that phone call..."

"You mean when Madison was talking to the detective? About the incident up in Mammoth Lakes?"

Bridget goes still. All except the tears that continue to fall. "I don't know what it means. I just don't... I don't understand. Since the break-in happened, I keep asking *why*. Why was it me they chose? Why my house? And now this, and things make even less sense. I just want to know." She looks up at me with her red-rimmed eyes. "*Please*. Tell me what it means. What do I do?"

I don't understand either. But what Bridget's told me is all kinds of wrong. It doesn't fit into what I thought I knew. That must be what Bridget was talking about earlier. That sense that the world has suddenly shifted on its head. And now, I know exactly how she feels.

Steve. *Steven*. Her stepdad's name is Steven. She's mentioned it before, and when Kent Kaylor said that name, I didn't think for a second there could be a connection.

It's a common name. A coincidence.

But the dents on his car? The absence over the weekend?

"Is Steve at home right now?" I ask.

"He's supposed to be, yeah. My mom has a shift at the hospital tonight. My baby brother should be with him."

"Does Steve park his car out here on the street?"

"No, the garage."

"What's his last name?"

"It's Wrey. W-r-e-y."

A dozen possibilities roll through my brain. I have enough probable cause to arrest Steven Wrey on a charge of domestic violence. Anything more is still speculation. *Wild* speculation. So bizarre I can't begin to dream up a theory of how this makes sense.

But the clues we need could be inside that house. Or in the garage.

I look from Bridget to the house, then to her again. "Can you wait here a moment while I go take a look? See if he's home?"

"You're going to leave me here alone?"

"Just for a moment. I need to know if your stepdad and baby brother are in the house. I'll lock the doors to the car, and I won't be gone for more than five minutes."

"What will you do if they're home?" Her eyes are pleading. It took incredible courage for her to tell me what she has. She knows there will be consequences. But she's a kid, and she's still scared about causing trouble.

"I won't approach him on my own. Not yet. But I need to find out if your brother's in the house with him right now. Then we'll figure out what to do next."

"Okay."

I start to get out of the car, but then she says, "Sergeant Jennings?" Bridget digs into her pocket and pulls out a key ring. "Just in case you have to..."

She doesn't finish the sentence, probably because she's not sure where this might lead. I'm not either. But I hold out my hand, and the key drops onto my palm.

"I'll be back in a few." I walk calmly along the sidewalk like I'm out for a nighttime stroll. I go past Bridget's house, pulling my ball cap down to obscure my face as I glance from the corner of my eye.

The windows are still black.

Once I reach the shadows just beyond the house, I melt into the darkness, dashing along the home's perimeter. The windows on this side look equally dead. I reach a gate and pop open the latch, stepping into the back yard. If anybody asks, I'm doing a welfare check on Bridget's stepdad and brother. At her request. She's a minor, but old enough to give legal consent to a search.

There's not even a flicker of light inside. I remember how the TV splashed colors over the walls the night of the break-in. But tonight, the place looks deserted.

It's possible Steven is asleep inside. That's probably my best-case scenario—if this wife-beating asshole is snoozing peacefully with no clue he'll be arrested soon.

But if he's not? If he's already in the wind?

My eye catches on the garage.

Keeping to the shadows, I cross the yard and try the pedestrian door into the garage. It's locked, so I use Bridget's key. I slip inside and switch on the light on my phone.

The place is empty. No car.

I glance around at the shelves, which hold the usual yard supplies and tools. Then a gleam of metal hits my phone-light. I step closer.

It's a rifle round. 30-06 caliber.

Bridget said Steven was out hunting this weekend. Is this all a coincidence? A misunderstanding?

Or is it a hell of a lot more?

I take out my phone to send a quick text to Madison and Emma.

Me: Something came up at Bridget's house. I'll be a bit longer. Keep the doors locked and stay there, okay? I'll see you both soon.

I almost add, *I love you*. Because suddenly, I feel it in my bones. I love them both. But I'd rather say those words to Madison in person.

I need to sort out this mess, make sure Bridget's safe, and get home to them. There's no place else I'd rather be. Home with my girls.

Next, I call Detective Holt. When he answers, he sounds exhausted. "I'm really starting to dread your calls," he says. "What now?"

"I've got a weird theory about who could've shot at us in Mammoth Lakes. But you won't believe it." Not even sure *I* believe it. Because if Steven Wrey shot at us during that storm, he's also the prime suspect in the murder of Kent Kaylor.

Why would Bridget's stepfather have anything to do with all that?

Holt curses as I explain what Bridget told me. Any trace of humor in his tone disappears. "Are you with Bridget now?" he asks.

"She's waiting in my car. I did a walk-by on the house. No

sign of her stepfather here. No car in his garage. But there's a rifle cartridge. If we can get it collected properly into evidence, we could compare it to the ones from the shooting scene in Mammoth Lakes."

"Leave it there for now. I want to be careful." Holt blows out a breath. "This case has been fucked-up from the beginning, but this is going a little far."

"There's more we're missing. All I know is that we need to bring Steven in and get a search warrant for his car and his residence. Right?"

"I agree. I'll look up his vehicle info and put out a BOLO. For now, we'll consider him a person of interest who's potentially dangerous. I'll wait on an arrest warrant for the DV charge until we have Ms. Hanson's statement that he hit her."

"Got it." I leave the garage, closing the door silently behind me. My foot sinks into the grass as I head back into the shadows on the far side of the house. "It's also possible Steven has his infant son with him."

"Shit, that complicates things. I'll put it in the BOLO. I'm sending more units your way. We need to get Bridget Hanson to her mom, and I'll touch base with victim/witness services. I'll see that we offer the Hansons an alternative place to stay."

Holt hangs up, and I head back to the car. Bridget's slumped in her seat, but she jerks upright when I open my door. "Your stepdad isn't here. Do you have any ideas about where he might've gone? Do you have access to the GPS on his phone? Anything?"

"No. Nothing."

I figured it wouldn't be that easy. Holt might be able to get Steven Wrey's phone location, but only if a judge signs a warrant.

Meanwhile, we have no clue where Steven has gone.

This is a high-risk situation. A powder keg waiting for a spark, and there are a thousand different ways this could explode.

41

Madison

*I*n the dark, I hear Emma gasp. *"Madison?"*

"I'm here." I rush toward her voice. I find her and pull her down with me into a crouch. I can barely see her outline. "Where's the breaker box?"

"Out...Outside," she stammers. "The backyard."

I lift my phone and unlock it. The glow from my screen illuminates Emma's frightened features.

No service.

I curse.

"What is it?" she asks.

"Do you have your phone? Do you have service?"

She checks. "No."

Someone's got a signal jammer. This is bad.

"Listen to me. I want you to hide."

"Hide? *Why?* What's happening?"

"I think there's someone in the back yard. They threw the breaker and cut power to the house. I'm going to distract them, and I need you to get as close to the front door as you can. When you hear me shout, leave through the front door.

Run to a neighbor to get help. Try to call your dad. Can you do that?"

"I...think so. Yes. But what about you?"

"I'll be fine. Don't worry. You do your part, I'll do mine."

Her hands are shaking as she holds onto me, but she nods.

"Focus on what I asked you," I say. "Find a place to hide, then wait till I shout. That's when you'll run."

"Okay." She's breathing heavily through her nose. "I can do it."

"I know you can." I squeeze her shoulder and switch off my screen. I don't want the light to attract whoever's out there. We have to assume he can see inside.

I glance back and forth across the living room, keeping in my crouched position. I still can't see anything unusual through the windows. Just a dim nighttime view of the back-yard, the neighbors' houses. The wooden fence that borders Nash's property.

But then, there's a scraping sound. It sets my teeth on edge.

Emma whimpers behind me.

"Hide near the front door and be ready," I repeat. *That's the plan*, I think, trying to channel what Nash might say. I wish he were here. But I'm the only one around to take care of Emma.

I am going to protect her if it's the last thing I do.

Adrenaline infuses my body with energy.

I dash across the room toward the hallway, then stop and listen. Nothing. I hear Emma breathing heavily.

"It's clear," I whisper. "Go ahead."

She crawls across the room toward the entryway of the house.

Glass shatters in another room. Emma screams. "What's happening?"

"Hide," I hiss.

I turn and rush toward Nash's bedroom. I have to get my gun.

But a shape rears out of the doorway, slamming me backward into the wall. My head bounces and my vision blurs. My phone drops from my hand.

"Emma, run!" I cry.

The intruder's wearing all black. I lunge for him, grabbing him by the legs as he tries to get past me down the hall. He crashes to the ground. His boot kicks at me. Makes contact with the side of my head. There's a sharp pain in my ear.

A bright gleam of metal. He's holding a knife. The blade slashes toward me. I roll away, trying to protect myself.

The man scrambles upright.

I haven't heard the door open. Is Emma still here? Has she gotten away?

Two choices. Go for my gun in the bedroom, or follow the intruder. But I don't have time to weigh those options. I don't have a moment to think.

I have to stop him before he can reach Emma.

I throw myself after him, careening down the hall toward the entryway.

Emma's got the door open. The man shoves it closed. She screams. In a second, he's got an arm hooked around her neck. He spins Emma to face me, using her as a shield.

"Stop." His voice is harsh, guttural. "Not another move."

My breaths are loud. My heart's beating so hard, the room pulses in my vision. But my eyes have adjusted enough that I can see.

The terrible image burns into my mind.

He's wearing a ski mask. And he's got a knife pointed at Emma's throat. She's shaking and crying. I want to reach out to her. Hide her away so this maniac can't touch her.

Nash. Where are you?

"Officer Shelborne," the man says. "It's time that we talk."

"Are you working for Landon Cowling?" I choke out.

His eyes are lifeless inside the holes in the mask. "I guarantee Cowling wants nothing to do with me."

"Then who are you?"

"Who do you think?"

"You're Bridget's *stepdad*," Emma cries, struggling against his grip. "I know your voice."

Her stepdad?

His cold eyes don't waver from mine. Keeping the knife on Emma, he uses his other hand to tug the ski mask free. My insides turn liquid.

This is the man who looked so distraught at the mayor's press conference. Brown hair, brown eyes. Average height and build. Yet there's no trace of the worry he displayed at the press conference.

This man's expression is empty. I remember Tonya's words. *There was something off about him. Soulless.*

"I think Officer Shelborne can guess," he says. "I believe Kent Kaylor told you about me? He tried to deny it, but I didn't believe him."

I'm hit with an overwhelming wave of nausea. "You're Steven. *That* Steven."

An average name. He used it back in Mammoth Lakes, too, when he was Kent Kaylor's neighbor. Before he stole Kaylor's knife.

No. No, no, no.

I don't understand. How is this possible?

Steven nods at me as if he's saying, *Go ahead. Tell me the rest of it.* But I can't say it. I don't want those words in my mouth. I'm already trying not to retch.

I thought I understood how it all unfolded. Cowling, Nichols... The Crimes Uncovered blog.

But I was wrong. So fucking wrong.

Somehow, Bridget's stepfather is the *real* Midnight Slasher.

The tip of Steven's knife moves an inch closer to Emma's neck. "Please. Let me go." She wriggles, and he tightens his arm around her.

The fear and panic inside me ratchet upward. I just barely keep myself from lunging at him.

"What do you want?" I cry.

"Information. How much does West Oaks PD know about me?"

"*Everything*. They have a casefile on you. They're tracking your phone and your car. If anything happens to me or Emma, they'll know instantly it was you."

His lip curves up. His smile is as sharp as his knife. But the rest of him just seems *blank*. Like he could fade into the background of any picture. Easily forgotten.

"Then why did you arrest Landon Cowling today?" he asks.

"For assaulting me."

"I saw the video online. The man barely touched you. So that was just an excuse to hold him overnight. What do you really want him for?"

"You talk like you know law enforcement."

"I have some experience."

"Such as?"

"If you want me to answer questions, you'll have to answer mine. An exchange of information."

"Fuck that," I snarl. "I want to know what you really want."

His face stays blank. No reaction. "We're going to wait for Sergeant Jennings to get here. I know he left to drive my stepdaughter home. I saw them leave. I've been watching."

Goosebumps break out over my skin. "And what then?"

Emma trembles and tears gather in her eyes. Steven's knife is just millimeters from the vein at her throat.

"I assume Nash will be armed. I need Emma to make sure he gives up his weapon. And then... I'm sure you can guess."

He'll kill us. And he's being so matter-of-fact about it. The shock steals my breath. This man is the definition of cold-blooded.

"But the waiting will be far more pleasant," he says, "if you tell me what I want to know. And I'll return the favor."

"Don't!" Emma screams. "Madison, don't tell him anything! My dad's going to come here, and he's going to—"

Steven drags the tip of the knife along Emma's chin. She shrieks, and blood wells from the cut.

"No!" I step forward, hands outstretched. "Please, please don't hurt her. I'll talk to you."

He moves the knife away from Emma by a centimeter. Waits.

My pulse races. If I could get my hands on Steven's neck, I'd squeeze the life out of him right now.

Somehow, I need to get her away from him.

"I'll answer your questions," I say. Steven nods, the tiniest smile appearing on his lips. "But you have to take me as your hostage instead of her."

That brief glimpse of a smile disappears. "You're in no position to negotiate."

"And I can't stand here and watch you hurt her," I say through gritted teeth. "I won't be able to think. Let her sit over on the couch, and you can hold the knife on me instead. Nash cares about me. I'm just as good a hostage as she is."

Those lifeless eyes don't shy from me. He stares, making me wait. Droplets of blood slide down Emma's trembling chin along her neck.

"I accept your offer," he finally says. "Stretch your arms

out and walk toward me. If you make a wrong move, you won't like what happens. And Emma, if you try to run after I let go of you, she'll die."

Emma's eyes are wide. "Madison, *no…*"

"Stay still. Okay? I'm doing what he says." I hold my arms out. My foot takes a step. Another. Slowly, I cross the room toward where they're standing.

With a sudden, violent movement, he pushes Emma away and grabs hold of me. Spins me around. The knife presses into my shoulder hard enough to slice through the fabric. I feel the metal tip against my skin. He pulls me closer, and the knife settles against my neck.

Steven is standing behind me, my back to his chest. My skin crawls everywhere he's touching me. I hate that I can't see him. But my nostrils fill with his scent. Sweat and something sour.

"Now it's you and me," he says.

Emma's right in front of me, hands pressed against her bleeding chin. She's crying. Shaking her head.

"It's okay, Em," I say softly. "Sit on the couch. It's going to be all right." I put every ounce of mental energy into my gaze, trying to beam my thoughts into her brain. *I will find a way out of this.*

I have no intention of just standing here and waiting to die.

Emma backs up until she reaches the couch. Then she sits and wraps her arms around her knees, facing me. Her expression turns hard. The tears stop. I can feel her determination as she gazes back at me with an answer to my silent message.

We're in this together.

She's only fifteen, but she's Nash's daughter. She's strong. I nod, almost imperceptibly.

"Ask your question," I say to Steven.

"Why did West Oaks PD really arrest Cowling?"

I breathe out, trying to slow my pulse. Trying to focus. "Because he had a motive to kill his father. We thought Cowling hired Jeffrey Nichols to do it. They created the 'Midnight Slasher' persona based on your crimes in Mammoth Lakes."

Then Steven does something I don't expect. He laughs. It's a belly-laugh, full of genuine mirth. Like he's not the cruel killer I thought. But I guess even a sicko can have a sense of humor.

"And how, exactly, did Nichols end up targeting my house?" he asks.

I'm wondering that myself, because it doesn't make sense. Not one bit. Even if Cowling somehow knew Steven's true identity, why would he send Nichols there?

"Did Cowling want to kill you because you're the real Slasher?"

Steven just laughs. The sound makes my stomach feel like it's turning inside out.

I decide to ask something else. "I know you stole Kent Kaylor's knife. You used it against the victims ten years ago."

"And a good knife it was, too. I was sorry to lose it. Had to get myself a new one."

"Where have you been since you left Mammoth Lakes?"

He brings his mouth to my ear. "That's the answer to everything, isn't it? I don't think you've earned that yet."

"Then...why do you do it? Hurt people like you do? What is the *point* of this?"

The cold metal blade scratches against my neck. I cringe away from it. The blade bites into my skin, and a hot trickle runs down to my collar.

"I do it for the same reason that you and Sergeant Jennings can't escape each other," he murmurs. "An experience like that, it binds you forever to someone. There's always been a part of me that was…missing. This is the only way I've ever found to fill it. A connection to someone that neither of us will ever forget. It's a greater intimacy than anyone who hasn't experienced it can imagine." His lips brush my neck. "Isn't it?"

"That's why you don't kill them. You want them to remember."

"When you hunt an animal, they don't really understand. But a person? They'll carry a part of me forever, just as I do of them. I don't want to sever that connection unless I have to."

Emma's eyes are steady on me. Dark amber, like her dad's.

"What about Eugene Cowling?" I ask. "Was it Nichols who killed him? Or you?"

"The old man…" Steven sighs, as if this topic exhausts him. "It wasn't supposed to be him in the house that night. I expected to find his son."

"Why go after Landon Cowling?"

"I've said enough. It's your turn. Who else did you talk to about me in Mammoth Lakes?"

Tonya. He doesn't know about her. "No one."

"I don't believe that. You and Jennings had to take shelter in the storm. I went back to Kaylor's house. Where did you go?"

"We broke into an empty cabin. The owner was out of town."

"And you spoke to no one else? No one helped you?"

"Nash and I are plenty resourceful."

A pause. Blood continues to seep from the scrape at my neck. I decide to push ahead. "Tell me why you wanted to go after Landon Cowling. Had he already guessed your tie to Mammoth Lakes?"

"You're giving him too much credit. Cowling wrote his

little articles about my time in Mammoth, but when I started hunting in West Oaks, he didn't see the connection. He came up with that stupid 'Slasher' name, trying to take credit for me, and I couldn't let that go unanswered."

"But Cowling hid the fact that he owned the Crimes Uncovered website. How did you know it was him?"

"I've made friends over the years. People who know the less legitimate side of the Internet. They helped me figure out who was behind the website. Cowling was so eager to capitalize on my story that I thought he'd enjoy becoming a real part of it. It turned out his father was inside the house instead, but oh well. One lesson's as good as another."

"But then Eugene had a heart attack."

"It was too bad, because I think Eugene really understood me by the end of our time together. I nearly got caught earning that connection, and he died on me. You would've thought I'd be more careful after what had happened before."

"Before?"

"A mistake I paid for dearly. With eight years of my life."

Eight years? What does that mean? He goes on before I can ask.

"I've been planning to pay Landon Cowling a visit, especially after his book deal announcement. Still trying to benefit from my story. I doubt he's mourned his father at all. But if he goes down for his father's death, that would be punishment enough. Losing your freedom isn't for the faint of heart."

The answer slams into my brain.

"You were in prison."

That's why he knows law enforcement procedures. And it could explain the decade gap between the Mammoth Lakes crimes and now. Just like...

"Well done, Officer Shelborne. After I left Mammoth

Lakes, I thought nobody could touch me. I was overconfident. I got sloppy once, and it cost me. A guilty plea to felony burglary, fourteen-year sentence, released after eight served. But have you figured out the rest of it yet?"

More realizations hit me all at once.

"You knew Jeffrey Nichols," I say, breathless.

Across the room, Emma squints at me. In my head, suddenly everything's becoming clear. There's no way I could've seen it coming, yet I'm sick over all the ways I've gotten this wrong.

"Keep going," he says.

"You met Nichols in prison."

"You're good at this. He was my cellmate for a few years. I've told you, it's a special kind of bond when two people experience extremes together. I told him some of the deepest truths about me. I thought I could trust him. When I got out, I tried to start a new life, new last name. Leave the past behind. I met Bridget's mother here in West Oaks, and she got pregnant."

He pulls me closer, hissing into my ear. "I wanted to stop. I wanted to be *different*."

"But you couldn't."

"I held out as long as I could. The past is never gone, as much as we try to let it go. That craving, it never goes away. I'm sure you're starting to understand that. Understand *me*."

I recoil at the idea that I share anything with this man. But I do need to keep him talking. I have to know the rest.

"You started breaking into homes again," I say. "Cutting people. And Nichols heard about it. He realized it was *you*."

"Nichols got out about a year after I did. When he heard the media talking about the West Oaks 'Slasher' a few months back, he guessed it was me. He decided to take advantage of that. It took him some time, but he managed to

find my new name and my new address. After Eugene
Cowling died, Nichols contacted me. Tried to blackmail me. I
refused to deal. I knew he'd never go to the police. But you
know what he did instead, don't you?"

"Nichols brought his half-brother Lipinski and broke into
your house. Was he looking for money?"

"I assume so. The little brother was upstairs, searching
for cash or jewelry, while Nichols was trying to terrify my
stepdaughter. He probably thought that would pressure me
into doing what he wanted. Nichols thought he had me
under his thumb. He'd use *my* methods against me. But he
never counted on you and Sergeant Jennings turning up. You
probably saved Bridget's life that day. And you saved *me*. I
was grateful. Nichols became the Slasher in my place, and I
was going to move on to a new hunting ground. I never
would've touched you if you'd left the rest of it alone."

But Nash and I questioned the official decision that
Nichols was the Slasher. We were right. Even if that knowledge is no consolation.

"You followed us to Mammoth Lakes," I say.

"I followed you other times, too. Everyone else wanted to
believe that Nichols was the Slasher. They were happy to see
the case closed. But Emma and Bridget talked about how you
and Jennings were still investigating. If anyone was going to
figure it out, I knew it would be the two of you. In a way, I'm
glad. You finally know that you're connected to me, too."

My eyes sink closed, disgusted by the idea that the
Midnight Slasher was around Bridget and Emma. Hiding in
plain sight all this time.

"And you killed Kent Kaylor."

"He could've identified me. I came here tonight because I
needed to know what he'd told you. If he'd given you
anything you could use against me. But I guess that doesn't
matter now, does it?"

No. Because Emma recognized his voice and we know who he is, and he can't leave us alive. My throat is so thick I can hardly breathe, much less speak. My heart is winding tighter and tighter, like a spring.

I have to get us out of here. How? *How?*

A memory flashes through my mind, so quick I struggle to place it.

We set charges and blew our own exit path.

It's the story Nash told us at the Shore Lounge a month ago. His war story from the SWAT team, about the time they had no way to reach a group of hostages, so they used brute force. Blew holes through the walls in between.

Now, I'm on the other side. I'm the hostage, and I can't see a way out.

Make your own exit path.

"It's really too bad," Steven whispers in my ear. "Now you know me. *Truly* know me, better than any of the others. And that's a rare thing. I'll be sorry to see you go. I always seem to lose the things I like the most."

The fury that's been building inside of me explodes.

Screaming, I slam my head backward. There's a sickening *crunch* that I think was his nose. The knife slices into my neck, cold and sharp. But I knock it away.

Steven loses his grip on my waist, and I wriggle free. "Emma, go! Back door!" It's the closest way out for her position.

We both run toward the door. Emma gets there first, her momentum crashing her into the wall. Her hands slip on the latch. Finally, she gets it open. Throws the door wide and dashes out into the dark.

I'm two steps behind her. Hot blood pours down my neck and soaks my shirt. *Go,* I tell myself. *Go. Hurry.*

There are footsteps behind me. A bellow of rage.

Steven's weight lands on me, knocking me down. He

crawls on top of my back. I'm trapped against the floor. I kick and try to buck him off, but he's too heavy.

He grabs me in a headlock and forces my chin up.

The blade slots against my throat.

42

Nash

*P*atrol units arrive, setting up a perimeter around Bridget's house. Detective Holt roars up in his truck. He checks on Bridget first, chatting quietly with her. Bridget takes my hand and squeezes it as she recites what she knows.

"You consent to a search of your house?" Holt asks her. She says yes, and he nods at the officers waiting nearby. "Let's do this by the book. Check for signs of where Steven Wrey might've gone."

Chills cascade down my vertebrae as I watch units go inside the Hanson residence. Wave after wave of memories passes through my mind, impossible to stop. Nichols holding a knife to Bridget's throat. Madison staring up at me from the entryway, her eyes glassy after she was shot.

"Sergeant Jennings? Are you okay?" Bridget's trembling.

"Yes, sorry. Why don't you wait in the car until your mom gets here? I'm sure it won't be long."

I stand outside on the sidewalk, responding to my fellow officers' questions and staying attentive as this scene gets ever-more chaotic. But thoughts of Emma and Madison distract me. The two people who mean the most to me in the world.

Neither of them has responded to my texts. Why? It's not like them.

And when I call, both numbers go straight to voicemail. As if they've got their phones off.

I don't like it.

A sedan tears up the road, honking its horn. It stops at the police perimeter. The driver's side door opens, and a woman jumps out, shouting when the officers try to stop her.

"That's my house! Where are my kids?"

It's Bridget's mom. Catherine Hanson.

I hurry over. Ms. Hanson looks thinner than the last time I saw her. Shadows ring her eyes from lack of sleep. "Let her go," I tell the officers. "She's the suspect's wife."

"*Suspect*?" Her eyes are wide with terror. She seems to recognize me, and grabs hold of my shirt. "Sergeant Jennings. You called me. Where are Bridget and Stevie?"

"Bridget's here. She was with Emma tonight. But I don't know where your son is. That's part of what we're trying to find out. We need to find your husband."

"Why? What's going on?"

I take Ms. Hanson over to the sidewalk. Neighbors are outside their houses, staring. Bridget's waiting in the passenger seat of the rental car, cowering like she's afraid of what her mom will say.

"Bridget told me that Steven hit you."

She blanches. Her mouth opens, then snaps shut.

"I know this is difficult," I say. "But our daughters are friends. I want to help. *Please*. Tell me what's going on so I can do that. You can trust me."

Her throat works as she swallows. Her voice is a dull monotone when she speaks. "I found jewelry in his things. Expensive stuff that I've never seen before. That made me want to go through *everything*. Then I found the papers he'd hidden, way at the bottom of a box. My husband is Steven Wrey, but he has a birth certificate with a different last name. And…" She drops to the barest whisper, and I have to lean in. "I paid for a background check online with his real name. I just got the results a couple days ago. He was in prison for *eight years*. He never said a word about it. I don't even know the man I married. The father of my son."

The world telescopes in front of me. Suddenly, the twisted pieces are unfurling, sliding together. Large parts are missing, but it's enough to change my entire view.

"What was his conviction?" I ask.

She bows her head. Her voice shakes when she answers. "Felony burglary. The jewelry I found…God, it made me think…"

Shit. I need to get Holt over here. *Now*.

I start to step away, but Ms. Hanson grabs my arm. "Wait. I put an Air Tag under a floor mat in his car so I could see where he goes." He takes out her phone and hits an app icon. "If you need to know where he is, I can find him."

The map loads. I'm holding my breath. A result comes up.

And my heart implodes.

No.

I run toward the nearest patrol car and shout at the officer standing beside it. "Light it up and *drive*."

Please, God. Let them be okay.

∾

I DON'T THINK I TAKE A SINGLE BREATH AS THE squad car screams through the neighborhood. I've got my gun in my left hand, muzzle aimed toward the floorboards of the passenger seat. I've texted Holt for more units, but I'm not waiting.

What if I'm too late?

"Stop here!" I yell at the officer who's driving.

I'm out before the vehicle stops moving. My boots slam into the pavement as I run toward the house. All the windows are dark.

But I hear shouting. Screams. They're shredding my skin.

My daughter barrels into me, coming around the side of the house. "Emma! What's going on? Where's Madison?"

Her expression is wild with terror. She's bleeding. I want to scoop up my little girl and protect her, make all this go away.

But the next thing she says turns me to ice.

"He's got her, Dad! Help her, please!"

My grip tightens around my gun. "Where?"

"By the back door. Madison saved me. She helped me so I could escape. But she's in there alone with him. He's the Slasher, he's got a knife, and—"

I steer Emma toward the street. My backup is coming down the sidewalk, trying to catch up. "Get my daughter to safety," I tell him. "Armed, dangerous suspect inside. Possible hostage."

The patrol officer nods. "More units are on their way. But Sergeant—"

I'm already racing for the back door to my house. I don't care about protocol or plans.

If Madison's in trouble, nothing is going to keep me from her.

If Steven Wrey hurts the woman I love, I swear to any power that's listening, I'm going to fucking end him.

I round the side of the house, and an eerie quiet falls. The huge window overlooking my yard is just as dark as the rest. Anyone who's inside would see me out here. I'm out in the open, not even trying to stay hidden. My left arm is outstretched, gun aimed ahead of me.

Then my heart stops beating altogether.

The back door yawns open. Madison stands there motion-less. A figure looms behind her, a hand pointing a knife at her jugular. The skin of her neck is painted a garish dark red.

"Come a step closer, and she dies." His voice is thick. I can barely see his face, but it looks like blood is pouring from his nose.

"Nash," Madison says carefully, "he's the Slasher."

I shift my weight from foot to foot. "Steven Wrey."

"So you know my name."

The fingers of my right hand are twitching, desperate to lift the weapon and kill this bastard. I have never felt so powerless.

"I know it's not your real one. Police are searching your house as we speak. All your secrets. All your lies. Just a matter of time before we know everything. It's over."

My finger caresses the trigger of the gun. Wrey is hiding behind Madison. I can barely see him. And even if I could line up a shot, could I take the risk of firing when Madison is so close?

I'm nowhere near as accurate left-handed.

"You've got a couple of choices, Jennings," Wrey says. "Either you lower your weapon and let me walk out of here. Or I'll slit her throat and run, and you can decide whether to go after me or let her bleed out."

Madison's eyes bore into mine.

I'm not going to let him hurt you, I think.

But how the hell do I do that?

Sirens wail. The knife at Madison's throat jumps, and she flinches. A new stream of dark blood flows from the cut.

"No more time," Wrey spits out. "Lower the gun or she's dead."

"*Nash*," Madison says, and I know she's thinking the same thing I am.

He claimed I have choices, but I don't. The Slasher won't hesitate to use that knife. If I lower my gun, he's going to slit her throat anyway.

I've got nothing but the barest hope. A risk built on pure instinct.

One false move, and I could lose her.

"I'm putting the gun down." But my eyes tell Madison something different. *Be ready*.

I lower my aim by an inch. Another.

The sirens are getting louder.

"Hurry up," Wrey snaps.

My pulse slows, and the moment hangs. *Wait... Wait...*

I raise the weapon and fire.

At the same time, Madison ducks to the side, the blade slicing anew across her skin. A bullet slams into Wrey's arm. He screams. The knife drops from his grasp.

Wrey tries to run from the doorway, cradling his wounded arm, but Madison's already on him. She tackles him to the ground.

In seconds, we're surrounded by tactical operators in full body armor, their AR-15s at the ready. It's my SWAT teammates. And fuck, am I glad to see them. They swarm over Steven Wrey, pinning him and reading his rights.

I don't relax until I've got my arms around Madison. My hand presses to the bleeding cuts at her throat.

"Nash." That one word is textured with all she's feeling. Terror and relief.

"I've got you," I murmur, covering her face with kisses. One of my SWAT teammates hands me a cloth, and I hold it to her wounds to staunch the blood. "We need medical over here!" I shout.

"Is Emma okay?" Madison asks, just as my daughter runs up. I pull her into a hug. Emma's crying.

"I'm here. Madison, I'm here."

Paramedics appear a moment later. They tell me to step aside, but I don't care what anybody says. I'm not letting go of either one of them. Never, ever again.

~

EXCEPT, THE DOCTORS AT THE HOSPITAL HAVE other ideas.

The three of us ride together in the ambulance. In the emergency department, doctors stitch up Madison's and Emma's wounds. Madison's are worse, but not life threatening. I hold both their hands and give them as many hugs as I can manage, while also staying out of the doctors' way.

I insist on having every test run so we can make sure there's nothing else wrong. With *either* of my girls. My arm is also killing me—the pain has been slowly increasing since the car accident days ago, though I've tried to ignore it—so I get an X-ray to check the placement of my fixator. I turn down any pain meds, and so does Madison.

I'm expecting a patrol officer to turn up and take our statements. Or maybe even Detective Holt.

But I'm surprised when Chief Liu himself walks into our room.

"Officer Shelborne. I believe your mother's in the waiting room, demanding to see you?"

Madison groans. "How'd she even find out I was here? I haven't said a word to my family. It's the middle of the night."

Emma looks guilty. "I might have texted her." Madison glares, and Emma throws up her hands. "She made me promise, if you were ever injured again…"

Chief Liu almost smiles. "I just need a few minutes. Then you can have all the family time you require. I'll have the nurses send Mrs. Shelborne straight back here."

"Is that really necessary?" Madison mumbles.

Emma gets up. She was sitting on one side of Madison, while I'm perched on the other. "I'll go see your mom, Madison. I'm sure she's worried."

"You sure?" I ask. I'm not about to let the chief drive my daughter away.

But she nods. "Yeah, it's all good. I wanted to call Bridget too. Make sure she and her mom and brother are okay."

I've been thinking of Bridget and Mrs. Hanson as well. Officers found Stevie asleep in a carseat in the back of Steven Wrey's vehicle. It was parked down the street from my house. He had a bag packed, as if he'd planned to leave town after finding out how much of a threat Madison and I posed.

If Emma hadn't recognized his voice, would Steven have pretended to be a hit man hired by Landon Cowling? It would've been a perfect way for him to shift the blame yet again. There's a lot that's still not clear to me, and it might never be.

But once it was clear that Madison and Emma knew his true identity, he couldn't resist opening up to them. They've explained what Steven Wrey told them. How he and Nichols went to prison together. But I can't understand Wrey's decision to marry Catherine Hanson and have a family. Maybe it was his attempt to live a "normal" life. His true nature came through in the end, yet he never hurt his own son or daughter.

He went after *mine*.

If Bridget's mother didn't tell me where Steven Wrey was, I might've been too late.

Emma gives Madison a hug, squeezes my hand, and then heads for the door. "Just the waiting room," I say. "Stay with Mrs. Shelborne. Don't go anywhere else."

"Okay, Dad. I'll text you when I get there." She rolls her eyes at me, but she's smiling.

Part of me wants to follow her and make sure she's safe. But she's not going far. Eventually, I'll have to come to terms with her growing up and leaving my protection. But after what happened tonight, it's going to take me a while longer. I'm still her dad, and she's my little girl.

I almost lost her and Madison both. It's more than I can fully process right now.

But one thing I'm *not* in the mood for? A lecture from the chief about how we disobeyed his orders.

Chief Liu sits in a chair beside Madison's hospital bed. He unbuttons his suit jacket. I don't think I've ever seen him wearing anything else. "You two have been busy."

"Because we were *right*," I snap. "Madison was right. Nichols wasn't the Slasher, and if she hadn't insisted that we keep investigating, then we wouldn't have a clue. You should be thanking her."

"Relax, Sergeant," the chief says. "I'm not here to chew either of you out."

"You're not?" Madison asks.

"No, I'm not. Though the mayor has been on my phone nonstop since Cowling's arrest this afternoon, wanting to know what the hell's going on. And that video of you two at the coffee shop didn't help." He crosses his legs. "I'm here to check on my officers. How are you doing?"

Madison tells him about her injuries. The chief seems genuinely concerned. But I'm not ready to let my guard down yet.

"The revelations tonight have shocked us all." Liu rubs a hand over his face, and I notice the redness of his eyes. "Steven Wrey being the Slasher. We've found evidence at his house showing his involvement in the burglaries. Jewelry stolen from the victims, more hunting knives, a rifle that I imagine will match the one used against you in Mammoth Lakes. I expect plenty more evidence will turn up as we finish our forensics. Detective Holt has been keeping me informed. But I'm curious why you went to see Kent Kaylor. Was it something in the casefile from the Mammoth crime scenes?"

Madison glances at me. Neither of us says anything.

The chief smirks. "You think I don't know you had copies of the files? I'm the one who left them for you."

"It was *you*?" Madison sputters. "But why?"

I'm ready to leap off the bed at him. Forget the fact that he's my commander. "You're the one who closed the official investigation! Who ordered us to stay out of it! You set us up?"

"Because I guessed Officer Shelborne wouldn't listen to me, anyway. She has a bit of a reputation. I was less sure about you, Sergeant. But I'm glad you stuck with your fellow officer. Though perhaps she's more to you now than just a colleague? Or a student of your SWAT training?"

I feel the muscle in my jaw pulsing as my teeth grind. Guess there's not much I can say to that.

"As for *why*, I was concerned about the holes in our case against Nichols. I didn't like that the mayor had shut down our official investigation so soon. But I didn't have the political cover to stick my neck out. I assumed you'd track down more leads to fill in the gaps so we could complete our file. I thought, at most, that Nichols could've had another accomplice. But I never thought there was a different Slasher out there who'd go after you."

I keep my mouth closed, trying to hold back the torrent of accusations I'd like to throw. The chief just looks calmly at me, like he's waiting for me to decide how pissed I am.

Madison puts her hand over mine. "Are you saying we won't be disciplined for defying your orders?" she asks the chief. "Or for pissing off the mayor?"

A smirk widens on his face. "Yes, Officer Shelborne. I'd say that's a fair exchange for your service to your community.

You're both welcome back on active duty as soon as you're ready. After a generous paid leave, of course. Sergeant, we'd love to have you back on SWAT or in some other capacity. We can discuss options later once your medical situation becomes clear."

Maybe that's all the thanks, or apology, we're going to get.

When I don't say more, he goes on. "Steven Wrey must've had some tie to Nichols, right? Is that why Nichols targeted Wrey's stepdaughter?"

Madison recounts how Nichols realized Wrey was the Slasher, and that Nichols tried to blackmail his former cellmate.

The chief nods along. "So the differences in the crime scenes finally make sense."

I've been thinking the same. Nichols and Lipinski didn't bother to wear gloves because they never expected the police to get involved. Steven Wrey wasn't likely to report the break-in. Their use of ski masks, the k-bar knife—it was all theater, designed to prove to Wrey that they knew the key details of the Slasher's M.O. That they could destroy Wrey's new life and new family if they wanted.

It disgusts me that Bridget got caught in the middle of it.

If Madison and I hadn't stumbled upon them, Nichols and Lipinski might have succeeded in pressuring Wrey to pay them off. Or, more likely, Steven Wrey would've hunted them down and killed them both.

The chief sighs. "Well, now we've got Wrey in custody and the district attorney can take over building a case against him."

"What about Cowling?" I ask.

"I just gave the word to release him. I didn't want to wait until morning, given what we now know."

I scowl as I remember how Cowling grabbed Madison earlier. "What about the battery charge against him?"

The chief tilts his head sardonically. "That's not worth our time. The man isn't going to win any awards for citizen of the year, but he's innocent of murder. Let's just leave it at that." He stifles a yawn. "I'll probably be up a while longer dealing with this mess, but the two of you should get some rest. You deserve it."

"Thanks," I grumble.

The chief takes off, and Madison rests her head on my shoulder. I run my fingers through her hair, then along her cheek and to the bandages over her neck.

"I'm okay," she murmurs. "We're all okay."

"I'm supposed to be comforting *you*."

"You are. You always do. But you need comfort sometimes too." She presses a kiss to my jaw. "Promise I won't tell anyone."

It's our first moment alone since we were at my house. Since she nearly died helping Emma escape.

I still don't know how I made that shot left-handed. Hitting Wrey's arm from yards away. It was more accuracy than I've been able to manage at the shooting range. But I guess I did it simply because I had to. It was the only way I could save the woman I love.

Everything I feel for her wells up inside me.

I've spent so much of my life choosing to stay quiet. That's just how I am, and I don't think it's a character flaw. But Emma and Madison have both taught me there are times I should open up. Let certain people in. Tell those who matter how I truly feel instead of letting it go unsaid.

"I love you," I breathe.

It isn't hard to say those words. Loving Madison is one of the most natural things I've ever done.

Her green eyes lift. There, I see a reflection of all that's within me. Longing and joy and an ache that only the other person can satisfy.

"I love you too. I think I've loved you since I moved in with you and I saw how caring you are. Looking out for Emma, for me. Not saying you're *perfect*, but I always feel better when I'm with you."

"I think I've loved you since you tried to arm wrestle me in the hospital."

She laughs, and I kiss her softly, fitting our lips together the way that our hearts already are.

43

Madison

After I'm discharged from the hospital, my mother takes charge. And tonight, I'm happy to let her.

Or is it tomorrow already? I've completely lost track of time. All I know is that I've gone past exhausted. I'm delirious from lack of sleep and from the shocks to my system in the last twelve hours. The wounds to my neck and to my soul from those endless minutes I spent with Steven Wrey and his twisted mind.

Yet somehow, I'm deliriously happy too. Because I love Nash, and he loves me.

We might've forged this connection on the night we were both shot a month ago. But it's so much more than that now. It's all the days and nights we've taken care of one another. Comforted each other. Loved one another, even when we tried to deny what was happening between us.

What Nash and I have has been tested by fire. We're unbreakable now. Not because of sharing an awful experience, but because we overcame it together. And that's something that Steven Wrey, with his twisted view of human connection, could never begin to understand.

We caravan to my parents' house just as the sun is rising. My siblings show up too, and then Bridget Hanson, her mom and baby brother. The house is way overfull, but I think my mother lives for these moments. She's like a general visiting with her troops, handing out pillows, spare toothbrushes, and plenty of hugs. Especially to me, Nash, and Emma, who hardly leave my side.

The Hansons take a guestroom. Nash, Emma and I hole up in another, crowding into a single king-sized bed. Emma falls asleep almost as soon as her head hits the pillow. She's in between Nash and me, knees pulled up to her chest, mouth slightly open like a little kid. Nash and I hold hands, resting them at Emma's waist.

We whisper I-love-yous and gaze into each other's eyes until I can't fight sleep any longer. I'm afraid of meeting Steven Wrey again in my nightmares.

But with Nash and Emma beside me, I don't have any dreams.

∾

WE WAKE UP IN THE AFTERNOON. MOM AND AIDEN make a huge spread of food. Scrambled eggs, sausage, French toast and baked apples, all breakfast foods even though we've slept away most of the day. We eat with everyone else around the folding tables in my parents' backyard, smiling and laughing as my niece and nephew do silly dances and tell knock-knock jokes they've just made up. Jake's golden retriever runs around and barks.

Emma stays beside her dad, but Bridget huddles at her other side. The girls whisper and show each other videos on their phones, snickering. I don't know how they can hear anything over the racket of everybody else.

I lean into Nash. "You surviving? It's hectic around here."

"I don't mind hectic. I've survived crammed into quarters on a submarine with a dozen other operators, and they were nowhere near quiet. As long as I don't have to get up and give a speech, I'm fine."

I actually think Nash is great at talking, but I get what he means. He doesn't enjoy it, and he never will. "No toasts then?"

"Please. No."

When Nash and I got shot a month ago, I didn't want to subject Nash and Emma to the craziness that is my family. But I shouldn't have worried. In fact, I'm feeling pretty lucky. I'm part of the Shelborne clan, and I'm part of Nash and Emma's family too. And the Hansons are here with us, trying to find their own peace after what they've been through. It's not going to be easy. But I can't imagine a better place for us all right now, surrounding each other with love and support.

Then my mother pulls me aside when I'm carrying a stack of plates to help wash up in the kitchen. "Madison, I've hardly had a minute with you. Can we talk?"

I grit my teeth. With my mother, there's no telling what she needs to say.

"Sure." I pass my plates to Emma and Bridget, and I follow my mother into the study. Mom shuts the door, blocking out the noise.

When she turns around to face me, tears are flooding her eyes.

"Oh sweetheart, you've been through so much." She pulls me into a hug. "Nash told me you saved his daughter's life."

"He did?" I saw him and my mom chatting earlier, but I had no idea what about. "I think Nash is the one who did the saving."

"That's not how he told it. He wanted to make sure I knew how incredible you are. It's cute, because of course I already knew. But that man cares deeply for you. It's obvious."

"I care about him too. I'm in love with him." My heart lifts. I really like saying that out loud.

"I guessed as much."

"Is this where you warn me to be careful? I haven't known him long enough, and I'm making a rash decision?"

"Madison, no. I'm trying to say that I'm pleased. You've found a man who just might deserve you."

"I *found a man*?"

"Oh, that came out wrong. I'm just happy for you. And so proud of who you are." She frowns. "Why do you look like you don't believe me?"

I'm not used to all this unconditional approval. "There must be *something* you'd change about me."

"Nope. Not a thing."

"Aren't you disappointed I became a police officer instead of working for you?" The wounds in my neck pulse with the beating of my heart. I've never come right out and asked her this before. Probably because I thought I knew the answer.

"I do wish I got to see you every day. But you've always been independent. I admire that."

I'm so surprised that I laugh. "Never thought I'd hear you say that."

"Of course I worry about you, just like I worry about Jake. Every time any of my kids is hurting, I feel it. But I have *always* been proud. I thought you knew that. You are the strongest woman I know." She cups my face with her hands. "Much stronger than me."

"Thanks, Mom." I don't *need* her approval anymore, but it feels good to have it. She's tearing up again, and I start the hug this time. "I love you."

"I love you too. And I love Nash and Emma for making

you happy. They're part of the Shelborne family now. Whether they like it or not."

"*Please* just stay out of their underwear drawers. And let them buy their own toilet paper."

We both laugh and brush away each other's tears.

AS THE DAYS TICK OFF TOWARD CHRISTMAS, THINGS settle down.

Nash, Emma, and I stay with my parents a little longer. It's a great chance to spend time with my family, and for Emma and Nash to get to know them. Emma babysits my niece and nephew, and she fits in with the Shelborne clan like she was always meant to be here. Nash bonds easily with Jake, but he's more awkward with the others. Yet everybody adopts him into our jokes and conversations—as much as Nash will go along—simply because they know I love him. My family is great like that.

When we can, Nash and I sneak off to be alone together, though it never lasts for long. I'm going a bit crazy with the urge to get naked with him, but that will have to wait. There's always somebody interrupting with an offer to have a drink, watch a movie, play a game.

Our phones have been ringing nonstop with media requests. The news is out—Steven Wrey is the real Midnight Slasher. West Oaks currently has custody of him, so their charges against him will be prosecuted first. But Wrey's cell phone data also proves that he was in Mammoth Lakes the day Nash and I were attacked and Kaylor was murdered. Tonya has identified him as the same neighbor who lived near Kaylor ten years ago.

However the legal side of this goes down, I have no doubt Steven Wrey will never see the outside of a prison again.

After a public outcry over Landon Cowling's ties to the Crimes Uncovered blog, the publisher who bought the rights to his story has rescinded the deal. Cowling is still posting articles over on his website, though under his own name now. He even had the nerve to ask me for an interview. He left me a long, rambling voicemail, insisting he didn't recognize the Slasher's connection to Mammoth Lakes. *I realized the Slasher went after my father because of what I'd posted on my blog,* Cowling's message said. *That's why I didn't want anyone to know. I did feel guilty, but not for the reasons you believed.*

I didn't bother to respond. The guy is pretty shameless, but at least he didn't kill his father like I thought. I'm not going to apologize for accusing him, but I'm not going to speak out against him either. I'd be happy if I never hear the name Cowling again.

Mayor Ackerman has been staying especially quiet about all these developments. He hasn't been seen in public in days. But Chief Liu held a press conference of his own, declaring that the case against Jeffrey Nichols had been reopened. He left my and Nash's names out of it. I was thankful for that. I'd much rather Detective Holt and the rest of major crimes get all the credit for this one. I didn't even solve the case until Steven Wrey was holding me hostage, so I hardly deserve any accolades. If anyone deserves all the appreciation, it's Bridget for being brave enough to speak up.

After a few days, the Hanson family moves to a new rental. From what I hear from Emma, Bridget and her family will be leaving West Oaks permanently soon. They'll probably need to testify against Steven Wrey, but there are too many memories and too much scrutiny here for them to stay. They'd rather sell the house they shared with Steven and start fresh someplace else. I can't say I blame them.

On Christmas Day, we're surrounded by festivity and noise. Nash and I cuddle up on one corner of the couch, while Emma goes on a marathon streak of baking and cooking, getting chef lessons from Aiden. The whole clan descends for a turkey dinner. Emma shouts and laughs with the others, adding to the general chaos. Nash keeps pulling me into deserted rooms or hallways for a quiet make-out session.

I don't think I've ever had a better Christmas.

The day after the holiday, the three of us pack up and head to Mammoth Lakes to get his SUV, which is now repaired. We spend the night at Tonya's, eating steak and baked potatoes and playing with Captain Jack. Tonya's thrilled to meet Emma, and the four of us stay up late chatting like old friends.

As we leave Mammoth, we head straight back to Nash and Emma's house. We've already packed up and said goodbye—for now—to my family. Nobody asks if I'll go back to my apartment, and I don't mention it either. I can't imagine going back there and living a life separate from Nash and Emma. We're too deeply connected now. I need to be with them, and I know they need me. It would be silly to pretend otherwise or try to fight it. I'm going to give notice to my landlord as soon as possible.

It's a little strange, walking in the door. The last time I was here, Steven Wrey was holding a knife to my throat. After the police arrived on that night, someone nailed a piece of plywood over the broken window and closed up the house. But other than that, the place isn't as much of a mess as I expected.

We spend a couple of hours cleaning up and setting everything back where it belongs. Nash has already scheduled the window repair for tomorrow. Then we make dinner together in the retro kitchen, maneuvering around each other as pasta boils and the sauce simmers.

"Remind me again why you didn't accept your mom's offer to stock the fridge?" Emma asks.

I grab the olive oil to add it to the sauce. "Because I'm a grown adult, and I told her I don't need her to provide for me."

Emma shakes her head. "I don't get it. But whatever."

Smiling, Nash hooks his arm around my waist. "It's because she wanted to make something with us." We brush noses.

"And I did," I say.

Emma makes a retching sound. And then we're all laughing.

After dinner, Emma says she's going to Chad's house. "Do you need a ride?" Nash asks.

"Toby's going to pick a bunch of us up. We're not going far. Please, Dad? I really want to go." She puts her hands together. But Nash just shrugs, all casual.

"Sure. Have fun. Be back by ten."

Her grin is a mile wide. She doesn't even argue for a later curfew. Emma gives us both a kiss on the cheek, then heads outside when Toby honks his horn. Nash watches the car drive away through the window.

It's the first time Emma's been away from us since the attack.

"You're handling this well," I say.

"Trying. I know I can't hold on to her forever. If she feels ready to be away from us, then I have to let her go." He spins around and grabs me by the waist. "Plus, it means we have a few hours alone. *Finally.*" Nash dips his head, trailing kisses down my neck. "I'm planning to make love to you."

"*Are* you?"

"Assuming you're interested?"

Shivers cascade through me. "Oh jeez, yes. I've been dying."

"Hold onto me. Arms around my neck." Nash taps my thigh, and I jump up, my legs tight at his waist. He carries me to his room, then shuts the door and locks it.

Nash settles onto the edge of my bed with me in his lap. For a few minutes, we just kiss, our lips and tongues moving slowly and sensuously. Drawing out the anticipation.

"You've never spent the night in my bed," he says. "Well, not *in* my bed. You slept in here that once, but we were on top of the blankets."

I giggle, remembering that. "I can't wait to spend the night here under the covers with you."

I've never been this happy. There's a thread of sadness, too, because of what else happened in this house the last time we were here. But we'll just have to make a thousand good memories here to drown out the bad.

"I can't wait for *everything* with you," he says. "I love you. So damn much."

"Then show me," I whisper.

For ages, we kiss and caress one another. Giving each other all the affection we've been saving up.

Sex with Nash is hot, but this might be my favorite part of being with him. These intimate touches, all comfort and sweetness, that aren't even R-rated but are things we share only with each other. The kind of touching that's possible only for people in love.

I hold tight to his shoulders and kiss his jaw. His beard's getting longer and softer. My fingers run over his whiskers. My thumb traces his lower lip, and his tongue darts out, sucking the thumb into his mouth.

Heat pools in my belly and moves downward. My clit throbs.

And just like that, I'm not feeling so sweet.

I reach between us, palming the erection in his jeans. "What are your orders, Sergeant?"

His deep brown eyes turn to molten fire.

Nash

"UNDRESS."

With a wicked grin, Madison scoots backward off my lap and stands. Her hips shake back and forth in a sexy, teasing dance.

If I keep smiling this much, I'm not going to be the grumpy guy anymore. But I think I've already been undermining that image. The past week or so, I've been telling her whole family how much I love her. That's how far gone I am for this woman. She's got me talking about my feelings to anyone who'll listen.

I bite my lip when her hands dip under her shirt, slowly lifting it an inch at a time. Her creamy skin appears. All her soft warmth that I can't wait to trace with my tongue.

Her arms raise, taking the shirt with them and sliding it off. Her nipples poke at the fabric of her bra.

"What next, Sergeant?" she asks, palm pressed flat on her belly.

My eyes flick downward. "Jeans."

She pops the button. Her legs shimmy, the denim lowering bit by bit. When the jeans reach the carpet, she steps out of them and kicks them aside.

"Now the bra."

Madison kneels over me where I'm sitting on the

mattress. She unhooks the back strap and lets the undergarment fall from her shoulders.

I rest my hands at her lower back, guiding her to arch her spine. Her nipples jut out, bright pink like cherries on a sundae. My tongue swirls around one of them.

She moans, hands flying to my shoulders.

My jeans are usually roomy, but they don't leave near enough space for how thick and long my cock is right now.

I stand and lift her up with me. In just a couple of steps, I've crossed the room and set her on my dresser. Breathing heavily, I ease back, adjusting my pants and looking down at her.

Madison's perched on my dresser, knees bent coyly. "Your orders, Sergeant?" she whispers.

Ughn. It shouldn't get me so hot when she calls me that. "Take off your panties and spread your legs."

She shifts from side to side to work the scrap of lace over her hips. Spreads her legs wide and shows me *everything*.

Damn, how am I this lucky? I drop an open-mouthed kiss to her knee.

My hand braces against the dresser. I bend forward, keeping eye contact until the last second.

My tongue darts out over her slick, sweet folds. Her answering cry is so loud, my neighbors probably hear it. But my heartbeat is nearly that volume, at least in my own ears.

This is who I want. Who I crave. Who I couldn't possibly give up.

Madison rests her feet against my shoulders. I flick my tongue over her clit. Her scent, her taste—it goes straight to my head and to my cock. I want to memorize every detail. Her long blond hair trailing down her back in the mirror, the way she pants my name.

I want to live here, right between her legs. Maybe after my kid leaves for college, I'll have to retire from West Oaks

PD altogether and devote myself to making Madison lose control. Wouldn't be a bad way to spend my time.

I lick her through every shudder of her orgasm, until she goes still and slumps against the mirror behind the dresser.

I take my time undressing, my eyes drinking her in. Inner thighs scratched red from my scruff. Breasts lifting and falling as she breathes. My shirt and jeans end up in a pile next to hers. I push down my boxer briefs, and my dick slaps into my stomach.

Before I realize what she's doing, Madison slides off the dresser and sinks down to her knees in front of me. Her tongue runs along my happy trail, and then her hot mouth closes around my cockhead. I shout a curse. Holy hell. She swirls her tongue around my tip, and her hand raises between my legs to play with my balls.

Pleasure moves up and down my spine like an electric guitar. Like white lightning and unbearable heat. Every coherent thought flees from my brain except one. Madison. In this moment, she's everything.

I tap beneath her chin. "That is *amazing*, but I want you up here."

She pulls off of me with a pop and stands.

I spin her around to face the dresser and nudge her thighs apart. "Bend over for me."

Madison arches her back to give me better access. I trace her vertebrae, then dip down, down, down, seeking her center. My fingers push inside her to make sure she's ready for me. She's wet from my tongue and her own arousal.

"Nash," she pants. "I need you."

I line up my swollen cock with her opening, and my shaft slides into her pussy. Fireworks are going off in my balls and my brain. Tiny explosions all over my nerve endings. Being inside of her is overwhelming, all-encompassing.

I take a moment to caress her back, her hip, her thigh. Waiting for myself to back off the edge.

Then I slide almost all the way out of her before slamming back home again, balls deep. Madison tips her head back, mouth open, throat and breasts exposed. I'm getting a damn good view in the mirror.

She opens her eyes. Finds mine in the reflection.

I hold her gaze in the mirror as I pound into her. Madison whimpers and shouts, tits bouncing as she takes my cock, and I can't get enough of it.

I don't stop until her body clenches around me with another orgasm, wrenching my climax out of my cock. My shaft pulses, filling her with my release. I grunt and curse through it.

I do sound like a fucking caveman. That's what Madison does to me.

I wrap my arm around her and stand her up. Dropping kisses onto her shoulders, I walk us backward toward the bed. We fall onto the mattress in a messy heap. I come down from that incredible high with three words repeating in my head.

I love her.

I'm never going to stop loving her, as long as she'll have me.

A WEEK LATER, I BLINK AND OPEN MY EYES. TWO beautiful, smiling faces are the first thing I see. One with my dark hair and eyes. The other pale blond.

In the background, machines beep and whir.

"Hey, Dad," Emma says. She squeezes my left hand. My other is encased in bandages.

Madison leans forward over the bed railing and kisses me

on the cheek. "Hey, sexy," she whispers in my ear. I try to smile. But I make an injured animal noise instead.

"*Urg.* I feel like shit." I hate anesthesia.

"Don't whine, Dad."

"You made me promise to share what I'm feeling. Trying to follow through."

Today was the day. The dreaded surgery. I look down at my bandages. No sign of the external fixator. It's finally gone, which is encouraging.

Madison's green eyes are bright. "They said it went really well."

"You're not Robocop anymore," Emma says.

"How do you know what Robocop is?" My words are slurring a little.

She shrugs. "Some old movie? Detective Holt told me."

The doctor comes in and confirms the news: the surgery went as well as we'd hoped. My bones were healing well enough to allow him to put the permanent plates and screws into place inside my arm. I don't need the fixator anymore.

"It's looking great," he says after checking the swelling. "Next, it'll be on to occupational therapy. That will take months, and it won't always be pleasant. But I have the feeling you can take it."

"Will I be able to get back to where I was before?" That's what I've wanted to know since the moment I was injured six weeks ago. The doctor has never been able to give me a sure answer.

He takes a breath, and glances at Madison and Emma, who are listening anxiously and biting their lips. "If you put in the work, I think the answer is yes. You'll make a full recovery."

Emma and Madison both hug me. I'm beaming. I'll be able to go back to operating on the tactical team. Being a sniper. Exactly what I've longed to hear.

But in a way, this isn't the groundbreaking moment I thought it would be. Looking at my two girls, I know I already had everything I needed. This is just a bonus.

When we finally head home from the hospital, Emma and Madison have a cozy spot set up for me on the living room couch. I sit down, and Emma sets pillows all around me and fluffs them. "I don't need all this," I say.

"Too bad. I'm going to take care of you. Or do you have a problem with that?"

Madison stands behind Emma, smirking.

The Christmas tree is still up in the corner. We haven't bothered yet to take it down. There's a small wrapped present under the tree that I don't remember seeing before.

"Dad, there's one more thing for you. It was supposed to be for Christmas, but I thought today might be better." She grabs the box and brings it over.

"You didn't have to do that." I've never been big on gifts, especially ones that are for me. Besides, having Emma and Madison with me was the best gift I could ever have received. This year, or any year.

Emma's rolling her eyes. "Just open it already."

Madison sits next to me, propping her elbows on the pillows.

I tear off the paper and open the lid on the box. There's a silver chain inside, with small metal circles attached to it. It's masculine, but also still delicate.

"Em, this is beautiful."

"You don't wear dog tags anymore since you left the Navy, so I wanted to make you something to replace them. Bridget has a metal stamping kit, and she helped me. At first, I made it with just an 'N' and 'E'. For you and me. But then, I realized it needed one more."

I finger the metal circles, turning them over. There's the N initial, and the next has the E.

The last circle has an M.

Madison gasps, her hand covering her mouth.

I put the necklace over my head, and the charms fall right over my heart. "It's perfect," I say. "Come here. Both of you."

We hug, Madison on one side of me and Emma on the other.

When I left the Navy, I wasn't naive. I thought I knew a lot about the world. How harsh and unforgiving it could be. But I had no idea it was possible to have this much love, too. That's what Madison and Emma have taught me.

Loss can happen in a moment. But something wonderful can happen that quickly too. And I know as I look at them that the best parts of my life are only just beginning.

EPILOGUE

Madison

"*Alpha team is in position*," Nash says over the radio.

I walk across the narrow space of the mobile command center, heading for the negotiation team sergeant, who lifts his gaze from the array of screens showing drone footage.

"What've you got?"

"Sir," I say, "I made contact with the suspect's girlfriend. She's locked herself in the back bedroom."

We've got the target barricaded inside his house with his girlfriend. This started as a high-risk arrest and progressed quickly into a potential hostage situation.

But this is no training. And I'm not part of the tactical team.

A lot's changed in the past year and a half that Nash and I have been together. It took him six months to get his arm fully recovered, faster than the doctor had anticipated. Probably because he was religious about his therapy and always pushed himself hard. For almost a year, he's been back in charge of the SWAT tactical team.

As for me, at first I returned to patrol. I was happy just to work with major crimes again. Tracking down leads, flexing my investigation skills. But after a while, Nash talked me into trying out for SWAT, but this time as a negotiator.

I guess I shouldn't have been surprised that I love this role. It's never been a secret that I'm a fan of talking. Of course, negotiations isn't just about talking to suspects and getting them to surrender. It's a lot of intel gathering too. I get to use all my skills.

Just now, I was listening to a throw phone inside the suspect's house. We broke a window in a back bedroom and placed the phone inside, loaded with special software to eavesdrop on the interior of the home. But a few minutes ago, the suspect's girlfriend found the throw phone and started chatting me up on the other end of the line. *Is this the police? I want to get out of here.*

I was more than happy to help, especially because the suspect hasn't been willing to back down.

"She's confirmed there's nobody else in the house," I tell the negotiation sergeant. "No kids, no pets. The suspect is still in the front room."

"Good work, Shelby." He shares this intel over the comm line with Nash—or rather, Sergeant Jennings.

I never mess that up when I'm speaking aloud, but in my head, he's always just Nash.

The operation moves from the negotiation phase to tactical, and now it's Nash's turn. He's great at what he does. Yet I can't help being nervous during this part. Sometimes, I still wish I could have his back out there with the rest of his team. But not because I'd prefer tactical. Nah. I realize now that my skills fit perfectly into this side of things.

I haven't got anything to prove anymore, but either way, I wouldn't trade this job if I could. My life still has plenty of ups and downs—um, helping raise a teenager? not easy—but I wouldn't change a single part of it.

Except maybe one *small* thing. But that'll happen tomorrow, and I can't wait.

I step down from the mobile command center. It's a beautiful night, the moon full, the scent of summer jasmine heavy in the air. I'm sticking to the perimeter of the scene, but I can still see the tactical team approach the suspect's house, kitted out in all their gear, including gas masks.

I spot Nash right away by his frame, his confident movements that I know so well. He's motioning to the others, and I know they've got all their plans mapped out and rehearsed to precision. These days, he makes a bit more allowance for instincts, as long as those instincts are honed by practice and experience.

One of his teammates breaks through a window and launches a teargas grenade inside. I breathe a sigh of relief when the suspect emerges a few seconds later, holding his hands up. Nobody hurt, no shots fired. The tactical team helps the girlfriend outside and takes her immediately to the paramedics to get checked out.

Now that the suspect is in custody, we can start shutting things down. Tonight isn't going to make our list of war stories. But this is the way it's supposed to be. No injuries, no unwelcome surprises. I've had enough of those.

Lia walks toward me, tugging off her mask and helmet. She joined the tactical team around the same time that I became a negotiator.

She high-fives me. "Made that look easy, didn't we?"

"It went like clockwork. You had a good plan."

"With Sergeant Scary in charge? You know it."

We both laugh. Just then, Nash walks by on his way to mobile command, giving me a wink and a sexy *see-you-later* smirk.

"Officer Shelborne," he says.

"Sergeant." I turn my head to watch him pass.

Lia nudges me with her elbow. "You two are the worst."

I shake my head and smile. Lia stopped being skeptical about me and Nash a while ago. There was some talk about our romance at work, but not as much as I'd expected. People were a lot more interested in how we found the real Midnight Slasher.

And Steven Wrey? I don't like thinking about that man, and I don't have to. He's serving an eighty-seven year sentence in a maximum security prison. Bridget Hanson and her family have settled into a new town and are finding happiness in their lives. Emma, Nash and I have visited them a couple of times.

"Want to grab drinks with tactical later?" Lia asks. "Maybe you can get Jennings to join the team outing. He never comes along."

"Afraid not. We can't stay out late. We've got an appointment tomorrow morning."

Lia tilts her head, scrunching up her face. "Oh, right. I remember something about that..."

Clint, our former classmate from SWAT training way-back-when, pops up behind Lia. He's in his patrol uniform. He moved into my spot in major crimes after I joined SWAT. "Hey, am I supposed to wear a suit tomorrow?"

Lia smacks his chest with the back of her hand. "What part of 'backyard casual' do you not understand? It was on the invite."

He scratches his head. "Right. I threw that away."

Lia recites the invite details again, though I'm pretty sure he was just kidding. After Clint wanders off, Lia puts an arm around my shoulders. "You sure about this settling down thing? Not too late to back out."

I snort. "Don't let Sergeant Scary hear you saying that."

"He'd know I'm giving you shit. But seriously, are you ready for this?"

I look down at the ring on my left hand. It's simple, with a green emerald and a tiny diamond on either side.

"I guess it's all about meeting the right guy," I say.

"Or having the right instructor?"

"That too."

A year and a half ago, my goals were all about my job. Making my parents proud, proving who I am. I thought I wasn't ready for a husband, mortgage, and family. But now, my career is exactly where I want it to be, and I'm making *myself* proud of what I can accomplish. My job isn't what truly fulfills me, day in and day out. It's Emma, who's become one of my very best friends. And it's Nash.

Marrying Nash doesn't feel like a big step. Because we're already living the happily-ever-after.

Nash

GARLANDS OF GREENERY AND FLOWERS DECORATE the backyard of the Shelborne house. A string quartet—some of Emma's friends from her school orchestra—plays classical music, and guests mill around on the grass, sipping champagne.

Thank goodness I don't have to stand up at the front yet, because I'd hate to have all those eyes on me.

Then Madison's brother Jake spots me. Smirking, he makes his way over to where I'm standing. "You look like someone who's trying to hide," he says. "Not great on your wedding day, man."

"Not hiding." I may have been behind an orange tree, but that's just because I needed to gather my thoughts. "If I was hiding, you wouldn't have seen me."

Jake rests a hand on my shoulder. "Nervous?"

"That's possible."

He nods. "Because this isn't your first time around?"

I blow out a breath. "Can you see inside my brain right now?"

"Did you forget I've been there, too? Got the ex-wife to prove it."

"I'd rather not compare those notes."

He laughs. "You're right, bad idea."

I asked Madison to marry me in December, after just over a year together. I did it in front of her entire family on Christmas morning, like a million TV commercials. But if it works, it works. Emma helped me pick out the ring. An emerald to match Madison's eyes.

That was definitely my best Christmas ever. Especially because Emma stayed for a couple days with Madison's family, letting Madison and me have the house to ourselves. It was a very merry Christmas indeed.

Sean Holt and Janie Simon were already engaged by then, but they had a huge soirée when they got married. Madison and I opted for a short engagement and a more casual event instead. I knew I wanted to marry her outside during the summer. And having it here at the Shelborne house made perfect sense. Madison turned over the reins to her mom for most of the planning, which made everybody happy. Madison's mom recruited Emma, and they bossed me and Jake around as we hauled in flowers and hung the decorations according to their design.

But the sweat rolling down my sides inside my white linen button-down? That's all me.

I see so many people we know, like Lia and Clint from

West Oaks PD. It turns out that I'm not a bad mentor to my younger officers, as long as none of them is named Madison Shelborne. I'm even starting to be known as an approachable guy. I think they still call me Sergeant Scary, but now it's mostly a joke.

My parents and sister are chatting with Simone and her new husband. I think Simone's homebase is Portugal now, but I've lost track. I've been slightly distracted.

I'm still afraid of making the same mistakes. But I've spent the last year and a half building a relationship, a *life*, with Madison. She's the person I've been waiting for. The love of my life.

"I want to make her happy," I say to Jake.

"Sometimes, the second time around is when everything clicks. I can attest to that. You and Madison? You click. Everyone can see it."

And it's what I feel.

Emma appears, right behind his shoulder. "Dad, it's time."

I swallow a brief surge of panic.

The next few minutes are a blur. I'm standing beneath a pergola that's draped with flowers. Emma walks toward me, looking beautiful and grown-up in her black dress, a bundle of wildflowers in her hands. She's smiling ear to ear. She turns and stands beside me after giving me a quick kiss on the cheek.

"You look like you're constipated," she whispers in my ear. "You're going to do fine. Relax."

I take a deep breath and smooth out my expression. I'm not worried about the commitment. That was never my issue. I just want this so much. I want to be everything Madison and Emma need me to be.

Today is symbolic, but it's still a big deal. I'm standing up in front of all our friends and family, showing them who I am. Who I love.

Suddenly, a sense of calm takes me over. That's what it's all about, isn't it? Madison and Emma mean everything to me. I love them both. It's just that simple, and just that incredible.

And then, there she is.

The woman I intend to spend the rest of my life with.

I love Madison in all her different forms. When she's kitted out as a negotiator or when she's wearing sweats on a Sunday morning. Or when she's dressed up to go out with her friends, with red lipstick and glittery eyeshadow.

But there's something about seeing the woman you're going to marry walking toward you down the aisle. She's never looked more stunning. Like, bowl-me-over beautiful. Her dress is sleeveless, made of some kind of shimmery, soft fabric that makes me imagine sliding it off of her. Her hair is down, framing her face and falling over her shoulders.

I try to memorize this moment as she reaches me. Madison hands her bouquet to Emma, giving my daughter a tight hug. They both have tears in their eyes.

Then, she takes my hands.

I chose simple vows. I wanted to keep to the essentials—how I promise myself to her, how she completes my family.

Madison says more, but I've got a confession. I don't hear much of it over the chorus of *Damn, I love her* in my head. Guess I'll have to watch that part on the video that somebody's cousin is making.

"I'm thrilled to pronounce you husband and wife," the officiant says. "Well, go ahead. Kiss her!"

I dip Madison backward to kiss her, pressing my smile to hers.

All I can think is that I'm happier than I've ever been. We're already planning to have more kids. After spending so much time with the Shelbornes, I like the idea of a crazy, noisy house. But I'm not going to be the grumpy dad in the corner. I'm going to be sharing every moment with them. Telling them all how much I love them. And through it all, Madison will be there beside me.

No matter what life throws at us, we'll face it together.

The end.

∿

Up next from Hannah Shield—
THE FOUR DAY FAKEOUT.

Jake Shelborne goes undercover with Harper, his high school crush. But the danger is almost as intense as their chemistry…

ALSO BY HANNAH SHIELD

Last Refuge Protectors Series

HARD KNOCK HERO - Coming soon

~

The West Oaks Heroes Series

THE SIX NIGHT TRUCE (Janie & Sean)
THE FIVE MINUTE MISTAKE (Madison & Nash)
THE FOUR DAY FAKEOUT (Jake & Harper)
THE THREE WEEK DEAL (Matteo & Angela)
THE TWO LAST MOMENTS (Danny & Lark)
THE ONE FOR FOREVER (Rex & Quinn) - Coming soon

~

The Bennett Security Series

HANDS OFF (Aurora & Devon)
HEAD FIRST (Lana & Max)
HARD WIRED (Sylvie & Dominic)
HOLD TIGHT (Faith & Tanner)
HUNG UP (Danica & Noah)
HAVE MERCY (Ruby & Chase)

ABOUT THE AUTHOR

Hannah Shield once worked as an attorney. Now, she loves thrilling readers on the page—in every possible way.

She writes steamy, suspenseful romance with feisty heroines, brooding heroes, and heart-pounding action. Visit her website at www.hannahshield.com.

Made in the USA
Coppell, TX
06 February 2024

28655904R00215